To Adam—
*for being wonderful
and always loving*

GLORIOUS DAWN

# PROLOGUE

E yes wild with shock, Johanna fought the hands that held her. She saw the trees swaying, dancing; the shadowy figures moving slowly in the glow of the raging fire. Twisting around, she saw tears glistening on the cheeks of the black man who held her in his great muscled arms.

"We can't help 'em, missy," he whispered. "We can't do nothin' but hide 'n' pray."

Johanna was no match for the old man's strength as he held her fiercely against him, his callused hand clamped over her mouth. Her father lay dead in the yard and her stepmother lay nearby, the flames from the burning cabin already licking at her body.

"I'd a gone to hep yore daddy if'n not fer keepin' you still, missy," Eli whispered. "Yore daddy would'a wanted me to keep you still. Them is bad men, missy. They do terrible bad things to white gals."

Hysteria spread through Johanna's brain like a writhing serpent, wholly engulfing her, when her sister was dragged

out of the darkness, stripped naked, and thrown on the ground.

"Yo' can't do nothin', missy. You can't hep her. Oh, Lordy! Be still—"

"'Spead yore legs, *puta!* Don't ya die on me!"

Johanna heard the heavily accented voice, and watched in frozen terror the humping body of the man on the top of her sister, and saw the three blood-crazed men waiting their turn on the slight, thrashing body.

Jacy screamed as the man entered her, plunging, pushing, with knifelike jabs and jerks that shook her whole body. Johanna prayed her sister would sink into merciful unconsciousness, but each time she seemed to be drifting away, one of the black-clad renegades gave her a resounding slap in the face, bringing her back, making her aware of what they were doing to her.

There was nothing for Johanna and Eli to do but wait in the murky darkness for the renegades to leave and pray that Jacy would live through the torture that the grunting, slobbering animals were inflicting as they emptied themselves inside her. Johanna thought wildly of the snorting, wild hog that had run across her path that very morning. *Think about anything,* she commanded herself, *think about anything to take away this horror.*

It seemed a lifetime ago that Johanna had run down the path to Eli's shack with an invitation to come to the house. Her father loved to visit with the old black man. He had told the family tales of the great sailing ships and about such places as Australia and the South Sea islands. They had been returning, Eli carrying a basket of green chili peppers for her stepmother, when the first shot rang out. Instinctively he had grabbed Johanna by the arm, dragged her into a thicket, and covered her mouth to hold the screams inside her aching throat, saving her life.

Peering through the bushes, Johanna had watched in horror as the men stormed the house. She saw her sweet and gentle stepmother cut down as she ran to aid her sister. Johanna's ears rang with her stepmother's screams and her nose filled with smoke from the burning cabin. In that one horrible moment, life as she had known it was gone forever.

The frenzied barking of a dog caught the attention of the bandits. They gathered in a tight group and talked. Then three of them quickly mounted their horses. The fourth stood over Jacy's still body, pulling up his britches. He cursed the men as they started to move away, then picked up the limp body of the girl, flung her across the neck of his horse, and rode after them.

Johanna tried to break free of Eli's arms so that she could follow. After what seemed an eternity, she was released. She whirled on Eli, beating at him with her fists and screaming.

"How could you let them take her? How could you stand there and do nothing? Papa liked you . . . and you didn't do anything to save him, or Mama, or Jacy. They'll kill her, too—"

Alternately sobbing and screaming her anguish, Johanna began to run, stumble, fall, and pick herself up until she fell on her knees beside her father.

"Papa! Oh, Papa!"

"It's a good sign, missy. It's a good sign the little 'un is live or they'd not of took her." Eli's voice came from above her, but Johanna was vomiting now, and swaying as she fought to remain conscious.

It had not been a nightmare after all. It was reality and she would never, as long as she lived, forget a second of it.

The citizens of San Angelo were outraged by the murders of their schoolteacher and his wife and the abduction of his daughter. They formed a posse to hunt down the murderers, but the area was vast and almost impossible to cover fully. Three days later they returned with Jacy, mute, and teetering on the brink of insanity.

# CHAPTER
## *One*

The small platform at the end of the room seemed miles from where Johanna paused to summon the strength necessary to walk to it. Standing in the doorway, she tried to collect herself, to contain her conflicting feelings. What was she doing in a place like this? she asked herself. She was a schoolteacher, daughter of a schoolteacher, reared with a love of learning and a sense of purpose. And here she was in a dingy saloon with people who had little interest in books or in any of the other things she cared about. The frantic clamor of her frightened heart bordered on sheer panic and she closed her eyes for a second, blocking out the scene before her.

The Wild Horse Saloon thundered with male voices and drunken laughter. It was a long room, dingy, and without light, without color, without women. The men were drovers, drifters, cattlemen, gamblers, and soldiers from nearby Fort Davis, from which the town got its name. A bar with shelves behind it took up one end of the room. At the other end a young man with a twirled black mustache and wearing a once-fashionable but badly scuffed derby was playing an out-of-tune piano. His chaps and boots proclaimed him a cowboy, but in the melting pot of the West there was no estimating the talents hiding behind the rough clothes and scraggly beards.

"Here she comes!"

The loud, boisterous voices of the men, the scraping of boot heels on the plank floor, the clinking of glasses and the piano, all ceased suddenly and every head turned to Johanna. Every eye in the room was focused on the white face framed in silvery blond hair.

She stood very still and swallowed dryly. *These men are not my enemies*, she told herself sternly. *They are lonely, hardworking men; rough but just, according to their code. They are ruled by the events in their lives just as Jacy and I are. Some of them may not want to be here any more than I do.*

Bracing herself and shutting out thoughts of her parents' murder, her sister's rape, and the consequent baby the now-mute Jacy carried, Johanna swept into the room, her chin held high, a smile tilting the corners of her soft lips. Fragile though she might appear, she had deep inner resources and strength, which constant use had intensified of late, and she faced the sea of male faces calmly. A sudden hush fell throughout the room. The loud voices ceased, as did the scraping of boot heels on the plank floor. Not a hand reached out to touch her as she edged through the crowd. This was still Texas, where a man could be shot for bothering a "good" woman. Johanna's bearing and dress proclaimed her that.

Thoughts swam through her mind as she seated herself and adjusted her guitar and the skirt of the modest dress that covered her slender figure from chin to toe, a costume she'd insisted on despite the owner's plea that she show a bit of cleavage for the men. Days ago she had run the gamut of feelings over this job—embarrassment, resentment, self-pity. But she was calm now, because this was something she had to do. This was Johanna Doan, schoolteacher, singing in a saloon! She remembered her father saying, "If you're born to hang, you'll never drown." She had not been born to sing in a saloon. She was sure of that. This was a stopgap, a way to earn money so that she and Jacy could move on.

"How 'bout singin' 'Sweet Kate McGoon'?" a slurry young voice came at her.

Johanna's cheeks turned scarlet at the mention of the well-known bawdy song. There was a censorious murmur, then a chair crashed to the floor as the offender was tipped over and silenced.

"Sing 'Believe Me If All Those Endearing Young Charms,' " one of the young soldiers called out.

Johanna smiled at him gratefully, adjusted her guitar on her lap and began the introductory bars. Her slender fingers stroked the strings and then her sweet, clear voice filled every corner of the room.

The audience was attentive, almost reverent, as she sang. Even the bartender stopped pushing the wet cloth over the grimy bar to listen to the haunting melody.

Ending the song, she stood. Pounding the whiskey bottles and beer glasses on the tables, the audience proclaimed its appreciation. She curtsied to acknowledge the "applause," then swung into a lively tune, her lips curved in a smile, her fingers moving rapidly over the strings.

> "Once I had a charming beau,
>     I loved him dear as life.
> I thought the time would surely come
>     and I would be his wife.
> His pockets they were lined with gold,

> I know he had the cash.
> He had a diamond ring, gold watch and chain,
> And a . . . charming . . . black mustache.''

The lively tune changed the mellow mood of the crowd to one of rollicking gaiety. They stamped their feet to the beat of the music.

Johanna's next song was about a Spanish dancer with dark, flashing eyes. The song, sung in perfect Spanish, delighted the Mexican customers, who joined in the chorus, loud and off-key.

An older, gray-whiskered cattleman, sitting alone at a table near the platform, raised his hand. Johanna knew his request would be the same as it had been the three previous nights. She sat back down in the chair. Her azure eyes took on a dreamy faraway look.

> ''In a little rosewood casket,
> sitting on a marble stand.
> Is a package of love letters,
> written by my true love's hand.''

Her voice was soft and husky and ideally suited to the songs. These were her favorites and always worked their magic on her as well as her audience. If only she could sing until the stroke of midnight, she thought. Then she would be free to return to the rooming house. But that was not part of the bargain she'd made with the saloonkeeper. She had agreed to serve drinks to Wild Horse patrons after she had entertained them with her songs.

Finally the performance was over and she laid her guitar on the piano. She moved toward the tables to refill empty glasses. Cringing inwardly, she passed among the tables, knowing her presence dominated the room. For the most part, the customers were respectful, although they stared at her fresh beauty and the boldest among them tried to engage her in conversation. The first night when this happened, a fight broke out and her confidence was badly shaken. She didn't know if she would ever be able to return to the saloon, but when evening approached she found the courage to make her way down the street and through the swinging doors.

Now, three nights later, she was better able to cope with the sly winks from the bleary eyes and the softly murmured invitations. She endured with one eye on the clock behind the bar. She would never become used to the sounds and smells, the raspy voices, the tables covered with whiskey bottles. But she smiled at the right times and kept herself distant and reserved.

"Sit down. I'll buy ya a drink." The man had a mustache that drooped past his mouth, puffy cheeks, and a whiskey stink. Johanna shook her head. He planted his hand on the top of the glass she was about to remove from the scarred table. "Ya work here, don't ya? Ya ain't so hoity-toity as ya make out. Ain't I good enough fer ya?"

Despite the thump of boots, the mumbled voices, and the mangled notes of the piano being played by the man in the derby, most of those in the room heard the remark. Activity in the saloon came to a halt. In the silence that followed, even the hiss of rapidly shuffled cards died away.

Johanna summoned a mask of haughtiness to cover her face protectively.

"I'm paid to sing for the customers and serve them drinks. That doesn't include listening to their drunken conversation."

The drover glanced about the room. Faces, uncharitably cold, stared back at him. His eyes flickered with uneasiness.

"No offense, ma'am," he mumbled and stared down at the table.

"Ya don't bother ladies, mister, if'n yore wantin' that mangy hide t'hold yore bones t'gether," a bearded man said threateningly.

"Ah . . . he sure as hell ain't no Texan or he'd know it fer a fact," someone muttered.

Johanna approached the bar with a tray of glasses. "I'll be going now, Mr. Basswood."

"Stay another hour and I'll pay another dollar," he said hopefully.

"No. It's almost midnight," she said firmly.

"You'll be back tomorrow night?" He took a dollar from the money drawer and handed it to her.

"I'll be back."

"Introduce me to the lady, Basswood."

The gray-haired, portly man who had spoken moved down the bar to stand beside Johanna. She glanced at him, taking in everything about him in one glance: his carefully brushed silver hair, the dark suit, and the gold watch chain draped across his ample chest.

"Sure, Mr. Cash." The bartender looked pleased. "This here's Miss Doan. Miss Johanna Doan."

Johanna nodded coolly and turned to the piano to pick up her guitar. "Excuse me. I've got to be getting home."

"Miss . . ." The bartender leaned toward her. "Will you go out the back way? When they see you leave, they'll all go over to—" He jerked his head in the direction of his competitor.

"No. I'll not go into that dark alley." She shuddered at the thought of slinking out the back door.

The portly man finished his drink and set his glass on the bar.

"Basswood, I'll escort the lady, with her permission, of course."

"That's right kind of you," the bartender said before turning to Johanna. "Mr. Cash is the lawyer here, Miss Doan. You'll be safe with him."

The lawyer followed Johanna through the back door and down the dark alley. He didn't speak until they stepped onto the boardwalk fronting the stores on the main street.

"I'll walk you to your door, Miss Doan. I'm rather surprised Mrs. Scheetz is allowing you a room in her house, considering your . . . er . . . profession."

"Mrs. Scheetz has already given us notice to move."

"This is your first experience singing in a saloon, isn't it?" Not waiting for her to reply, he went on, "You were fortunate to pick Basswood's. He runs as decent a place as is possible in this lawless town."

"I visited every respectable business in town asking for work before I approached Mr. Basswood." Her voice was taut, strained.

They walked in silence, the heels of their shoes tapping on the walk. The lawyer glanced covertly at the girl beside him and he marveled at the beauty that nature had bestowed upon her: fine-boned yet delicately curved; flawless skin; wide-set azure eyes. Her exquisitely shaped face was crowned with soft-spun hair of a curious mixture of silver and gold. She was slender to the point of fragility; but the set of her mouth and chin, the candor in her eyes, and the way her head rode proudly on her slender neck all showed strength of character. This was no empty-headed beauty but a strong-willed, determined woman, and he felt instinctively she was the right person for the proposition he intended to make.

They reached the gate leading to the porch of the boardinghouse, and Johanna turned to the man.

"Thank you." She smiled politely. "Good night."

"Are you interested in other employment, Miss Doan?"

"What kind of employment?" Her eyes looked unwaveringly into his.

"Perfectly respectable employment," he said evenly. "That is, if you have no objections to living out of town."

"My sister goes where I go." It was a flat statement.

"I've taken your sister into consideration, and also the fact that she is expecting a child."

Surprise flickered across Johanna's face, and her lips narrowed.

"I know quite a lot about you and your sister. I watched you get off the stage a few weeks ago. I went to Fort Stockton and talked to the banker. He told me you were asked to leave your teaching job, asked to leave town and take your sister with you."

Johanna drew herself up rigidly. Sparks flared in her eyes.

"Did they tell you," she snapped, "that the renegades who murdered my mother and father also carried off my seventeen-year-old sister and kept her for three days? Did they tell you that she is mute; that she hasn't uttered a single word since she was found wandering on the prairie?" Johanna paused to collect herself but could not still her temper. "The good people of Fort Stockton turned us out. They wouldn't believe Jacy's pregnancy was the result of her ordeal."

"I believe it."

Johanna was, for a moment, taken aback by the statement. "Why would you believe it when practically every person in town did not?"

"Because I took the trouble to find out why you left San Angelo. You wanted to get your sister away from the place where your parents were killed, where she suffered . . . violation. You left San Angelo and found the teaching job in Fort Stockton, but the Mrs. Scheetzes of Fort Stockton didn't believe your sister had been raped. You were too honest, Miss Doan. You should have said she was a widow." He waited for her to speak, and when she did not, he continued,

"It will be difficult for you to find decent lodgings here, and your money must be almost gone." He added the last apologetically.

Her mind was racing. No use pretending; the money was nearly gone and the landlady had given her two days to find another room.

Johanna's wide, candid eyes looked directly into his. The straightforwardness of her stare slightly unnerved the lawyer and he felt a pang of indecision about offering her the job in Macklin Valley, but he shrugged it off. He had looked too long for the right woman to go soft over this girl.

"My office is above the dry goods store, just west of the bank. Will you come there in the morning? I may have an answer to your . . . problem."

"I'll be there." She started to turn away, then turned back and thrust out her hand. "Thank you," she said softly.

The lawyer looked into the young woman's face, so open, so beautiful, and felt again a slight twinge of conscience. He shoved it aside.

"See you in the morning, miss. Good night," he said in his most professional tone and quickly walked away.

Johanna felt her way up the darkened stairway and down the hall to the small room in the back of the house. Quietly she opened the door and let herself in. She frowned when she saw that the oil lamp was still on. Mrs. Scheetz would have considered that still another reason to complain, had she known. She set her instrument in a corner and walked over to the bed where her sister lay sleeping, brown hair spread over the pillow, dark lashes shadowing her pale cheeks. Her face was so young, so stirringly beautiful, and for the moment relaxed. Her body was so slight that it seemed hardly to make a depression in the big bed.

"What a cruel twist of fate." Johanna said the words

softly, her mind racing down a well-traveled path. Usually she tried to block the memory of the raid from surfacing, as if it had all been a bad dream; but it was real, it had happened, and she would never forget a second of it.

She sighed in introspection and let her mind probe once again for a reason for the tragedy that had befallen her family. If only her father hadn't wanted to come west, if only they hadn't taken the house so far out of town, perhaps her father wouldn't have been surprised by the band of Mexican renegades and they could have held them off until help arrived.

The calamity of Jacy's pregnancy had driven the girl into an even deeper depression. Knowing that she carried the child of one of her parents' murderers wiped out any progress she had made since being found and returned to Johanna. She sat for hours staring into space. She seldom smiled, and at times Johanna found her pounding her small fist on her slightly protruding abdomen.

Johanna blew out the light, undressed in the dark, and slipped into bed beside her sister. She closed her eyes and tried to sleep, to forget for a while the problems that faced her. But there was no relief. Her thoughts continued to flow. It was plain now that the biddies in this town were no different from those in Fort Stockton, only this time their prejudices were directed toward her, for she had, indeed, told Mrs. Scheetz that Jacy was a widow. Perhaps, Johanna reasoned, Mr. Cash would provide the solution. Whatever he offered would be better than attempting to stay on here at Fort Davis.

Johanna was up and dressed by the time Jacy awakened. "Get up, sleepyhead. Get up and get dressed. We have an appointment to see about a new job."

Obediently Jacy rose from the bed, but she remained expressionless and showed no interest in what Johanna had said.

She dressed, washed her face and hands, brushed her hair, and coiled it into two buns over her ears.

Johanna chattered on as though Jacy were eager to hear what she had to say. "There was a crowd at the saloon last night, Jacy. The same man asked me to sing, 'Rosewood Casket.' You could have heard a pin drop in that saloon while I was singing that song. Oh, how those big, rough cowmen like a sad song! It's hard to believe unless you see it. Big men with guns strapped at their waists, whiskey in their hands, and tears in their eyes over a sad song." Johanna's voice trailed away. Once again, she had failed to engage Jacy's interest. She tucked a handkerchief into her sister's pocket. "Come along—we've got to get down to breakfast before Mrs. Scheetz clears it away."

Johanna put a protective arm around Jacy's shoulders as they entered the dining room. Mrs. Scheetz was sitting at the head of the table, her grim mouth pressed into a tight line of disapproval. The other two occupants at the table—middle-aged male store clerks—acknowledged the young women's entrance by half-rising from their chairs, but upon seeing their landlady's disdain they quickly sat down. Soon they finished their meal and left.

The three women sat in silence, the tension gradually building. Finally Mrs. Scheetz pushed herself from the table and stood up.

"Be out of that room this afternoon." The words were hissed at Johanna. "I run a respectable house. This is the last meal you'll have at my table. The idea . . . a saloon singer living in my house and eating at my table. I'll never be able to hold my head up in this town again!"

Johanna calmly continued to eat. "Our rent is paid until tomorrow. We'll not be leaving until then."

"You'll leave today!" The words burst from the woman's tight mouth and reverberated in the small room.

Johanna wanted to laugh. The woman's face had turned a plum red, and she suddenly felt a vengeful need to further antagonize her.

"We'll stay until tomorrow, and if you make any trouble for us," she said softly, "I'll tell the men at the saloon you're sleeping with Mr. Rutledge." She glanced up to meet the woman's astonished eyes. "I know it isn't true, but they won't know, will they?"

Mrs. Scheetz seemed to swell up, her face took on an even deeper color, and her eyes rolled back in her head. For a moment Johanna almost regretted what she had said. Perhaps she had gone too far and the woman would have a seizure.

"But . . . but . . . you, you . . ."

"I was sure you would allow us to stay, Mrs. Scheetz. Thank you."

The woman gasped and walked unsteadily from the room.

Johanna turned and saw Jacy looking straight at her, an unmistakable glint of amusement in her eyes. Johanna could have cried with joy. Jacy had finally reacted.


A few minutes before nine o'clock the girls left the boardinghouse. Johanna had dressed carefully for the meeting with the lawyer. She wore a demurely styled, light-blue cotton dress that fitted snugly over her tiny waist and full breasts. Her one and only hat, a stiff, natural-colored straw decorated with a pink satin rose, sat squarely atop her soft piled hair. Jacy wore a dark brown dress attractively brightened by a white collar and cuffs and a light shawl that she draped about her shoulders.

Satisfied that they were presentable, Johanna looked around the street with interest. Several wagons were standing in front of the mercantile store. The horses, with blinders attached to their bridles, stood patiently, their long tails swishing at the pesky flies that tormented them. Two cowboys rolled toward the young women, their high-heeled boots beating a hollow tattoo on the boardwalk. They lifted their wide-brimmed hats and murmured, "Mornin'."

Jacy turned her eyes away, but Johanna nodded a greeting.

They walked to the corner and across the dusty street, dodging a tumbleweed whirling on the gentle breeze, and went past the bank, then stopped under the sign that read: SIMON CASH, ATTORNEY AT LAW. Johanna took Jacy's hand and they climbed the wooden stairway that clung to the side of the building.

Simon Cash rose from the chair and stood before his massive rolltop desk.

"Good morning, ladies."

"Morning. This is my sister, Mr. Cash. Miss Jacy Doan."

"Morning, miss."

Jacy ignored the greeting and turned away. The man gave her a puzzled glance.

"Is there someplace where my sister can wait for me?"

"Certainly. My living quarters are in the next room. She can sit by the window and look down on the street."

Johanna took Jacy by the hand and they followed the lawyer into the next room.

"Look, Jacy. You can see the whole main street from here." Jacy sat down in the chair, her eyes reflecting a hopelessness that tore at Johanna's heart.

Johanna and Mr. Cash returned to his office. He offered her a chair by his desk, then seated himself.

"Is your sister always like this?" he asked kindly with a glance toward the closed door.

"Yes, since we found out about her pregnancy. But this morning I was quite encouraged—she smiled at me after Mrs. Scheetz and I had a little tiff."

Cash didn't react. He leaned back in his chair and absently

took out his gold watch, flipped open the case, glanced at the face, and returned it to his pocket. He smoothed his hair, which was already slicked down, then sat up straight in the chair and looked sternly and silently at Johanna. A wave of despair swept over her. It was obvious that he was skeptical about offering her the job.

When, to her relief, he finally spoke, Johanna leaned forward eagerly.

"I have been debating with myself. I had almost decided not to offer you the position, but knowing you are in need of work away from this town . . ." He paused. "Oh, yes, I know the ladies are going to ask you to leave. Mrs. Scheetz exercises a powerful influence over the ladies. If you were a different type of woman you would move to the other side of town and continue working in the saloon, but then if that were the case I wouldn't be considering you for the job."

Johanna's hopes began to rise, not only because of what he had said but because she sensed a softening in the sharp eyes that studied her.

"Let me put the facts to you, Miss Doan, and then we'll talk about it. My client lives in a distant valley. Over thirty years ago, when he was a young man, a determined young man, he found a valley. Out here a man has only what he can hold. He fought Indians to get that valley. He fought Indians, outlaws, and Mexican renegades to keep it. He went there before any other white man dreamed of anything but going on to California and getting rich in the gold fields. They came through here in droves, taking everything, building nothing. They wanted only to get to where the picking was easy.

"But Mack Macklin was different. He stayed. He worked—worked hard—and carved himself out an empire. He built a house, a dam, dug irrigation ditches where he wanted them. He put up bunkhouses for his drovers and houses for the Mexicans who worked his land. He drove a herd of cattle west when there were no cattle in this part of the country. It wasn't an easy chore to drive cattle to his valley, but he did it. He turned the cattle loose, and now they've bred into some of the biggest herds in the Southwest.'' He paused and rocked for a moment in his desk chair. "He's old now. His foot was taken off a few years back and he gets around on his sticks. He's ornery and cantankerous, but I figure he's earned the right to be.''

Cash fell silent for a moment and looked directly into Johanna's eyes. "He has asked me to find him a housekeeper. A pretty young woman with blond hair and blue eyes. It seems he knew a woman years ago who had blond hair and blue eyes, and in his old age he would like to have one around to look at and to care for his home.'' His voice trailed off and he sat looking at Johanna.

Johanna sank back in the chair and her heart did a little flip-flop of relief. She closed her eyes for a second while the tension flowed out of her.

"Oh, saints be praised! You were so stern. I was afraid it was to be something I couldn't do. A housekeeper! It's perfect for me. I love to keep house and I'm a good cook.''

"Miss . . .'' He made an effort to look stern to put force behind his words. "The valley is a long way from here. A very long way.''

Johanna didn't allow her spirits to drop. Indeed, laughter bubbled up in her throat. "I don't care how far it is. I'll work hard. I'll work very hard to pay for Jacy's room and board. Oh, you don't know how relieved I am.'' Impulsively she reached across the desk and clasped his hand. "When do we go? How do we get there?''

The lawyer studied the young woman and a smile played about the corners of his mouth. He liked her—liked her quiet determination. She had courage. He hoped she had the stamina to cope with old Mack. The tough old man had told Cash,

"By God, I don't want no milk-and-water lass—no milksop that'll weep and cringe. I want a strong lass with guts. Guts! Guts is what made Macklin Valley."

Old Mack would be madder than sin when he first saw the girl. She wasn't the big-boned, hefty type of woman he wanted, but she did have the blond hair and the blue eyes, and she wouldn't fold up under the first attack of the old man's wrath. The thing that bothered the lawyer was the sister, who was obviously part Mexican. Old Mack hated Mexicans with a cruel passion that Cash had never understood. That was something Johanna would have to deal with when she reached Macklin Valley, he decided.

"Every six months a train of ten to twelve wagons comes in from New Mexico. The valley is closer to El Paso, but it's easier to bring the freight wagons over the plains than to cross the mountains. It will take about three days for the men to blow off steam and to load the wagons. Besides their usual load of supplies, this time they're taking back lumber to build a windmill. I suggest you and your sister stock up on whatever you'll be needing for the next few months. You'll be going back with the train. Do you realize, Miss Doan, that you'll be traveling over very rough country? You'll cross over three hundred miles of every type of terrain imaginable. It will be a hard trip for any woman, and doubly so for one in your sister's condition. I'll talk to Mr. Redford, the head teamster, and see if he can fix up something a little more comfortable than a freight wagon for you to ride in."

"I assure you, Jacy is in good physical condition, Mr. Cash. Oh, I wish you could have known her before. She was so lively, so bright and pretty. The doctor in San Angelo said that there's a good chance that someday she'll be well and speak again. He said that sometimes a second shock can loosen the vocal cords. She's terribly frightened of men, especially Mexican men, and justifiably so."

"There'll be at least two dozen men on the train, and a good number of them will be Mexican. You have nothing to fear from them. Danger may come from outlaws, renegade Apaches, or Mexican bandits—although it would take a good-sized gang to dare to attack a dozen wagons and two dozen guns." Cash looked at her sympathetically. "I've told you exactly what you will face because I want you to know it won't be easy."

"I don't expect it to be easy," she said simply. "If I've learned one thing, Mr. Cash, it's that the good things in life seldom come easy."

# CHAPTER
## Two

The big, covered wagon rolled down the dusty street, past the curious bystanders lounging in front of the stores, then began the long curve out of town. Ahead of it the freight wagons waited. It pulled alongside, then passed the string of wagons to take the lead. With a warm smile Johanna acknowledged each driver as the covered wagon passed the others, and the men, eyes dancing with excitement at having the women along, tipped their broad-brimmed hats. Several riders were on the trail ahead, some were beside the train, and a few more were leading strings of mules, replacements for those hitched to the heavy wagons.

Johanna sat on the high seat beside the driver, a ranch hand named Mooney. Redford, sitting astride a powerful sorrel, waved them on, and the pace picked up. When the wagon swerved, Johanna clutched at the seat, then turned to look back at Jacy lying in a hammock stretched across the inside of the wagon. Her eyes were closed.

There had been a rough moment when Mooney attempted to lift Jacy onto the wagon seat: she'd struck his hands and cringed behind Johanna. The incident stiffened Johanna's resolve to ask Mr. Redford to explain Jacy's situation to the others so as to avoid a repeat of that scene.

The days since their meeting with Simon Cash had sped by. He had brought Redford to meet her. He was a short, heavy-shouldered man with iron-gray hair and a drooping mustache. His face was brown and seamed with wrinkles. His flannel shirt was ragged and sun-faded, and his boots were even dustier than the hat he held in his hands.

Johanna told him everything, beginning with Jacy's ordeal and ending with the possibility of being asked to leave the so-called decent part of town because of her job in the saloon. She saw the kind eyes turn cold with fury, then soften when she told him about her hopes for Jacy's recovery. He suggested that they rig up a hammock for Jacy with heavy springs on each end to cushion the jolts of the rough trail. He said he'd seen it work before and was sure that he could make the contraption.

The night before they were to leave he brought the wagon to the boardinghouse and loaded their trunks, pushing them to one side so that they would have room for the hammock and a place for Johanna to bed down. He made them acquainted with Mooney. He told them, with a twinkle in his eyes, that they would be safe with Mooney. He was his oldest driver and far more trustworthy than the other young scutters he had. Mooney had laughed and hit Redford goodnaturedly on the back with his dusty hat.

"By gol', I ain't that old!"

Now Johanna untied the strings of her stiff-brimmed sunbonnet and took it off. The breeze stirred her hair and felt cool on her neck. The sun had begun to climb over the horizon and promised the kind of warm, early-September day that Texas settlers knew well. She watched the slow, rhythmic steps of the mules. Each step stirred up a fine white dust that grew into a cloud above the wagon train, settling over the animals and caking the nostrils of men and beasts. The miles stretched on before them, and to Johanna on the swaying wagon seat, they seemed endless and timeless.

The driver sat with one booted foot on the guardrail, his hat pulled low over his brow. It would be a long, silent trip unless she could get him to talk.

"Have you made this trip many times, Mr. Mooney?"

"More times than I could shake a stick at, I reckon."

"Mr. Redford said it would take about two weeks to get to the valley."

"Yup. Red's got it figured 'bout right."

"Please don't be offended at how my sister behaved this morning, Mr. Mooney. She suffered a terrible shock a few months back, and it will take time for her to get over it. I'll ask Mr. Redford to tell you about it so you'll understand why she's the way she is."

Mooney leaned out over the side of the wagon and spat onto the dusty trail. "Don't let it worry yore head none. Red done gathered us all 'round and told us 'bout what was done to your sister. He didn't want anybody t'be a-scarin' her, you see. It was just pure-dee ol' ignorance on my part what I did. If I'd'a give a thought to it I'd'a knowed better."

Johanna smiled, relieved. "I'm glad he told you, Mr. Mooney."

"You don't have to be addin' no mister to my name, ma'am. I'm just plain ol' Mooney." He looked at her and his leathery face creased with a grin.

"All right, Mooney, if you'll call me Johanna. Tell me about this valley where we're going. Is it big?"

"Pert' nigh fifty miles long."

"Does the ranch cover the whole valley?"

"Yup, and then some."

"Mr. Cash told us that Mr. Macklin lost a foot a few years

back. It must be difficult for him to oversee such a large spread."

"Ol' Mack don't oversee nothin', 'cept a few things."

"Well . . . who does?"

Mooney shifted uncomfortably in his seat and adjusted the reins in his hands. Finally he spat over the side of the wagon again. It was evidently what he did while he was considering what he might say.

"Burr runs things. Goddam good at it, too. Better'n ol' Mack ever done."

"Tell me about Mr. Macklin," Johanna prodded, eager to know more about the man for whom she would work.

"Ain't much to tell. He's an ornery ol' coot."

Mooney's description of their employer made her laugh.

"Ornery or not, it took courage to build a ranch way out there."

"He's got grit, all right. There ain't no doubt about it. He was good at fightin', gettin', and holdin', but he ain't no good atall at managin' what he's got. Burr's got him beat all hollow."

Johanna already knew that Mr. Macklin was difficult and that the ranch was huge. It had to be to support the largest herds in the West, as the lawyer had said. She hadn't known, however, that he had a ranch manager. It she had stopped to think about it, she would have known. After all, he was an old man. She wondered if the manager had a wife. If so, had she been keeping house for Mr. Macklin?

The day went quickly. The sun arched high overhead and then went on its relentless path until it was a glowing orb hung low over the western edge of the world. When finally it was no more than a faint, rosy tinge, the freighters circled the wagons for the night. Mooney stopped the big covered wagon beneath the fanning branches of a huge old pecan tree. The drivers leaped from their wagons and stretched, then unhitched their teams and led them to the water wagon. Lids were removed from the wooden barrels and each animal was allowed to drink before being turned loose inside a roped area to roll in the dust and eat the sparse prairie grass. Minutes later a fire was built in the center of the circle of wagons and over it was hung a huge iron pot. On one side of the fire a very black coffeepot soon was sending up a plume of steam.

Johanna helped Jacy climb down over the big wheel of the wagon. Redford put his horse inside the rope corral and came to them.

"We'll help get supper if someone will tell us what to do." Johanna began to roll up her sleeves.

"Ain't no call fer that, ma'am," Redford said with a grin. "Ol' Codger over there is 'bout to bust a gut a-tryin' to fix up a decent meal for you ladies. I don't know if'n I ever did see him get so high behind."

She laughed, and the men, unaccustomed to a woman in their midst, paused to look at her.

"There's somethin' you *can* do, ma'am, if'n you're of a mind to. You can sing fer us tonight. It'd sure be a treat. We heard you sing at the saloon, and we was mighty taken with what we heard."

"I'd be pleased to sing, Mr. Redford." Her voice must have carried in the stillness of the evening, because from several wagons away came a wild Texas yell.

Red shook his head and tried to look stern. "I'll swear," he said, "some of 'em ain't got no manners atall."

The light disappeared from the sky while they ate. Codger, the cook, brought the young women each a plate of smoke-flavored beans and bacon, then returned with two tin cups and the coffeepot. Surprised at her hunger, Johanna attacked the meal with relish. The food was wholesome and filling. Jacy too seemed to enjoy the meal. They emptied their plates and sipped at the hot black coffee. Night sounds filled the air with pleasant and familiar harmonies, and Johanna relaxed, enjoying the rustle of the leaves of the pecan tree above their heads and the crackling of the wood in the campfire. It was comforting too to hear the quiet rumble of masculine voices keeping up a steady stream of talk while they finished their third helpings of food.

Johanna heard the sound of running horses and looked up in alarm. She was relieved to see that the men continued to eat and showed no concern. The riders pulled their mounts to a sudden halt just outside the circled wagons, leaped from their saddles, and draped their reins over the wheels of a wagon. They were laughing and teasing one another as they approached the campfire.

Without warning, Jacy sprang to her feet and looked wildly about. Her eyes became huge with fright and her hand flew to her face, trying to cover it. Blindly she darted toward the fire, then back to Johanna, and crouched behind her like a cowed, small animal, ready to spring away into the darkness. Before Johanna could stop her she leaped up onto the crate and tried to claw her way into the back of the wagon.

"Jacy, no!" Johanna held on to her, murmuring soothing words, and gradually was able to pull her back and into her arms. Jacy clung to her sister, trembling. "It's all right, honey," Johanna said gently. "There's nothing to be afraid of."

The three riders who had come so boisterously into camp stood stone-still, a bewildered look on their young, dusty faces. They started to back away.

"Please stay," Johanna urged.

They stood uncomfortably, shifting their weight from one foot to the other.

"Jacy," Johanna said softly. "Look at them. They work

for Mr. Macklin, just as we're going to do. Turn around and look at them. They would never hurt either of us." Firmly she took Jacy's shoulders and turned her to face the men.

The only sound to be heard, while the men stood still, allowing Jacy to look at them, was the blowing and stamping of the horses. Two of the men turned their eyes away, but the tallest of the three looked directly at Jacy as if his eyes couldn't leave her face. Johanna thought him the most handsome man she had ever seen. He was tall, whiplash-thin, with finely chiseled features. His hair was as black as coal, and his eyes, under a heavy fringe of black lashes, were a bright crystal blue. He was dressed in tight black pants and wore a loose, embroidered vest over his shirt. His boots were Mexican style, as was his hat; a black sombrero held by a cord about his neck rode on his back. He had two silver pistols in holsters strapped around his slim hips.

Johanna turned her attention back to Jacy. She was looking directly into the man's eyes as if mesmerized. She was quieter, and Johanna drew her down to sit once more on the box beside her.

The tall man didn't move, even when the others left to go to the cookfire. He lingered to look at Jacy.

"Thank you," Johanna said quietly.

He looked at Johanna as if seeing her for the first time, tilted his head, and walked away.

Red detached himself from a group of men by the fire and came to squat in front of the two young women.

"Ma'am," he said earnestly to Jacy, "there ain't a man jack here what wouldn't lay his life right down on the line fer ya. Ya don't have nothin' to be feared of long as you're with us, and that's the God's truth."

His kind, homely face and sincere manner must have gotten through to Jacy, for she timidly held out her hand to him and he gripped it with his big, rough one. A lump rose in Johanna's throat that threatened to choke her, and tears sprang to her eyes. To hide them she reached into the back of the wagon and brought out her guitar. Red carried the crate closer to the campfire and she and Jacy moved out into the center of the circle.

When Johanna began to strum the strings of the instrument with her slender, knowing fingers, all conversation ceased. She flashed a sudden, bright smile around the circle and began to sing an old ballad her father had taught her when she was a child.

> "Two little children, a boy and a girl,
>  stood by the old church door.
> The little girl's feet were as brown as the curls
>  that lay on the dress that she wore."

She sang the ballad in English, then repeated it in Spanish. Her voice had a kind of sweet, husky throb that drifted gently on the cool night breeze. She sang song after song, and never had a more attentive audience. She let her eyes roam over the faces of the men. Most of them were of Mexican descent, as was the tall, handsome man with the silver pistols. He had moved back in the shadows and was sitting very still. The brim of his sombrero was pulled down over his eyes, but he was facing toward her, and Johanna could almost feel the impact of his sharp, blue eyes. Something about his manner gave her a moment of uneasiness, but she pushed the thought away and gave her attention to entertaining the men who had made her and Jacy feel so welcome among them.

That night, for the first time in her life, Johanna slept in a covered wagon. Although tired, she felt strangely more contented than she had since her parents' death.

* * *

"H'yaw! Hee-yaw!" Mooney shouted at his team and cracked the bullwhip over their backs. The yell was echoed down the line as the drivers started their teams and the cumbersome wagons began to move. The camp had been stirring since an hour before daylight, when Codger had banged on the iron pot. "Come 'n' git it before I throw it away!" he'd yelled.

This was their fifth day on the trail. About them lay vast, immeasurable distances, broken by a purple tinge, the hint of the mountains ahead. The sun sent its heat waves shimmering down on the train as it moved sluggishly across the desert of sparse prairie grass and baked earth.

Johanna fastened her eyes on the notch in the mountains toward which they were heading. Mooney had pointed out that they would have to cross the river before they reached the mountain pass. All travel on the plains was governed by the need for water. When they reached the river they would fill their barrels, and the water would have to last until they reached the mountain pass, where there was a water hole. Between the river and the mountain pass was the meanest stretch of country God's sun ever shone on.

"Land out here ain't fit fer nothin' but tarantulas, centipedes, and rattlesnakes," Mooney had told her.

Later in the afternoon they encountered one of the latter.

They were rolling along at a steady pace, Johanna drowsing on the seat beside Mooney, Jacy in her hammock. Suddenly the two lead mules whirled off the trail, bringing the wagon to an abrupt stop.

"Right there's gotta be the granddaddy of all rattlers."

Johanna's eyes followed Mooney's pointing finger. In the middle of the trail was a large snake, coiled in striking position. Its head was up and swaying, its beady eyes looking directly at them. The rattles on the end of its body were in constant motion. Johanna shuddered but couldn't take her eyes off the snake. Jacy, standing behind her, clutched her shoulders and stared with horror at the squirming monster whose rattles could be heard by the teams pulling up behind.

Mooney was having difficulty holding the badly frightened mules. Johanna turned her eyes to them for only an instant, then heard the shot. She looked back to see the snake, now minus its head, uncoiling in its death throes. A rider astride a horse as black as midnight was shoving his silver pistol back into its holster. He turned in his saddle, and his somber blue eyes slanted across Johanna to rest on Jacy's pale face and shiny brown hair.

"Thanky, Luis." Mooney leaned over the side of the wagon and spat in the dust. The mules ceased their restless movements and stood trembling in their harnesses. Mooney wound the reins about the brake lever and jumped down from the wagon.

The body of the snake was as thick as a man's leg, and stretched out it was well over six feet long. Mooney grabbed it by the tail and pulled it off the trail.

"It'll make good eatin', Luis, if Codger'll pick it up."

"Sí—I will tell him." He turned the black horse and looked at the girls once again before he headed back down the line.

It was the first time Johanna had seen the slim, good-looking cowboy in daylight. He always came into camp after dark and was gone when the wagons rolled out in the morning. She had wanted to ask Mooney about him, waiting until the time was right. She turned to him now.

"That was real shooting, Mooney."

"Yup. But that warn't no chore atall fer Luis. I seen him shoot the eye outta a jackrabbit at full gallop."

Johanna expected him to turn and grin at her as he did sometimes when he was exaggerating, but his face remained serious.

"Is he a gunman?" She didn't know why she asked the question and wished she could rephrase it when she saw the look on Mooney's face.

He let loose another stream of tobacco juice. "'Pends on what ya call a gunman."

"You know what I mean. Is he hired by Mr. Macklin because he's good with a gun?"

"Ain't hired," was Mooney's clipped reply.

Before she realized it, Johanna let out a sigh of exasperation.

Mooney grinned.

"If'n you're a-wantin' t'know 'bout Luis, why don't ya just come right on out and say so 'stead a beatin' 'round the bush?"

"Mooney, you are the beatinest man!" Johanna said heatedly and then laughed. "All right, I'll stop beating about the bush. Tell us about Luis."

"Luis is a breed of his own. He ain't like nobody else I ever knowed."

"Why is he with the train if he isn't working for Mr. Macklin?"

"He makes the trip once in a while. Likes to look over the horseflesh in town. He's got know-how 'bout horses. Hates cows."

"Does he live in the valley?"

"Yup. He lives there." Mooney waited, but Johanna decided to ask no more questions. He would tell her as much as he wanted her to know, in his own good time. After a lengthy pause he said, "Built a nice little hacienda down the valley a ways. Got a string of horses, all good stock. Right steady feller, Luis, and in a fight he ain't got no quit atall."

Now that Mooney had started talking, Johanna held her breath for fear he would stop, but he continued on.

"I recollect a time when Jesus Montez—he was a powerful mean Mexican—come a-raidin' up and 'cross Texas and got into New Mexico territory. He raided and burned out Mex and gringo alike. Then he come to Macklin Valley. Hit the Mex village when most of the men was out gettin' strays fer roundup. Men what was left turned tail and run for it. All but Luis. He stood alone till Burr got there and the two of them cleaned out the whole kit and caboodle of the varmints. I'm thinkin' them two birds together could lick their weight in wildcats."

He glanced at the women to see if they were impressed. They were.

"I didn't realize there was a village in the valley," Johanna said thoughtfully.

"Ain't exactly a village. All the Mex what work fer Burr kind of live together like. Burr's got it fixed up real nice. Women got a place to wash, even. Them Mex women are the washingest women you ever did see. Always got clothes a-dryin' on the bushes. Good folks, I'd say, even if ol' Mack do hate 'em like poison."

"But . . . why?" Johanna asked the question immediately.

"It's a long story and an ol' one. I ain't even sure if it's the real one, but it's the only one I know of. Ol' Mack wrestled this range out of Indian country. He talked peace when he could, fought when he had to. Twice all the Mex deserted him and all he had left was Calloway, and him green as grass 'bout fightin', fer all his book learnin'. Ol' Mack, he say he ain't got no use for a goddamn Mex. Allus worked the hell outta 'em, give 'em a little corn for tortillas and a lot of cussin'. Burr sees it different. Treat 'em decent, he says, and they'll more than likely stand by you when the hair gets in the butter."

He pulled down the brim of his hat, and the way he settled back told Johanna he wanted to drop the subject.

"Thank you for telling us about Luis and about Mr. Macklin. I'm relieved to know he's got a kind and thoughtful foreman. Burr sounds like a very nice man."

"Jesus H. Christ!" Mooney swore, and for once he didn't spit beforehand. "I ain't never said nothin' 'bout Burr bein' kind and thoughtful. He ain't got hardly a kind bone inside his ornery hide. Get right down to it, he's 'bout as loco mean as ol' Mack, but different somehow. He'd just as soon knock ya down as look at ya if'n ya cross him. Do yore job, shut yore mouth, and stay outta his way is the way t'get along with Burr. Any *kind* thing Burr does is fer the good of the valley, and that's 'bout the size of it."

Johanna looked at him sharply, measuring his sincerity.

"You . . . don't like him?"

"Hell, yes, I like him. A man don't have t'be soft as mush fer me to like him. Burr's hard as nails and rougher than a cob, and the way things is, there ain't no reason fer him t'be anything else." Mooney gave her a disgusted look that shut off any more questions.

Johanna had a lot to think about. For the first time since she had accepted Cash's offer, she felt a nagging little cloud of apprehension in her mind. She pushed it to the farthest corner and covered it with the thought that no matter how disagreeable Mr. Macklin was, she would be able to handle it. Jacy would have her baby in Macklin Valley, and when they left the valley it would be with most of the wages she'd earned. This job was going to give them the time they needed to work things out.

Jacy climbed onto the seat. Johanna put her arm around her sister and gave her a little hug. Jacy smiled at her. The change in Jacy during the past week was almost a miracle. She was eating better than she had for several months and was taking an interest in things around her. Johanna no longer had to coax her to wash or to comb her hair. The doctor had said to treat her normally, not to urge her to talk but to give her time to get used to the changes in her body. Johanna had obeyed the doctor's instructions and added an abundance of love and devotion.

Suddenly she was almost happy. The sky was bluer, the breeze cooler, the landscape more beautiful. Things would work out. They were just bound to.

# CHAPTER
## Three

The "settlement," as Mooney referred to it, was a couple of adobe houses and a lean-to shed, set in the lowland near the river. Farther out were several abandoned dugouts. There they would cross a swiftly moving stream. Mooney explained that the riverbed at this point was solid rock and one of the few places within a hundred miles where the heavily loaded wagons could cross. There was a plume of smoke coming from the chimney of one of the houses and Johanna was disappointed when Red circled the wagons some distance from the settlement.

"Who lives here, Mooney? Who would want to live so far from everyone else?"

"That's a mean outfit, Johanner. Small-caliber, but mean. We don't usually have no truck with 'em."

It had been a long day, and evening began to settle its purple darkness about them when the cookfire was built and the large pot containing beef and potatoes was swung over it, as well as the ever-present black coffeepot. Johanna and Jacy sniffed appreciatively.

When the stew was ready and the plates were filled and passed around, Red brought his dinner to where Johanna and Jacy sat on a wooden box.

"We'll ford the river come mornin'. Luis was across and back. He says the rains up north has raised it a mite, but still ain't nothin' to worry 'bout."

Across the campfire from them Luis sat back in the shadows, as he did each night, silently watching, his face expressionless. Tonight his face was turned away from them as he visited with his companions, and they could see his profile clearly in the flickering firelight. Jacy's eyes dwelled on the man often, and Johanna wondered if she was attracted to him or just curious about him, as she herself was.

Red adjusted the dusty hat on his head nervously. "Ma'am, I been a-wantin' to tell you this, and I guess now's as good a time as any. If'n you get to the valley and it ain't what y'all thought it would be and if'n you want t'leave and go back t'town, all y'all got to do is say the word. There ain't a man jack here what wouldn't sign on to take you and the young miss back, and that means Luis, too."

While his craggy face showed no emotion, the sincerity of his words conjured images of doubt within Johanna.

She turned the full force of her troubled eyes on him. "What makes you think we'll want to leave?"

"Well . . . I just thought you might. These lawyer fellers can paint a pretty picture with their smooth words, and I . . . just thought . . . well . . ." his voice trailed off, then he added, "you might not want to stay."

Johanna laughed with relief. "I'm used to hard work, Red. I know it won't be easy to get along with Mr. Macklin, but I can do it. Surely he can't be so mean as not to want me to have my sister with me. Don't worry about us." She put her hand on his arm. "But . . . thank you." Their eyes met and he looked away, embarrassed.

Red was taking their empty plates back to the cookwagon when the horsemen approached the camp. They stopped outside the circle of light and called out, "Hello the camp!"

"It's Burris and a couple of Mex, Red." The soft, slurry voice of the night guard came out of the darkness.

"Come on in, Burris." Red's voice held a touch of annoyance.

The men came forward slowly, dismounted, and tied their horses to the wheel of a wagon. One of them came to the campfire and shook hands with a reluctant Redford.

"Jist thought I'd ride over and say my howdy and see if'n there's anythin' I can do fer y'all. Anythin' atall."

"Thanky," Red said curtly. "We're a-makin' out just fine. You're welcome to some coffee before ya ride out." Red turned his back and walked away.

Codger brought three tin cups from the chuckwagon and set them on the ground near the coffeepot. He motioned the Mexicans toward the fire. None of the men sitting around the campfire made any attempt to get up or to greet the visitors. It was obvious that they were not welcome, but the unwritten law of the prairie demanded that they offer the minimum of hospitality.

The man called Burris was bearded, heavyset, and gray-haired. It was difficult to tell where his hair left off and his beard began. His clothes were typical range clothes, dirty and ragged. The two Mexicans looked much like hundreds of men Johanna had seen lazing around the saloons in San Angelo, unkempt and shifty-eyed. These two had guns strapped about their hip with the holsters tied down.

The evening was cool, and after a glance at the men she turned to the wagon to fetch shawls for herself and Jacy. She had started to climb inside when she heard a mournful wail that pierced her heart like a dagger.

"Maa . . . maaa!"

As Johanna turned from the wagon, her heart seemed to stop beating. Jacy was standing with her hands clasped tightly over her ears, her gaze riveted on the two Mexicans squatted by the coffeepot, their features clearly outlined in the flickering light of the campfire. They were staring at Jacy with something like disbelief on their faces.

The plaintive cry came again and trailed away on the evening wind.

"Maa . . . maaa . . . !" The call to her mother came repeatedly in the seconds that follow. Jacy's eyes were wide with terror, her body paralyzed with fear. For an instant the scene around the campfire was suspended in silence, although the echo of Jacy's hauntingly hopeless cries hung in the evening's stillness.

"Johanna! It's them! It's them! They shot Papa . . . and hurt Mama. Mama begged them not . . . to hurt me—"

The two men stood up in unison as if mesmerized by Jacy's stare.

*"Madre de Dios! La hija, la virgen!"* Mother of God, the daughter, the virgin. The words tumbled from the man's lips.

Johanna's mind scrambled for comprehension. She stared at her sister as if transfixed. The fact that she had broken her long silence had not yet penetrated her senses. Johanna ran to her and put her arms around her. Jacy's anguished eyes never left the men beside the fire.

"Oh, Johanna, it was so terrible what they did. I wanted to die, prayed to die! I'm sick! I'm going to throw up!" The contents of Jacy's stomach came up and out and covered the front of her dress. Johanna tried to draw her back, but Jacy turned, pointing a shaky finger at the Mexicans. "You'll burn in hell! You'll . . ."

A black-clad figure, moving with incredible speed, emerged out of the shadows as Johanna pulled Jacy toward the wagon.

The Mexicans shifted their attention to the man, awareness of their desperate predicament plainly visible on their faces. The men behind them faded into the background, and they stood alone beside the fire. Luis faced them, feet apart, his body bent slightly forward, his face expressionless but for his narrowed eyes. His hands hovered over the twin guns on his hips.

*"Perros!"* Dogs. The word, when it came, was hissed though tight lips.

The two men glanced quickly at the men standing around them, and then at Burris. There was no help there. Then they looked at the slim, black-clad figure facing them. They knew in that awful instant that they were going to die. In desperation, they reached for their guns.

Luis's hands flashed down and his guns sprang up. Their guns had scarcely cleared their holsters when he fired. One of the men was flung back as if struck a tremendous blow. The other staggered and went to his knees, his face wolfish, teeth bared in a snarl. He lifted his gun and Luis fired again. A hole appeared between the man's eyes and he fell backward, the back of his demolished head disappearing in the short prairie grass.

The roar of the guns was so unexpected that Johanna and Jacy were paralyzed with shock. They gazed with horror at the two dead men and at Luis, who was shoving his guns into his holsters. The reality of what they had just witnessed began to take hold, and they clung to each other.

Burris stood as if his feet were planted in the ground, then slowly lifted his hands, palms out.

"Where do you stand?" Luis waited, his stance loose, his eyes missing nothing.

Burris shook his head and his hands at the same time. "I stand alone, señor. I stand alone."

"When I see you again I will kill you." The words were softly spoken, but the import was heavy.

"Now see here . . . I ain't never set eyes on them afore they come ridin' in a few days back. I don't know nothin' 'bout what they've done, hear?" Burris looked at Red. "I ain't never had no trouble with Macklin riders, Mr. Redford, you know I ain't."

Red looked at him coolly. "Only 'cause you was afeared to, Burris."

"I ain't like them Mex—"

"Sleep with dogs, you'll get up with fleas," Red quoted dryly.

"But . . . this here's my place and . . . I ain't no gun-fighter."

"Then I guess you'd better clear out of the country. Luis ain't one to repeat hisself."

The men watched him go. Not a sound was made until the sound of hoofbeats dimmed, then a few angry curses were flung after him. Red walked over and looked down at the dead men by the campfire.

"Carlos, you and Paco see what these varmints was a-packin'. Get the guns off 'em and anythin' else anybody wants. Ain't no use lettin' Burris make a profit off 'em. Some of you get shovels—not that they deserve buryin', the dirty, murderin' bast—" He broke off and looked guiltily around. "We'd ort t'a strung up the sons of bitches," he muttered.

"Hangin' woulda been too good for 'em, Red," Paco protested. "What we ort t'a done was nail their balls t' a stump 'n' shoved 'em over backwards."

"What Luis done was right," Mooney said. "He give 'em a chance. But, dadburnit, he was sure takin' hisself a chance takin' on both of 'em."

Behind the wagon, Johanna held her sobbing sister in her

arms. Then she bathed her face with a wet cloth and talked quietly to her until she calmed. Then Johanna lit a candle, lowered the canvas flap, and helped her sister undress for bed.

"Keep talking, darling. Please keep talking. I'm so afraid you'll stop. Tell me everything. We'll talk it out and then it will be a part of the past and we won't have to mention it ever again."

"How can you say that?" Jacy sobbed. "You know I can never forget it. I've got this . . . thing growing inside me. I hate it, Johanna! Hate it! Why won't it die? I'm ruined, and you know it. Every time anyone looks at me they'll . . . know." Jacy turned her face into the pillow and sobbed.

Johanna sat beside her, searching for comforting words to say.

"Jacy, dear." With gentle fingertips she turned the tear-wet face toward her, and a pang of anguish shot through her heart. There was such futility in Jacy's eyes. "We'll face what comes together," she said. "Our parents are gone, but think about this, Jacy. You're going to have an extension of Papa and Mama. They'll live on in the baby."

"No." Jacy shook her head and Johanna saw in the forlorn look the death of a young girl's dreams. "Johanna, I'm so ashamed I can hardly look anyone in the eye. Oh . . . I miss Mama so much!"

"I know you do, and so do I. Mama wouldn't want you to hate the baby. She was a wonderful mama to me. I owe her so much. She took me to her heart and loved me when my own mama deserted me and Papa."

Tenderly she pushed Jacy's brown hair back from her face. It had been a long day and one full of emotions. Jacy was exhausted but so keyed up that she couldn't relax. Nature, however, was strong enough to cope and finally

Jacy fell asleep, her hand still holding Johanna's in a tight clasp.

Johanna sat beside her sister for a long time before she blew out the candle and left the wagon. The moon was up and flooded the camp with light. The small fire in the center of the circle of wagons burned low under the coffeepot, left there for the night guards. The silence was absolute except for the sounds of horses cropping the short grass and an occasional blowing and stamping. Without these famililar sounds, Johanna thought, one might think the world had gone away, except for herself, on a tiny island in a sea of straw-colored grass.

Slowly she sank down on the crate and leaned her head back against the wagon wheel. She was weary and closed her eyes for a moment. When she opened them she saw a figure come out of the shadows and walk across the center of the camp toward her. As he passed the campfire she saw the gleam of the silver-handled pistols. She rose to her feet and stood waiting for him to reach her. He approached to within a few feet of her and stopped. She could see only his silhouette as he stood with his back to the fire.

"The señorita? Is she all right?" His voice was soft but deep, his accent Spanish.

"She had a terrible shock, but it was for the good. She'll be all right now." Johanna spoke to him in fluent Spanish. "Thank you for what you did." She added the last hurriedly, because he had turned to walk away. He looked back at her now.

"Good night, señorita."

"*Buenas noches*, Luis."

Johanna watched the tall, slim figure slip back into the shadows and disappear. She sat down again. The silence of the night made itself felt after he left her and she knew, without analyzing it, that here was a man who shared only a small part of himself with other people.

The next day was unbearably hot, but they were moving toward the mountains, whose purple shadows seemed to reach toward them promising cool breezes and a relief from the relentless sun and clouds of dust that hovered over them.

The river crossing began when the first faint streaks of red appeared over the eastern horizon. The air was alive with excitement, and for Johanna and Jacy, so long under their own dark cloud, the challenge to reach Macklin Valley across the miles of desolate, dangerous terrain spoke of adventure and lifted their spirits.

At the point of their crossing the riverbed was solid rock, and though the water barely reached the bottom of the wagon, the current was swift enough to be a real danger. Even with Luis guiding them and the extra precautions of heavy ropes secured to either side of the wagon and outriders alongside, the vehicle skidded on the moss-covered stones. Finally, the wagon rolled safely onto the riverbank and Luis wheeled his black stallion to plunge back across for the dainty sorrel mare that had been tied to one of the freight wagons. It was evident from the way he handled her that he was immensely proud of the horse. He led her up to the wagon where Jacy and Johanna sat as they watched the heavier wagons make their crossing, then swung out of the saddle and approached the excited mare. He talked to her softly, gently stroking her nose and neck.

Jacy never took her eyes off the man and the horse, and when he saw her looking at him, he smiled. He led the mare over to her and held out the lead rope.

"She's beautiful!" she cried out involuntarily, then

laughed. Johanna felt tears spring to her eyes. The sound was so familiar and so . . . dear.

"*Sí*, she is!" Luis spoke softly and gave Jacy a searching look, so penetrating yet so filled with understanding that she was compelled to meet his eyes.

As the significance of his words dawned upon her, color flooded her cheeks. Her breath seemed to stop, and her pulse to accelerate. For what could have been an eternity, their eyes held, and then he smiled. It was as if they had reached an understanding that needed neither words nor actions to make it more real.

He mounted the stallion and looked at Jacy once again before he splashed back across the river, leaving her holding the mare's lead rope.

"Well, now." Mooney tugged at the brim of his battered hat. "Luis sets a mighty big store by that mare, missy."

Jacy gave the rope a tug. The mare bobbed her head up and down and moved close to the hand that reached out to pet her. The young woman turned a beaming face toward Mooney.

Johanna couldn't believe the change in her sister. Just twenty-four hours ago she had been a silent, brooding girl whose spirit appeared to be broken. Now it seemed as if the floodgates had been opened by last night's tears, and a large portion of the depression that had gripped her for months had been washed away.

The wagons and the horses had all crossed the river, and still Luis hadn't come for the mare. Mooney climbed down and led the horse to the rear of the wagon and tied her rope securely to the tailgate. Jacy moved to the back so she could be near the mare. Johanna could hear the murmur of her voice and occasional laughter. After months of her sister's silence, Johanna treasured every sound that Jacy made.

The trail followed a torturous route. This was the "mean" country Mooney had talked about at the beginning of the trip. It was a baked and brutal land, sun-blistered and arid. The trail snaked through stands of organpipe cactus, prickly pear, and cat's claw. The desert throbbed with its own strange life and death. The desert allowed no easy deaths, only hard, bitter, ugly ones. They traveled on in silence, while the sun grew hotter as it rose higher in the sky.

The swaying, bouncing motion of the wagon was conducive to drowsiness, and Jacy lay in the hammock, her face turned so that she could watch the mare trotting along behind the wagon. When she was sure Jacy was sleeping, Johanna spoke to Mooney.

"Does Luis have a family in the valley?" She asked the question abruptly. Mooney said nothing. He cut off a chew of tobacco with a long, thin blade and didn't look at her. Johanna turned on the seat so that she could look into his face, hoping to read something from his expression. "Is there some reason why you don't want to talk about Luis?" she asked quietly, and waited patiently for him to shift the cud in his mouth.

"It ain't that . . . exactly."

Johanna took a long breath and held it. "Well, go on, Mooney." She said it lightly, with a small laugh, in an attempt to ease the tension between them.

"Luis is the ol' man's son." Mooney said the words right out and looked at her to see her reaction. She was smiling.

"Is that all? I thought he was an outlaw, or something worse."

"It ain't nothin' to smile 'bout, Johanner. The ol' man hates him worser than a rattler."

Johanna looked startled. "Hates his own son? I find that hard to believe." And remembering their meeting beside the campfire the night he had killed the Mexicans, his concern for Jacy, and his quiet dignity, she added, "He can't be that bad, Mooney."

"Well, it's the God's truth, and you'll find out once you get to the valley. Ol' Mack's a hard case. He hates most thin's he don't understand. Guess that's why he's got such a powerful hate for the Mexicans."

"Luis is Mexican," Johanna said, now aware that Mooney had more to tell. "That's obvious to me despite the blue eyes and his height. But why would Mr. Macklin marry a Mexican if he dislikes them so much?"

"He ain't never married."

It was something Johanna hadn't thought of, and it shocked her into silence for a moment. Why did she suddenly think of Jacy's baby? There could be no comparison in the situations, she was sure, because Luis knew his father, something Jacy's baby would never know.

"Poor Luis," she said at last.

"There ain't no call to feel sorry fer Luis, Johanner. It's the ol' man what's got his tail in a crack. He never did have no use fer Luis, 'cause his ma was a Mexican, but after him 'n' Burr took off his foot t'keep the ol' fool from dyin', he ain't got no use fer nobody. Luis keeps the ranch supplied with horseflesh 'n' Burr does the ramroddin'."

"Are you saying that Burr is Mr. Macklin's son, too?" Johanna asked.

"Yup. You'll know soon's you clap eyes on him. Spittin' image of the ol' man."

"And," she went on, although she hesitated to ask, "Mr. Macklin didn't marry his mother, either?"

"Nope. Said he never married."

"I don't think I'm going to like Mr. Macklin very much."

"It ain't all that bad. Don't seem to set very heavy on Burr. Luis is a mite shy, but could be his nature. The only thin' 'bout it is . . . nobody goes 'round callin' nobody a bastard.

It just ain't done in Macklin Valley. Course, now, the ol' man—he ain't got no sense atall when he's riled, and that's the first thin' he says. Don't bother the boys none, leastways they don't let on.''

Johanna was convinced by now that she would not like Mack Macklin and she told Mooney as much.

"Never figured ya'd take to him. Ya thinkin' a goin' back?''

"I need this job, Mooney," she answered slowly and sincerely. "I'll work for Mr. Macklin, but I'll not tolerate any abuse of Jacy because of her mixed blood." Johanna lifted her head, and the defiant look in her eyes brought a chuckle from Mooney.

"Glad to hear it." He punctuated the statement by spitting a long stream of tobacco juice into the dust. "You'll need spunk to stand up to the ol' man.''

Johanna had much to think about as the hot afternoon wore on. They crossed a virtual desert and overhead the inevitable buzzard soared with that timeless patience that comes from knowing that sooner or later all things that live in the desert become food, and he had only to wait. Despite the heat, a roadrunner poised beside the trail and flicked his long tail and took off, running on swift feet along in front of the wagon. A tiny lizard, its little throat pulsing with the excitment of seeing the train go by, raced across a hot rock and paused in the shade. These things that would have been interesting to Johanna passed unnoticed, as absorbed as she was in her thoughts.

That night they made camp in a narrow, oddly shaped arroyo. It was an easy place to defend, Mooney explained. This was Apache land.

"Nope," he said, when asked if they expected an attack.

"But where 'paches is concerned they don't never do what you think they're goin' to."

The wagons were drawn in a tighter circle and the horses staked out closer to the camp than on previous nights. The cook prepared the pinto beans and chilies quickly so that the fire could die down sooner. There was a feeling of tension in the camp, although the sisters seemed not to notice it. They excused themselves as soon as they finished their meal and went to bed.

In the privacy of their wagon Johanna told Jacy all the information Mooney had given her about the Macklins. Jacy's interest centered around Luis, and she pressed Johanna for any details she could remember from her conversation with Mooney.

"I've told you everything I know, Jacy."

"Don't you think he's handsome?"

"Yes, dear, I do," Johanna said after a short pause. "He's very handsome, and brave, too. Facing two armed men takes exceptional courage, but . . . we don't know anything about him except that he's Mr. Macklin's son. He may be a gunman for all we know."

"He isn't anything bad, Johanna. I know that. I think he's been alone a lot and he's shy. He didn't say a word to me when he came for the mare. He just looked into my eyes the way he did before, untied the horse, and went away."

The sound of running hooves broke the stillness of the night. Johanna lifted the canvas flap and peered out. An outrider had come into camp and was talking to Red. It obviously wasn't Luis, as this man sat low in the saddle. The conversation was in Spanish.

"There are three of them, señor. The same ones Luis saw before we cross the river. All gringos. Got good horses, one pure Arabian, Luis say. Black as midnight, got deep chest and strong legs. Luis say he ain't seen a horse to compare."

"Sounds like an Arabian. Not many of that ilk in these parts. The gringos are a-ridin' in our dust 'cause they're feared of the 'paches. If they want to trail us, ain't nothin' we can do 'bout it but keep our eyes peeled. Where's Luis?"

"He make sure they bed down." The man laughed. "Luis hate like hell to have Apaches get that horse."

Luis left the camp before daylight and headed west toward the hills. He rode cautiously along the dim trail. It was rugged, lonely country where stunted cedars and gnarled oaks clung to the ridges of the canyon and the low-spreading shrub with its hooklike thorns thrived. He was tired and the sun was hot. He went off the trail and into the rocks, to give himself better cover.

He had come to this place for two reasons. He could see along the trail for almost two miles, and he was accessible if Gray Cloud wished to contact him. The unpredictable Apache had been trailing the train for the last two days, and that puzzled Luis. He knew Gray Cloud didn't have enough men to attack the wagons, and he supposed his surveillance of the three gringos following discouraged him from attacking the camp.

Settling into a comfortable position against a rock, he lowered his head and waited. Soon there was movement on the trail below. Luis recognized both mounts and riders. Gray Cloud and two of his men were headed toward him.

Luis's horse scented them and grew skittish at the intrusion.

"It's all right," Luis said softly to his horse. "It's all right."

When the Indians reached the spot where the trail started upward again, the two braves stopped and Gray Cloud came on alone. The mare the Indian was riding lifted her head, and her nostrils flared when she became aware of the big black. Unhurriedly, Luis left his observation spot and stepped into the saddle, keeping a firm grip on the reins of his excited stallion.

He held up his hand in greeting and spoke in Apache dialect. "Greetings, Gray Cloud. My brother is far from his lodge."

The Indian stared at him silently with dark, fierce eyes. Luis knew that the man had strength and courage. He was also a shrewd trader, but for the last few months Luis had found trading with him distasteful. Gray Cloud had become difficult, bitter. Luis suspected that he was not receiving the recognition from his people that he felt he deserved.

"Why does my brother bring whites to Apache land?"

"We promised to bring no whites into the valley of the stone house, and we bring none."

"What of the woman who sits on the wagon? I will barter for the one with hair like a cloud."

Luis was surprised, but his face and voice didn't register the feeling. "The woman is not mine to trade."

The Indian stared into his eyes. "Whose woman?"

"My brother's woman." Luis knew that the Indian was testing him, and he never took his eyes from the stern face.

The Apached glared at him with burning intensity. "He can have other woman," he spat out heatedly.

"Other woman is my woman. I keep my woman," Luis said, matching his tone to that of the Indian.

Gray Cloud turned his eyes down the trail where the freight wagons had raised a dust that drifted against the cloudless sky. The dark eyes moved back at Luis, his eyes glittering with hatred.

"I could take pale woman." His expression changed to one of arrogance. "Mescalero wait in hills."

Luis watched closely and chose his words carefully. "A Chiricahua Apache brave has need of the Mescalero to take a woman?" He put a touch of scorn in his voice.

"Because of Gray Cloud, Mescalero stay in hills." A look of cunning came into the dark eyes. "I will trade mare for rifles and talk to my brothers, the Mescalero."

Luis had no doubt that he could draw and kill Gray Cloud and at least one of the braves. But if there were Mescalero in the hills and if Gray Cloud did have influence with them, there was a chance they would seek revenge on the train. He studied the situation carefully before he spoke.

"I thank you, my brother Gray Cloud, for holding off the Mescalero. Come to the place near my lodge and we will trade horses for food, blankets, tobacco. We have traded together many times. Your chief is a friend to the whites of the stone house. We will be friends and barter as before." Luis purposely omitted mention of the rifles.

The expression of hatred appeared again on the Indian's face.

"Soon we will kill all whites and take your pale-skinned women. I, Gray Cloud, will lead my braves against the stone house and take what you have." He paused, but Luis knew he was not finished and waited for what he knew would come. "I will kill Sky Eyes and take his woman to be my slave."

Without waiting for Luis to reply, the Indian wheeled his horse around and trotted back down the trail. His braves fell in behind him.

Luis waited a full five minutes before moving his horse out. Gray Cloud and his men didn't worry him, but the information about the Mescalero did. He headed his horse into the hills, scouting the area with care until he found a spot where six ponies had been tied to a few clumps of brush. The leaves on the brush had been freshly cropped, Luis determined, which indicated that the Indians, riding unshod ponies, had definitely been trailing the wagons.

Mounting up, he took the most direct route to the train, to warn Red of the possibility of an attack. He considered it would be no more than harassment if only the six riders were involved, but there was a chance that they were part of a larger party.

The freight wagons circled once again for the night. Johanna and Jacy had kept up a steady flow of conversation all day, and the time had passed so quickly that they were surprised to notice that night had fallen.

The drivers squatted around and ate the meager meal the cook prepared over the tiny semblance of a campfire. They talked in hushed tones. Johanna and Jacy's wagon had been drawn closer inside the circle, and gradually Johanna came to realize that something peculiar was happening. As time passed, she became more and more uneasy.

"Mr. Redford?" Her voice was low but managed to reach him.

"Yes, ma'am?"

"Is something wrong?"

The old cowboy took off his hat and scratched his head. "You might say that, ma'am. Luis spotted Mescalero in the hills. Might be they'll try to steal horses. If it comes to it, and I ain't a-sayin' it will, I want you women to stay down in the wagon, keepin' your heads below the sideboards."

"Are the men still following us, Mr. Redford?" Johanna felt a sudden spurt of worry for the three white men and their Arabian horse.

"They've pulled up a mite closer." Red grinned. "They be all right. You go on to bed and don't be worryin' none."

"It's hard not to worry."

Johanna glanced at her sister, dreading to see fear in her face. To her surprise, Jacy was calm.

"We'll be all right, Johanna."

"That's right, little lady," Red said gently. "We'll all see to it that nothin' happens to you."

It was dawn when the sound of gunfire woke Johanna from a sound sleep. Her first instinct was to jump up and see what was going on, but remembering Red's words, she hugged Jacy to her and lay flat on the floor of the wagon. Her heart beat rapidly with fear and she felt a flash of guilt for having brought her sister into danger. She prayed that God would protect them and the men who were fighting to keep them safe.

Off in the distance a shrill cry broke through the roar of the guns and she felt Jacy's hand, tightly held in hers, tremble. A horse whinnied and a man, close by, cursed. But they heard nothing more.

The gunfire stopped in a matter of minutes, and the waiting became almost unbearable.

"Is it over?" Jacy whispered.

"I don't know."

"Can we get up, Johanna? Oh, I hope Luis is all right!"

"Johanner?" It was Mooney's voice just outside the wagon. "Ya can come on out if'n ya want to."

Both of the women stuck their heads out of the canvas flap.

"Was anyone hurt?" Johanna asked.

"None a us," Mooney said dryly. "Rag-tail bunch of Mescalero a-tryin' to steal the mules. We be a-gettin' started soon's coffee's been had. Gettin' to the valley today, and they ain't goin' to follow us in there—that's Chiricahua country."

# CHAPTER
## *Four*

The wagons wound their way down the rocky side of a canyon that widened gradually and soon the horses were walking in knee-deep, rich green grass. Alongside the stream they followed, birds flitted from bush to bush, some scolding the intruders, others singing happily. A startled deer raced into the trees, its white tail standing straight up. Johanna caught her breath and laughed with pure pleasure.

The long, magnificent sweep of the Macklin Valley lay before her, green and shining in the morning sun. It was breathtaking, overpowering, beyond anything she could have imagined. The slopes on either side of the valley were blanketed with stately pine trees, and beneath their branches was an abundance of wild flowers and ferns. The green was a startling contrast to the snow-capped ridges that towered above them.

Johanna turned her head quickly and looked at her sister's glowing face. Jacy seemed to be even more impressed with the beauty of the landscape than she was. She reached for her hand and gripped it tightly.

"Just look at it. It's magnificent!" Jacy's voice was joyous.

Johanna looked down the long valley again and suddenly became uneasy. Silent as the wagon made its way deeper into the lush valley, she kept turning over in her mind what she had learned about Mack Macklin. Thinking about it now gave her a twinge of doubt that she allowed to linger for a troubling moment before she thrust it from her mind.

The outriders raced past the wagon, waving their hats and shouting at Mooney. They prodded the work mules they were leading into a gallop and were soon far ahead.

Mooney chuckled good-naturedly. "Everybody'll know 'bout you before we get thar. The young scutters is jist a-dying t'tell it. Yup, by granny, you'll be looked over good 'n' proper by ever' livin' critter by the time we get thar." He chuckled again.

"How long have you been in the valley, Mooney?"

"'Bout five, six years." Mooney spat out a mouthful of tobacco juice, a sure sign he was about to say more. "Red 'n' me, we met up with Burr 'n' Luis in El Paso jist after the war, 'n' we liked their way a doin' things. Burr, he tol' us 'bout the valley 'n' ask us to hire on. We did 'cause we didn't have nothin' else t'do. Red, he's tied up with a Mex woman now 'n' they got 'em a little young'un 'n' another on the way, so he ain't never gonna leave. Me, I don't have nobody nowhere, so I'll stay as long as I can work."

Jacy had been quiet. She turned often and looked back at the string of wagons behind. Most of the outriders had gone on ahead. Johanna knew she was waiting for Luis to pass. When he rode up beside the wagon he was leading the sorrel mare. He put his fingers to his hat brim and smiled.

"Señorita, you like?" he asked, indicating the mare.

"Oh, yes, very much." Jacy's eyes shone with excitement. "She will bring new blood to my herd."

"Are you going to breed her to the black?" Jacy asked with the uninhibited frankness of youth.

"No, señorita. He is too big for her. I have the perfect mate at my hacienda. Would you like to see him?"

"Yes, very much," she said again.

"Then I will come for you. *Adiós.*" He tipped his sombrero to Johanna, then his eyes swung back to Jacy. His face was different, more alive. His eyes seemed to caress her face for an instant before he spurred the black horse and raced down the trail, the flowing mane and tail of the mare standing out as she sped along behind the powerful black.

Mooney chuckled knowingly and slapped the team with the reins.

Johanna looked at Jacy's beaming face and glowing eyes. *She's smitten with him!* she thought. *Please, God, don't let her be hurt. Don't let him break her heart all over again.*

Involuntarily she reached out for her sister's hand and squeezed it tightly.

The wagon topped a small rise, and for the first time Johanna caught a glimpse of buildings. A cluster of sun-bleached adobe dwellings, surrounded by a patchwork of garden plots, shone brilliantly in the noonday sun. Even as she watched, the houses emptied and people ran out toward the trail. There were women in brightly colored skirts with small children clutched in their arms, while older children ran alongside, laughing and chattering. They lined up beside the wagon track, heads turned toward the approaching trail. Quietly, shyly, they waited for a look at the strangers. Dark, solemn eyes gazed at Johanna and Jacy. Some of the children hid behind their mothers' skirts.

"*Buenas tardes*," Johanna called out gaily. A few smiles appeared at the use of their language. Most of the two dozen or more women who lined the trail smiled back at the new-comers, and a few answered their greetings.

Johanna remembered her hat and reached for it. She placed it squarely on top of her high-piled flaxen hair. She felt better. Somehow the hat gave her courage.

The trail curved around the adobe houses and the rest of the ranch buildings came into view. Johanna's spirits sank.

Seeing it on the whole, Johanna's first impression was that the place looked like an army post. The buildings and the ranch house were made of stone and blended with the land as if they and the mountains that framed them had been created together. The peaked roof of the house extended down and out to form the roof of the porch, which was supported by the husky posts that fronted the house. Several hide-covered chairs stood along the wall. There were three doors at the front of the building and three glass-paned windows. Stone chimneys, one emitting a weak plume of smoke, protruded high above the roof on each end of the squat stone structure. While the place looked permanent, there wasn't a bush, flower, fence, or anything else to lend warmth or humanity. Several large trees stood well back from the house, and under their spreading branches was the hitching rail.

Mooney stopped the wagon and waited for the freight wagons to pass. They veered off toward the buildings behind the bunkhouse, which was as long as the house but not quite as deep. Beyond that was a network of split-rail corrals and several small stone buildings. All activity centered around the bunkhouse. The returning outriders were putting their tired horses into the corral, and there was much shouting and blackslapping as the men were greeted by those who had stayed behind.

Red rode up beside the wagon. "Take 'er on up, Mooney. I'll go on ahead and tell the old man. I see he's a-waitin' fer us."

Johanna adjusted her hat again, then gripped Jacy's hand and smiled reassuringly. She had steeled herself for this meeting with her new employer, and despite her uneasiness she was determined to face the man boldly.

"He didn't know I was coming," Jacy said nervously.

"Don't worry about it, dear. Mr. Cash was sure it was all right for you to come. You stay with Mooney and I'll go speak to Mr. Macklin."

"That's a good idey, missy. You stay with me till Johanner gets the lay of the land."

Mooney pulled the wagon to a stop beneath the trees. Johanna glanced nervously at the house, where Red was talking to a man sitting in a huge chair. First impressions are the most important, she told herself, and called on all her inner resourses to help her put a cool, confident expression on her face. She patted Jacy's hand, once more straighted the straw hat on her head, and turned to climb down over the wheel.

Her foot found the spoke and she was about to jump lightly to the ground when the horses suddenly lurched forward. She teetered for a breathless instant, hopelessly grabbing for a way to save herself, before she fell heavily, striking the ground with such force her hat bounced off and rolled beneath the wagon. She sprang up quickly and out of the corner of her eye saw a small boy disappear around the corner of the house. Badly shaken from the fall, her face flooded with color, she smoothed her skirts and patted her hair into place.

Jacy leaned over the side and stared at her with horrified eyes. "Jo! Johanna! Are you hurt?"

Johanna felt like a fool and wished the ground would open and swallow her.

"That goddamn Bucko!" Mooney cursed as he held the frightened horses. "I'll get me some skin off his butt!"

"I'm . . . all right." Johanna tried desperately to compose

herself. "I'm not hurt, just embarrassed." She laughed nervously and glanced at her hat under the wagon; a wheel had run over it. The crown was crushed and the lovely satin rose was beyond repair. She refused to bend her dignity still further to retrieve it. Her legs were unsteady, but her shoulders were square and her back was straight as she walked up the path to the ranch house. Red gave her a sympathetic look and another wave of color flooded her face. She had no doubt that both men had witness her inelegant sprawl in the dust.

The big man seated in the cowhide-covered chair had thick white hair and a mustache, stained with tobacco juice, that curved down on each side of his mouth. Closer now, she could see in his lined face a lifetime of struggle against man and the elements. His bright blue eyes were compelling and tinged with impatience. She met his hard, discerning stare and started to look away, then forced herself to return his appraisal with a measuring look of her own. He wore a faded flannel shirt with rolled-up sleeves under a sleeveless leather vest, and a high-heeled boot beneath one pant leg while the other pant leg hung limply. The hands that gripped the arms of the chair were huge and gnarled, but the flesh on his large forearms was loose and sagging, as if the years had worn away the muscles of youth. His sunken blue eyes were narrowed and cold. Johanna met them unflinchingly.

"I'm Johanna Doan, sir. I . . ."

"I know who the hell you are," he broke in rudely. "I've got a letter here from that goddamn Cash. I told him I wanted a woman, a real woman, not a prissy miss that can't get out of a wagon without fallin' on her arse!"

Johanna was stunned into silence but never allowed her eyes to waver from his. His hard words had hit her like stones, but she stiffened her back and answered him sharply.

"I assure you, sir, I *am* a real woman and I know how to work like one. And as for my . . . ungraceful descent from the wagon, the child who threw the stone at the horses should be punished.''

''I doubt if the bastard was aimin' at the horses, miss. 'Twas that silly thing atop your head he was aimin' for.''

Johanna was speechless. His attack was unsettling and unwarranted and totally unexpected even after all Mooney had told her about him. She could feel her knees weakening again, but not from terror. The anger that started down in her stomach surged upward, but before she could retort Red broke in, a questioning frown on his weathered face.

''I think we'd better unload the trunks, Mack, so Mooney can take the team on down to the sheds.''

The old man's grunt was noncommittal as his gaze swept up and down the slender figure of the woman standing before him.

''I hope t'hell you got all the parts of a woman. You got the hair and eyes. You're here and I ain't got much more time to be a-dallyin' 'round. I wish to God you wasn't such a skinny bitch.''

Johanna took a deep, hurtful breath and looked at him with disbelief. ''I'm not going to like working for you, Mr. Macklin. You're rude and you're crude.''

The man's eyes were cold, but there was a strange sort of smile tugging at the corners of his mouth. He nodded in Red's direction.

''Well . . . bring in her gear.''

Johanna forced herself to appear calmly contemptuous of his rudeness, and soon her anger gave way to pity for the crippled old man whose heart was so corroded with bitterness that he couldn't even be decent to a stranger in his home.

''Cash says your sister's goin' to whelp and it'll be a bastard. There's plenty here, one more bastard in the valley ain't gonna matter none. Does she have hair and eyes like yours? Is she heftier than you?''

Bluntly Johanna answered him. "No, she's small, and no, she doesn't look like me because her mother was Mexican." She said the last deliberately, then clamped her mouth shut and waited for an explosion.

"Another bastard!"

"No," Johanna said firmly. "My father and I loved her mother dearly, and I want you to understand this: I'll not allow you to mistreat her because of her mixed parentage. I insist that she not be subjected to any unpleasantness. Do I make myself clear, Mr. Macklin? She is the dearest thing in the world to me, and if she's not welcome in your home, now is the time for you to say so before Mooney brings in our things."

The look on his face was surprise, then smoldering anger.

"I ain't got no use for a goddamn Mex. You'd better swaller that and keep her out of my way!"

"That will be impossible if we are to live in your home," Johanna said calmly. "So I suggest that *you* learn to control your prejudice."

His eyes narrowed and he glared at her. He seemed to be taking a second look at the slender young woman, aware now of her defiant stance, the eyes that met his unafraid. He had sent men scampering off the porch with his roar, and this woman stood firmly in front of him and gave *him* an ultimatum. The silence was heavy between them as they took each other's measure.

Still looking at her, the old man opened his mouth and bellowed, "Calloway!"

A door opened at the end of the porch and a small, neatly dressed man came toward them. He was not as old or as weather-worn as Mack Macklin.

"This here's the woman," old Mack said by way of introduction.

As she offered her hand, Johanna's eyes roved the lean

features of the small man. His eyes were piercing and showed slight surprise, but his clean-shaven face was kind. In his youth his snow-white hair would have been black, the brown eyes daring, and his body slim and wiry. There was an air about him that spoke of education and breeding. She waited for him to speak.

"B. N. Calloway," he said. There was a noticeable lack of a southwestern drawl in his voice. "Call me Ben. Only Mack insists on calling me Calloway."

"Hello, Ben." Johanna held out her hand and looked into faded brown eyes that were on a level with her own. "My name is Johanna Doan."

"Johanna," he repeated, and his eyes flicked at old Mack. "Lovely name," he said softly.

Red came to the porch holding Jacy by the arm. It was obvious that he wasn't sure about the reception she would receive and looked at Johanna to indicate what he should do. Johanna came forward and put her arm around her sister. She led her to the old man as if the words they had spoken about her had never been said.

"Mr. Macklin, my sister, Miss Jaceta Doan."

"Good afternoon, sir," Jacy said, with a frightened tremor in her voice.

Old Mack grunted, turned in his chair, and looked off toward the mountains.

Trying desperately to excuse his rudeness, Johanna introduced her sister to Ben, who smiled, clasped her hand warmly, and bowed gallantly.

"Two lovely ladies in the house," he said. "I'm over-whelmed."

He led them through the middle door and into a hall that ran the length of the house. There were two doors on each side of the hall and a small, steep stairway at the end. A door to the back of the hall opened onto what appeared to be another porch. The first two doors in the hall were closed, but looking into one of the last doors, Johanna saw a large kitchen with a black iron stove and a long trestle table with two benches. On the other side of the hall was a room with several chairs, a table, and a huge fireplace full of cold ashes. The place was stark and bare and dirty. The floors were stone, the same as those of the porch patio, and were covered with dust so thick it looked as though it had been there for years. She glimpsed several lamps, their chimneys black with soot.

Ben painfully climbed the steep stairway to a room tucked under the roof. Johanna could walk upright only in the middle of it, because of the sharp slant of the ceiling. It looked larger because its only furnishings were a bed, a table, a ladder-back chair, and an old trunk. Pegs for hanging clothes lined the wall at one end. A faded quilt in what Johanna recognized as the "flower garden" pattern covered the sagging straw mattress on the rope bed. Jacy looked at the ill-kempt room in dismay.

Forcing a lightness in her voice, Johanna said, "After a good cleaning we'll be very comfortable here."

Ben smiled, but his voice was anxious as he said, "This house needs a woman. I'm glad you're here."

"Thank you," Johanna said, then asked hesitantly, "Is Mr. Macklin always this difficult, or is this just one of his bad days?"

Ben's brows went up. "I'm sorry to tell you this, Johanna, but Mack is always difficult. He's an unhappy, unfulfilled man, and this is one of his better days. If you can do it, close your mind to his cruel remarks, for he's to be pitied. He's never allowed himself to be happy. He cares for no one and nothing but this valley. He feels it's a sign of weakness to show either mercy or compassion to another human being."

* * *

When the sisters were alone, Jacy came to Johanna and rested her head on her shoulder.

"That old man is horrible, Johanna. I can't believe he's Luis's father."

"Neither can I, but Mooney said he was." She took hold of her sister's shoulders and held her away from her so that she could look into her face. "We won't be discouraged, Jacy. Mr. Macklin isn't used to having women around. He'll soften up, but in the meantime, we won't let that mean old man think that he's smart enough to get our goat!" She laughed, and Jacy couldn't help but smile.

"Oh, Johanna, you're just like Papa. You can paint a silver lining on the blackest cloud."

"We can make this dreary, dirty room livable," Johanna said with determination. "Get out our sheets, towels, dresser set, and mirror. I'll go down and get a pail of water and a broom."

Johanna changed into a faded brown work dress and tied an apron around her slender waist. She secured her blond hair in a knot atop her head, then took her first tentative steps down the stairway. She entered the kitchen and stopped short. She stood in the middle of the room and gazed with despair at the disorder, wrinkling her nose at the offensive odor coming from the spittoon by the hearth. The cooking range and a very long work counter were covered with piles of earthenware plates, pots, and an assortment of cutlery. The floor was constructed of smooth stone slabs and littered with grease and scraps of food embellished with chunks of dried mud that, Johanna assumed, had been tracked in by the men. Soot hung like Spanish moss behind the cookstove, and cobwebs floated from the ceiling beams. She felt a flicker of anger at the thought that the ashes in the hearth had probably been there for months.

As she hesitated, hard footsteps, accompanied by the jingle

of spurs, resounded on the stone floor outside the house, then into the hall. Seconds later came the murmur of male voices that escalated into a storm of angry words, unintelligible and rumbling. She could distinguish the cold, harsh voice of the old man, and a second, equally cold voice rising in argument. Johanna was gripped with curiosity. Who would dare raise his voice to the formidable old man?

The hail of angry words grew louder until the antagonist and the old man were shouting at each other. The old man's angry voice rose and his words reached the kitchen.

"You'll do as I say, you bastard, or you'll not get one foot of this valley!"

"I've already got the whole goddamn thing, you old fool! You've gone too far this time."

"You've got nothin'! Hear me! You got nothin' but what I'll let ya have!"

"You're dreamin', you ornery old cuss. You got only what I'll let *you* have!"

"This valley is mine and I'll do with it as I goddamn please. You ain't runnin' things yet, by God! Come back here, you bastard, I ain't through—"

The words were cut off by the sound of a door slammed so viciously that the walls of the house shuddered. Silence fell, and Johanna drew a long breath of relief for the end of the barely restrained violence.

She moved to find the broom and a pail, then heard the hard steps and the soft jingling of spurs coming down the hall. She stood, apprehension holding her motionless, wishing desperately that she didn't have to face another difficult Macklin. It was too soon. She needed time to adjust to this family, to their violent tempers, and to the drab, unfriendly atmosphere of the house.

A huge man with hard blue eyes and white-blond hair filled the doorway. Speechless, Johanna stared, her startled eyes questioning his apparent anger at her for being there. His face was twisted with bitterness and a smoldering rage that was directed at her.

Arrogantly her stare was returned. He stood with his feet apart, balancing on the high heels of his boots. His long legs seemed to stretch up forever before reaching his slim hips, about which was strapped a wide gunbelt. His shirt, opened at the neck, revealed a chest tanned toast-brown. A head of curly, wind-tossed flaxen hair reached almost to the top of the doorway. Piercing blue eyes gleamed diabolically over his blade of nose.

His tightly compressed lips opened and he bit out, "So you're the one that's come to stud!"

Johanna had no idea how many seconds went by while she stood and stared at him with open-mouthed astonishment, his words echoing through her mind.

"What did you say?" The words came out of her as if someone else had said them.

"With outraged virture, too!" he sneered. "A saloon girl with outraged virture! Well, I never thought I'd live to see *that*!"

Johanna was so surprised by his attack that she felt faintly giddy. Her face paled.

"Why are you talking to me like this?" She swallowed with difficulty. "Who are you?"

He strode forward until she had to arch her neck to see his face. He searched her pale, distraught face for a hint of duplicity. Without softening his expression, he hit her with angry cutting words.

"Is it possible the old man hasn't told you about the bastards of Macklin Valley? I'm surprised!" he said angrily, sarcastically. "Let me introduce you to one of them. Burr Englebretson Macklin. My mother's name was Englebretson, but I've taken the name Macklin, not for any love of the old bastard but because it sticks in his craw for me to do so. I've taken it from him, just as I'll take this valley for my own by the right of having been unfortunate enough to be sired by that old man—and because I've ridden hard, driven hard, and worked until calluses covered my hands and I almost dropped in my tracks. That's my right of ownership, and I'll not have a scheming woman shoved down my throat in order to keep what's already mine!''

Johanna gasped at the onslaught. ''I don't understand any of what you're saying.''

He looked down at her with cold eyes filled with scorn. They flicked over her face as if he were looking at something beneath his contempt. She could almost smell the anger that radiated from him. Without being aware of it, she stepped back, but his hard eyes held her bewildered ones as if they were caught in a snare.

''Don't tell me you didn't know of the old man's plans! We're pawns. Pawns, in his plan to populate the valley with legitimate grandsons made in his own image. Look at yourself and you'll know why you were chosen for this honor. Blond hair and blue eyes, same as mine. He'll see to it that we're wed, all proper and legal. No more bastards . . . Macklin Valley will never be left to a bastard.'' His chin jutted and he taunted, ''How does it feel to know you've been brought here solely to act as brood mare?''

''No! I don't believe you!'' Johanna was on the edge of hysteria.

''Believe it!'' He glared into her rebellious face, his jaw muscles pulsing as he fought to contain his anger. ''If you're eager to put out the fire burning in your britches, I'll oblige, but that's as far as it'll go. I'll not wed you. The old man is as devious as the devil, but bastard or not, I don't give up what's mine, and I choose my own women.''

He was gone before she could voice the retort that sprang

to her mind, but his presence remained in the room long after his giant strides swallowed up the length of the hall. The sound of the door being slammed echoed throughout the house.

Johanna swayed. The walls of the room seemed to recede. The insults he had heaped upon her were the hardest thing she'd had to bear aside from her family tragedy. She stood with her arms clasped around her shuddering body in an effort to dispel the effect this overpowering man had left on her. She collapsed onto the bench by the table and buried her face in her hands.

Burr Macklin was every bit as rancorous as the father he so obviously despised and who so obviously despised him. How could Mr. Cash have sent her to this place knowing what the old man had in mind? This man was so far removed from her imaginings of the man she would someday marry that she felt she would prefer to face plague, pestilence, or starvation rather than become tied to him for life. He was heartless, uncivilized, and savage; and there was not a speck of difference between him and old Mack Macklin, who had sired him.

# CHAPTER
## *Five*

"**S**o you've met him."

Johanna spun around on the bench, a picture of flagrant outrage, her classic beauty enhanced by the high color in her cheeks and the sparkle of tears in her eyes. Ben hesitantly came through the doorway.

"Yes, I've met *him*!" Her voice was shrill with anger. "There's not an ounce of difference between father and son."

As he took a seat opposite her, he sighed. "I'm sorry," he said gently. "It's unfortunate you had to meet him just now. He——"

"To meet Burr Macklin under any circumstances would be unpleasant," she retorted. "He's detestable, arrogant, and uncivilized, besides being boorish and . . . self-centered! I'm no meek little mouse, Ben, and I refuse to be intimidated by a loud voice and crude language. I resent that man's implying that I came here for any reason except to do the job I was hired for. And from the looks of this . . . pigsty, a housekeeper is sorely needed!"

"Lass, Burr was as unaware of Mack's plans as you were.

70

It's natural for him to be resentful.'' For a brief moment a small flicker of pain showed in his eyes.

Johanna tried to steel herself against softening, but it wasn't her nature to stay angry for long.

"Ben, what can I do?" She looked pleadingly at him. "We have almost no money left. And my sister—"

"Red told me about your sister. He thought that perhaps she should stay with him and Rosita."

A lump of fear came up into her throat. "Do you think that he . . . that Mr. Macklin will be unkind to her?"

"I'm sure he will, if the opportunity presents itself. We must try to keep them apart."

His use of the word *we* had a soothing effect on Johanna. She reached across the greasy table and clasped his hand. His fingers were long and slim and his nails trimmed and clean. It struck her how out of place he was in this house, but for now her mind was too crowded with impressions to wonder why he was here; it was enough to know she had a friend.

"She mustn't know about the . . . other thing, Ben. This reason Mr. Macklin wanted me here. She's just beginning to accept her condition, and I don't want her upset."

"We'll do all we can to keep her from knowing. I'll speak to Burr."

Johanna got up. "I'd better get back upstairs. I came down to get a broom and a pail of water," she said with a dry smile, "and what I got was a blow, right between the eyes."

Back in the attic room she set to work with vigor, making as little noise as possible lest she wake Jacy, who was curled up on the bed. She swept down the walls with the broom before sweeping and mopping the floor, using strong lye-soap water. When she finished she was exhausted, but the room was clean and smelled of soap and scrubbed wood.

After giving the room a satisfied glance, she carried the pail of dirty water down the stairs and out the back door. She walked past a small boy leaning against the house, watching her. He lowered his eyes when she looked at him. Appearing to ignore him, she went to the end of the porch and threw the water out into the yard. The boy didn't move. She started back toward the door, then veered off toward him. Johanna loved children and missed the contact she'd had with them in the classroom. She was particularly curious about this child, eager to know why he so obviously disliked her.

"Hello."

The boy neither looked up nor answered.

"*Hola*," she tried.

He continued to look down. His dark brown hair was long and looked freshly washed. She couldn't see much of his face, for his chin rested on his chest, but he was rather light-skinned and his features were sharp. The bright flannel shirt he wore, obviously new, was much too large for him, and the sleeves were turned up at the cuffs. She reached out a finger and lifted his chin.

"No English? No *español*?" she asked gently.

The boy jerked his head away from her hand and looked up at her. She almost recoiled from the venom that shot from the child's cold blue eyes. The shock of seeing the vivid blue eyes between thick dark lashes left her speechless. Quickly she concealed her surprise and smiled at him.

"You gave me a fright when you threw the stone at the horses," she said in Spanish.

"I no want hit horses!" His small face was tight and he looked at her defiantly.

Still smiling, Johanna said, "You didn't like my hat?"

"I no like you!"

The smile left Johanna's face. "How do you know you don't like me? You don't know me."

"Old Mack want you be Burr's woman. He said to Ben when wagon come. Burr don't want no woman." The little boy's lips were trembling and he was trying hard to stare her down and keep the tears from his eyes.

Johanna heard a door open at the far end of the porch.

"And that's the reason you don't like me?"

The boy didn't answer.

"Well then, there's no reason why we can't be friends. I'd rather be afflicted with horns and a tail than to be . . . Burr's woman. I wouldn't have your precious Burr if he were served up to me on a silver platter." She laughed lightly.

Still the boy said nothing.

"You believe me, don't you?"

"Bucko!"

The boy jerked around at the sound of the sharp voice. Then he turned back to Johanna.

"Burr say to me, say I sorry."

Johanna looked steadily at him. "But you're not sorry, are you?"

"No."

"Then I don't think you should have to say so."

The boy glanced at the man and back to Johanna. He moved away from the wall and went toward the man, who was waiting at the end of the porch. He lurched as he walked, and Johanna noticed that his foot was bent outward at the ankle. The man was watching her over the boy's head, waiting to see her reaction to the boy's deformity. She didn't allow her expression to change until the man turned his back and, taking the boy's hand, went toward the bunkhouse. Only then did she let surface the digust she felt for Burr Macklin. He had expected her to show revulsion. Because he lacked compassion, he didn't believe such an emotion might be found in others.

"Just like his father!" she hissed under her breath.

Then Ben came out from the kitchen. "You've met Bucko. Both of them are quite a dose to take in one day, eh, lass?"

"Are there any more hostile members in this family, Ben?" she asked wearily.

"Don't you think three are enough?" His eyes twinkled.

"I'm not worried about the child—he's young enough to be won over. It's the father and the grandfather that worry me."

"Burr's protective of the boy and keeps him out of Mack's way as much as possible."

Not wanting to get on the subject of Burr again, Johanna asked, "About the evening meal, Ben. Will I be expected to prepare it?"

"No, lass, you've done enough for today. We can eat over at the bunkhouse."


Johanna slept badly that night. She was exhausted both physically and mentally. After the bewildering meeting with old Mack, climaxed by the meeting with Burr Macklin, her mind was plagued by an even greater turmoil than that which she'd experienced at Fort Davis. When sleep finally claimed her, nightmares came to torment and confuse her.

Once in that deep blackness she awakened to a strange, unnerving feeling that brought her to full awareness. A poignant loneliness possessed her for the first time in her life. Careful not to wake Jacy, she got out of bed and went to the window. She was filled with uneasiness, and thoughts raced around in her head. Had the scene with Burr Macklin really happened? Did old Mack really think she would marry that overbearing, arrogant man? Thank God the idea didn't appeal to Burr. And the little boy whose eyes were so like Burr's . . . how many more children in the valley had blue eyes? She could ask Red to take her and Jacy back to town, but she was afraid another trip would be harmful to her sister. So she would stay, because of Jacy's condition, until the next supply wagon went into town. That thought held, and she resigned herself to it. In the meantime, she wouldn't allow these loathsome men to intimidate her. Maybe it would be best for Jacy to be with Red and his wife, but, oh, she would miss her! Ben had promised to help keep her and old Mack apart, so maybe she would wait and see how things worked out.

Johanna paced the room restlessly, then lay back down on the bed, closing her eyes wearily. She dozed and eventually fell into an uneasy sleep.

When dawn brushed the sky with the first faint streaks of light, Johanna got up and went down to the kitchen. She found Ben bent over a tub of dishes.

"Sit down, lass." He picked up two of the freshly washed cups. "Let's have some coffee."

Johanna sat at the trestle table, and Ben set the coffee in front of her, then slowly eased himself onto the bench opposite her. The grimace of pain that crossed his face caused her to say, "Ben, you shouldn't have been bending over that tub."

"It's been a long time, lass, since I've been chided by a woman. Sounds kind of nice." His eyes twinkled, and he reached into his pocket for his pipe. "Burr ordered this tobacco all the way from South Carolina. I was surprised when it came on the train, and I'm like a small boy with a bag of stick candy."

"My father was the same with his favorite tobacco."

"You haven't always lived in Texas, have you, lass? I don't recognize your accent."

"I should have a Texas drawl, Ben. I lived there from the time I was five years old. My father and I came from St. Louis. He was a teacher and pronounced his words very distinctly, and I probably acquired the habit from him." She sipped her coffee, her face thoughtful. "Are there any more surprises waiting for me, Ben? This is a very strange family." She gave a nervous little laugh.

Ben puffed on his pipe for a moment, saying nothing, his expressive features sobering. When he answered her his voice was without warmth.

"It isn't a family, Johanna. There's Mack, and then there's Burr, Bucko, and Luis."

"And you, Ben? Where do you fit in?" Johanna felt a lump in her throat when she saw the pain in his eyes.

"Ah, lass, there's me. It's natural that you would wonder why I stay on with this tyrant. There's not an ounce of friendship between us, no respect, and no liking."

"It's obvious you're an educated man, Ben," she said, thinking of the waste of his life.

Once again Ben paused before he spoke, his lips curved over the pipestem, his eyes alight with admiration for her.

"Educated in every way except in how to take care of myself in this savage and unpredictable land. When I was a lad I left my home in Massachusetts. I had become involved in some unpleasantness, and my family felt that I had disgraced them. I arrived in El Paso as green as grass and completely unequipped for the life in that lawless, brawling town. To make a long story short, Mack saved me from being stomped to death by a bunch of drunken cowhands. It was a purely selfish act on his part; he needed me to guard his back. Nevertheless, I was grateful and came back to New Mexico with him. I've been here ever since, except for a few trips I've made outside."

"But . . . why do you stay?"

Ben stirred uncomfortably and knocked the ashes from his pipe. "Well, I stayed at first because I had no other place to go. Then Mack went out with a mule train and came back with a young girl." His face closed and he looked away.

"Mack had only contempt for her." He paused. "She was never strong enough to leave the house after Burr was born." A wistful note crept into his voice. "Anna died when he was four years old and I stayed on." Then he added softly, almost under his breath, "I promised her I would."

For a moment Johanna was quiet, then she put her hand on his. "You stayed because of Burr?"

"Yes, I stayed because of Burr."

Johanna refilled the coffee cups. She felt a sadness, and it reflected in her eyes.

Interpreting the look, Ben said cheerfully, "You're not to feel sorry for me, lass. I had more in a few short years than most men have in a lifetime. And I've had the pleasure of seeing Anna's son grow up to be a fine man." His eyes flashed with amusement when she lifted her brows in question. "Despite what you think now, Burr has many admirable qualities."

Johanna decided it would be wiser not to argue the point.

"Why do he and his father hate each other so?"

"They always have," Ben said matter-of-factly. "As a little fellow, Burr was scared to death of Mack—not that he came near him very often. There was a time when Burr was about fourteen that Mack took sort of an interest in him. He took him out to El Paso, and, I found out later, to a sporting house. At fourteen he was a man, and one day he found Mack laying a horsewhip on Luis and he fought him like a tiger. Course, Mack almost beat him to death. Ever since that day there's been open antagonism between them."

So many things crowded into Johanna's head that she found it hard not to keep asking questions.

"Why did Burr stay?"

"He left after a while," Ben said slowly. "He was gone for a few years, fought in the war, and saw a lot of the world. He came back a few years ago and found Mack with a crushed foot turned putrid with rotting flesh. He and Luis took off the foot and saved Mack's life. Not that they ever got any thanks for it—just the opposite. Mack's cursed them every day since then. But Burr says he's set on staying. He says he's never seen a place to compare with this valley. Luis feels that way, too. Nothing Mack can do will run them off. They've worked hard and made a lot of improvements these past few years.''

''What will Burr do, Ben, if Mr. Macklin doesn't leave the land to him?''

''He'll fight for it,'' Ben said simply.

The statement gave Johanna food for thought as she worked beside Ben, finishing washing the tub of dishes. Perhaps Burr did have a reason to feel bitter, but her opinion of him remained the same. Fine man indeed! Fathering children just as his father had before him. And the boy, Bucko, would undoubtedly do the same.

''Ben, does Mr. Macklin spend most of his time in his room? Shall I make breakfast for him?''

''Mack gets up at dawn and sits on the porch and watches the men get saddled up for the day's work. Codger brings him coffee and, later, breakfast if he wants it. I don't know what the arrangements will be now that we have a house-keeper.'' He smiled mischievously.

Johanna smiled back. She was becoming quite fond of this slight, gentle man. He had lasting qualities, as had her papa, a calm confidence, sense of humor, and compassion.

It was midmorning. Jacy had come down, eaten breakfast, and helped with some of the lighter cleaning before Johanna suggested she go out and look around. Ben offered to accompany her, and she went readily enough. Johanna suspected that Jacy sensed she was unwelcome and was glad to leave the house, if only for a little while.

Alone in the kitchen, Johanna found the work satisfying. She placed the freshly washed dishes on the trestle table and filled a large wooden bowl with hot water from the kettle on the cookstove. After rubbing a chunk of hard lye soap between her hands to build up suds, she scrubbed the shelves, then replaced the dishes. The cupboard at the end of the room held a few supplies; she scoured that and replaced those foodstuffs that were still edible. The tin of flour was full of weevils, so she dumped it and washed the tin, leaving the lid off so that the can would become thoroughly dry. She scoured the trestle table and the benches before she poured the soapy water into a tub to use on the floor. She felt she was making progress and hummed softly under her breath, almost forgetting the brooding, hate-filled household. The call, when it came, couldn't have startled her more.

"Girl!"

Johanna straightened her tired back and waited for her thumping heart to settle into its regular pattern. The old man called again, his roar filling the house. Johanna took her time drying her hands and smoothing back her hair. After pausing in the hall to make sure her features were composed, she calmly walked out the door and confronted the old man sitting in his cowhide chair.

He looked even more disagreeable than he had the day before. His gray hair was long, hanging almost to his shoulders. His mustache drooped on either side of his wide mouth. The rest of his face was covered with a stubble of gray beard. He had once been a powerful man. His shoulders were broad, his torso long, but age and inactivity had thickened his waist, and his soiled shirt barely came together over his protruding stomach. However, his eyes, beneath bushy gray brows, were sharp and penetrating, and his lips were set defensively.

"Did you call?" Johanna asked cheerfully. "By the way, my name is Johanna."

The old man was still. Only his eyes were alive, and they examined her from head to toe as if searching for a way to dig into her to make her squirm.

When he didn't say anything, Johanna continued, "You should have a small bell, Mr. Macklin. Then there would be no need for you to shout when you wanted to speak to me." She smiled at him, determined not to let him think he frightened her.

"Hush your foolish prattle and sit down," he snapped.

"Thank you, I'll be glad to sit and rest awhile." She turned one of the chairs so that she would be facing him and sat down, crossing her legs at the ankles. While she waited for him to speak she fanned her face with the tail of her apron.

He slumped in his chair and stuck out his booted foot in a deliberate, childish way, she thought, but she refused to look at it and continued to look him straight in the eye. Finally he turned his eyes away and looked out over the valley.

"Do you like this place, girl?" he asked begrudgingly, as if it pained him to inquire.

"I've been here only two days, Mr. Macklin. That's hardly time enough to decide whether I like it or not," Johanna said innocently.

He glared at her. "You've been here long enough to know if you like the valley and the house," he said impatiently.

"It's a lovely valley." She smiled pleasantly.

"Speak up," he ordered sharply. "Do you like it or don't you?"

Johanna turned her eyes from him and looked out toward the ranch buildings before she answered.

"Yes, I like the valley very much. It's a beautiful place. I don't like the house; I'm sure no woman designed it. But I'll make do while I'm here, which won't be for long." She looked him straight in the eye, determined not to back down, to meet him on an equal basis whether he liked it or not. She needed to stay in the valley awhile, but not at the expense of her pride or peace of mind.

Anger tightened the muscles in old Mack's face, and instinctively Johanna knew he was holding back his rage at her criticism of the house.

"What's wrong with it? It'll last. It's every bit as strong as when I built it thirty years ago. There ain't a better house this side of the mountains."

Johanna smiled sweetly. Somehow she knew her smiles irritated him.

"Oh, yes, it's built to last, I'll grant you that. But it's an unhandy house. I will say, though, it has potential. Water could be piped up into the house from the spring, and a washhouse built for washing and bathing. The place certainly needs a good cleaning and rugs on the floors and curtains at the windows and a few more lamps. A few flower beds in the yard would add a pleasant touch. And, oh yes, one more thing . . . an outhouse. This ranch could certainly use an outhouse."

He didn't say anything at first, and Johanna thought maybe she had stunned him with her frankness, but she saw his lips quirk at the corners, and although she was sure he hadn't smiled in years, he seemed very close to doing so.

"An outhouse, aye? Can't a gal from town go out in the bushes and shit like the rest of us?" he jeered, and spat a stream of tobacco juice into the can beside his chair.

Knowing his words were meant to shock her, Johanna kept her face composed as though this were an everyday topic of conversation.

"Oh, yes, and I'm sure I can manage it easier than, say, an . . . older person. I was thinking of your convenience, Mr. Macklin, as well as my own."

They stared at each other, and suddenly Johanna felt good. This arbitrary old man knew she was no spineless creature who would scurry away when he bellowed.

"You ain't got no folks to go back to. You ain't got nothin'," he said suddenly. "Stay here and the valley can be yours." His probing eyes searched her face, but she showed no reaction to the offer.

She smiled and got to her feet. "Thank you, but no. My sister and I will be leaving when the next supply train goes to town. Mr. Redford tells me the trip is made every six or eight months."

Stung to anger by her blunt refusal, he threw back his head and spat out, "Ain't good enough for ya, is that it? You don't need to be actin' so uppity with me, gal. I know what ya come from and I know you ain't got a pot to piss in. I'm offerin' you a chance to own the best valley in the Southwest and money to fix the house the way you want it. I'll give it all to you and not to that bastard you'll have to wed to get it."

Johanna crossed her arms and lifted her head. Sparks of anger danced in her eyes.

"No!" she said firmly. "When I wed, if ever I do, it will be under circumstances entirely different from the ones you offer. Thank you for your most *generous* offer," she said sarcastically. "But I want no part of your son or your valley."

Her scorn cracked like a whip across his pride. He jerked erect and gritted out viciously, "Ya goddamn snotty bitch! Who the hell do ya think you are? I know ya ain't nothin' but a goddamn saloon gal!"

The vehement roar of his voice filled her ears. She backed away from him, opened the door, and walked into the house.

"Don't walk away from me, you bitch! I ain't through with you!"

The hall was dark and cool. She placed a hand over her

madly thumping heart and leaned against the wall in an effort to compose herself.

"So the old man put the proposition to you, did he?" The cold voice of Burr Macklin broke the stillness of the hall.

Instinctively Johanna lifted her chin and a fiercely defiant glint came into her eyes. It seemed that her ordeal was not yet over. He lounged in the kitchen doorway.

"He offered the ranch. Why didn't you accept his offer? Of course, the gift would include his bastard son served up on a silver valley!" His cold blue eyes pinned her glance. "Now that I think about it, it might not be such a bad idea. It would save me a trip to El Paso to visit the whores."

Johanna would have gone past him and into the kitchen, but his bulk filled the doorway, barring her path. Coldly she stared at him, taking her time, her contempt no less obvious because it was mute.

"It doesn't appear to me that you've deprived yourself, Mr. Macklin," she said stiffly, and turned to walk up the stairs.

He gripped her wrist so viciously that she barely withheld a pained cry as he spun her around.

"What do you mean by that remark?" he asked through lips taut with suppressed anger. "You've got guts to be throwing accusations around. You're fresh out of a saloon! A singer? A whore, if the truth were known!"

Her heart hammered wildly. The fingers that circled her wrist tightened their grip, discouraging any attempt to break away. They stood like that for several seconds, saying nothing, her expressive features giving some indication of what was going on in her mind. Then she shook her head slowly.

"That's the second time you've called me a saloon girl," she said frigidly. "Do you think that makes me unsuitable to be Mr. Macklin's housekeeper? Are you waiting for me to defend myself? All right. I did work in a saloon for a while.

It was necessary for me and my sister to have money to live on. It was honest work and I was paid for services rendered.''

He threw her hand from him in a gesture of contempt. ''I bet you were,'' he sneered.

Johanna's control snapped. Her hand flashed up and she struck him a resounding slap across the face. She was as stunned by her action as was the man who stood before her. It was the last thing she ever expected to do; something she had never done in her entire life. These Macklins were far different from the men she had known. They seemed to bring out traits in her that had never surfaced before.

''Damn you!'' His arms were around her and she was pulled forcibly against him even before he finished speaking, and one large hand entwined itself in the hair at the nape of her neck, pulling back her head. ''Is this what you're wanting, Miss Prissy? Are you an old maid, starving for a man?'' Using the hand in her hair to hold her head, he covered her mouth with his, hard and angrily.

Johanna struggled to free herself. She wanted only to strike out at him, to treat him as violently as he treated her, but she was forced to yield to his superior strength and the cruel demand of his mouth. His arms held her so tightly against him that she could feel the wild beating of his heart against her breast. She was aware of the tangy smell of his freshly shaved face, and his mouth, as it ground into hers, tasted of tobacco. She was sure she would swoon from lack of breath when he released her mouth at last, and for a moment she stood locked in his embrace, breathing deeply and erratically as though she'd run too far too fast.

''Let go of me!'' Her voice rasped huskily. She pushed against his chest, feeling that she would suffocate if she didn't get away from him. ''I said . . . let go of me!''

Slowly he let his arms slid from around her, and she saw

a hint of a smile on his face that did not quite reach the cold eyes.

"Now you can say you've been kissed by a bastard," he said softly.

Johanna felt choked with a bitterness that almost matched his. She allowed her lips to form a contemptuous sneer, but then she realized the futility of the gesture, for he had turned away.

"Do you think that's something to brag about? Being a bastard is no excuse for bad manners," she informed him in as cool and steady a voice as she could manage.

"Bad manners?" He laughed. The sound was short and dry. He turned and touched her cheek lightly with his fingertips. "I might point out, Miss Priss, that bastards are not supposed to have manners." He tapped her cheek and laughed when she jerked her head away. "You came here thinking you'd found the pot at the end of the rainbow and all you found was a lot of bullshit thrown out by a crazy old man. Didn't anyone ever tell you that bastards are survivors and that a lot of great men in history were bastards?"

Johanna felt her heart throbbing under her ribs in a strange and urgent way that alarmed her. Almost unconsciously, she raised her hand to wipe it across her lips, still warm and tingling from his kiss.

"Are you making a bid for my sympathy, Mr. Macklin?" she asked quietly, rashly uncaring that she might arouse his anger again. "You have so much to be grateful for, and yet you're bitter and angry because . . . because your father didn't marry your mother."

It took her only a minute to realize that this time she had gone too far. She stepped back when she saw his mouth tighten and the twitch of the muscles in his strong jaw. His eyes bored into hers and his large hand tightened into a fist.

He shook his blond head sharply as if to clear it, and when he spoke, the harshness in his deep voice chilled her.

"You little fool! Don't you ever pity me, you hear?"

Johanna was not aware, as he was, that Ben had come into the hall from the back of the house and had caught those last few words. He came up to them, his face creased in an uneasy grin, his anxious eyes going from one to the other with the unasked question of why they were quarreling.

"Burr, did you tell Johanna her sister is going to spend the evening at Red's and that she wants her to come down later with her guitar and the violin?"

Burr swung around, his features still hard and unrelenting. "No," he snapped. "I hadn't gotten around to it. We were busy, talking about . . . other things. What I came in to tell our . . . housekeeper, is this—Bucko and I will take our meals in the ranch house from now on, as is our due!"

He turned and strode out the door, his steps hard, his spurs leaving a musical sound trailing him as he crossed the stone floor of the porch and headed toward the corrals.

# CHAPTER
## Six

**B**en watched Burr leave, then swung around to face Johanna. She shook her head. Nothing would stop her tears, and Ben would probably misinterpret their meaning.

"That's the most detestable, uncouth man I've ever met!" She turned swiftly and went into the kitchen. It was ridiculous to cry, she told herself, but there was nothing she could do about the tears rolling down her cheeks.

Ben followed her, his face full of concern. "What did he do, Johanna? What did he do to make you cry?"

She turned on him, not wishing to include him in her anger, yet unable to subdue it. "I'm just so mad, Ben, that's all. I'm just so mad!"

"Sit down and we'll have coffee," he said soothingly.

Johanna wiped her eyes on her apron. Her thick lashes were spiked with tears and her lips quivered. She swallowed convulsively.

"I'm sorry, Ben. This must be embarrassing for you. I don't know what's the matter with me. I'm not a crying woman. First I cry because I'm mad. Now I just cry. I don't know what's the matter with me."

"It's perfectly understandable," Ben told her quietly. "Beauty in a real woman is the capacity to feel things very deeply, and that includes pain as well as joy." He clasped her hand warmly. "Don't judge Burr too harshly, lass. He's had so little of what really matters in this life."

Her cheeks warm and pink, she looked at him with eyes that shone brightly through her tears, and her brain whirled with emotions from her contact with Burr. She couldn't bring herself to pour out her feelings of disgust for the man Ben so obviously loved like a son, and yet she had to voice her disapproval.

"But . . . he's so crude, Ben. He's not like you, he's arrogant and . . . demanding."

"He is that, lass, but it's due to his battling all these years with Mack. He resents his beginnings, girl, and who can blame him? Anna wanted me to tell him the circumstances of his birth as soon as I thought he was old enough to understand. She never wanted her son to think she had willingly submitted to a man like Mack. I told Burr as much as I knew, but there's a depth to Mack that no one knows, possibly not even himself. He's not a man who explains his actions. I only know he came riding in one day with Anna, and my life took on a different meaning."

*It had been an unusually wet spring in 1843. Mack Macklin was tired. He had been away from his valley for two months. It had been almost that long since he'd had a woman and the ache in his loins, added to his discomfort, made him impatient and irritable.*

Hugging his rifle against his shoulder, the big man took careful aim at the rock and fired. The rock splintered and the boulder tilted. The boulder was propped by a small rock and piled behind it was a heap of debris and in front of it a steep incline. At the bottom of the slope the Indians were grouping for the next, more than likely final, assault on the wagon train.

Carefully, Mack Macklin took another sight and fired. He never knew if the second shot was necessary, for the instant his finger squeezed off that second shot the whole pile of rocks broke loose from the wet hillside and came thundering down. There was an instant of panic among the Indians, then a startled yelp, followed by another and another. Two Indians raced into the open and Mack Macklin calmly drilled the first through the chest, and dropped the second with a bullet from his six-gun. The stones tumbled down, bouncing off a shoulder of rock in their rush to the arroyo below.

Swiftly, before the Indians had time to adjust themselves, the big blond man positioned himself so that he had a view of the short gully leading into the main canyon. He grinned. A shrewd, experienced Indian fighter, he knew just exactly what the Indians would do. They would be on the trail fast, and he'd get them one by one.

Grinning with satisfaction, he leaned against the rock, reloaded, and methodically fired into the canyon. He picked off four men, being careful not to hit the horses, then he stopped firing and waited until one of the Indians commenced to crawl toward the bush, leaving a trail of dark, wet blood on the sand of the creekbed. The giant man smiled wryly.

"Bastard," he muttered and squeezed off a shot. The Indian's body jumped, then lay still.

Mack took off his hat and wiped the sweat from his brow with his shirtsleeve. He checked his rifle, replaced his hat, and with catlike agility moved across the rocks toward the horses. His blue eyes narrowed, bringing his sun-bleached brows together over his beak of a nose. His wide, thin-lipped mouth twisted in a sneer as he gazed with contempt into the canyon.

He shoved his rifle into its holder on the saddle bow and mounted his big sorrel, which carefully picked its way among the rocks as it descended. The man who had just calmly killed a dozen or more men felt his pulses quicken. If his eyes hadn't deceived him, and it wasn't likely they had, there was a blond woman with the wagon train. He had seen the sun shining on her blond hair as he peered over the rim of the rise after hearing the shots. It was then that he had decided to take a side in the skirmish between the Indians and the greenhorns, who had formed a half-assed circle with their wagons and were, in his opinion, doing a piss-poor job of defending themselves.

As he rode toward them he removed his hat. He didn't want the sons of bitches to think he was an Indian and open fire. One thing he had learned in his almost five years in the territory was that greenhorns were unpredictable. He squinted against the sun and searched the site for a glimpse of the girl. He saw her bending over a figure sprawled in the dirt beside an overturned wagon. A look of smugness settled over his hard features. From the looks of things, it wasn't going to be hard to get her.

Now that he had spotted what he had come for, he took his time riding toward the train and looked around. They had about ten poorly equipped wagons and hardly any know-how at all. If they got out of Texas it would be a miracle. Good thing he'd come along when he had or the woman's long shiny hair would be hanging from an Apache's belt by now.

A group of pilgrims were waiting for him. All farmers looking for the promised land, he thought sarcastically. One of the group moved toward him and held out his hand. Mack ignored it until he had looked the man up and down, then shook it without interest. The man was thin, and his pointed beard bobbed up and down on his chest when he talked.

"We sure do thanky, mister, yessiree, we sure do thanky," he blubbered. "We'd'a probably got ourselves together and got the heathens, but you comin' like you done helped. Yessiree, with God's help we'd'a done it, but he saw fit to . . ."

Mack stared coolly down into the man's face. "You'd'a shit, too!"

"I ain't a-takin' nothin' away from you, mister," the man hastened to say. "I ain't a-takin' nothin' away atall. It was God's will, was all I was a-sayin'."

Mack's look dismissed him, and after hesitating the man shrugged and stood aside. Mack then urged his horse into the circle of wagons, dropped the reins, and dismounted. His sharp eyes missed nothing. Two horses and two oxen had been killed. Three men lay dead with arrows in their backs and a fourth lay dying, his blood pouring out rapidly. The blond girl, his reason for being here, was bending over him. Mack went to her and without preliminaries squatted down beside the wounded man.

"You this girl's pa?"

"Uncle," he gasped.

"You're done for, you know that," Mack said coolly.

"Aye." The word was whispered.

"The Indians'll be back. Too many braves died here. There'll be weepin' and wailin' in the villages and they'll have a need for revenge. Are you wantin' this girl to stay here and be scalped or to come with me and live?"

The man's eyes were beginning to glaze over, but with an effort he said, "Go, Anna. Go with him."

Mack got to his feet and motioned to the leader of the group. "Tell this man what you want," he said to the dying man.

"Anna, go with him and . . . live," he gasped, and his eyes swung to the girl's tear-wet face, then closed. The girl's bowed head rested on her uncle's breast and she sobbed.

Mack turned to the group standing behind him. "You heard him," he said curtly. "Get me a shovel." Mack's almost forty years had brought him a better than average aquaintance with fools, and he had no patience with them.

An hour later he lifted the still-crying girl onto the back of a horse, strapped her trunk onto a mule, and rode away without a backward glance. He wanted to be as far away as possible when the Indians attacked the train again, because with or without his help they didn't stand a chance.

For the first time in a long time Mack felt a sense of well-being. He had his valley and he had a woman to produce the sons he wanted. The girl was younger than he had first believed, and thin, but with luck and good food he could fatten her up. God, he wished she would hush the damn bawling. What was done was done, and no good could come from whining about it. He'd give her the rest of the day and the night before he started using her. He felt a stirring in his loins. Jesus Christ, it'd been a long time since he'd had a white woman.

The morning after their first camp, Anna Englebretson lay exhausted. The emotional shock of the Indian attack, her uncle's death, and her sudden departure from the train with this silent, overpowering man had left her physically and emotionally fatigued. He was up before first light, and after a cup of coffee they broke camp and headed away from the rising sun. Anna had not ridden a great deal, and never astride. As the morning progressed, pains began to shoot through her body until the struggle not to cry out consumed her every thought. Despite her efforts an occasional cry did escape her lips. The big man finally turned and his blue eyes bored into hers with such intensity that she almost fell from the horse, for fear and anxiety had robbed her of her energy. Determined not to draw attention to herself again, she doggedly held her lips together and shifted her weight often in an attempt to alleviate the shooting pains running up her thighs and into her buttocks and back.

The first day they rendezvoused with a mule train. The Mexican drovers had rounded up the Indians' horses and were driving them along with their own spare mounts. Anna came to realize that she would get no help from them. They didn't come near Mack's camp and stayed well behind, but never out of sight of their employer.

Anna hadn't wanted to leave her home in upper New York State to come west with her uncle. Her life on the small farm, if uneventful, had been pleasant. She had a small circle of friends, her house to keep, her needlework. But when her uncle—her only living relative—had caught the fever to go west and sold their farm, she had no choice but to go with him. Anna was a gentle person who had led a sheltered life. Nothing in all her sixteen years had prepared her for the violence and hardship she had experienced during their trip.

The second night Anna looked into the darkness surrounding their small camp and realized that she was completely at the mercy of this strange man, who had not even asked her name. A feeling of foreboding froze her heart as she crawled into her bedroll, outside the circle of light. She watched as Mack added a piece of mesquite root to the small blaze, and when it flared he got to his feet and came toward her, his intentions perfectly clear even to the naïve young woman. She fought off panic.

"You ever been with a man, girl?" the rough voice asked.

Anna felt a rush of heat in her face, and she looked up at him, her eyes pleading.

"I see that you ain't," he said curtly, "but it makes no never mind."

He unbuckled his gunbelt, laid it on the ground, and placed his hat over it. His big hands commenced to work at the buttons on his breeches.

"No!" Anna pleaded. "Please no!"

His eyes held hers and his fingers continued working until they released the swollen, rigid member between his legs. He stood gazing down at her for a long moment, his hands on his hips, his legs braced apart, allowing her the full view of his extended sex, rising straight and hard out of a thatch of blond curls that matched the curls on his head.

Anna gasped, her entire body shaking violently.

"I ain't sayin' you're goin' to like it," he said harshly. "but you're goin' to have it. It's the way of things."

Anna whimpered like a small animal caught in a trap. Dimly she was aware that he was pulling down his breeches and that his hands were pulling up her skirt and forcing her legs apart. Something hot, hard, and throbbing was pushed into her.

She lay under him, feeling his crushing weight on her breasts and the searing pain of the rod he was thrusting so rapidly into her. He grunted and his large body arched and heaved, then jerked in spasms. His breathing was loud in her ear, and an acrid smell of perspiration came from him as he stirred and lifted his weight from her slight body. Closing her eyes tightly, she wished fervently that she would die.

When he removed himself, the night air felt cool on her wet thighs, and she painfully brought her legs together and covered them with her skirt. The pain between her thighs was excruciating, and her lower legs and ankles smarted from the contact with his rough boots.

"That's the worst of it, girl," he said and strapped on his gunbelt. "You'll get used to it in time. Ain't sayin' you'll like it. I never heard of no woman a-likin' it but a whore. I aim to get sons out of you for my valley. Sons, big and strong like me with yellow hair and blue eyes. If you breed for me, I'll wed you. If you don't . . . well, we'll sweat on it when the time comes.''

He kicked dirt onto one side of the fire to dim the blaze and stretched out, broke wind crudely, and soon was snoring.

In the days that followed, Anna was used each night. Once when she protested he gave her a resounding smack that threw her head to one side and sent a flashing pain through her jaw. Her life took on a pattern of unreality. When the man came to her, she docilely lay down and spread her legs and detached her mind from her body.

By the time they approached the valley, Anna had been with Mack Macklin for six weeks. She had become even thinner and so weak that her heart pounded from the slightest exertion. Mack seldom looked at her. Days went by without a word spoken between them, but each night he poured his seed into her. His contempt was obvious as he drove her relentlessly across the sea of barren arroyos, thirsty creeks, and sandy gullies.

They arrived at the stone ranch house in his high green valley late one afternoon. Anna was sick. Her head throbbed and her body ached. She had thrown up while still on the horse because she didn't wish to bring attention to herself by asking to stop. Vaguely she knew when they reached their destination, but she sat on the horse, dazed, looking at the stark stone house.

''Get off the horse,'' Mack commanded sullenly.

Anna fought back tears. ''I don't know if I can.''

''Calloway,'' he bellowed, ''where the hell are you?''

A small, slight young man came toward them with quick sure steps.

''I'm here, Mack. If you'd looked you could have seen me coming.''

"Get her off the horse. She's sick, I reckon. Puked out her guts a ways back."

The young man came to her and put his hands on her waist and gently lifted her down from the horse. His soft brown eyes were filled with compassion, and at the sight of the first sympathic face she'd seen in weeks, Anna's eyes flooded.

"I got her off a wagon train before she got her hair lifted by the Apaches," Mack growled, and started unsaddling his horse. "I was goin' to make her my woman, but she ain't any stronger than a pissant, and I can't abide a whimperin', pukin' woman. If she don't shape up you can have her." He stomped off toward the bunkhouse.

"Please," Anna whispered, "may I lay down?"

The room to which he led her was cool and clean, and Anna's pain-dulled eyes found a row of books on a shelf by the bed. She looked at him; his dark crisp hair framed a serious young face, and his voice was gentle and his accent reminded her of home. Tears filled her eyes again.

"I'm afraid I'll throw up," she whispered.

"Don't worry about it," he said. "I'll get a bucket and then leave until you can get into bed. I'll be back with something to make you feel better."

Later he sat beside her and placed a damp cloth on her fevered brow. She smiled her gratitude and reached out a thin hand. The man took it in his and immediately lost his heart to her. Anna's eyes closed. It all came flooding back, and she began to shake with dry sobs. The man held her close, smoothing her hair back from her face and murmuring soft words of comfort. The tears came and her body shook convulsively. He held her tightly, and she buried her face against his shoulder, clinging to him to give her some sanity in a world that had suddenly gone insane.

In the weeks that followed, Ben devoted himself to her, stayed with her night and day. They talked for hours, revealed their every secret thought, and their love and devotion for each other grew until it was all-consuming and the only world they knew existed was in that one room of the stone house.

"Ben," she said one evening as she sat by the fire, her feet puffy and cold, and a light shawl draped about her shoulders, "if your name is Burnett, why are you called Ben?"

"Because, my lovely," he said teasingly, "my name is Burnett Nathan Calloway. My father called me by my initials, B.N., and it just worked into Ben."

"I think Burnett is a lovely name for a boy," Anna said. She looked at him with glowing eyes. "What would I have done without you, Ben?"

"After you have the babe," he said, ignoring the question, "we'll leave here and find a place of our own."

"Do you think he'll let us go?" she asked wistfully.

"I don't know, Anna. We'll just have to wait until the time comes and see."

"I don't care where we are, my love, as long as I'm with you."

"You'll always be with me, Anna. Always."

The baby was born on a cold windy night. Ben sent down to the Mexican quarters for a woman to help Anna. The women were afraid to come, because Mexicans were never allowed near the house. With the help of a ranch hand, a woman was brought up and slipped into the room where Anna lurched and screamed in the agony of childbirth.

It was a long night for Ben as he watched his beloved give birth to another man's child. Her suffering was his suffering and her pain was his pain, until at last the woman held out a wet, wriggling mass of humanity for him to hold.

With her son, clean and wrapped, lying beside her, Anna smiled weakly and held up her lips for Ben's kiss.

"I'm going to call him Burnett," she said. "Burr for short. A burr that will stick in the craw of that . . . that man. Don't ever leave him to Mack Macklin, Ben. Promise you'll stay with him and teach him that brawn alone won't make him a man.''

"We'll teach him together, my darling. We'll teach him together.''

She closed her eyes, and Ben gazed at her fragile beauty and then at the red-faced baby in the curve of her arm. His heart quickened and a lump rose in his throat. She was so weak, he thought with despair.

Anna lived until her son was almost four years old. She seldom left the room, except to sit on the porch when Mack was away. She was content, basking in Ben's love and tender care. Her son was the joy of her life, a strong, bright boy with a mass of blond curly hair. During the day she used most of her strength to teach and play with him, and in the evenings Ben would read the stories he most loved to both mother and child. It was a peaceful, comforting life, although obviously confined, since their time was spent solely in Ben's room. By now Ben and Anna were resigned to the fact that she would never survive the trip out of the valley.

Mack's activities kept him away from the house much of the time, but when he was there he seemed to accept the relationship between Ben and Anna. For the most part, the strange master of Macklin Valley ignored them. He maintained a grudging civility toward Ben because he needed him. Ben kept all the ranch records and acted as buffer between him and the Mexican workers. Furthermore, he was reliable and could be left in charge while Mack was away. Ben knew this, but he suspected that Mack also allowed Anna and him to stay because of the boy. Occasionally he caught Mack watching the miniature of himself, a quiet, solemn expression on his face, as if he was remembering events from his own childhood.

On a bright summer day, Ben held the cold hands of his

beloved and kissed her serene lips for the last time. Holding tightly the hand of the small boy, he followed her plank coffin to a grassy knoll above the ranch house. The men lowered the box, then stood with hats in hand while Ben read from Scripture. Somberly and silently they filled the grave with warm earth and walked away to leave Ben and the boy alone.

The breeze that came down from the mountains stirred the boy's blond curls and rippled the wild flowers he clutched in his hand. Ben took the flowers from him and scattered them on the grave. He and the boy got down on their knees. Ben put his arms about the bewildered child, and they wept together.

Ben's depression was deep. No one could know what the lovely, frail woman had meant to him. For days he could not eat, and at night he walked the floor. After a while he began to realize that his time with Anna had been beautiful and fulfilling but now it was time to get on with what needed to be done. Anna had left him with her most precious possession, her son, and through him Anna would live. With quiet determination he went about the task of raising Burr. He committed himself wholly to the boy's welfare and education, all the while planning revenge for what Anna had suffered. Someday he and Burr would wrest from Mack Macklin this valley— the only thing Macklin had ever loved.

# CHAPTER
## Seven

Johanna tucked her fresh blouse into her skirt and secured the belt around her minute waist. She brushed her hair and carefully recoiled it, pulling loose a few tendrils of curls about her face. Scrutinizing herself in the mirror, she decided she looked coolly conventional, yet informal enough to suit her position in the house. With nerves firmly under control she marched down to the kitchen, ready to do battle with Burr when he came in for the evening meal.

The kitchen was spotless. The trestle table had been scrubbed with a stiff brush, dried, and oiled. The seasoned old wood gleamed after being polished with a soft cloth. Lighting one of the freshly washed lamps, Johanna placed it in the middle of the table, then set plates and cutlery for five, thinking it better to set a place for Mr. Macklin although Ben didn't believe he would come to the table.

There was an abundance of food on the ranch. Codger and a young Mexican lad brought up from the cookhouse flour, cornmeal, sugar, rice, dried beans, dried fruits, and numerous seasonings. He had shown her the smokehouse, which was filled with slabs of bacon, sides of beef, venison, and even a portion of bear meat that he swore was good eating if cooked long enough. There was a chickenhouse, so fresh eggs were available as well. Codger had proudly shown her a cave in the rocks near the spring behind the house where milk and vegetables were stored.

Johanna was astonished at how well organized the ranch was outside the house. It seemed to her that the ranch house was like a desolate island in a sea of plenty.

Evening came early. When the sun passed over the crest of the mountain, its long shadows engulfed the valley, cooling it. The cookstove made the kitchen pleasantly warm, and the shining chimneys on the lamps gave the room a rosy glow.

Ben sat in the chair by the hearth and watched Johanna. She moved from stove to workbench, her color intensified by the heat from the stove.

"We'll have to set a time for supper, Ben. I work better if I have a schedule." Not wanting to admit to herself that she dreaded hearing the thud of Burr's boots on the stone floor, she chattered on. "Tomorrow I think I'll start cleaning the room across the hall." She looked up. Burr and Bucko had come quietly into the room. She glanced at them and quickly took in everything about them.

It appeared that Bucko had come unwillingly, judging by his pouting expression. However, he was dressed in a clean shirt and his hair had been combed. His small hand was engulfed in Burr's large one. The reason she hadn't heard Burr come in was that he was wearing Indian moccasins. He had also put on a clean shirt, minus his ever-present vest, and had attempted to control his mop of curly hair, but without much success. His expression was not friendly but not surly either. Johanna decided that his look could only be described as determined.

"Supper is almost ready, Mr. Macklin," she said formally.

"And I would like to know if this is a convenient time for the meal. If it is, I'll have your meal ready at this time every evening." He didn't answer her immediately, but instead let his eyes travel the room, taking in every change she had made. When he'd finished, he met her cool gaze.

"If it isn't, I'll let you know." His voice was barely cordial.

"Thank you," she said in a voice equal to his, then glanced down at Bucko. "I hear you met my sister today, Bucko. Did you know she's quite good at making a slingshot?" She spoke to him in Spanish.

"Speak English," Burr said harshly. "Bucko must learn English."

"Yes, of course he should." She smiled, refusing to let his manner shake her confidence. She took a pan from the oven. "Come, Ben, the biscuits are done. You and Bucko sit down, Mr. Macklin." She was delighted to see a flush of anger come into Burr's face at being invited to sit at his own table. After she placed the food on the table, Johanna whipped off her apron and went to call old Mack.

When she didn't find him on the porch, she knocked on the door of his room, but there was no answer.

"Supper is ready, Mr. Macklin," she called out. There was no reply, so she went back to the kitchen.

Burr was seated at the head of the table, with Bucko on one side and Ben on the other. Johanna couldn't help but wonder what would happen if old Mack came to the table. She sat down beside Bucko. Ben was waiting for her, but Burr had placed food on Bucko's plate and his own and had started to eat. It was difficult for Johanna to keep from smiling at the childish act of defiance. It was plain that her cool reserve had gotten under the skin of the confident Burr Macklin. She smiled at Ben; his eyes twinkled back at her. There wasn't much that he missed.

After a failed attempt to start a conversation, Ben sat quietly, eating and observing. Johanna could tell that he was enjoying the meal. He had faultless manners, and she was surprised to discover that Burr's manners were also good. Probably the result of Ben's teaching, she thought. Judging from the quantity of food that disappeared, Burr too enjoyed the meal.

At the end of the meal Johanna refilled coffee cups and brought milk for Bucko before she set a large platter of bear claws on the table. Bucko looked disbelievingly at the warm, sugar-coated cakes before his eyes found hers. She winked at him, and she was almost sure she saw a flicker of friendliness before he lowered his eyes. She rounded the table to take her seat and her gaze collided with Burr's. His sun-bleached brows were drawn together, and the look on his face was one of puzzlement.

"Later I'm going down to Mr. Redford's, Bucko. Will you walk with me and show me the way?"

The hand reaching for a bear claw halted when he heard her words. He looked at Burr, as if hoping he would answer for him. Burr reached over and placed a cake on Bucko's plate.

"If you want to go, Bucko, say so. If you don't want to go it will be all right."

Johanna couldn't believe the gentle, patient voice had come from the man who had only a few hours ago been so boorish. She looked at him and saw a softening in his face that completely changed his countenance. Evidently Ben and Bucko saw nothing unusual in his manner of speaking, because Ben continued eating his bear claw and Bucko turned big, serious eyes in her direction.

"Yes," he said in a voice so low she barely heard the word.

"I'm glad," Johanna said with mock relief. "I'll need someone to carry my guitar."

The little face lit up almost instantly. Johanna's heart lurched. He's lonely, she thought, and realized that there was one Macklin, at least, who was human and reachable.

The meal was more pleasant than Johanna anticipated, yet she was glad when it was over. It irritated her that Burr's presence made her nervous. Each time he looked at her the bold, masculine magnetism he emitted aroused a sense of excitement in her. She blamed it on the antagonism between them. She would never in a million years be comfortable with this man. It was unthinkable to imagine being married to him.

"Burr, come talk to me while Bucko stuffs himself with cakes." Ben excused himself and got stiffly to his feet.

When Burr stood he seemed to fill the room, and in reaction Johanna sucked in her breath until he moved away. He sat by the hearth, opposite Ben, and brought out the makings for a cigarette. Bucko remained at the table, eating slowly and steadily.

While preparing a tray for Mr. Macklin, Johanna listened to the conversation at the hearth.

"Have you decided what you're going to do about the men who followed the train in?"

"For the time being, nothing. Luis is keeping an eye on them and if they move from the spot where they're camped, or if it looks like they plan to stay, then I'll act. Meanwhile, we have plenty to do getting the stragglers down out of the hills and breaking the string of horses Luis brought in, and there's the windmill to put up."

"Did Luis find anything in town to add to his string?"

"Yes, he did." When Burr answered, Johanna held her breath, for the change on his face was miraculous. The stern lines relaxed when his lips spread in a smile that showed his white teeth. He was undeniably handsome and no doubt well aware of it, she told herself. She attributed her quickening pulse to the fact that she was surprised he could even smile.

"He found a fine-boned little mare he wants to put to the stallion he got from the Apache. He thinks he'll get a colt with the speed of lightning."

Could that chuckle in his voice be affection for his brother? Johanna asked herself.

"I think he'll get just what he thinks he'll get," Ben said. "Luis knows horses."

"I wish I knew half as much," Burr admitted.

"Did you find out any more about the two Mexicans he killed?"

"No. He didn't say much about it, except that they gave themselves away and they needed killing. You know how Luis feels about such as that. He gave them a chance at him, then killed them as though they were a couple of rattlesnakes. He didn't see any need to wait for the men to get out a rope and hang them."

"He's practiced for years with those guns, Burr. I thought the day would come when he would use that speed here on the ranch." Ben knocked the bowl of his pipe sharply against the stone hearth.

"It'll not come to that now, Ben. Luis will have his horse ranch and Bucko will have his chance too. I'll see to it. Nothing and nobody is going to prevent it."

Johanna thought he said the last for her benefit, and a brief flash of anger swept over her. She wanted to blurt out that he had nothing to fear from her, but she kept her head turned so he couldn't see the flush that flooded her face.

The tray was ready. She had put more food on the plate than she thought the old man could eat, but she wanted it to be ample. While covering the tray with a clean cloth, she felt a sudden rush of uncertainty and looked helplessly at Ben. She wondered if she would be able to bear another encounter with the frightful old man.

Ben reached for his tobacco can to refill his pipe and said,

"All I can tell you, lass, is take the bull by the horns. Rap on the door. Mack won't answer, but open it and go in. You'll find him propped up in bed. Just place the food on the table and leave. He may swear at you, but he'll not strike you. At least I don't think he will."

"Of course he won't!" she scoffed. She picked up the tray. Not for the world would she let that overbearing dolt by the hearth know that Mack could cause her even a moment of concern. She walked calmly through the door, but paused in the hall to prepare herself for the old man's onslaught. He didn't answer her knock, as Ben had predicted. She hesitated only a second, then opened the door. The room was in semi-darkness, but she could see the bed at the end of it. The offensive smells of sweat, unwashed body, and a spittoon that badly needed to be emptied assailed her. She heard the sound of heavy breathing but wasn't sure whether the old man was asleep.

"Mr. Macklin," she called softly.

The bed creaked as he shifted his weight. As she walked toward him her foot struck an object on the floor, and she just barely managed to keep her balance and the tray upright. Moving aside a lamp, she placed the tray on the table near the bed.

"Shall I light a lamp for you, Mr. Macklin?"

There was no answer. She felt along the table and her fingers found a box of sulfur matches. She lit one, lifted the chimney from the lamp, and applied the flame. The old man was propped up in bed watching her. His sunken blue eyes were cold, and his mouth was open to gulp air.

"I've brought your supper."

"I ain't blind," he growled.

Johanna smiled. "Is there anything else I can get for you?"

The lips snapped shut and the look on his face was one of

distaste. Johanna was reminded of a puma ready to spring on its prey. Perhaps it was the growl, or it might have been the glow in his eyes that followed her every move. Resisting the temptation to run from the room, she walked slowly to the door, where the sound of his voice halted her.

"About what I asked you today," he said caustically. "Are you still of the same mind?"

Johanna thought she should get this settled once and for all.

"Mr. Macklin, I never even considered your proposal. What you suggested is absolutely out of the question."

With surprising agility the old man swung up to sit on the side of the bed.

"You goddamn slut!" he bellowed. "You goddamn whorin' slut! What more are you wantin'? Are you wantin' me to go down on my knees and beg? That goddamn lawyer! I been waitin' six months for you to get here. Waitin' six months for a bitch to stand there and tell me my valley ain't good enough for her." His face was almost purple with rage. Johanna had never seen a person so angry that he frothed at the mouth like a mad dog.

"You'll wed the bastard, or I'll sell the whole goddamn valley out from under him," he roared. "I'll not have a goddamn bastard have my valley, not a goddamn bastard that robbed me of my foot. He'll wed you and bed you, I say! Once he gets you on your back he'll know what to do. I seen to that!"

Johanna went through the door and closed it behind her. She could still hear his voice through the closed door.

"You ain't nothin' but a goddamn bitch, hear?"

She stood in the hall, her hands pressed tightly over her ears. Humiliation surpassed her anger and almost crushed her determination to withstand whatever came in order to keep a roof over her and Jacy's heads. How could she face Ben and Burr now? They most certainly had heard the old man's insults.

Burr came through the kitchen door. The light was behind him so she couldn't see his expression, but she thought he was smirking. Her features clearly showed the strain of the encounter with the old man.

"If you're going to get the honey you must expect to get stung by the bee," he said softly as he passed her.

"You . . . you shut up!" she hissed at him, and the soft chuckle that followed infuriated her.

"Damn him!" she muttered as she entered the kitchen.

Ben sat puffing on his pipe. Johanna knew he and Burr had heard every word old Mack had said to her, but she decided not to mention it. In all her life she had never been subjected to the kind of abuse she had received since she'd come to this valley. She could never even have imagined such behavior, nor did she know how to deal with it. Dear, dear Ben! Maybe his calm assurance would help her to survive in this house of evil. She had regained her composure by the time he spoke.

"You'll never get used to such talk, lass, but don't let it touch you."

"I won't, Ben. The problems here have nothing to do with me."

Johanna worked swiftly and when the last clean dish was put away she smiled down at Bucko, who sat in the chair Burr had occupied.

"I'll run up and get my shawl and the instruments and we'll go." At the door she said, "Ben, will you come with us?"

"No, girl, but I may come down later. I'd like to hear the music."

* * *

Bucko was waiting at the foot of the stairs when Johanna came down. She handed him the violin case, because it was the lighter and less bulky of the two instruments. They went out and across the front of the house.

From the rooms at the end of the porch a path of light shone out onto the stone patio. Johanna glanced into the room as they walked past. Burr was sitting in a chair facing the door. He looked up and then jerked down onto his lap a young Mexican girl who had been standing beside him. Her pleased laughter rang out as her arms circled his neck possessively. Stung by unexplained anger, Johanna quickened her steps.

The night was dark, the moon not yet high enough to provide much light. Bucko led her down the smooth, well-worn path that started at the back of the bunkhouse.

"Can you read, Bucko?"

"*Sí*. Burr teach me . . . and Ben."

"Good. Would you like to learn to play my guitar?"

Although they were walking slowly, he stumbled. His affirmative answer came clear and strong, with more emphasis than she had heard from him before.

"I'll teach you, then. We'll start next week."

A large fire burned in the center of the semicircle of adobe houses. People lounged around the fire laughing and talking, and the children ran about, shouting to one another. The scene caused Johanna to feel a pang of homesickness for the happy home she'd had before her parents were killed. The children, seeing Bucko with the strange light-haired woman, stared in awe. Bucko lifted his head proudly and clutched the handle of the violin case.

Jacy came to meet them. Johanna noticed at once the lightness of her step and the eagerness in her voice.

"Johanna, we've been waiting for you. Come, I want you to meet Rosita, Red's wife."

Jacy pulled her toward the fire. She seemed happy. Actually happy. Johanna was delighted, and a large part of the heaviness she had carried for so long lifted from her heart.

A small, plump woman with shiny black hair and large expressive eyes came toward them. She smiled her welcome, her bright eyes moving from Johanna's striking blond hair to Jacy's dark coloring.

Jacy laughed. "I told you she had hair like a silver cloud."

"*Sí*, Jaceta. You were right."

"Good evening," Johanna said. "Thank you for allowing Jacy to spend the day with you."

"Ah . . . her *español*, it is good like yours, Jaceta." Rosita rolled her eyes at Jacy and laughed.

Rosita's friendly, lighthearted disposition had affected Jacy, and Johanna could hardly take her eyes from her sister's smiling face. *It's worth it all . . . it's worth it all.* The words kept repeating themselves in her mind.

"Are you a-makin' out, Johanner?" Mooney appeared beside her.

"Just barely, Mooney." She laughed, and then said seriously, "I'm glad you prepared me, or I'd have been struck dumb."

"I figured ya was in fer a jolt."

Bucko stood shyly beside her, and Johanna gently took his hand. A bench had been cleared for her, and as she sat down she pulled the boy down beside her. Jacy took her violin from the case and plucked the strings to be sure they were in tune.

"Let's play some Spanish music."

"You lead off, as Papa used to do, and I'll follow." Immediately Johanna wished she hadn't mentioned Papa, but a quick look at Jacy's face reassured her that she hadn't upset her.

Jacy struck up a lively Spanish tune and Johanna played the accompaniment. Exhilarated, she soon had her fingers flying over the strings of the guitar. Bucko, sitting beside her, watched intently, his eyes bright and the corners of his mouth turned up. Johanna was surprised by his interest in the music and how the changing tempos affected his expression.

After several numbers the audience began to clap their hands and sing. Some of them were calling out, *"Bueno, bueno!"*

Johanna watched her sister carefully for signs of fatigue, but Jacy was totally carried away by the vibrant music she played and the utter joy and freedom of the moment. To the delight of everyone, she swung into a fiery, rousing piece, and a shout went up: "Isabella, Isabella, come dance for us."

A girl stepped out of the darkness and raised her arms over her head. It was the girl who had been reclining so languorously on Burr's lap. With animallike grace she poised on tiptoe, then pivoted and twirled. Around and around the circle she went, pirouetting and posturing, her movements inviting attention to her lovely body. Hands clapped in unison, keeping perfect time with the throbbing beat of the music. The girl's feet were bare, and as she stamped out the rhythm of the music she whirled before each group, arms raised, boldly provocative. She halted briefly before Johanna, her flashing black eyes sending forth a challenge to the woman she thought her rival. Then with an insolent flick of her lashes she dismissed her. Johanna's intuition told her that this girl resented her and her action was a warning that she didn't intend to be cast aside. Her suspicion was confirmed a moment later when the girl's searching eyes settled on the face of the man standing out of the circle of light.

Isabella, her dark hair whipping around her, whirled and swayed her body sensuously as she dance toward Burr, displaying every seductive curve of her body before his smiling gaze. Her hard eyes beckoned, invited. She wriggled her hips in wild abandon, and her full skirt billowed and flounced with every move. Her dance became wilder and more intense. The tempo rose and the clapping was so fast that Isabella's whirling skirt showed flashes of bare thigh.

Johanna felt embarrassment, tinged with pity, for the girl. Obviously she had been intimate with Burr or she wouldn't have been in his room. No doubt he found her an amusing plaything, and Johanna conjectured that he more than likely used her in the same way he had used and discarded Bucko's mother.

She caught Burr watching her with a glint of mockery in his eyes that said her thoughts were plainly written on her face. Angry with herself and with him, she gave all her attention to the guitar.

Waves of laughter and applause followed the end of the dance. Jacy swung into the less feverish "Greensleeves," and when Johanna looked up again neither the dancer nor Burr was there.

Jacy finally put down the violin and sat down. She had been playing for an hour, and although she was tired her eyes were bright and she was still smiling.

"It's almost like it used to be, isn't it, Johanna?"

Before Johanna could answer, a voice drawled, "Sing us one of them songs of yourn, ma'am."

"Sing us a ballad, Johanner," Mooney called.

"All right. I'll sing first in English, then in Spanish."

Her fingers stroked the strings of the guitar, and then she sang, her voice sweet and clear. The song was a sad story about a small boy who wanted to ride on the train but didn't have money to pay his fare. Her audience listened attentively, and she sang the chorus.

"Oh please, Mr. Conductor, don't put me off of
    the train.
The best friend I have in this world is waiting for
    me in pain.

Expecting to die any moment, she may not live
    through the day.
I want to kiss Mama goodbye, sir, before God takes
    her away.''

Her next song was about a young cowboy killed during a
stampede and his sweetheart who waited for him in vain. The
tragic lyrics were popular with young men who spent many
lonely hours on the prairie. She also sang the touching war
ballads "Lorena" and "Just Before the Battle, Mother," and
the best-known of all the songs to come out of the War
Between the States, "Dixie."

Her eyes roamed over the faces before her. Luis was there,
standing quietly beside Ben. Red, Mooney, Codger, Paco,
and Carlos: all there. The only person who hadn't put in an
appearance was the old man who had discovered the valley,
fought for it, developed it, and become bitter because of it.

Johanna finished singing and handed her guitar to Bucko.
She was tired, the weariness of her flesh equal to the weariness
of her spirit.

"Señorita?" Luis spoke from behind her. She turned and
saw him standing beside Burr. Suddenly she was angry that
Burr was there when she thought he had gone. Ignoring him,
she smiled up at Luis.

"Your sister say I must ask your permission to walk with
her."

There was no hesitancy in his voice, nor did he seem
reluctant to speak in Burr's presence. He was an extraordi-
narily handsome man whose face showed not only strength
but character. Had it not been for his deep-blue eyes, she
would have thought it impossible that he had been sired by
old Mack. However, looking at the brothers standing together, she could see that their features were somewhat simi-
lar, yet the chiseled lips that in Luis curved easily in a smile

in Burr became an almost malevolent sneer that engendered a lack of trust. Both men were tall, but Burr was taller and more heavily built.

Johanna's eyes found Jacy, standing slightly to the right and behind Luis, her eyes anxious.

"Jacy?" she questioned. Then she addressed Luis: "It is the custom to ask permission and I thank you for the courtesy, but Jacy is a grown woman and the decision is hers."

Luis turned toward Jacy and held out his hand for her violin case. She smiled up into his face, and they walked off into the darkness together. A sharp feeling of apprehension struck Johanna as she watched them.

Burr was watching her. His eyes rested on her face for a long time without movement, without any discernible emotion; his expression was calm and confident. She felt hot, uncomfortable, and unsure of herself. She cursed him under her breath. Reading her thoughts, he tilted his head toward her.

"Galls you, don't it, to see your sister enjoys my brother's company," he taunted softly.

She had thought the extent of her dislike for this man had reached its peak, until now. She had to fight the impulse to slap him again, to mar that handsome countenance with her nails. She struggled with the primitive desire to hurt. The murderous impulse increased as his blue eyes, with more than a hint of malicious amusement in their depths, looked into hers.

"I'll thank you to keep your observations to yourself!" she said frigidly. She was surprised and pleased that her voice was so calm. She braced herself for another mocking jibe, but when he spoke it was to Bucko.

"How about a piggyback ride, cowboy?" He lifted the boy to his shoulders and walked away.

Anger flared anew in Johanna at his rudeness, before she

dismissed him as mannerless, overbearing, ignorant, and completely self-serving.

"You two really *do* strike sparks off each other." Ben moved up beside her.

"Yes, we do," Johanna admitted.

As she and Ben walked down the path, Johanna adjusted her stride to his slower pace. The shimmering glow of the moon illuminated the landscape, and the night sounds took over. Somewhere an owl hooted, and the crickets sounded loud in the darkness. The faint murmur of voices came from behind them as families separated to go to their homes.

"Ben," Johanna said when she was sure they were out of hearing of others. "Tell me about Luis. Is he a gunman?"

"Are you bothered that Luis wants to court your sister?"

Now the suspicion that she had been pushing to the back of her mind was out in the open. She laughed nervously, unwilling to voice her thoughts.

"I doubt that he's courting her, Ben," she said lightly. "I'm just curious to know what kind of man he is."

"Luis isn't a killer," Ben said after a while. "He's killed, as most of the men in the valley have at one time or another, but never without just cause. I consider Luis a good man. Not a perfect man, none of us is, but a good man."

"With Mr. Macklin's dislike for Mexicans, it hardly seemed likely that he would have . . . would have . . ." She fumbled for the words needed to phrase the question.

"I understand what you're saying. Mack took his pleasure and didn't consider it any more than his due. It was the same with any woman."

"And his son is following in his footsteps."

"You mean Luis, or Burr?"

"It's obvious."

"Don't be so quick to judge Burr. He bought Bucko from the Apaches; gave six ponies for him. I don't know how he managed it, because the Indians almost never give up a child, even a malformed one. The boy was nothing but a bag of bones when Burr brought him here about four years ago. They told him the boy was six summers at the time. He was so weak he couldn't walk and so cowed he cringed every time he heard a human voice. That's probably the only reason they let him go. They're very intolerant of the old and the weak."

Johanna walked along in silence, then said dubiously, "I find it hard to believe Bucko is ten years old. I've had ten-year-old boys in my class who were almost as tall as I am."

"When I first saw him, he was like a babe in arms. Burr's brought him a long way."

"You talk as if Burr had done him a favor," Johanna said contemptuously.

Ben didn't answer for a long while, and Johanna's anger and disgust for Macklin's older son flared anew.

"He could have left him there," he said quietly.

"Indeed!"

# CHAPTER
## *Eight*

L uis rode his tired horse down the dusty street of El Paso and paused before the shambling two-story hotel that had its sign dangling askew.

He sat his horse and his eyes took in every detail around him. The Mexicans in their loose, light breeches, and full shirts, their straw sombreros set straight on their dark heads, paid no attention to him. Three gringos in dusty trail clothes, leaning against the unpainted building, eyed him, but Luis dismissed their looks as mere curiosity. Chickens squawked and scampered from the road as a freight wagon went past with several dogs trailing it, barking and trying to catch the rolling wheels with their snapping teeth. Down the street a door opened and a drunk, with a well-placed boot at his back propelling him, went sprawling in the dust.

Still cautious, but satisfied that the street scene was as it appeared to be, Luis walked his horse to the rail and dismounted. The gringos turned to watch him, more than casual interest on their faces.

"Ain't that the Mex they was talkin' about up at Las Cruces?"

"By God if it ain't!"

"What about him?" The third man picked his teeth with a long, thin-bladed knife. "He don't look like nothin' but a Mex to me."

"Shut up!" the man standing next to him muttered.

"God, yeah!" The man who had first recognized Luis shifted his weight uncomfortably. "He's a fightin' son of a bitch! Fought in the Battle of Glorieta in '62, and the general, he said he was just a wet-eared kid, but if'n he'd'a had six more like him he'd'a whipped the shit outta the whole Yank army."

"They say he's faster than greased lightnin' with those guns."

"Gunfighter, huh?"

"Wal, I don't know if'n that's what he is. Feller didn't say he hired out or nothin' like that. He said he ain't touchy, but ya better not crowd him."

"He seemed kinda spooked when he come in, kinda like somebody was trailin' him."

"Probably jist natural spooky. Them fellers allus got some fool wantin' to try 'em."

Luis walked up the worn steps to the porch of the hotel, paused and looked around, then went through the open door into the dim lobby. Beyond the desk a grossly fat man dozed. His dirty shirt lay open, revealing a hairy chest, and greasy whips of hair straggled across a nearly bald pate.

Startled, he peered through watery eyes, then struggled to his feet.

"Room?" And looking toward the street, "I can put your horse up, too." The man thumbed his triple chins and the watery eyes became evasive. "Air ya stayin' long?"

Luis signed the register.

The fat man looked at the name he had written, then squinted up at him. "Stayin' long?" he asked again. Luis didn't answer him, but the hotel man kept prodding. "Come a long ways?"

"Is the stable out behind?" Luis asked coolly.

"I'll get a boy—"

"I care for my own horse." Luis left the lobby, the heels of his boots sounding loud on the bare plank floor.

Later, in his room, he lighted a lamp on the scarred bureau and tossed his hat onto the sagging bed. He removed his gunbelt, then peeled off his shirt. The cracked mirror above the bureau showed his naked chest with its long red wound. He uncorked a bottle, had a swallow, then poured whiskey into his palm and applied it to the knife cut where a little dried blood indicated that the wound had opened. Next he spilled water from a cracked pitcher into a crockery bowl and washed. The mirror showed his lean, tired face, eyes bloodshot from days of dusty travel. He decided he was more tired than hungry. After checking the door, he stretched out on the bed, got up to blow out the lamp, then lay down again, hands folded across his stomach.

It was dawn when he came instantly awake and sprang to his feet. The floorboards in the hall had creaked. Quickly he put on his shirt, buckled on his gunbelt, and went to the window. The street was quiet. The hotel was quiet, but then the creak came again, followed by shuffling sounds. Luis edged to the side of the door. He had meant to camp out tonight and give his tracker the opportunity to catch up; but now that he was here, there was no need to delay the inevitable.

His door opened slowly and a rifle barrel appeared. In one quick motion, Luis kicked the door wide open, gripped the barrel, and jerked hard. With a startled oath the person holding the weapon was pulled over the threshold. The rifle fell to the floor as a bullet from the six-gun the man held in his other hand whizzed by Luis's head. Luis drew his gun and fired. He heard the bullet strike the man.

Quickly he twisted through the doorway and went into the hall. He flattened himself against the wall and waited. He didn't expect to find an accomplice, but it was best to make sure. A pale light came from the dirty window at the end of the hall. As Luis made his way along the corridor, the doors to the other rooms opened to reveal the cautious, curious faces of other lodgers. They watched calmly as the tall man with the silver-handled gun scanned the stairs, then, satisfied, turned back toward his room. They could see the dead man sprawled on his back, his arms and legs flung wide, and they had no intention of tangling with his killer.

Luis shoved his gun back into its holster, stepped over the dead man, picked up his hat and saddlebags, and left the hotel.

Wariness tightened his nerves as he stepped out onto the boardwalk. He looked both ways along the walk, then moved toward the cantina at the end of the street. The heels of his boots sounded loud in the morning stillness.

The cantina was empty except for a Mexican woman working over a stove and two customers bent over plates of food. He ordered tortillas and eggs and took a seat at a table with his back to the wall.

"*Gracias, señora*," he said when the woman set the food in front of him. Her plump face wrinkled into a smile. Few strangers who were polite came into the cantina.

Luis ate hungrily. The woman, keeping an eye on the plate of the handsome stranger, brought him an additional egg wrapped in a hot tortilla and filled his tin cup with strong coffee.

The morning wore on. He sat quietly looking out the door

and down the busy street. No one approached him, but he was eyed by everyone who came in. He suspected that his presence was the reason for the smile on the face of the plump señora as she served the customers and collected their pesos. Luis was used to sitting with his back to the wall or looking over his shoulder. That he had fought well in the Battle of Glorieta, not as a member of the Confederate Army but as a volunteer, had earned him a reputation as a fighter. More times than he cared to admit, he had been forced to prove his skill by facing some reckless fool who hoped to earn a reputation. That wasn't the case, however, with the man he had killed this morning.

Sudden impulse had caused him to ride out of the valley and head for El Paso. His thoughts of late had been completely taken up with the small, dark-haired sister of the old man's housekeeper. This protective longing he felt for her was a new feeling, and he needed time to think, to try to understand, to find out if it was just a woman he craved, or this particular woman.

The second night out he met two drifters. They seemed to be friendly enough and he endured their company. The first night he realized there was a suspicious intimacy between the two men. He was accustomed to sleeping with one eye open and was surprised to see one of the men creep over to the bedroll of the other. He watched long enough to become sick with disgust, then dismissed it as their business. The next night he was awakened by a hand caressing his hair. He came awake instantly. The man reached down to touch his face and then reached quickly for his crotch. Luis pushed the man away but the man persisted. Nauseated, Luis drew back his hand and slapped the man across the face. He sat back and whimpered, then swiftly drew a knife and slashed Luis across the chest. Luis's reflex was instant: he pulled his gun and shot him.

The other man sprang to his feet and stared with horror at the dead man, then dropped to his knees and cradled his lover's head in his arms and sobbed. Luis gathered up his gear, saddled his horse, and mounted. The man looked up, his dirty face streaked with tears.

"I'll kill you. I swear I'll kill you!"

He had tried.

Luis sat in the cantina and watched the children play in the street. They were a ragged but happy lot. Their shrieks of laughter drifted into the cantina, and the fat señora smiled indulgently and shook her head. Childhood memories came flooding back to him, sweeping him again into the good times and the bad; forcing him to remember his mother, the lovely and gentle Juanita Gazares, and his own tortured beginning.

*Summer of 1844 . . .*

*Evening was drawing in. For one wildly desperate moment Juanita Gazares clung to the hope that the señor wouldn't come. The weird shape of the trees against the evening sky, the endless shadowy folds of the tree-covered hillside, and the soft sound of the clear creek water as it traveled over the stones on its way to the river; it was all too peaceful. Her people now would be drifting along the dusty road toward their quarters, enjoying the pleasure of doing nothing after a hard day's work. Even the half-naked niños were playing in the road or were being carried on strong shoulders. If she allowed the señor the use of her body they would have corn-*

*meal for tortillas and pinto beans to boil in their pots. If she didn't submit to him they were certain to go hungry. Her uncle believed it and said as much, and her aunt was of the same mind; and so her degradation had come about.*

Juanita leaned her dark head back against the tree trunk and closed her eyes briefly. He was later than usual and she thanked the Virgin Mother for it, for it gave her time to recover her senses; time to control the screaming inside her, the revulsion she felt for what he did to her body. She heard a sound and her eyes flew open. It was only a ground squirrel scampering among the rocks.

She closed her eyes again. It was futile to believe that the señor would not be angry when he discovered the wee *niño* growing inside her slender body. Had he not sworn not to give life to a "Mex bastard"? He had taken the only precaution known to him to prevent such an occurrence.

Always he played on her body for as long as possible before allowing his seed to spurt on the ground between her parted thighs. The times when he had been unable to remove his swollen, throbbing member and had filled her with his life-giving fluid, he had forced her to squat in the flowing stream and wash herself. He would know soon about the *niño*, perhaps today, for her waist had thickened and her small breasts were swollen. In a sudden flurry of panic she prayed for the strength to climb the steep cliff and throw herself onto the rocks below. But she knew she wouldn't do it, even if she'd had the strength. It would be a cardinal sin and her soul would burn in everlasting hell if she destroyed herself and the tiny *niño*.

Her ears caught the sound of a horse's hooves on the stones that bordered the stream. Any vague hope she had nurtured that he would fail to come was dashed, and her heart thudded hard against her ribs. Her eyes, now without expression, were turned in the direction from which he would come.

* * *

Mack Macklin, mounted on a dun gelding, left the ranch buildings and walked his horse past the stone house with only an uninterested glance. Calloway and the milk-pale bitch were sitting on the porch in the hide-covered chairs. His lips curled with scorn. Calloway could have her. A lot of pleasure the skinny slut would give him, he thought, and a caustic smile hovered about his mouth.

He turned his horse toward the stream, urged it to cross, then followed the stream down to where it widened and the grass and bushes grew thick and lush. He felt an excitement in the pit of his stomach and a hot ache in his loins. It was always the same when he was on his way to meet Juanita. He didn't understand it, but when he thought of her his passion flared. At times he was disgusted with himself that he would give a second thought to a damn Mexican other than plowing her, but this woman's body drew him like a magnet.

He remembered the first time he had seen her and was so aroused that his buckskin breeches became uncomfortable. He had been sitting on his horse watching a family of Mexicans come into the valley to work his irrigation ditches. She was plodding along on a little burro, sitting erect as a queen. He continued to stare at her for a long time, then she turned and looked at him. Her eyes were as black as night and as full of concealment. They rested on his face, then moved away. He felt hot and cursed her under his breath.

"Goddamn mestiza bitch!"

He couldn't forget her. "A nice little piece of hot baggage like that with no stud bull in the barn!" he told himself wryly. This would take some thinking about.

It had been amazingly easy. A few hints to the uncle, a few extra days of hard work for him, and Juanita waited for him by the spring. What started out as a way to relieve himself developed into uncontrollable lust; he craved her, he hungered for her. At times he was so angry with himself for wanting her that his temper flared and he struck her. She accepted his blows without a whimper. She never cringed or cowered, nor did she allow him access to her personal thoughts or to arouse her so that she was a willing partner. This too infuriated him. During these angry periods he would force his thoughts to dwell on another time and another place, and he would use her roughly and ruthlessly, then push her from him and ride away.

He rode into the clearing and his pulse quickened. There she stood waiting for him, as she had every evening for the past few months. Her thick, coal-black, waist-length hair hung free, just as he liked it. She wore the thin off-shoulder blouse and the full skirt, also just as he liked. He dismounted, threw the reins over a bush, and came toward her.

"Did you think I wasn't coming?" he asked in the voice he used only in speaking to her. It wasn't the harsh voice he used when talking to other Mexicans, but it wasn't soft. It was restrained, as though trying to be gentle.

"No, señor, I knew you would come." Her voice had music in it, he thought, and any man who ever heard it would not forget it.

He lifted her full skirt and ran his rough hands up and over her soft hips. He had never felt anything as smooth as her flesh. Taking his hands from beneath her skirt, he pushed aside the soft blouse and wrapped his arms around her legs just under her hips and lifted her up until his face nuzzled against her soft breasts. He rubbed his face with its stubble against the smooth flesh, neither knowing nor caring about the pain he inflicted. He took one of her nipples between his lips and pulled on it hungrily, then grinned up at her.

"You're some hot little pepper, Juanita," he said huskily. Holding her with one hand, he pushed one of her legs up into his crotch and held it there between his thighs.

"Feel it," he breathed. "I'm fair about to bust."

He set her on her feet, and she walked away from him and lay down. His hands, clumsy with haste, worked with the lacings on his breeches, then pushed them down beneath his hips. He fell on her and without any preliminaries entered her and commenced to thrust furiously. She felt his jerking spasms, and he uttered soft animal sounds as his fluid gushed into her. He stayed inside her, embedded in her, his breath coming in gasps. Finally he lifted his head and whispered hoarsely in her ear.

"Jesus Christ! I done it again. Lay still—can't be no worse if I do it some more."

Juanita clenched her teeth and turned her face away so that she wouldn't smell his breath. *Madre de Dios*, she prayed, help me. Help me!

Mack worked feverishly to satisfy himself. He placed his hands beneath her hips and thrust into her slender body. When it was over he rose immediately, pulled up his clothing, and strapped on his gunbelt. Juanita covered herself with her full skirt, then got up and walked to the stream. Mack reached out and pulled her to a stop by tugging on her hair.

"Take off your clothes, Juanita." His narrowed eyes gleamed angrily, and fear quickened her heartbeat.

With her back to him she unfastened her skirt and let it drop, then pulled her blouse over her head and walked quickly into the water until it reached her thighs. She squatted down and let the cool water flow around her, washing the thick semen from her thighs. *He knows! He knows*, she thought, and her frightened heart pounded so loud it echoed in her ears. Dulce Madre de Dios, *let him kill me quickly. Please let it be quickly.*

"Stand up and turn around!" It was the harshest tone he had ever used with her.

She got up slowly and turned to face him. She stood as tall as she could, her head held proudly, her eyes looking straight into his. He inspected her thoroughly and silently for a while, then his breath came out in a long, low whistle.

"I thought as much! I thought there was somethin' different about them titties. You goddamn whorin' bitch, you're gonna whelp! I told you I ain't havin' no goddamn Mex bastard. Get outta that water!" he roared.

Juanita walked slowly out of the water. The air hitting her wet skin would have felt coolly pleasant had she been sensitive to any feeling. She stood on the bank, her long hair her only covering. Finally one of his big hands lashed out and he struck her. She went down on her knees, but got back to her feet and raised her head.

"It ain't mine! You've been fuckin' them goddamn Mexicans." The words were bellowed so loudly that the echo resounded far down the valley. He took a handful of her hair and pulled her up close to him. "Ain't you? You been a-spreadin' your legs for *them*! You bitch! You *hija de puta*!"

"No, señor. I lie with no one but you." Her voice was calm and steady and convinced him that she was lying.

Still holding her by the hair with one hand, he drew back the other and struck her with the back of it on one side of the face and with the palm on the other. Blood spurted from her nose and covered his hand; still he continued to hit her. Finally he pushed her from him, and she fell heavily on the stones by the stream.

"You lying, whorin' bitch. If I ever see your face again, I'll kill you. Do you hear? I'll kill you!"

Juanita sat up slowly, her black eyes filled with pain and terror. Her face was cut and bruised and blood oozed from a hundred scratches on her knees, thighs, and hips. Slowly and painfully she crawled to the edge of the water and bathed her face. Tears she had not allowed to come in his presence now rolled down her cheeks, mingling with the blood on her face. She washed her body while the tears washed a small part of the misery from her soul. She dressed herself, then got painfully down on her knees.

"Our Father," she prayed silently, "and our Holy Mother, who has compassion for sinners and those of us who are weak. Why have you put upon me, thy lowly one, the burden of the wee *niño* growing in my belly? *Madre mia*, why? Help me to face my uncle. Help me to face my friends, who will know I gave my body outside thy holy sanctions. Oh, *Madrecita mia*, have pity. Have pity upon me!"

Juanita rose and draped her rebozo over her head and wrapped it about her face and shoulders. With resignation she went up the dirt track to her uncle's house.

Remembering was painful for Luis. Hatred and resentment burned anew in him as it did each time he thought of what his mother had endured to give him life. If not for Burr and Ben he would have killed that rotten old man years ago. Killing him, Ben had said, would be too easy an end for Mack Macklin. Long years of drawn-out pain and misery, and then to know he'd lost what he loved most, was what he deserved. Burr had agreed and so the years had rolled by.

Luis rode out of El Paso, headed north, then veered across the badlands toward the mountains. He was eager to get home to Macklin Valley to the lovely sad-eyed young woman who constantly occupied his thoughts. He had a purpose now. He knew exactly what he was going to do.

# CHAPTER
## *Nine*

Jacy waited at the door of their room while Johanna felt her way to the table and lit the candle.

"We should make a curtain for the window, Jacy."

"Luis has been gone two weeks, Johanna." Jacy was unable to hear anything but her own thoughts. "I thought he liked me!"

A pang of fear struck Johanna's heart. She went to the wall peg to hang up her shawl. She had suspected that Jacy's depression had something to do with Luis's absence. Now her statement had confirmed it.

"Don't jump to conclusions, Jacy. Walking you back to the house didn't mean he was courting you."

Jacy sat on the edge of the bed. "It was the way he looked at me that made me think he liked me. And he talked about himself, as if he wanted me to know about him." Sudden tears filled her eyes. "Do you think . . . he could want *me*?" She stumbled over the words as if afraid to utter them.

"Jacy Louise Doan!" Johanna was almost angry. "You've got a lot to offer a man. Why . . . you're educated! Papa taught you and you're as good a teacher as I am. Mama taught both of us how to make a house into a home. You're sweet and you're pretty, but most of all you have integrity. I won't listen to you doubting yourself. We're just as good as we think we are, and don't you forget it."

Engrossed in her own thoughts, Jacy continued as if she hadn't heard. "He told me about his horses and the hacienda. He wants to breed a lighter, faster strain of horses. And, Johanna, he never once mentioned what . . . happened to me or about . . . what he did." There was a kind of a desperate note in her voice when she added, "You like him, don't you?"

Johanna looked into the anxious face of her sister, heard her disjointed statements, and was filled with uneasiness. *She's already fallen in love with him,* she thought. *She's afraid I'll disapprove. Dear God in Heaven! What kind of man would pay obvious court to her, then go away without a word? Is he only playing with her?* Of the two brothers he seemed the kinder, the more understanding, and he had seen Jacy when she was mute. He wouldn't, he couldn't, be so cruel to her, to give her hope merely to amuse himself. One more emotional upheaval in her life would be more than she could endure.

"Of course I like him," she said, perhaps too emphatically.

"No, you don't," Jacy replied stubbornly and looked as if she was about to cry. "Is it because he's a . . . bastard?"

"Jacy! You know better than that. Papa didn't bring us up to be self-righteous snobs. He always said the best people can be found in the most unusual places. Luis can't be blamed for something his father did."

"I wish he would come back." Jacy's voice was wistful and her lips quivered as she tried to keep from crying.

"Ben expects him back soon. But, Jacy, please don't read too much into the attention he gave you. You'll be able to tell what his intentions are toward you when you see him again. This is a good place for us right now. We'll stay until after the baby comes, then we'll decide what to do.''

Resigned, Jacy got up and took off her dress.

Moonlight shone through the small window. Jacy lay awake, but motionless lest she disturb Johanna. Jacy wished she were more like her older sister. Stable, practical Johanna could always be depended on to put things in their proper perspective. It had been wildly impulsive of her to think that Luis was interested in her. The evening they'd spent together now seemed no more than a dream. It was like the story about the prince and the beggar maid. Luis was so handsome and gentle. She could see him now, tilting his head toward her and listening so intently to what she was saying, as if it were really important to him. He had watched her all evening and hadn't looked away when their eyes met. *I was so sure he liked me*, she thought despairingly as tears rolled down her face.

Morning came suddenly. Jacy awakened to see sunshine streaming into the room. She heard activity down by the corrals and went to the window to peer out. Men were driving in a herd of horses, and her eyes searched for Luis's slim figure. Disappointed not to see him, she forced herself away from the window and dressed.

Jacy always dreaded leaving the room. The house had an eerie, cold feeling that disturbed her. It was as though a heavy curtain of invisible mist cloaked her and moved with her about the house. She longed to leave it, to run down the path to Rosita's cheerful home, but she couldn't leave Johanna with the backbreaking work of cleaning this ghostly place by herself.

The sound of angry voices came from the front of the house

as Jacy started down the stairs. Johanna came out of the kitchen.

"Jacy, go out to the back porch and I'll bring your breakfast," she said in a low, anxious tone.

Johanna followed her to the bench at the end of the porch, her face creased with a worried frown and her chin tilted just a trifle higher than usual. Johanna was angry. Jacy knew the signs.

"That old man is the most impossible creature I've ever met, bar none," Johanna sputtered angrily. "He's rude, demanding, and unreasonable. He's been cursing and shouting all morning, and the language he uses is just awful. I don't blame the people on this ranch for hating him. I'll probably end up hating him myself."

"This place makes me uneasy, Johanna. I can't explain it, but I know this house has had unhappy times. It's so dark and gloomy and sad. Sometimes I'm afraid."

"There's nothing to be afraid of here, love. Nothing at all." Johanna's manner softened. "Red invited you to come and stay with him and Rosita. Would you rather go there?"

"No. I'll not leave you here alone."

Johanna hugged her briefly. "I'd miss you, love." In a lighter tone she said, "There's something you can do for me. I promised Bucko I'd teach him to play my guitar, but I can't seem to find the time."

"I can do that. I haven't taught for such a long time, and I need something to take my mind off other . . . things. He's such a sad little boy. I'd love to teach him."

Jacy drank her coffee while sitting on the bench. Burr came around the side of the house, his steps a bit hesitant when he saw her sitting there. In one of his big hands he held Johanna's straw hat, its pink satin rose crushed and hanging limply.

"This thing was blowing down by the corral and scaring

the hell out of the horses,'' he said gruffly, holding up the hat for her inspection.

Jacy giggled. She liked the big, gruff man even if Johanna didn't. He and Luis had real affection for each other. It was obvious when she saw them together.

Burr pushed the hat down on a peg that stuck out high over the door. The peg came through the crown of the hat and the faded pink rose tilted down at an odd angle. He stepped back and cocked his head to one side, his eyes mischievous.

"I bet it looks better there than it did on her head," he said confidentially.

Jacy's eyes danced and she laughed behind her hand. "She'll be fit to be tied when she sees it there!"

Burr lifted sun-bleached brows and looked at the hat again. "Yup, she will."

Johanna came through the door carrying a plate of buttered biscuits. Burr stepped aside to let her pass, winked at Jacy behind Johanna's back, and disappeared inside the house.

Johanna handed the plate to Jacy. "I can see that he has an entirely different effect on you than he does on me," she said curtly.

"I like him." Jacy bit into a biscuit.

"Well, I don't!"

Johanna went back into the house, and Jacy's puzzled eyes followed her.

From where she sat on the porch Jacy could distinguish the harsh, angry words coming from the front of the house. It seemed the argument was about the windmill and where Burr was building it. After a while he came out of the house, showing no signs at all that he had been involved in a violent argument. He glanced up at the hat above the door.

"I guess she didn't see it."

Jacy's eyes twinkled up at him. "She liked that hat a lot."

"She can still wear it, if she likes it so much." He started to walk away.

"Señor," Jacy called. "If you see Bucko, will you tell him to come to see me here? I'm going to teach him to play chords on the guitar."

Burr paused and turned back. "Whose idea is this?"

"Johanna's. But she's too busy, and she didn't want to disappoint him, so she asked me to do it. Don't you approve, señor?"

He squatted on his heels beside her. "Yes, I approve. I approve of anything that'll help Bucko. Ben and I have been teaching him to read, and he can write some. I don't suppose you'd take on that chore, too?"

"Johanna is a much better teacher than I am, but I'd like to try."

"Perhaps I'd better ask Luis first." His teasing smile turned to deep, soft laughter when the crimson tide flooded her face.

"Señor!"

Burr got to his feet. "Call me Burr. And, Jacy, speak English to Bucko."

"*Sí* . . . Burr," she said as he began to walk away.

Briefly he turned, flashed her a smile, and said, "I'll round up your pupil and send him up."

Bucko was an interested if not a talented pupil. Jacy showed him how to pluck the strings, but his small fingers pinched and pulled. She soon discovered that Bucko liked the sound that came from the strings—any sound; the louder the twang, the better he liked it. Finally she gave up and allowed him just to play with the instrument. Physically, Bucko was the size of a seven-year-old; and although he was unusually bright, he was emotionally immature.

"Bucko," she said suddenly.

The wide blue eyes that looked at her were so like Burr's that she was startled. Now was the time to ask him about his mother, but the words wouldn't come. The thin little body, the bent ankle, and the sad look on his face touched her heart. She decided she couldn't do it—couldn't awaken memories better forgotten.

"Would you like me to teach you to read?"

"Burr teach me to read," he said in halting English.

"You can read? Well, in that case we can play a game where you read a little and write a little. We can start tomorrow. Would you like that?"

"*Sí, señorita!*"

It was the mention of a game that caught his interest. It was a trick her papa had used. *How wise he was*, Jacy mused. *I wonder how he would have handled old Mr. Macklin?*

They sat on a big flat rock, the sun warm on their backs, and Jacy showed Bucko how to lace his fingers together to form a church, to lift his thumbs to form a steeple, and to fold back his hands to show the people.

She was explaining the purpose of the steeple when she saw Luis. She looked up and there he was.

"*Buenos días*, Jaceta. *Buenos días*, Bucko."

Jacy's heart beat a mad tattoo against her ribs. She got to her feet, but found herself standing so alarmingly close to the head-tossing stallion that she sat down again.

"Good morning." Her voice was slightly breathless.

Luis moved the restless horse back a few steps and looked down at her, almost as if he knew the reason for her momentary confusion. She expected him to say something, but instead he simply sat there as still as his restless mount would allow and looked at her steadily.

He wanted to tell her that he had thought of her every minute during the long ride back from El Paso, that she was nothing like any woman he'd ever known. She was warm and sweet and gentle; lovely beyond compare. But couldn't say any of those things to her yet. He would have to move cautiously, wait until the time was right, lest he frighten her.

Jacy found words at last. "You've been away."

"*Sí*," he said softly.

Bucko carefully laid the guitar on the boulder. "*Puedo cabalgar Rey?*"

"Speak English, Bucko," Luis said gently.

"Ride on King, Luis?"

"*Sí.*" Luis was still looking at Jacy. "I came for your teacher, *hombre*. I want to take her to my hacienda. But first you may have a ride on King."

He spoke a soft word to the horse, who ceased his restless movements and stood perfectly still. Bucko limped forward, and Luis bent from the saddle to grasp him and lift him up to sit in front of him. The usually quiet boy was laughing, almost shrieking, in his excitement. He grabbed great handfuls of King's mane, and Luis withdrew his supporting arms and allowed him to hang on by himself. The big horse, as though aware of his responsibility, walked slowly and evenly along the trail. In a moment they were out of sight and Jacy allowed herself to relax.

Luis's words echoed in her mind. He had come for her! She fervently wished her wildly throbbing heart would behave so that she could think. After a quick glance down at her wrinkled skirt, she looked away, not wanting to see her protruding abdomen. She smoothed her hair and reached around to feel if her hair ribbon was in place. She closed her eyes tightly, and a quiver ran through her slender body. Even with her eyes tightly closed she could still see his face, which was like a sculpture she had seen in one of her papa's books. She could hear him talking to Bucko before they came back into view.

"I have not forgotten, *vaquero*, about the pony, but you

must grow some so you will not fall as you go racing like the wind." He stopped the horse beside Jacy and dismounted, allowing Bucko to sit alone atop the big horse. He looked so small on the powerful animal that Jacy became anxious. Luis saw her concern and sought to reassured her.

"King will behave, señorita, so you need not worry." His voice was deep and quiet, speaking fluidly in his own tongue.

Jacy felt her heart race wildly once again. His voice was a part of his undeniable attraction and Spanish did its deep, soft tones far more justice than English.

Luis lifted Bucko from the saddle and set him on his feet.

"*Hombre,*" he said seriously, "I have an important job for you. I need a man I can trust to take a message."

"I can do it, Luis. I can take a message. I am a man to . . . to . . ."

"To trust," Luis finished for him. "I know that, Bucko." The child nodded his head gravely.

"Go and tell Señorita Jaceta's sister that she is going with me to my hacienda, that she will be safe with me, and I will return with her before the sun goes down. Do you understand?"

"*Sí,* Luis," he said proudly and turned to leave.

"Bucko," Jacy called. "Will you take the guitar to Johanna?"

Luis picked up the instrument and handed it to the boy. "Be careful, *vaquero,* and do not fall on it," he cautioned.

When they were alone, Jacy found herself more tongue-tied than ever. Her mind went blank and she couldn't think of anything to say. Her eyes sought his face and found him staring at her. Her face colored and she looked away.

"I like to look at you, Jaceta."

The softness in his voice brought her eyes back to him briefly before a swift new wave of color filled her cheeks.

"Do you mind, *querida,* for me to look at you?"

Her heart gave a lurch. He couldn't have said what she thought he had: *querida*—beloved. She bowed her head and shook it.

"You will come with me?"

"*Sí*," she finally managed to say; then, "Is it far?"

"Not for King. Will you ride with me?"

She shook her head. "Can't we walk?"

"It is too far for you, Jaceta." He looked down at her, a speculative glint in his eyes. "Do you not ride?"

"Not . . . very well," she said, not wanting to admit to a fear of riding since she had returned to consciousness on the back of her abductor's horse.

"I will teach you."

She shook her head. "Oh, no, not . . . now," she said hastily. "I can't . . . I can't! Not like . . . this."

He swung easily into the saddle, and Jacy felt a flash of fear that he would ride away.

"Do not be foolish, my little Jaceta," he scolded gently. "Later I will teach you. Now you will ride with me on King. Come," he invited softly. The horse tossed his head, blew, and pawed the earth. Luis spoke sternly and the stallion stood motionless again. Luis's hand was extended and he smiled, a challenging smile that was reflected in the bright gleam of his eyes. "I would not let you be hurt, *mi pichon*," he assured her. "You need have no fears up here in front of me. Give me your hand. Come, I will not let you fall. I promise you."

Jacy responded to the persuasion of his quiet, seductive voice, and obediently she reached out and put her hand in his and placed her foot on his boot. She let out a small cry of surprise as she was pulled swiftly up in front of him. A strong arm encircled her while the horse shifted restlessly in protest at the extra weight. Another sharp word from Luis and the horse stood still again. Then he adjusted her position so that she was sitting across his lap.

The nearness of him was something she hadn't anticipated. She could feel every nerve in her body responding to his lean hardness. She pressed close to his chest, and his powerful arms not only held her safely in front of him but controlled their lively mount as well.

"You like it up here, *pequeña*?" He spoke close to her ear. She nodded a little uncertainly, for she had to cope not only with the unaccustomed sensations of being on horseback again but with the effect of his tender words and the physical intimacy of the way in which he held her.

"I don't know," she said, then looked down to see how far she was from the ground and immediately shut her eyes.

He laughed at her timidity. "*Tímida*," he teased as he put his heels to the flanks of their mount. The animal responded willingly, and before she realized it she wrapped her arms about Luis and buried her face against the warm, sensual comfort of his chest.

"*Querida mía!*" His voice vibrated with tender concern. "I will let nothing hurt you."

Jacy dared not look up. Her face was pressed against his shirt, and she kept it there, not wanting him to see the tears that had filled her eyes when he had called her his beloved. She was aware of the smooth easy stride of the horse as he carried them easily across the open ground, and of the wind that stirred her hair. She ventured a brief, hesitant peek at the trees going past and realized that they were not going fast. She raised her head and the wind lifted her hair and cooled her cheeks. She looked into his eyes and smiled. Her fear was gone now in the sheer exhilaration of the ride. She tightened her arms around Luis, hugging him, her face nestled against his strong body.

Jacy would have been content to go on like that forever. They didn't talk, and looking up at Luis she no longer felt shy. His eyes held hers and her heart thudded heavily in her breast. He brushed the hair gently from her forehead and she reached up and placed her palm against his face. He turned his lips into it, his eyes holding hers.

"Does it make you happy to be with me, Jaceta?" His voice was barely above a whisper.

Jacy could feel his heart beating strongly and she could see the throbbing pulse at the base of his strong, brown neck; she was mesmerized by it and didn't answer.

"Jaceta?" Strong fingers lifted her chin.

"*Sí*, Luis. Very happy."

He continued to look down at her and ran his fingers lightly over her mouth and down her cheek; his hand cupped the back of her head and he held her firmly against him.

"*Mi bella querida!*" he whispered, then repeated it in English. "My beautiful beloved."

Jacy squeezed her eyes tightly shut as tears welled and glistened brightly on her dark lashes. Her heart swelled and she thought she would choke with the effort of keeping the sobs from her throat.

"*Querida mía*, you weep," he said anxiously.

Her eyes still closed, she shook her head, swallowed convulsively, and tried to control her quivering lips. Luis lifted her chin, then wiped the tears from her cheeks with his fingertips.

"Why?" he asked hoarsely. "Why weep, my little Jaceta?"

Unable to answer and knowing she owed him an explanation, she took his hand and placed it on her abdomen. She was vaguely aware that the horse had stopped. The fingers lifted her chin again, gently but insistently, and she could feel his warm breath on her wet cheeks.

"Look at me," he urged.

Jacy opened her eyes, but tears blinded her. She tried to

wipe her cheeks with the back of her hand, but he moved her hand away and held it in his.

"Weep if you must, my Jaceta, for you have been truly sinned against."

She turned her wet face into his shirt, and her voice when it came reflected the misery in her soul.

"I . . . I'm . . . soiled!"

As his arms tightened about her, the flood of emotion she had kept in check for so long broke. She cried as though her heart would break. Luis held her tightly against him and stroked her hair until she was quiet.

"*Dulce, dulce,*" he crooned against her hair. "You are immaculate!" He tilted her head against his arm and his eyes devoured her face. "Believe me, *amante*, you are as unblemished as the babe unborn."

Heavy lashes lifted from tormented eyes only inches from his, and the look she saw in them brought a great swell of joy within her. She was too confused to hide her secret feelings, and her eyes glowed with love.

"You could . . . love me?"

"Can and do, *amada!*" His eyes laughed at her, and she cherished a joy she had never expected would be hers. If at this moment he had asked for it, she would have given him her soul. "Somehow I knew when I first saw you that we were meant to be together."

Jacy took a deep breath. What had to be asked must be asked now. "The . . . babe?"

Luis lowered his head, and his warm lips caressed her forehead. "The *niño* will have *madre* and *padre*." He moved his hand down and gently stroked the mound that was the unborn babe. "I came to life much as this one, *amante*, but this one shall have a papa to guide it, to teach it, and to love it."

Jacy felt tears coming to her eyes again. She raised her face for his kiss and felt for the first time the touch of a man's lips on hers. Soft and gentle in their seeking, they lovingly caressed, and then sipped at her tears, making them his. As she looked into his blue eyes soft with love, strength flowed into the forlorn void she'd carried within her for so long and filled the hollows her despair had dug. She was filled with love for this man who had accepted her as she was.

A feeling of faintness then swept over her, and she clung to him, wanting desperately to shield and protect him. She clasped her arms about his waist, and her lips gently brushed his chest.

With his lips in her hair, he said softly, "Rest now, *querida*. We will be home soon."

Luis's house was built from earth, like the houses Mexicans had been building for hundreds of years. Massive beams held the structure together and protruded from the sun-browned adobe walls. A stone patio extended across the front of the house, which was set on a rise with its back to a steep cliff. Water flowed through a crevice in the dark red rock and into the irrigation system that Luis had developed. He'd channeled the water so that it flowed past the house and formed a pool inside his fenced pasture. Near the house, where the stream curved, willows offered shade from the hot afternoon sun. The horses were corralled down a slight incline to the right of the house. There was a bunkhouse to the side and the unmistakable outlines of a smokehouse, and inside the network of pole corrals were outbuildings of various sizes. An enormous number of horses milled about in a stockadelike structure, and several *vaqueros* were working with them.

Luis turned the horse toward the willow trees and pulled him to a stop. He placed his hands under Jacy's arms and gently lowered her to the ground. He dismounted quickly, for she was hanging on to the saddle, her numbed legs having refused to support her.

"Are you all right?" he asked anxiously.

Jacy's heart was so filled with joy that her laugh came bubbling up from deep within her. "I'm so all right, Luis, I'm afraid I'm going to die!" The happiness she felt was reflected in her face, and he bent to kiss her. His kiss was gentle, reverent, as though she were something infinitely precious. Her arms closed tightly around him as their lips touched and clung. Her shyness was gone, and her uninhibited desire to show him her love set him trembling.

"Luis," she whispered huskily. "I love you."

"And I love you, my beloved. You are my soul. Your smile fills me with the warmth of the sun." The soft, caressing words were whispered in her ear. He led her to a seat under a willow tree. "I'll take King to the corral."

Jacy watched him go and her heart swelled with love and pride. She'd found her heaven at last. This peaceful hacienda, away from the ghost in the stone ranch house, was heaven. It was home. It was Luis.

# CHAPTER
## Ten

Willard Risewick sat atop the slick Arabian stallion and looked down at the distant stone house. The two men he had hired to accompany him sat their horses a distance away and talked in low tones. Willard neither knew nor cared what they talked about; their opinions were no concern of his. He was a man who had fought with the Union forces during the war and won a battlefield commission and two decorations. A shrewd man, he took no unnecessary risks, and he possessed an amazing knowledge of both military tactics and men. He had returned from the war with the reputation of being the best rifle and pistol shot in the command and an excellent swordsman as well. Ambitious but honorable, he had undertaken this mission with all the zeal he would devote to a major campaign.

He had followed the train of freight wagons from Fort Davis, in sight of the wagons, close enough to be seen but not close enough for contact. Risewick knew he and his men were being watched by the Macklin people, but it was of no importance to him. He carefully mapped the approach to the valley and then turned back to map and scout the entire area. Now he had returned.

He took out his glass to get a better look at the Macklin ranch buildings. A drab place, he mused, remembering the rich and colorful plantations he'd seen in the South during the war. He studied the country below and, as he'd expected, saw the rider hightailing it to the ranch to report on their progress. Boldness was the only policy now, so he swung his mount around, went over the rim, and started down into the valley. His men followed.

They went down through the forest. The trail was difficult to follow, but there appeared no other way to go. The trees around them were mostly Rocky Mountain nut pine and mesquite. Occasionally, when they rode out onto a knoll, over the tops of the trees they could see peaks and ridges at the timber line, and above that the white streaks of snow on bare rock.

Risewick set an easy pace. He calculated how far they had to go and how long it would take. He took a cigar from an inside pocket and bit off the end. It was then that he saw the Indians. They came like ghosts out of the shadowed trees, riding single file. There were four of them, and for an instant each Indian was starkly outlined against the sky as he reached the edge of the wash. In that brief moment a hoof struck stone and alert dark eyes swung in their direction.

The Indians wheeled and raced back into the shadows even as Willard's rifle leaped in his hands. Spurring his horse, he raced for cover behind a boulder. He jumped from the saddle as his men joined him.

"Hold your fire," he ordered sharply. Cautiously he studied the terrain before him. He gave it a quick glance, then scanned it methodically with his glass. He studied each rock, tree, and shrub with particular care, making allowances for the light and the length of the shadows.

He waited, his rifle ready, but there was no further movement or sound.

There was a stir behind him and one of his men moved up.

"Dirty, stinkin' Apaches," he whispered. "I ort to a-knowed it was too easy. What we gonna do?"

"Nothing," Willard said calmly. "Nothing, until we see what they're going to do."

Squatting in the shade of the boulder, Willard took stock of their situation. There was a chance that the Apaches might retreat down the valley, but there was a greater chance that they would make a fight of it. It was doubtful that he and his men would last an hour against an all-out attack. He had never fought Indians, and he was beginning to doubt the sticking quality of his companions, who had insisted they were experienced scouts when he hired them. The very silence worried him, because the Apaches knew exactly where they were. Even now they could be circling to attack from the rear.

He shifted his rifle in his hands and checked the chamber, then removed his hat so he could peer around the boulder. As he did so a faint whisper of sound reached him. "Pssst . . ." With rifle ready, he scanned the area behind and on each side. Not a twig or a leaf moved. The sound came again. "Pssst . . ." Seconds later a low voice with a Spanish accent came from somewhere behind them.

"Stay down, señores. When you see Apaches, be afraid; and when you see no Apaches, be more afraid."

"Who the hell are you?" one of the men growled.

"Luis Gazares. These men have come to trade with me, but they take your hair if they can."

"Goddamn! There ain't nothin' worser than a goddamn Indian-lovin' Mex."

"That's enough!" Risewick said sharply. Then, "Señor Gazares, we would appreciate your advice."

"*Sí*. I will circle around and talk with them. Wait until we move out, then make for the stone house. That was your intent, was it not, señor?"

"It was. And *gracias*."

"Go quietly, or it will be an insult that they let you go."

"Will I see you to thank you properly?"

"It is likely. *Adiós*."

Risewick settled down to wait. He was a patient man; he had learned to be so through experience. He sat still now, but alert, waiting to pick up movement. When the sound came, he motioned to the men. They mounted their horses and rode down toward the ranch.

Willard tied his horse to the hitching rail beneath the trees and walked up the path to the house. The old man sitting on the porch offered no greeting. He looked Willard up and down, then leaned over to spit in the can beside him.

"Willard Risewick, Mr. Macklin. It's a pleasure to meet you." He offered his hand. Mack took it and grunted a greeting. "I think you're fast becoming a legend in the Southwest. My respect for you grows, sir, now that I see with my own eyes what you've accomplished here."

Mack indicated a chair, but didn't speak until Risewick was seated.

"You got somethin' on your mind, or you wouldn't have followed the wagons, or stayed on in my valley."

Risewick hadn't expected to have to jump right into his reason for being here. The old man was blunt and direct, he had to give him that. Several thoughts whirled through his mind, ways to postpone the proposal, but he discarded all in favor of being equally direct. He opened his coat, took out his cigar case, and offered it to Mack. The old man ignored the gesture and Risewick put the case back in his pocket.

"Girl!"

The bellow was so sudden and so loud that it startled Willard. A minute or two and several bellows later, the door to the house opened. A tall, slim woman came confidently onto the porch. She was lovely, with a calm face, blue eyes, and silver-blond hair piled neatly on the top of her head. She moved as if she were in the drawing room of a townhouse. Seeing her in this setting was even more of a shock to Willard than hearing the old man bellow. He got quickly to his feet.

"Whiskey."

The woman walked toward Risewick. "I'm Johanna Doan, Mr. Macklin's housekeeper." She smiled and held out her hand.

"Willard Risewick, ma'am." He took her hand and found her handclasp strong.

"Excuse me. It will take only a moment." She went inside without even looking at the old man, and Risewick sat down again.

"You're fortunate to have such a lovely housekeeper, Mr. Macklin."

"Humph!" Mack snorted. "The girl's no concern of yours. What brought you to my valley?" His voice was now tinged with hard impatience.

"I'm here to make you an offer for your holdings," Risewick said briskly.

"They ain't for sale. Leastways, I ain't decided yet." Mack's eyes narrowed and he stared at Risewick, but Risewick had the distinct impression that the old man's mind was busy with other thoughts.

"It's my understanding, Mr. Macklin, that you have no family. I thought that perhaps you'd rather not have your holdings go into litigation until an heir can be found—that you would prefer to sell now and know that your life's work will be continued."

Mack was silent, and Risewick wasn't sure the old man was listening to him.

"It's understandable, sir, that you would wish to continue to occupy the ranch house. Our offer need not include the house and buildings."

The old man still said nothing, and it was impossible to tell from his expression what he was thinking. The only visible emotion was in the big hands that gripped the arms of the chair. Risewick decided to say no more until Macklin spoke.

Johanna came out of the house with a bottle of whiskey and two glasses on a tray. Willard got to his feet.

"Ain't no need for you to go a-jumpin' up and down like a jack-in-the-box for *her*. She's just my hired help. I got her outta a saloon in Fort Davis." Mack growled out the words, then lifted his sharp gaze up to Johanna's face. She was smiling pleasantly.

"Mr. Macklin is quite right, Mr. Risewick. Please keep your seat." She set the tray down and stepped back. "He's right also about my former employment. I was a singer in the Wild Horse Saloon. A very lively place, by the way. If you happen to be going back through Fort Davis you might wish to spend an evening there. If you do, please give my regards to Mr. Basswood, the bartender."

"I'll do that, ma'am." A glimmer of admiration flicked in Risewick's eyes, and he returned her smile. There was definitely animosity between Macklin and the woman. The old man had wanted to embarrass her, but she had turned the tables on him.

"What do you want with my valley?" Mack poured himself a liberal drink and shoved the bottle toward his guest.

Aware of the old man's rudeness, but ignoring it, Risewick uncorked the bottle and poured himself a generous amount of whiskey.

"The company I represent will bring in settlers to farm the land."

Mack looked at him with disbelief, then his hard face crumbled as he broke into a loud laugh. The sound came harshly from his throat, but it was genuine. It had been years since the old man had laughed. The sound stopped as abruptly as it started.

"Plow up my land?" he asked.

"That's the plan."

Mack leaned back in his chair. The half-smile on his face reminded Risewick of a lynx he had once seen exhibited in a cage. Folding his hands over his ample stomach, Mack looked down over the valley, then back at Risewick.

"I'll give it thought. Might be we'll deal."

There was a moment of silence while each absorbed the statement and its ramifications. Risewick's mind pieced together all the scraps of information he had gathered about the man, worried that his opinion of Mack would be shaped by the uneasy feeling of dislike Mack engendered in him. He never allowed himself to be influenced by personal feelings when taking a man's measure. He knew he must be dispassionate; he must examine the situation coolly before handing in his report.

"May I impose upon your hospitality for myself and my men? I'm sure a few days is all the time we will need to come to an agreement, one way or the other."

Mack had already retreated into himself but lifted his hand casually. "Tell the girl to find you a place to sleep."

Her control almost shattered, Johanna went back into the house after delivering the whiskey to the porch. The smile she had pasted on her face vanished the instant she stepped into the hall. For the first time in her life she felt hatred,

hatred for that cruel, vindictive old man. She was feeling the after-effects of the effort it had taken to appear calm in the face of the deliberate affront. Glad beyond measure that Jacy was away from the house, she walked slowly back to the kitchen.

Jacy was spending a lot of time at the hacienda with Luis. It wasn't proper for a young lady to go alone to a man's house, even though Jacy had assured her that an older woman kept house for Luis and was there most of the time. Such behavior could ruin a young woman's reputation. Oh, God, what was she thinking? Jacy's reputation! Johanna had no doubt that she would be safe with Luis, and she was away from the house, where the old man couldn't hurt her.

As the supper hour approached, Johanna grew apprehensive. Surely old Mack would come to the table if they had a guest. Would he make a scene with Burr? Would Burr control his temper? Ben had taken charge of Willard Risewick as soon as he left the porch. They had been closeted in his room for hours, and Johanna fervently hoped he had told him about the bitterness between the old man and his sons. She wished she could just set the food on the table then excape to her room, but she knew it wasn't possible. It's their affair, she told herself. Why should it matter to her if they went at each other hook and tong? It had nothing to do with her. Yet her fear of a scene remained as she prepared the food.

Burr and Bucko were the first to come into the kitchen for the evening meal. She smiled at Bucko and nodded coolly to Burr. He ignored her until he had built up the fire in the hearth. When it was crackling pleasantly he sat down in the fireside chair and rolled a cigarette. Johanna had her back to him when he spoke.

"Luis and Jacy are down at Red's. Sometime this evening Luis wishes to speak to you."

His calm voice plucked at her already taut nerves, and only

a momentary burst of common sense prevented her from snapping at him.

"He knows where to find me." She spoke calmly, but her insides were churning with curiosity as to why Luis wanted to talk to her.

"He wants to talk to you *outside* the house," Burr said slowly and firmly.

"I'll be here," she replied casually, to hide her mounting concern.

"You're the most mule-headed woman I've ever met!"

"And you're the most asinine man I've ever met!" The words were out before she could stop them. Never would she have believed that a brief encounter with a man could cause the turbulence she felt whenever she came in contact with Burr. Her pride had taken a beating at the hands of the Macklins, and she wasn't sure she was equipped to handle so much as one more abusive word. She put her hand to her head, her lips forming another retort, but before it could be voiced, Ben and Willard Risewick came into the room.

"Evening, Johanna." Ben's eyes flicked from her flushed cheeks to Burr.

"Ma'am," Risewick greeted her politely.

Ben had a soothing effect on her. She breathed a sigh of relief. Dear Ben would take over the conversation and leave her free to persue her own thoughts.

Burr got to his feet to meet the guest. "Burr Macklin."

The two men shook hands, and Burr urged Bucko forward, his hand on the boy's back. "Bucko Macklin," he said, and Johanna could swear she heard pride in his voice.

"Hello, young man." Risewick's eyes went from the boy to Burr. Burr looked steadily back at him, as if wishing he would voice the question about the boy's parentage that was in his eyes.

The last of the platters of food were being placed on the

table when Johanna heard the thump of Mack's walking sticks in the hall outside. She glanced at the table to be sure there was a place setting for him, then brought the biscuits from the oven.

"Evening, Mack," Ben said as casually as if Mack regularly came to the kitchen to eat.

Old Mack ignored the greeting and eased himself down in the chair at the head of the table, the one Burr usually occupied. He had shaved for the occasion and put on a clean shirt.

Burr motioned for Risewick to be seated on the old man's right, and Ben sat across the table from him. Burr took the chair at the other end of the table, and Bucko sat beside him. The place left for Johanna was on Burr's right.

She wasn't sure she would be able to eat. Her stomach was unusually tense and her hands felt as though they were weighted. She looked often at Ben's calm face. He chatted easily with the guest while old Mack sat at the head of the table watching and listening, his eyes unusually bright, his face flushed. Burr was civil when spoken to, and Johanna began to hope the meal would end without conflict. Bucko picked at his food. He looked frightened, Johanna thought. Perhaps he sensed the tension between Burr and old Mack, knowing that whenever the two had been together in the past, tempers had flared.

Burr leaned over and spoke to him. Bucko nodded, and Burr broke open a biscuit, put a piece of meat between the two halves, and handed it to him. The child got up as quickly as his lame foot would allow and without looking at anyone limped out of the room.

"Humph!" old Mack snorted scornfully.

"What brings you to the valley, Mr. Risewick?" Burr asked, and Johanna knew instinctively that Burr had sent Bucko away because he too was sure an explosion would come.

"I've come to make an offer for the land," Risewick said smoothly. "I represent a company that will bring settlers out here." Risewick glanced at the old man. "Mr. Macklin is considering my offer."

Johanna thought she would choke on her food; she couldn't swallow. She was unwilling to look at Burr's face, afraid of what she would see there. She did look at old Mack, and what she saw on his face brought a chill down her spine. His steely eyes were on Burr, and his mouth had a demonic twist.

Burr showed no surprise at the announcement and Johanna was sure that Ben had already told him the purpose of Risewick's visit.

"Mack may accept your offer and take your money," Burr said firmly. "But this valley belongs to me and my brother, Luis. He has no right to sell it to you."

"Mr. Calloway told me about you and your brother. I've no wish to become involved in a family conflict, sir." As he spoke, Risewick looked steadily at the big blond man. "But if we buy the land we will bring a large enough force with us to hold what is ours."

"I suggest you find other land and save yourself some trouble. I'll not only fight you with men and weapons, I'll go to the courts." Burr's voice had an edge to it.

"You just try!" Old Mack leaned back in his chair, his sunken eyes cold and a strange sort of smile on his face. "What good would it do you?" he jeered. "You and that damn Mexican ain't my legitimate heirs. I never married your ma, didn't need to. I saved her from a scalpin' by the Apaches, and I plowed her. 'Twas no more than my right, and more'n she deserved, common as she was." He looked pleased with himself, his eyes going from the fury on Burr's face to the horror on Johanna's to the shock on Williard Risewick's. He failed to see Ben's face; it was chalk-white and the hand that gripped his eating knife trembled violently.

Burr's mug came down on the table with a bang. He got to his feet, his eyes dark with anger, his voice more deadly because he spoke softly.

"I don't know how I've kept from killing you, but I swear to God, if you mention my mother again I'll kill you, even if I hang for it!"

"You ain't got the guts, you bastard. And if you did you still wouldn't get my valley. I done told you the only way you'll get it. Grandsons! Legitimate sons! If I could get this gal here in bed, I'd do it myself. If you don't, by God, I'll sell to Risewick and hope he brings back an army that'll blow you the hell out of here."

There was silence. A bitter, aching silence.

Johanna was perspiring with anger, not because of the reference the old man had made to her but because of the fiendish delight he was taking in humiliating the unconventional, white-headed giant standing beside her. Burr was huge in stature and passions, had been rude to her and seemed to enjoy taunting her; he had even made her angry enough to strike him; yet now she felt an inexplicable protectiveness toward him. She'd never before felt anything so passionate as her anger at this man and now because of him.

"I'll talk with you later, Risewick." Burr left the table, his meal still on his plate.

"Humph!" old Mack grunted. "Damn cur thinks 'cause he's running things around here the land belongs to him. Well, I'll show the bastard. Ain't no bastard ever gonna get this valley!" He reached down for his walking sticks and heaved himself up and out of the chair. "Goddamn the son of a bitch," he cursed. "The bastards took off my foot while I was laid up with a fever, but I'll see them both in hell before they get my land."

Johanna stole a quick look at him as he left the room. His face was blotchy red and he was breathing heavily. She could still hear him cursing as he went out the door and down the hall. Her heart was pounding and she closed her eyes for a moment. The silence was deafening, and when Ben spoke it seemed as though his voice came through a long tunnel.

"Please accept our apologies, Mr. Risewick. Mack takes some getting used to. I'll pour fresh coffee and we can enjoy these delicious pies Johanna made for us."

"I'll get the coffee, Ben." Johanna jumped to her feet, glad to have something to do for a few minutes so she could gather her wits.

"I'm mystified," Risewick confessed. "Don't think I'm prying, but I can't help but wonder about what Mr. Macklin said about his foot."

Ben took his time answering. "It's true," he said sadly. "Burr and Luis came back to the valley after the war and found Mack in the house Luis and his mother lived in until she died. He was raving with fever. They removed his crushed foot and saved his life."

"A strange man," Risewick said thoughtfully. "A very strange man."

"He is that," Ben agreed.

"Do you know where he came from originally, Mr. Calloway?"

Ben smiled before he answered. "I've known Mack for thirty years and in all that time he's never mentioned a family or any specific place where he spent his childhood, but I got the impression he was from back East someplace. It was as if he'd never had a life before he came here."

Johanna rose from the table and collected the empty plates. Her mind was flooded with troubled thoughts. The depraved old man enjoyed hurting Burr and Ben. She was sure of that. It must be that he was demented. No man in his right mind would do such terrible things to his child. He was evil! Evil . . . evil . . . evil. The words kept pounding in her head. Evil was all through this house; she could see it now, and feel it. The house was filled with brooding memories; memories of young Anna, saddled with the guilt of loving one man and bearing the illegitimate child of another. And of a small boy, lonely after his mother's death, neglected and hated by his natural father. Jacy had felt the presence of the ghost in the house, and it was her reason for not wanting to stay there. Wearily Johanna raised her hands to her head, and her fingers massaged her aching temples. She was grateful that her sister had not been there to witness the scene that had taken place at the table.

# CHAPTER
## *Eleven*

**W**ith so much on her mind, Johanna was almost finished with the cleanup before she remembered that Luis wanted to talk with her. She was disgusted with herself. This house with all its conflicts had so absorbed and muddled her mind that she had confused her priorities. Jacy was her first concern—Jacy and her welfare. She was convinced now that she and her sister should not remain in this explosive environment. The episode this evening had brought that realization clearly into focus.

Looking up from the pan of sudsy water, she groaned inwardly. Burr was lounging in the doorway, his big body filling it—making her feel closed in. *Now is as good a time as any*, she thought. *I'll take the bull by the horns.*

"Mr. Macklin," she said firmly. "I've decided to terminate my employment here and leave. Mr. Redford offered to escort Jacy and me back to town if the position wasn't suitable." She looked straight into his eyes, her determination clearly visible. "It's not suitable and I want to leave as soon as possible."

He looked at her thoughtfully, then moved his eyes slowly over her body. "You'd not be a bad-lookin' woman if you had some flesh on your bones. We like our women strong and healthy out here."

"Like your horses."

"Exactly." He sauntered into the room and sat down.

Johanna continued to work. "I'm not interested in your opinion of me. All I want from you is your cooperation in arranging our transportation to town, any town."

"You're not likely to be leaving, Johanna. You'll realize that shortly."

She breathed deeply in an attempt to calm her nerves. She should have known better than to try to carry on a conversation with him. She could feel his eyes on her but refused to turn around.

"If you refuse to help us, I'll speak to Luis."

Suddenly he was out of the chair and there behind her. He stood so close that she could feel his breath on her neck. She couldn't speak, couldn't raise her head, in fact couldn't do anything. He brought out a primitive urge in her to scratch and bite, and she knew that if he touched her she would turn and strike him.

"I've decided to wed you," he announced to the back of her head. "If Mack sells the valley all hell will break loose. I saw enough fighting during the war to last a lifetime. If all it takes to keep peace here is to wed you, I'll do it. I'm no prize, being a bastard, but you're no prize either. You're a headstrong, contrary, disagreeable woman. After we get used to each other, we should fit well together. Of course, we may kill each other first."

Johanna barely managed to check the urge to lift the pan of water and fling it at him. Her next impulse was to weep. She chose to do neither. She laughed, insultingly, and continued washing the dishes.

When he turned and went out the door, she took her hands from the water and held the sides of her head as if to squeeze him and what he had said from her mind. On no account must she let him suspect that he held such a powerful sway over her emotions. She also knew that marrying him was out of the question no matter the alternative. The feud between old Mack and his sons was not of her making, and she would not feel the least bit guilty if, by her leaving, it erupted into bloodshed. She and Jacy would go to El Paso, and if she couldn't get a teaching job she would take another singing job in a saloon. It would be far more pleasant than staying on here.

*Damn, damn, damn him!* she thought. *I wish to God we had never come to this godforsaken place.*

Burr was waiting for her on the back porch. A tremor shook her when she saw him, and she blinked nervously. His hand came out of the semidarkness and his fingers closed around her wrist, where she allowed it to stay rather than uncurtain the wild panic she felt at his touch. When she neither spoke nor moved, he slid his hand up her arm and gripped it with warm fingers. His touch evoked turmoil within her. She longed to jump away from him, but her limbs were stiff and unresponsive.

"Don't do anything to spoil my brother's happiness."

In the dark stillness that enclosed them, the statement moved sluggishly through her mind even as she battled the violent storm that pounded inside her, threatening to accelerate beyond control. She had to do something. She tried to pull free of him, and with all the coolness she could command said, "Don't . . . don't touch me!"

Instead of loosening his grip he moved forward to imprison her other arm and pull her against him. He loomed over her, so close she could feel his heart, a great dynamo of power, hammering against hers. She rallied her panic-stricken wits around her and looked him full in the face.

"Release me, please," she said with deliberate sweetness. "Luis and Jacy are waiting for me, and I suspect Isabella is waiting for you."

The grip on her arms tightened. She rejoiced because she knew she had provoked him to anger. After a tense moment the hands on her arms relaxed and his anger gave way to amusement. He chuckled, and his warm breath hit her face in little spurts.

"You *are* a shrew, Johanna, but then I never did like a tame horse." He moved his face closer to hers. "Do you expect me to be flattered because you're jealous of little Isabella?"

"I don't expect anything of you, Mr. Macklin. Now, if you don't mind," she said, carefully blending a touch of sarcasm into her words, "Luis and Jacy are waiting for me. I would like to continue on, or else go to my room."

"*We* will continue on and meet Luis and Jacy."

The trail he took inclined toward the cliff and the spring. Johanna bit her bottom lip in agitation as she stumbled along beside him, his hand so firm on her arm that it felt as if it had grown there. The evening was warm and alive with the soft music of cicadas and crickets. The moon, dim behind a wayward cloud, shed a pale light on the hard-packed earth. To her right a bluff of sheer rock rose darkly into the night; to her left and ahead, screening the spring, was a tangle of willows and junipers. The cloud passed, and ahead in the bright moonlight she could see Jacy and Luis standing so close that their shadows fused.

The intimacy of the image they made caused Johanna's heart to plunge, and Burr's words came back to stab at her, their implications sending a quiver through her body. A thin spear of moonlight slanting through the trees beamed on her sister's glowing face. Even while Johanna watched, Jacy tilted her face up as Luis whispered to her, then turned to look down the path.

"Johanna, Johanna!" Jacy would have run to her, but Luis kept a firm hold on her hand and pulled her back against him.

"Hush, hush," he scolded gently. "The telling shall come from me."

"Jaceta," Burr said, using the Spanish name with a teasing note in his voice. "I've brought your waspish sister to you. She's all wound up and ready to sting someone."

"I haven't seen you all day." Johanna finally found her voice and with it a new desire to be free of the hand clamped to her arm. She tried to move away without forcefully yanking her arm, but the grip tightened, and to her annoyance Burr drew her closer to him.

"Jaceta has been with me, señorita," Luis said. "We have been spending much time together and know we wish to spend all our lifetime with each other. You are the family of my beloved, and I ask your blessing."

The strength seemed to drain out of Johanna and her usually straight shoulders slumped. Her mouth suddenly went dry and she felt sick. Luis's words had wiped away all her plans for leaving the valley. Her head whirled giddily. Event had piled upon event until she was sunk in a welter of confusion. For the first time in her life she stammered.

"Ja-cy?" she said hoarsely. "Are you . . . sure th-this is what you want? You don't really know him."

"I know I love him, Johanna. I loved him even before we reached the valley, and I think loving him saved my sanity. Please say it's all right."

"I only want what's best for you." A tremor shook Johanna's voice. "It isn't for me to say what's right for you. I can only advise you to think carefully before you decide to spend the rest of your life here.''

''I've decided. Please be happy for me,'' Jacy pleaded.

''Of course I'm happy for you, darling.'' Burr had released Johanna's arm at some time during the conversation, though she couldn't have said when. Free to move now, she put her arms around Jacy, and their tears mingled as they held each other close.

''Señorita,'' Luis said when they parted, ''I know of your concern for your sister. She and the tiny *niño* will be my concern. I will care for the babe as if it were my own. Indeed, it is already dear to me, for without it Jaceta might never have come to the valley.''

''Thank you for telling me that. I've cared for Jacy for so long it's going to be difficult for me to let go and allow someone else to do it.'' Johanna spoke evenly, trying to keep her anguish out of her voice.

''Our home will be yours.'' Luis spoke sincerely and drew Jacy back into his embrace as if reluctant to have her away from him.

''That's kind of you, Luis, but I have my work with Mr. Macklin. I'll not leave the valley until my six months are completed. After that, there will be any number of teaching jobs I can choose from. You and Jacy are not to worry about my future.''

''You'd leave here?'' Jacy cried.

''Hell no, she won't leave!'' Burr's voice boomed in the quiet night. He reached out and took Johanna's two arms and almost hauled her off her feet as he pulled her back against his chest. ''She's gonna marry me, Jaceta. What'a you think of that?''

''Johanna?''

The question in Jacy's voice coupled with Burr's presumptuous announcement inflamed Johanna. "I'm not marrying Burr Macklin, Jacy. I haven't completely lost my mind!"

To add to her irritation, Burr laughed and nudged the side of her face with his chin.

"Yes, she will," he chortled confidently. "I've made up my mind I'm going to have this woman for my wife. She's willful, balky, and pig-headed, but she'll do nicely once I've broke her to halter."

Johanna stood still and allowed his words to wash over her. He was doing his utmost to anger her into making a fool of herself. She was not going to allow that to happen. Only when the soft sound of Jacy's giggle reached her ears did she feel hurt. Instead of being indignant with him for his insulting words, her sister had laughed with him . . . at her. Tears sprang to her eyes and she lowered her lids, hoping that in the dim light they wouldn't be noticed. Luis saw the trembling lips and realized how distraught she was. He turned the attention to himself and Jacy.

"Jaceta and I wish to marry as soon as possible, Burr. I am thinking of sending Paco and Carlos over the mountain to bring the *padre*. I would take Jaceta to him, but the trip may do her harm at this time."

"Have a couple of good men ride with them. The *padre* may hesitate to come. It's a good idea to bring him here—he'll have much to do. You can wed Jaceta and I'll wed her waspy sister—if I have to hog-tie her to do it." He laughed. "The *padre* can say a few words over the ones that died since he was here last, and who knows, we may have a few fresh ones for him before he's ready to leave."

"I hesitate to speak of this, señorita," Luis said to Johanna, "but I must. In the week or more it will take for the *padre* to come, I wish my *novia* to stay with Red and Rosita. I have asked them to do me the honor of caring for her until I can take her to my hacienda."

Johanna felt the hollow feeling in the pit of her stomach expand to include her heart. She was losing everything so fast! She looked from Jacy to Luis and finally said with a slight quiver in her voice, "She can stay with me at night and go to Rosita during the day."

"If Jaceta wishes." Luis ran his hand caressingly over the top of Jacy's head and down over her hair, which hung loose to her waist.

*He really loves her*, Johanna thought. *He's not in the least hesitant to show his love in front of his brother. He looks at her as though she were the most precious thing in the world. I'm glad for her, but oh, God, how I'll miss her!*

She shook herself mentally. This is what she had hoped for, prayed for—a man to love Jacy in spite of the cruel thing that had happened to her. It had just come so suddenly, and so soon, that she wasn't prepared for it.

"Thank you," she whispered, and she didn't know why she said it.

"We'll go on back and leave you two lovers alone," Burr said and pulled Johanna around. "You coming, Luis? Don't make it too soon, I want to do some sparkin' of my own."

"I'll bring Jaceta shortly, señorita."

Walking beside Burr, Johanna was hardly aware of him. The grip on her arm had loosened, and now his hand merely guided her. Her thoughts were full of the events of the last half-hour and their implications. She was trapped—trapped in this valley as surely as if her foot were caught in a snare. She couldn't leave Jacy now. Perhaps later, but not now. Meanwhile, she had old Mack and this younger version of him to contend with.

She stopped, shivering. It seemed as though her brain had refused to tell her feet what to do. Burr watched her but said nothing. When she became aware that she had stopped and was standing still she started to move on, but his hand stopped her.

"Luis loves her," he said impatiently. "When Luis loves, it's with all his heart, and it's the same when he hates!" He took her by the shoulders and shook her, not roughly, but not gently. "He loves her," he repeated. He waited, but when she didn't answer, he continued, "What more do you want for her? Luis is a *good* man. He'll take care of her. Believe me, no harm will come to her while Luis lives. He and Ben are the best men I know." His voice was sincere and had almost the same tone he used when talking to Bucko.

Thinking of Bucko, a new wave of anger stormed through her and her hurt feelings took refuge behind it. She twisted out of his grasp and faced him like a spitting cat.

"You've got a nerve! Telling Jacy I'm going to marry you. Do you think I'm stupid enough to sentence myself to a life of hell with you? I'd rather die!"

"You'd rather die than wed a bastard! Go on, say it. Say what you mean." He yanked her up close to him and barked the words in her face. "You'd rather die? How about your sister? You wed me or that old devil will sell to Risewick and this valley will flow with blood. She could very well die here right along with her babe, Luis, and Ben. Do you want that on your conscience?"

Involuntarily she recoiled from his cold, reasoned planning. Wildly, she said, "Conscience! You Macklins don't know the meaning of the word! What about Bucko? Do you have Bucko on your conscience? How many more children in this valley have blue eyes? And you have the gall to think I'd marry *you*?" she sneered. "I'm telling you, Mr. Macklin, I want more out of life than to be a brood mare to satisfy a selfish, demanding, cruel old man and his equally selfish, demanding, cruel . . . offspring." She couldn't bring herself to form the word that came to her mind and was forced to substitute.

Burr's hands slid up and around her soft throat, and for a brief second his strong fingers squeezed. His eyes were hooded as he peered down into her face and she knew that he was very angry.

She tried to swallow, found it impossible, and allowed her mouth to fill with saliva. She could feel the frantic clamor of her frightened heart even as some devil prodded her to goad him more.

"What about Isabella? What do you plan to do with her? Cast her out . . . after she produces another bastard?" She drew in a ragged breath. "You're the lowest form of man. The kind I despise. The kind that should be . . ." His fingers tightened about her throat and choked off the words.

"So that's what you think, eh?" For a long moment he looked down into the fragile white face. One slender hand came up and tried to pull his hands away from her throat. Realizing the futility of the gesture, she let it drop to her side. She stood quietly, her head tilted up, his thumbs beneath her chin supporting it. "Don't think that your opinion of me matters in the least," he said cruelly. "At this moment, all I'm concerned with is what I want."

Abruptly his arms were around her and she felt another rush of panic as they tightened their hold, until she was crushed against him so hard that she could feel every tense muscle in his body throbbing. His mouth was hard and angry, and she had time to make only a small murmur before his lips cut off both breath and sound. Moon and sky were blotted out by his dark, angry face as he swooped down on her trembling mouth and besieged it with all the fire and passion he had inherited from his lusty forebears. His kisses were not gentle and she suffered numbly, too shocked to protest. Later, she tried to turn her mouth away, but he would not be thwarted and held her prisoner by threading his lean fingers through the pale gold hair that tumbled down her back. His lips moved on hers, slowly at first, then hard and demanding. His tongue traced hotly the outline of her mouth before compelling her lips to open. Violently and ruthlessly he plundered her mouth until, defenseless, she could do nothing but drift helplessly upon the flood of emotions he had unleashed within her. She sagged against him, unable to stand.

His hand slipped down to her buttocks, holding her there, his muscular thighs forcing intimate pressure upon her. She resisted, a sob in her throat, but her movement only inflamed him more, and his lips pressed her mouth open, crushing all the resistence out of her. She tried desperately to stop herself from surrendering to his strength and magnetism, but the warm hand that found its way under her blouse began to caress her and she passed into a state of limbo where there was no sanity or reason; nothing but hard arms, warm lips, and stroking hands on her bare flesh.

She came out of a near swoon and was instantly aware that Burr was shaking. She could feel the tremor in the body pressed to hers. His mouth, warm and damp, moved down her throat, kissing, nibbling; sending showers of tingling desires, unfamiliar and uncontrollable, racing through her body. His mouth was unlike anything she had ever tasted or felt before and it awakened a thousand peculiar sensations inside her. She forgot who she was, who and what he was, and wished that the feelings he aroused in her could go on forever. As pleasant as it was, a small corner of her mind insisted that she should protest.

"Please . . . I don't . . . Don't do this . . ." Her shaky voice was not convincing. She knew suddenly that although she hated him she couldn't resist him. How could she want him to do this? Was she depraved? Wanton? *Just this one time*, she thought. *Just this one time—*

Delicately, but with deep passion, she brushed her lips along his cheek, quivering with the temptation to find his mouth with her lips. Burr raised his head and she looked up at him. Her heart stood still and crimson colored her face as she saw the mocking blue eyes observing her and realized he knew of the feelings that flooded her. For a moment she was unable to move or speak, trembling with humiliation and pain.

"You like it, eh?" When she only stared at him, his teeth showed a narrow smile. "You've got an itch, sweetheart, that's just begging to be scratched, and I'm just the bird that's going to scratch it for you." His arms dropped from around her and he firmly but gently moved her aside and walked away.

Johanna could hear him chuckling as he strode quickly down the path. She stood panting for breath, because her throat felt painfully tight. A thought struck her with the force of a blow. Burr Macklin would do anything to gain what he wanted, anything at all, and there wasn't a single thing she could do about it.

Sudden fatigue washed over her like a giant wave. She turned and walked slowly to the darkened house.


Jacy watched Johanna and Burr move out of the shadows and down the path toward the house, their blond heads shining in the moonlight. The joy she had felt before Johanna came was dimmed just a little. The look on her sister's face belied the words that she spoke. Johanna was worried about her staying in the valley with a man she had known but a short time. She turned in Luis's arms and pressed her cheek against his chest. Time didn't mean anything when you were sure of love. Papa had always said there was someone special for everyone and only the very fortunate were able to find each other. It had been that way with her parents, and it was that way with her and Luis. If only Johanna . . .

"Luis." Her whisper was soft and husky. "It would be wonderful if Johanna married Burr."

Luis took his time in replying, first kissing her eyes, the tip of her nose, the corner of her mouth.

"Only if they are in love, *querida*," he said against her ear. "I would wish my brother to know what I know, that he is loved by the woman he loves."

"Do you think he could love my sister? Oh, Luis, he looks so much like that old man! Could it be that he's like him in other ways?"

"Hush, *querida*, hush! Do not speak of it, do not think it. My brother must live with the fact that he was made in the old man's image, but only on the outside. On the inside he is a man much like me."

"He said he'd made up his mind to marry her. It was as if she had no say in the matter. Johanna won't marry him unless she loves him. He's so harsh, Luis. Not gentle like you. Oh, I'm glad it's me you want!" She lifted her arms and wound them closely around his neck, and he bent his head to kiss her throat and the softness of her neck and shoulders.

"Do not worry, *mi bella novia*," he told her. "What is meant to be will be. I waited for you, looked for you, my heart cried for you, and . . . you came. It will be the same with your sister and my brother, but perhaps not with each other. Come, you are tired."

"Not yet, Luis!" Jacy closed her eyes and slid her arms around him as she had done when they rode the black stallion together. "Luis, Luis!" She buried her face against him, then looked up at him, bright-eyed and feeling light-headed. Her wide eyes scanned her beloved's face and she cherished every feature. She laughed, tipping her head back until her dark hair fell past her hips.

"I love you, and I'm so happy! And to think a few weeks

ago I wanted to die. Oh, Luis, don't let me wake up and find it all a dream!''

He put his fingers over her lips. "If this is a dream, *amante*, I wish that neither of us wakes up.''


Long after Jacy was asleep, Johanna lay awake, unable to control the turmoil that filled her mind. Jacy and Luis were in love, Burr wanted her to marry him, old Mack was threatening to sell the valley. The ramifications of such a thing were almost beyond her imagination. Burr and Luis would not back down, of that she was sure. There would be bloodshed. The Mexicans who survived would be out of work and would have to move on. To some of them this was the only home they had ever known. So much depended on her willingness to sacrifice her future happiness. But how could she possibly stay on after tonight?

Just thinking about Burr's ridicule of the one small, soft gesture she had made toward him was mortifying, and tears dripped from the corners of her eyes onto the pillow. She put her fingers to her bruised lips. What was the matter with her? For some awful, inexplicable reason, she had enjoyed his advances. God help her, she had! Now that she had finally admitted it to herself that it had been pleasant leaning against him, having his arms hold her close, his face against hers, his lips hard, yet caressing, she attempted to face her feelings squarely. She was a woman with all the female instincts. She wanted to be loved, had dreamed that someday she would find a wonderful man who would love her to distraction. How could she be attracted to a man like Burr Macklin? Why did her heart hammer rapidly each time she was near him? Someone had said that people were attracted to opposites. That was it! She sighed with relief.

Johanna replayed in her mind each and every word that had passed between her and Burr. *It will save me a trip to El Paso to visit the whores!* He had said that the day they met. That was still all she meant to him! That and a way to keep his land without having to fight for it. Heaven help her if she should ever fall in love with him.

*Papa, Papa*, she cried silently. *You always said the Lord never puts more burdens on a person then he is able to bear. I know what I've got to do. I've got to swallow my pride and marry Burr Macklin, and I'd almost rather die than do it.*

Sleep was a long time coming. She closed her eyes and tried to empty her mind of anything pertaining to Burr Macklin and the valley. When sleep finally came it was in light snatches of naps, and dreams came fleetingly of a tall, blond, blue-eyed man who kissed her passionately, laughed, and walked away.

*Damn it all!* Burr swore silently as he walked away from Johanna. He was angry at himself for the biting remark he had made when she touched his face with her lips. There had been no need for him to humiliate her. The woman was as innocent as a babe when it came to sexual assault on her senses. Yet, he had known as soon as he kissed her that she was a passionate woman. It surprised him because she was always so haughty, so in control, so . . . prissy!

*Why don't you admit to yourself that you don't like the feelings she arouses in you?* his conscience asked. *Why do you always go out of your way to goad her and make her so angry that she tells you how rude and crude you are, and how much she hates you? Are you afraid you might come to care for her? No!* he scoffed. He'd be playing right into the old man's hands. *Hell, you're asking for trouble, Burr, messing around with her*, a voice inside him said. *But I'm doing it for Luis*, he told himself. *He's so in love, he doesn't know which end is up. If Johanna stays in the valley Jacy will be happy and content, which in turn will make Luis happy.*

*Luis, Ben, and Bucko are the only people in the world who mean anything to me*, he thought angrily. *And by God, it's going to stay that way.*

# CHAPTER
## *Twelve*

Johanna was awake and dressed the next morning before dawn. She was tired but forced herself to hurry down the steps and into the empty, chilly kitchen. She stoked the cookstove and put the coffeepot on to boil, then kindled a small fire in the hearth and sat down to watch it. The twigs caught and blazed, then spread to the larger pieces of wood. She sat back, enjoying the warmth and watching the shadows play on the walls. She was listless and had no desire to stir from where she sat. There was no rush to start the morning meal, so she closed her eyes and soon she was in that dreamless state between repose and wakefulness.

One second she was asleep and the next she was awake. Her eyes flew open. A big man stood beside the fireplace. His intense blue eyes were fixed on her. Her heart did a flip-flop in her breast and blood rushed like quicksilver through her veins. She opened her mouth to scream, but no sound came out. Her throat was frozen. She cowered back in the chair, her face ashen, her eyes large and blank.

Burr leaned toward her, his brows drawn together in a frown. He realized that she was terribly frightened. He had seen that dazed, empty look on men's faces during the war.

"Johanna!" he said sharply.

As her vision cleared Burr's face came into focus. "Oh . . . oh, it's . . . you—"

"I've no intention of attacking you."

Johanna looked up at him, dark circles emphasizing the blueness of her eyes. Her lower lip quivered ever so slightly, and there was a vulnerability about her that made her seem small and helpless.

"I thought . . . I thought . . . you were old Mack," she said, her voice barely above a whisper.

He recoiled. The look on his face was one of suppressed frustration. No!" he said sharply. "Anything but *that!*"

He was gone almost before the words left his mouth. Johanna continued to sit by the fire until dawn streaked the sky and it was time to start her daily chores.


Ben came in for breakfast and told Johanna that Burr had instructed Mooney to come to the house and escort Jacy and Bucko down to Red's, and that he or Luis would return with them this evening.

"The Apaches are coming into the valley for their seasonal camp. It's nothing to be alarmed about, Johanna," Ben told her reassuringly. "Luis and Burr are especially watchful at this time. They keep a wagonload of supplies ready, and the Indians know they're here. It's an arrangement that's worked very well for the past few years."

"Jacy is going to marry Luis," Johanna blurted nervously.

Ben puffed on his pipe for a few minutes. "Burr told me this morning." He paused, and Johanna didn't say anything, so he said, "This bothers you, doesn't it, Johanna?"

"No. I'm happy for her." She looked at him steadily. "Luis loves her and she loves him. It's just . . . just that she will be making her home here and the situation is so unsettled." She walked to the end of the room and stood with her back to him. "I guess you may as well know I've decided to marry Burr." She said it bitterly, as though the words tasted nasty in her mouth and she wished to be rid of them. She turned to gauge his reaction.

Ben looked at his pipe before she could see the hurt in his eyes.

"Don't do it, Johanna. Don't wed him if you don't wish to. There will be no happiness for either of you."

"I don't wish to, but I'm going to do it. If Burr can endure a loveless marriage, so can I. It's necessary . . . for a number of reasons."

"Marriage is forever," Ben said slowly.

"I've resigned myself to it."

The conversation ended abruptly when Risewick came in. Johanna was thankful for his presence. He talked with Ben while she prepared breakfast.

In the middle of the afternoon Johanna went silently down the stone porch and passed the window of Ben's room.

"Don't do this, Burr," she heard him say.

"Don't interfere. I know what I'm doing."

"You're going about this the wrong way. Given time—"

"There's no time," Burr said curtly.

"But it isn't what either of you wants," Ben insisted.

"Maybe, but . . ."

Johanna quickened her steps, not wanting to listen to the conversation, yet wanting to. She wasn't sure what Ben and Burr were talking about, but she guessed the marriage was the subject. She was sure that Ben had great influence over

Burr, but she was equally sure that if Burr had made up his mind to do something, it would be hard to change it.

She had an hour or so before she started the evening meal, so she walked down toward the cook shack, then past it toward the corrals. There wasn't anyone about, and she leaned on the rails and watched a newborn colt frolic around its mother. It spied her and stood for a moment with raised tail, then ran, kicking up its heels. Johanna laughed.

The day was like Indian summer, warm, with a smoky haze across the valley. A quail's cry came from the willows on the creek. Time seemed to stand still in the answering silence, suspended in the warm, bright afternoon.

Johanna strolled along the path to the spring, kicking up dust with her feet. The sky was a vivid blue, and for some reason it made her think of Burr's eyes. She suddenly felt something strange and frightening, yet vitally exciting, come to life in her. She had never been completely aware of her body and all the pleasures it had to offer until Burr had awakened it with his kisses. Her stepmother had said, "When a man and woman love, their bodies are in tune." Was it possible for bodies to be in tune without love?

Johanna was pondering the question and didn't hear the horsemen come up behind her. She looked up and he was there. Nodding, she expected him to pass on, but he slowed his horse and kept in step with her. He was one of the men who had ridden in with Willard Risewick. He grinned down at her, his teeth showing yellow when he parted his lips.

"Hello, purty thin'."

Shocked that he would speak to her like that, Johanna gave him a haughty look, then looked straight ahead.

"Yer a-meetin' somebody, girlie, or jist awaitin' fer somebody t'come along?"

Johanna didn't answer, but walked a little faster, hoping he would ride on.

He didn't.

"Ah, come on. I know what ya are—"

Johanna ignored him and kept walking.

"Little Mex gal tol' me ya come from a saloon. High-class whore, air ya? Ain't my money good as any?" His words shocked her and she glanced up at him, a look he interpreted as flirtatious. He moved his horse closer and reached out a hand. "Come on up, we'll find us a place. I got somethin' what'll pleasure ya good. No rough stuff. T'will be just like ya like it."

Johanna jumped back, frightened now, and looked wildly about, then turned quickly and started back toward the house, walking as fast as she could. The man wheeled his horse and came up beside her.

"Get away from me!" Panic made her voice shrill.

"Ain't no need to act skitterish. You ain't foolin' me none. Now, I just betcha my pecker's bigger'n that white-headed bastid's ya was with last night." With his horse he started crowding her.

"Get away!" she shouted. Her fear was making her breathless.

"Behind that little ol' buildin' will do just fine. T'won't take long, as horny as I be."

Panic-stricken, Johanna tried to break and run, but he used his horse as if he were dogging a steer, and laughed at her attempts to get away. He was between her and the house, edging her closer and closer to the small stone building. She ran back and forth, small, whimpering cries coming from her throat. Trapped between the building and this lust-driven beast, she was barely able to think.

Desperately, she whirled and bolted behind the horse. Then she saw someone running down the path. Frantic with relief, she leaped back from the horse's sharp hooves, and tried again to run.

Burr's long legs ate up the distance, and the man, enjoying his game, didn't realize Burr was there until he grabbed the horse's bridle and jerked it to a halt. The startled hatchet-faced scout looked down into the angry face with surprise.

"Get off that horse, you son of a bitch. I'm goin' to kick you to death!" The savagery of his tone reached the man, who was clearly scared out of his wits. He got off his horse, slowly, on the other side, and started backing away. Burr walked after him.

"She's only a whore, mister. I didn't think—"

Burr's huge fist sprang up and hit him squarely on the mouth. He was knocked flat on his back, with his arms and legs sprawled in the dust. Shaking his head, he rolled over onto his knees and got to his feet, spitting teeth and blood. He started to say something more, but Burr hit him again, lifting him off the ground, driving his broken nose back into his face. Blood spurted.

"Go to the house, Johanna!" Burr commanded, and she went, not looking back.

Her legs were so weak they could hardly carry her. Badly shaken from the experience, she went straight to her room and bathed her flushed face with a wet cloth. A whore! That's what they thought of her here. No . . . a "Mex girl," he'd said. Isabella. Isabella had told him she was a whore. But why would she say such a thing? But of course—Isabella was jealous, afraid she was going to take Burr away from her. The spiteful cat!

Johanna was mad. As mad and determined as she had ever been in her life. She took off her drab work dress, washed herself, then dressed again in a white blouse with a puckered drawstring at the neck. The soft gray skirt she took from her trunk fitted perfectly, and she buttoned it tightly around her slim waist. She felt better. She was dressed as though going to her classes. The clothes draped neatly about her body and, controlling her movements, also clothed her emotions. She brushed her hair and twisted it into a firm chignon, allowing only two tiny curls to escape and hover in front of her ears. Her lips were soft, her face smooth, and her heart determined. She left the room to find Mack Macklin and tell him her decision.

Willard Risewick spent the day helping to erect the windmill. He became so interested in the enterprise that he picked up a hammer and worked along with the men. When Burr had to leave to supervise another crew, Luis and Risewick took over. Luis translated his instructions to the Mexicans. It was enjoyable work, and Risewick got to know and admire Luis, who seemed to hold no animosity toward him for trying to buy the valley. When time allowed they talked horses and made plans for Willard to visit the hacienda.

Later in the afternoon Willard went back to his room and spent several hours writing the report he would take back to his employer. The people he had met in Macklin Valley were a complete surprise to him, a man who in his line of work met many people under other than normal circumstances. The five people about whom he wrote in his report all had forceful personalities, but each in a different way.

Mack Macklin, Risewick wrote, had allowed malevolence to erode his heart and soul and eat away any decent qualities he may have ever had. Burr Englebretson knew what he wanted and would fight to get it and keep it. A weaker man would have either killed the old man or left the valley. Luis Gazares was a man who hated deeply and when aroused would strike with the swiftness of a viper. Willard recorded what he'd heard about the vicious way Luis had fought at the Battle of Glorieta. It was hard for him to associate that man with the gentle one who was so knowledgeable and gentle with his horses and who had fallen so completely in love with a young woman who had been cruelly violated.

Johanna Doan would stand out in any society. Willard's pen paused here and he nodded thoughtfully. A beautiful woman. Dressed in the right clothes she would be a sensation in any Eastern city. He had learned, only this morning, she had accepted Burr's proposal of marriage. He felt a little guilty about that and shook his head sadly. One never knew the far-reaching results when one set a plan into motion. Burr would have his hands full with that one, he thought. He wasn't getting a weak-minded, submissive woman.

Risewick's most pleasant surprise had come in meeting Ben Calloway. The man's stature might be small, but he was the strongest of them all. A man of means, whose family headed a shipbuilding empire, he could have left the valley anytime he wished. But he had set his mind on a course and had not deviated from that course. Risewick stopped writing and chuckled. Ben Calloway would have his revenge. By using his wits he would win against the big-muscled Macklin. Somehow, it reminded Willard of the Bible story of David and Goliath.

Risewick was deep in thought when the door was shoved open and Burr came into the room. He knew immediately that the big man was boiling mad.

"I just beat the hell out of one of your men," he announced. "You might want to go down and take a look at him. He's unable to sit a saddle, or I'd have forked him on a horse and run him out of here."

Risewick got up slowly, a puzzled frown on his face. "What did he do?"

"He bothered Johanna!" Saying the words seemed to make him all the more angry. "Insulted her! I should have killed the son of a bitch!"

"Insulted . . . Miss Johanna?" Risewick's shock was genuine. "I'm sorry, Macklin. I'm very sorry. I'd have thrashed him myself. I may still do it." He picked up his notebook and put it in his pocket. "I'll go down and see about this."

"You do that," Burr said, "and while you're about it, you tell him that if he so much as shows his face outside that bunkhouse before you're ready to ride out of here, I'll gut him."

Burr stomped out of the room and went to the kitchen. He paused in the doorway and looked into the room. There was no one there, so he went in and poured water in the granite washbasin to soak his bleeding knuckles. He emptied the bloody water in the pail that had been set at the end of the washstand to receive the waste water and refilled the basin. He washed his face and dried it on the neatly folded towel that hung nearby. He could not remember there ever being a *folded* towel near the washstand. He looked about the room: it was spotlessly clean. The table was set and a clean cloth covered the dishes and other necessaries that were placed in the center of the table. The stove was clean as was the coffee-pot on the back of it. Lamp chimneys glistened and the copper kettle shone. Candles were placed conveniently on the mantel, and a small rug, dug up from heaven only knew where, was in front of the chair in which Ben usually sat.

A poignant longing struck Burr. He'd never missed these things because he hadn't realized they even existed. The thought struck him that a man needed a woman to be there in the evenings when he came in, tired and worn out, from a day's work. A woman who would be glad to see him, and greet him with a smile, a kiss, and a hot supper. A woman to talk to before a fire and to hold during long, endless nights when sleep wouldn't come. A woman who turned to him and wanted his lovin'. *A man needed that*, he thought. *Most men, but not me*.

"Goddamn," he said softly. "Goddamn."

Burr left the room, his boot heels ringing on the stone floor. He was irritated with himself for thinking such damn fool thoughts and irritated at Johanna for worming her way into his life and making him think the damn fool thoughts. He was out the door and onto the porch before he saw her sitting in one of the bulky chairs talking to Mack.

"The girl's come around," Mack said. "She'll wed you."

Burr looked from one to the other. Old Mack sat gloating. Johanna was calm and distant, her white face cold and haughty. Every hair on her beautiful head was in place, and her skirt was folded demurely over her ankles. Her calm reserve and icy appraisal sparked a dash of resentment in him. His pride was hurt, too, that she had chosen to tell the old man her decision before talking to him.

"Well, now, ain't that just dandy. Maybe I've changed my mind."

He saw the color come up in Johanna's face and grinned with satisfaction before he turned and walked away.

"Come back here!" old Mack roared. "Come back here, you bastard!"

Burr's steps never faltered as he disappeared around the corner of the house.

"He'll wed you, never fear. He'll wed you, if he knows what's good for him." The old man glared at the place where Burr had disappeared and muttered, "Stubborn son of a bitch, always a-buckin', always a-buckin'." He spat a stream of tobacco juice on the stone floor, making no attempt to use the can that sat beside his chair. "Must be my blood in him. That lily-livered thing that whelped him didn't have no more guts than a jellyfish."

"I've said I'll marry him, and I will," Johanna said firmly. "But I don't want to hear any more about the past or anyone in it. Is that understood?"

Old Mack looked at her and frowned. "You know, missy,

it's a good thing for you that I ain't fast on my feet no more or I'd'a boxed your ears more times than you got toes.''

Johanna leaned forward and looked him straight in the eye. ''You'd have boxed them only once, Mr. Macklin. The next time you tried I'd have laid your skull open with anything I could get my hands on.''

The old man sat back, and a sly smile played at the corners of his mouth. ''If I'd'a met a woman like you thirty years ago, missy, we'd'a stocked this valley with sons that would'a set the West afire.''

Johanna got to her feet and looked down at him with an icy stare. ''I can think of nothing more revolting than having to submit to you and give birth to your child.'' With that she turned and left him.

''You'll do, missy,'' he called after her. ''You'll do.''

Johanna went through the house and out onto the back porch. She stood by the support post and shivered at the thought of being touched by that lecherous old man. *Please God*, she prayed, *let me get accustomed to these people and this house*.

Her troubled eyes turned back toward the doorway and she barely choked off a profanity that sprang to her lips. High above the doorway, on a peg, hung her straw hat, the faded pink rose swaying gently in the afternoon breeze. Flushing with humiliation and pent-up fury, she saw the hat as a symbol of her treatment since she had come to the valley. She had no doubt who was responsible for putting it there and decided she would leave it as a reminder and a guard against any soft feelings she might have about the man she had promised to marry.

A door opened at the far end of the porch, and she whirled, thinking the recipient of her contempt was coming to enjoy her discomfort. It was Isabella . . . coming out of Burr's room, her arms loaded with his clothing.

"Isabella, come back here!" Burr's voice reached Johanna where she stood at the end of the porch. "You've not got nothing better to do than be with me, have you . . . sweet thing?"

The words stabbed Johanna like a knife, and she marveled that she could stand there so calmly while the Mexican girl's eyes flashed a clear message of victory. After Isabella turned back into the room, Johanna sagged momentarily, then pride came to her rescue and she went to the kitchen to start the evening meal.

# CHAPTER
## Thirteen

Burr was the first to come to the kitchen that evening. Johanna wasn't aware he was there until she turned and almost collided with him.

"Must you sneak about so quietly?" she said crossly.

"Sneak? Can't a man walk into his own kitchen without being accused of sneaking?"

About to retort, Johanna caught the glint in his eyes, and clamped her mouth shut. The big, blond devil was trying to irritate her.

Burr stood near the table and rolled a cigarette, then moved to the cookstove to poke a twig into the flame until it caught fire. All the time he watched her.

His attitude puzzled her. Today he had been murderously angry, then cynical, and now teasing. Would she ever learn to cope with his moods? Now was the time to thank him for coming to her rescue today. She had no doubt that he'd make some sarcastic remark and throw her thanks back in her face.

"Thank you for what you did for me this afternoon, Mr. Macklin."

He didn't say anything for a long while, and eventually she wished she hadn't bothered to thank him. His very presence made that shameful weakness creep over her again. She was determined not to give in to it and vigorously stirred the gravy in the iron skillet on the stove.

"Don't you think you should call me Burr now that we're going to wed?"

"I haven't given it a thought, Mr. Macklin," she answered coolly.

"I've never met a woman who could make me so angry," he said as if to himself, but he made sure that she heard.

"Then you've not met many women," she retorted.

"I've met enough," he said with a lift of his brows, and laughed when she tossed her head and banged a pan down on the stove. He watched her silently for a few moments. When he spoke again his voice was serious. "Usually you would be perfectly safe with any of the men who work here. It puzzles me why Risewick's man did the stupid thing he did. Had you met him in the saloon in Fort Davis?"

"He might have seen me there. But he said someone had told him I was . . . that sort of woman."

"Who would do a thing like that?"

"Ask him." Johanna looked directly into his frowning face. Her cheeks were slightly flushed from the cookfire and her eyes large and serious.

"He won't be talking for a while." The frown changed to a grin.

In spite of herself Johanna let a fleeting smile pass over her lips.

Ben and Risewick came into the room.

"I understand congratulations are in order," Willard said.

"Yes, I'm a fortunate man." Burr took the hand Willard offered.

Johanna raised her eyes to the ceiling in a gesture of disgust. The white-haired idiot was grinning like a cat and accepting the good wishes as if . . . as if . . . She bit back the scathing remark that came to mind and turned back to the stove, but not before she saw the devilish glance he gave her.

Burr was all "sunshine and light" at the supper table. It was all Johanna could do to keep from kicking him. He talked of his plans to allow the "little woman" to fix up the house, and he said he supposed that now that he was going to have a wife he'd have to give up certain, he paused and his eyes flashed at Johanna, pleasures he'd enjoyed in the past.

Ben sat quietly watching, commenting only when forced to do so. Risewick listened attentively and Johanna wondered if he was aware of the act Burr was putting on. *As bad as this is*, she decided, *it's not as unpleasant as it would be if old Mack had come to the table.*

When the meal was over she prepared the tray for old Mack as she did each night and took it to him. Days ago she had stopped trying to be cordial to the cantankerous old man. Now, she kicked open the door, set the tray on the table beside the bed, and left the room without giving him a glance. He seldom spoke to her, but his hard eyes followed her every move.

Later in the evening she stepped out onto the porch to find Willard Risewick waiting for her.

"Ma'am, I asked Ben if I might have a word alone with you. I wish to apologize for what my man has said and done this afternoon and add that if Burr hadn't given the man a good thrashing, I would have done it myself. The only excuse I can give is that he thought his attentions would be welcome. However, he should have known that his information was false. I've seen men hung for doing what he did to you today."

"It was frightening, and I'd rather forget it," Johanna replied.

"Certainly. May I walk with you?"

They strolled to the end of the house and as they neared the benches outside Burr's room, she saw his blond head. He was sitting beside Luis and Jacy. Next to Jacy, sitting as close as possible, was Bucko. Johanna smiled. Children always loved Jacy; she drew them to her as honey draws flies.

Jacy came to her the moment she saw her, and Risewick moved off to find Ben.

"Johanna!" She was bubbling with excitement. "Burr told us! Now we'll be living here together. I can't believe how things have turned out for us. You are happy, aren't you, Johanna?"

"Of course I'm happy. Now, tell me, how is Rosita and her little one? I don't get to see her nearly enough."

"She's all right. Oh, Jo, I'm just so happy. I never thought it possible to be this happy. Sometimes I wonder if I'm alive."

"You're alive, all right."

Burr came up behind Johanna and put his hand on her shoulder. She turned and glanced up and tried to pull away, but his hand tightened and she was forced to stand still.

"*Buenas tardes, señorita,*" Luis loomed up out of the darkness to stand beside Jacy.

"Evening, Luis." Johanna thought her face would crack soon from her forced smile. She looked around for a diversion, saw Bucko, and whirled to go to him. Burr's hand continued to hold her, so she brought the heel of her shoe down on his instep. She was pleased to feel the bone beneath the soft leather of his moccasins. His hand released her, allowing her to take a few steps . . . then she felt a sharp pain. He had pinched her! Pinched her, viciously, on the bottom!

"Don't try that again, sweetheart, unless you want Jacy to know how we really feel about each other," he murmured in her ear.

"Stay away from me and keep your hands to yourself," she hissed.

"Don't you two want to be alone?" Burr called to Luis. "Johanna and I do."

Johanna heard Luis's soft laugh and Jacy's giggle as they moved away.

With a firm grip on her arm, Burr maneuvered her toward the shadows of the house. Johanna fumed. He's impossible, insufferably arrogant, a real . . . mule's ass! Good heavens! she thought, soon I'll be just as crude as he is.

And yet, at the same time, she had to admit there was something about him that fascinated her. She felt attracted to him and she resented it and rebelled against it, and that brought out a childish side of her that she hadn't known existed.

They stopped and Burr pushed her up against the wall, one hand on either side of her. She wanted to look at him but couldn't. The coil of hair at the back of her neck caught in the rough stones. She put her hands on his chest to push him away, but he didn't move. It was like pushing against a mountain. She could feel his breath stirring her hair, and he moved still closer until her hands were captured between her breasts and his chest. Still he said nothing. He smelled smoky and of freshly washed, sun-dried clothes, which brought Isabella to mind.

"Will you please move back and give me room?"

"You're like a little fox I once had. I built a nice little cage for him, thinking I could tame him and have him for a pet. He'd stand in the middle of the cage, too proud to try to jump out because he knew he couldn't make it. But one day I let the barrier down and he was gone; quicker than a flash, he was gone. He was all gold and silver and warm, like you. But smart and sly and quick . . . like me."

"Just what are you trying to say?"

He drew in a deep breath. She could feel his face against her hair. She closed her eyes and forced herself to breathe evenly. After a moment he moved away and she felt the tension go out of her.

"Do you want your sister to know why you're marrying me? Ben and Luis know. Luis would rather Jacy didn't know, but it's up to you. I don't give a damn one way or the other."

"You don't care for anyone, do you?"

"Yes, I care for Ben, for Bucko, and for Luis. Now I care for Jacy for Luis's sake."

"And I care for my sister. Not for anything do I want her to know that I've made this sacrifice for her."

Johanna knew immediately that she had used the wrong word. He grabbed her and pulled her to him, lifting her off the ground so that their faces were level.

"Sacrifice!" he said angrily. "Do you think I want to marry a prissy old-maid schoolmarm, turned saloon singer, turned housekeeper? Do you want to know what you are? You're a cold bitch! God only knows why I'm willing to marry you!" He sat her on her feet with a jolt.

She rubbed her arms. "Then talk to your father. Make him understand we don't want each other." She put in her voice all the scorn she could manage.

"Don't call him . . . that!" he said hoarsely. "Ben's the only father I've ever had. I wouldn't ask that old man to piss on me if I were on fire!"

Johanna was shocked by the intensity of his anger. She turned away from him, miserably conscious of how angry she had made him.

"I don't want Jacy to know," she said in a muffled voice. "I don't know what she would do."

"All right." He came to stand behind her. "But don't get

so all fired up when I touch you." He pulled her back against him and folded his arms around her waist. She stiffened and he laughed softly.

Would she ever get used to his quick-changing moods? she wondered. One minute he was angry, the next teasing, or gentle as he was with Bucko, or expressing his love for Ben and Luis. She was too confused and weak to cope with all the anger inside her. And this other thing . . . this awful physical attraction she felt for him. She stood still and allowed him to nuzzle her. His lips were soft against her face, his cheeks slightly rough with beard. She could feel his heart pounding against her back and the ripple of muscles in the powerful arms that closed around her. He placed soft kisses along the line of her jaw and the spot beneath her ear.

"That didn't hurt much, did it?"

Johanna tried to step out of his embrace, but he refused to let her go.

"Why do you want to leave me?" he whispered, his tongue dipping into her ear. "You liked it?"

She could feel a blush flooding her face. What he'd said was true and he knew it. He laughed at her struggles to free herself and nibbled playfully at the lobe of her ear.

"Admit it. You like my kisses."

Furious with herself and with him, she dug her elbow into his ribs.

"Stop!" She strained away from him, and he loosened his grip just enough to turn her around in his arms.

"You'll have to get used to my lovin', Johanna. I'm a lusty man."

"Oh! . . . You . . ."

Burr laughed at her outraged cry; Johanna could feel it rippling through his body. She wanted to weep.

"You'll fill the nights with excitement, Johanna. I just might have found me a treasure." The words were spoken against her lips. Then savagely he kissed her. His arms possessed an incredible strength and he bound her still closer to his hard body until she felt she would be crushed to death. His lips softened and his kisses became caresses, sending a surging warmth flowing through her like a river. Her lips began to cling, to move, to seek, and she felt once again the sharp stab of pleasure in her middle and a weakness in her limbs. Then he lifted his head, looked down into her face, and laughed, a low, savage, triumphant laugh.

Passion's blinding, deafening spell faded instantly, and anger, like bile, came up in her throat. She emitted a strangled noise and her hand flashed up and she slapped him, taking him and herself by surprise. He loosened his hold and she scrambled back, but his arms snaked out to wrap her again in his strong embrace. Then, to her consternation, she was quickly pulled through the doorway and into his room. Effortlessly he scooped her up into his arms and kicked the door shut. Ignoring her protest, her flailing arms and legs, he carried her across the moonlit room until he reached the bed. His face was suffocatingly close, and his arms imprisoned her like a vise. She could feel the anger that radiated from his body and for the first time she was physically frightened of him. She opened her mouth to scream.

"Scream," he hissed. "Scream and bring your sister running!" He dropped her on the bed and fell on top of her, his body stretched out and pressing down against hers. He held her wrist in one hand and grasped her chin in the other, his fingers digging into her cheeks. His lips were only inches from hers when he spoke in a harsh whisper. "You make me so all-fired mad that I want to twist your head right off your stupid neck."

The fury of his attack had left Johanna speechless with fear. She knew he was capable of violence, and she could tell he was genuinely angry. Jacy's soft laughter and Luis's voice came from beyond the porch, and she tightened her lips and silently struggled against the powerful body holding her.

"I'm going to teach you a lesson, little fox. You're going to learn not to bait the bear."

She tried to struggle, twisting her head from side to side, but there was no escaping the lips that came smashing down on hers. The hand cupping her chin moved slowly down to the bodice of her dress. The strong, firm fingers slipped inside and moved caressingly over her soft flesh, then halted as they reached the nipple, and slowly squeezed.

"I'll not rape you," he whispered. "I won't have to. I'll make it so good for you that you'll want me. You don't believe it? Well, I'll show you. . . ."

His lips touched hers, lightly at first, then with longer and more intense kisses. He concentrated all his attention on doing just this. He kissed her eyes, her cheeks, her mouth, traced it with his tongue, licking and nibbling and then hotly kissing. Her body untensed, melted against his, and she began to enjoy the sensation of his hand on her naked flesh. Her hands found his head and her fingers moved in his hair, pulling his lips harder against her open mouth. She felt the first thrust of his tongue, and when her kisses became wetly passionate, his hand moved to shove her skirts up to her waist and his quick fingers found the slit in her drawers.

*My God, my God! I'm forgetting to hate him.* Her brain pounded with a million thoughts, and somewhere inside her a warning was screaming to be heard. She could not listen, would not listen, not now, when his fingers were giving her spasms of unfamiliar joy that obliterated all else. She wanted him in a way she had never wanted anything. She could feel her muscles tightening, her insides straining, reaching out, longing for fulfillment of the strange, delicious hunger he had aroused in her. His caresses drove every thought from her brain. She felt hot and cold all at once. She wanted him to stop, and she wanted him to go on. She moaned softly and opened her legs.

His kisses became more insistent, and his hands roamed freely. She could feel his pulsating hardness against her thigh . . . this was what she wanted. She lifted her hips toward him, her hands clenched in his hair. He kissed her hard, hungrily, bruisingly. He was between her thighs, rubbing his elongated hardness against her pubis, and unconsciously she began rubbing with him. She threw back her head and strained upward, and still he waited, bringing her nearly to the brink of madness.

"Is this what you want, little fox?" he whispered, and moved the tip of his swollen sex just inside to explore the warm, moist chasm of her being. "Say you want me . . ."

"I want . . . I want . . . Oh, darling—" she whispered on his mouth. She moved and he was inside her.

They came together with the combined force of their passions and created a fierce, explosive, all-compassing world. The hardness plunged inward and upward and began to move within her.

"Oh . . . I can't! I shouldn't!" The feverish words came from her lips even as they sought his. She felt a sharp twinge of pain and whispered, "Please . . . please . . . please."

A giant wave of white-hot pleasure surged over her, and she sank down into a well of shooting stars, fighting to keep her screams of pleasure silent. It was heaven . . . it was hell . . . it was fire, lightning, the pounding of a thousand drums. It was everything, and she clung desperately to the body united with hers. Surely she would never be the same again.

Burr's breath came in short, hot bursts. The hammering urge to release his passion was acute. He had waited, holding back, listening to her soft, startled cries, feeling her orgasm as a jolting triumph. And then he was free to plunge wildly toward his own fulfillment, and it came like a surging river.

When it was over, Johanna lay gasping and spent, bewildered by the explosion that had rocked her senses. Burr lay on top of her for a moment, his heart pounding against hers, his breath ragged in her ear. When he moved, it was slowly. He pulled himself out of her and, careful not to crush her, sat up on the side of the bed. He looked down at her, and in the dim light she could see that he was smiling.

That smile, or smirk, as she interpreted it, brought her to her senses. She yanked her dress down and sat up. Turning her back to him, she adjusted her bodice. She had behaved like a wanton, a whore, and she felt sick with humiliation. She scrambled to her feet and fought to keep back her tears until she could be alone. She felt revulsion, disgust, and hatred for herself and for him.

He caught her arm and she whirled on him in fury. "I hate and despise you," she sobbed. "You sicken me!"

He looked at her for a long moment, then chuckled. "I would have swore you loved me a few minutes ago. You called me darling." A short raspy sound came from his throat that was either a snort or another chuckle. "You may hate me, but you willingly gave me what I wanted. You wanted it, too. I made sure of that. I could've done a better job if I'd had more time. I bet you thought you'd have it the first time with a gentleman on a feather bed. Instead you were taken by a bastard on a straw tick. You know, sweetheart, you're not bad. Given a little time and practice you could get to be as good as Isabella."

Johanna ran out the door. She didn't care who saw her. Tears of humiliation almost blinded her as she sped across the porch and up the stairs. She made it to her room, snatched off her clothes, and crawled into bed.

Burr watched her go, a peculiar feeling moving through him. Why had he so desperately wanted her to enjoy his lovemaking? Why had he held back, tortured himself, until he was sure she had reached her peak? He knew she was a virgin, and he'd never have seduced her if she hadn't promised to marry him. He felt no guilt about that. Now, she really hated him. *I wonder what she thinks*, he thought. *Ladies are taught to act as if they don't like coupling.* He admitted to himself that he didn't know much about ladies, but Johanna was one . . . and she had liked it!

*But why should I care if she liked it or not?* he asked himself with the next breath. He felt nothing for her, nothing like what Luis felt for Jacy or what Ben had felt for his mother. What happened to them wasn't going to happen to him. He didn't want to be tied, heart and soul, to a woman. A man should have a woman to do all the things a woman was made to do, yet keep his heart free. That was what he was going to do with this one.

Burr stretched out on the bed and felt a strange envy when he heard Jacy's soft laugh come out of the darkness. For a moment he speculated on how it would be if Johanna had responded to him out of love and not just in response to his passion. How would it be if she whispered words of love in his ear, and there was a softening of her eyes when they looked up into his? He turned restlessly in bed and wondered about the strange, twisting feeling that churned inside him.

# CHAPTER
## *Fourteen*

L uis rode up out of the wash and halted the stallion so that the sorrel mare he was leading could scramble up the incline. He looked behind him to see if they had left a swirl of dust hanging in the air, then moved on toward the mountains. He had left his ranch at daybreak with the Arabian he had bought from Willard Risewick and the mare that was to be his gift to Jaceta. Of all his horses, he prized these two most. He intended to stable them in the stout barn behind the stone house while the Apaches were encamped in the valley. The rest of the *remuda* would be driven up by the *vaqueros* and put inside the pole corral. There they would be less tempting to the Indians.

Squinting under his pulled-down hat brim, he studied the terrain with care and thought about the small, bright-eyed girl who had come into his life. When he thought about her it was like breathing clean, fresh air after being long in the confines of a smokehouse. Sometimes the most important thing in a man's life comes at the most unexpected time. He hadn't believed himself capable of feeling this all-consuming love for another person. Now, no hour of the day passed that he didn't think of her, she was always with him, and even when they were together they didn't talk a lot because much of the time there was no need for words. It was something that existed between them that they both understood.

He moved out of the shadows and topped out on a rise. The ranch house lay below him. He stopped and studied the terrain again. It was hard to focus his eyes, but he took his time, measuring the sunlit vastness, the great shoulders of red rock, the splashes of green, and the splotch of brown that comprised the ranch buildings. It had been a long time since he had been this cautious. Nothing must happen to him now. His life, suddenly, had become precious to him.

He turned his eyes toward the southwest. Something stirred among the tall grasses growing along the creek. He waited, making no sudden movement. As he watched, the grasses moved in a motion against the breeze, and Luis kept his eyes riveted on the spot. When the grass was disturbed again, Luis knew the movement was too cautious to be caused by an animal. It must be an Indian, because only an Indian could move yet stir the grass so little.

Since his last meeting with Gray Cloud, Luis had had an uneasy feeling about the Apache. Something had been eating at him. Luis had traded with Gray Cloud for several years. It had started when the Indian had tried to steal his horse. Instead of killing Gray Cloud, Luis had whipped him and thereby gained his respect. An Indian would deal with a fighting man, but he'd kill without compunction a man who wouldn't or couldn't defend himself. It was unfortunate, though, that Burr had been present during the fight. Although he hadn't met Gray Cloud since, as far as Luis knew, the Indian hated Burr for having witnessed his defeat.

Luis watched until he was certain there was only one person moving furtively among the grasses and observed the direction he was headed. Luis dismounted and tied the horses under a slab of rock where they would be protected from view. He ducked into a narrow space between two boulders. Once he started down the narrow watercourse he walked slowly, for the trail switched and doubled back and was incredibly narrow in places. The sun was blazing hot and he didn't need to hurry. He was reasonably sure that he and the Indian would reach the spring behind the house at the same time.

Luis stopped and removed his hat, peered down the trail ahead, and wiped his brow with the sleeve of his shirt. Before continuing his descent, he pulled his shirt out of his pants to cover the glinting silver handles of his pistols. Silver reflects sunlight, and he'd be damned if he'd give the Indian a perfect target. He moved on around a jog in the trail and saw the spring. He also saw a flash of color, then heard a woman's angry voice—Johanna's. Burr and Johanna were at the spring. He could see their shining blond heads.

Slowly, methodically, Luis searched the area for the Indian. He spotted him, then with infinite care inched to where he could look out onto the place where the man would approach. Maybe the Indian was just curious about the two white people by the spring. He would wait.

The Apache came into view. It wasn't Gray Cloud but one of the braves who rode with him. Luis wondered if Gray Cloud had sent him to spy. The Indian ran in a crouch until he reached a clump of course gray shrubs, then knelt behind them. Swiftly and silently Luis followed until he was no more than forty feet behind him. He reached into his boot for a long, thin-bladed knife, his eyes never leaving the back of the kneeling warrior. The words Johanna and Burr hurled at each other were the only sounds to be heard, although Luis could not have said what they were saying, so intent was he on the Indian.

Several minutes passed before the Indian moved. Slowly he reached into the quiver on his back and removed an arrow. Luis waited until the arrow was in place and the Indian rose to shoot it. Luis let his breath out easily and stood. The knife shot from his hand with deadly accuracy. He heard the thud as the blade went into the Indian's back below the shoulder blade and threw him forward. There was the crackle of brush as the body fell, then no sound except for the angry voices coming from the direction of the spring.

Luis could not be sure he had killed the man. Cautiously he maneuvered himself toward the still form lying face down in the brush. In a matter of minutes he stood over the dead body of an Indian he recognized as one who had come often with Gray Cloud to trade. Luis decided that no doubt the young warrior wanted to be known for something other than stealing horses and thought to build his reputation as a great warrior by killing Sky Eyes and hanging his white hair from his belt.

Luis pulled his knife from the corpse, wiped it carefully, and returned it to his boot. His squinted eyes searched the landscape once more. Once he was satisfied that the brave had acted alone, he moved quickly and quietly away.

When Willard Risewick left the valley, some of the tension was gone from the ranch house. A Macklin Valley rider guided him and his men out of the valley and set them on a course across the mountains to El Paso.

The days passed slowly for Johanna. She cooked and cleaned during the day and spent her evenings remodeling a blue satin dress that had belonged to their mother into a wedding dress for Jacy. There were faint shadows beneath her eyes. Glad as she was for Jacy's happiness, Johanna was tormented by thoughts of her own future: an unloved wife living in a house filled with unpleasant memories.

Isabella flitted in and out of the house with a proprietary air, her long skirts swishing around her bare ankles. Burr made no attempt to keep her visits to his room secret. In fact, it seemed to Johanna that he flaunted his young Spanish mistress at every opportunity. It was both hurtful and humiliating for Johanna. Although she tried to ignore both of them, she could not ignore her feelings. It was as though the wound was opened afresh each time she saw them together. She began to see Burr's smiles as cruel and insensitive. The glances from his insolent blue eyes struck her in her most vulnerable place. No venom-tipped arrow could have pierced her heart more deeply. Johanna dared not show this inner turmoil, and so her face remained placid, even as Burr's penetrating gaze searched it for some sign of emotion. She never allowed a flicker of hatred or a glimmer of tears in her eyes; there was nothing for him to see but a cold, beautiful mask.

The subject of Bucko and his mother was constantly at the back of Johanna's mind. It was one subject Ben refused to discuss. He urged her to talk to Burr about the boy, but that was the last thing she intended to do. Anger and bitter shame began to churn within her each time she saw him. And each night, lying in her bed, filled with disgust and self-loathing, she would stare into the blackness of the room and hate him with a hatred that was part despair and part an unnameable something that caused her heart to beat faster. She knew that she would never forget or forgive the man who had taken the one thing that she could have freely given only once.

One morning on her way to the spring she heard the sound of horse's hooves behind her. She glanced over her shoulder and saw Burr on his big bay, his hat pulled down over his eyes, and slumped in the saddle as if he were very tired. Johanna stepped out of his way, thinking he wanted to pass, but he pulled the horse up beside her. She saw a thousand white lines around his eyes and his face was covered with stubble, but it remained as impassive as an Indian's while he sat silently looking down at her. He had been working hard. The hair that showed beneath his hat was wet with sweat and curled into tight ringlets, and his shirt had huge wet circles under the arms. He dismounted and reached for the wooden bucket she was carrying while he handed her his horse's reins. She walked beside him, leading the horse.

"Do you ride?"

The question startled her. She had expected him to give her a sarcastic lecture on the hazzards of coming to the spring alone. His orders had been for her not to do so while the Apaches were encamped.

"Yes, some. I don't ride well, but Papa taught me to ride astride. He thought it rather silly for a woman to perch atop a horse when she had two perfectly good legs to help her hold on."

After a pause he said, "Don't come here alone again. I'll see to it that water is brought up to the house."

They walked on toward the spring. *Is that all he's going to say?* Johanna thought. *Isn't he going to make the most of an opportunity to chastise me for being stupid?*

Burr filled the bucket with cool water, then tilted it up and drank deeply. He offered to hold it for her to drink, but she shook her head and drank from her cupped hands. He took off his hat, wetted his neckcloth, and used it to wipe the dust and sweat from his face and neck. Johanna glanced at him furtively. Lately his mood had been quiet; he only half-heartedly responded to the old man's baiting. Perhaps he was as sorry as she that they were being forced to marry. She decided to speak of it.

"Burr." She said his name quickly, and his head turned sharply toward her. "This is an awkward situation we're in. People shouldn't be forced to marry. I'm sure that you're not any happier about it than I am. I've been wondering if . . . if there is some way we could—"

"No!" He put his hands on his hips and gazed down at her, his dust-reddened eyes squinting at her, his brows drawn together. His opposition to what she proposed was obvious, and she felt impelled to speak rapidly before she lost her nerve.

"Why should we give up our future happiness so an old man can achieve his ambition? From what I've heard about him, he's never done a decent thing for anyone in his life." She pleaded for understanding with her eyes. Sweat glistened on her upper lip and her soft breasts rose and fell with her breathing. The look in his eyes told her his answer before he said it.

"When the *padre* comes we'll be married under the sanction of the church, Johanna. It's arranged and nothing you say or do can change it. You struck a bargain and, by God, you'll keep it. You'll be my wife. If you're planning to leave me after Mack is gone, I advise you to forget it. I'll come for you wherever you go. I don't easily give up what's mine." There was a note of cold finality in his voice that made her shudder. Still, a part of her rebelled.

"You'll . . . not own me as if I were a horse!" she sputtered. "A marriage is not a bill of sale! And . . . I'll not be . . . your wife! Why do you insist on marrying me? You've got Isabella. If you force me to marry you I'll not have that . . . your . . . that woman in my house, and I'll not . . . not . . ."

"Sleep with me," he finished for her. His hand flashed out, closed around her wrist, and he jerked her to him. "Do you think I'm the kind of man that lets a woman tell him what to do? Or what *not* to do? When you're my wife, you'll share my bed. You didn't mind it the other night . . . you didn't need much persuading, either," he said softly and smiled. "And you liked it, Johanna. You'll sleep with me all right. As for Isabella, she's no concern of yours." At his words her body went cold inside. She strove to pull back, but his grip was too strong, too painful.

She stood glaring at him, her head tilted proudly, her eyes like bits of blue glass. Something about the way she looked at him made him hesitate, and it brought to mind again the proud little fox he had captured and had wanted so badly to have like him and stay with him. He could see the rise and fall of her breasts, even though the shirt she wore was loose. He remembered the sweet softness he had felt when he held her. Suddenly he ached to hold her again with her soft arms about his neck. His eyes searched hers, and he wondered why this woman, of all women, aroused him whenever he was near her.

Johanna seemed to lose her will as they stood with eyes locked, the powerful attraction he held for her drawing her to him. He was less frightening now, but she trembled all the same when she felt his hand at the small of her back bringing her closer. Abruptly he folded her into his arms, his face so close she felt the scrape of his whiskers on her cheek.

"No," she whispered.

"Why not?" he asked against her lips. The puff of warm breath that came from her when he squeezed her warmed his mouth as he lowered his head to take hers in a deep, twisting kiss. His arms pinned the length of her against his body, and he kissed her hungrily, savagely, his tongue playing over her tightly compressed lips. She thought she would swoon; a strange, feverish pounding in her temples spread to her stomach and lower.

His hand went slowly up her back to the knot of silky hair,

and he threaded his fingers beneath its neat coil. It tumbled down her back as his mouth broke from hers and made a burning path across her cheek to her ear lobe, then hungry lips unerringly sought hers again, taking possession of them, stifling her words of protest when his warm fingers crept up under her loose shirt and closed about her warm, bare breast. His callused palm against her nipple sent a warning message to her brain. She struggled, but then she felt her desire to struggle slipping away from her to be replaced by something else—a ravening urge that flowed swiftly through her, spreading a burning flush over her whole body and an aching wetness between her thighs. She was drained of thought and will. He must have sensed her sudden surrender, for his fingers bit into her shoulders and he moved her away from him.

He grinned down wickedly into her white face. "Not now, sweet thing," he said lightly. "I don't have the time."

His voice came from somewhere far away, but it was his words, the endearment he used when calling Isabella, that brought her to her senses. She pushed away and stood free of him, trembling with shame and indignation.

"I never thought it possible to despise a person as I despise you." She sank to her knees, fumbling for the hairpins he had so carelessly discarded when he loosened her hair. She found them and knelt there, twisting her hair hastily into a knot atop her head. Her breath was still catching in her tight throat, and when her trembling hands touched her burning cheeks, they left streaks of red dirt on her white skin. "You're a low-quality, despicable, completely unscrupulous man, without a speck of decency in your whole body," she said calmly. "I realize that some of these hateful characteristics you possess are hereditary. Nevertheless, I find it hard to excuse your behavior for that reason, and I shall hate you until the day I die."

He jerked her to her feet and turned her toward him. She stood calmly, refusing to struggle.

"Take your hands off me. You've no right to touch me."

"Not *yet*! But I will! Then, don't ever tell me not to touch you. I will touch you when and where I please. And I don't give a damn if you hate me. Love or hate—what the hell's the difference under the blanket?"

She was jolted by his crude remark, but pulled together the shreds of her pride and dignity and said calmly, "I'll never agree to that part of the marriage."

"You think not." He laughed. "I could have had you right here in the dirt if I'd wanted too."

"You make it easy to hate you."

"I'm used to hate," he said harshly. "I'm not used to a woman who wraps her arms about my neck, moves her soft breasts against me, opens her mouth and her legs to me, then tells me she despises me."

Shame and anger seared through her. How could he be so vile as to remind her of her shameful behavior? For days now she had been torn between two desires. One was to reach out and touch him, feel, once again, the firmness of his skin beneath her fingertips, surrender to the ecstasy of lying close to him; the other was the desire to run, to put as much distance between them as possible before she became completely captivated by his animal magnetism.

"Oh!" She took a step backward, and the color drained from her face. "Is there nothing too low for you to say?"

"Is there a code of behavior for bastards, teacher?" He said the last word scathingly, as if it were something to be ashamed of.

"That's what bothers you, doesn't it?" she shouted. "You can't live with the fact you're a bastard. Well . . . you are one! You'll always be one, and marrying a thousand times won't change that fact. You use that as an excuse for every-thing! For begetting bastards of your own, for forcing me to marry you. You use the fact you're a bastard to be vulgar, brutish, and domineering! I will marry you to keep my sister safe and happy, and you may have access to my body, but you'll never have my respect. I'll detest you . . . if I live to be a hundred in this godforsaken place!''

At that moment Luis stepped out onto the path in front of them, seeming not to have heard Johanna's words.

"*Buenos dias.*"

Johanna collected herself sufficiently to acknowledge his greeting, picked up the half-empty bucket, and walked up the path toward the house.

Luis watched her go.

Burr turned his back, picked up his hat, and slapped it against his leg before slamming it down on his head. The bitch didn't care a damn about the raw feelings tearing up his insides. Of course, he couldn't blame anyone but himself for the position in which he now found himself. He *was* forcing her to marry him. With a sneer of self-disgust tinged by self-pity, he turned to Luis and said gruffly, "What'er you doin' here afoot?''

Luis knelt and drank long from the spring. He had seen the frustration on his brother's face. Something was eating at him, something he'd have to work out for himself.

"Apache, brother Burr. An Apache who wanted that white hair to dangle from his belt. He's back in the bush. We can bury him now.''

The weeks of hard work had taken a toll upon Johanna's strength, and with the tension at meal times she had been eating less and less. The brown work dress hanging loosely on her frame was evidence of her weight loss. In her despair she often felt tears in the backs of her eyes and found herself constantly thinking of the past, of the happy times spent with her mama and papa.

Suppertime was the time she dreaded most of all. The old man now came to the kitchen often. Sometimes he came to watch her prepare the food and after the meal he would stay to watch her clean up. He seldom spoke to her, but his presence and the aura of evil that surrounded him unnerved her.

That night Johanna was especially tired. Her nerves were frayed from the confrontation with Burr. Old Mack had come early to the kitchen and had watched her with such a burning intensity that she wanted to scream. Ben, noting her nervousness, had tried to draw him into conversation to divert his attention, but he had refused to respond and sat watching her like a giant toad ready to spring. Burr and Bucko came in and sat down at the table.

Halfway through the meal, old Mack took a leather pouch from beneath his shirt and tossed it down the table. The bag landed beside Johanna's plate with a thump, and the distinct clink of silver could be heard. Startled, she looked up.

"Your pay," he growled.

Johanna lifted the bag. It was so heavy it slipped from her fingers, fell to the table, and sent a spoon skittering to the floor. She was dumbfounded for a moment and then she looked up into the unwavering eyes of the old man.

"There's more than thirty-two dollars here."

"I hope the hell there is!" he said rigorously. "There's more than four hundred."

"I contracted for thirty-two dollars a month. Why this?"

"Ain't it enough?" he sneered.

"It's more than enough. It's almost a year's pay. Why?"

Her voice was sharp and cut into the sudden dead quiet of the room. Burr and Ben had stopped eating and all eyes were focused on her cold features.

Old Mack's face lit up and his faded eyes blazed brightly. "Why? I told you you'd have money to do some fixin'. Don't you want it? Are you weddin' the bastard 'cause you want him? Haw! Haw! Haw!" The unaccustomed laughter came scratchily from his throat.

"You know why I'm doing it," Johanna hissed angrily. "You promised not to sell the valley if I married him. That's the pay I'm getting, not your . . . blasted money! Are you trying to pay me so you can crawfish out of your bargain?"

"I keep my word. I don't crawfish!" he roared.

"No, you're too low to crawfish," she shouted. "You wiggle along on your belly like a . . . a snake!"

The old man leaned back in his chair and gazed with open admiration at her angry face. The look got through to her, and she realized she had been led into the shouting match for the old man's enjoyment. Appalled at her lack of control, she forced herself to speak calmly.

"I'll take thirty-two dollars for my pay and that is all."

"It ain't much for what you'll have to put up with." Old Mack's eyes darted to Burr to make sure she understood the meaning of his words.

"That is none of your business."

The old man laughed again, filling the room with the strange sound. Johanna gave him a searing glance and turned her attention to Bucko. The child was terrified. She reached out and pulled his trembling little body to her.

"It's all right, darling. There's nothing to be afraid of," she whispered.

"Humph!" old Mack snorted. He turned his beady eyes on Burr. "She ain't no milksop. I don't know as you're man enough to handle her." Burr helped himself to bread and

ignored him. "She's full'a piss and vinegar," he stated bellig-
erently, his overbright eyes going from Johanna to Burr and
back again. "Ain't you got it in 'er yet, you bastard?" he
finally shouted to Burr. "Ain't you man enough to get her on
her back and take the starch outta her? Been me, I'd'a been
between her legs before she got her hat off."

"Shut your foul mouth!" Burr pounded his fist on the table
so hard that the dishes fluttered and the lamp chimney swayed.
"Damn your rotten soul!" he shouted.

The old man laughed nastily. "So you ain't, and it's put a
burr in your blanket. I wouldn't think a big man like you'd
need help with a scrawny thing like her."

Johanna got up from the table and pulled Bucko up with
her. Her face was flaming and her heart felt as though it would
leap from her breast. She didn't dare look at Ben or Burr.
With the child's hand in hers she rounded the end of the table
and grabbed up the sugared pie crust she had been saving for
him. They had reached the hall and started up the steps when
Burr's voice reached them.

"You filthy old son of a bitch! Don't you have any decency
at all? You keep your foul thoughts to yourself, or, goddamn
you, as old as you are, crippled as you are, I'll break every
bone in your rotten body."

"You just try it, you bastard, and I'll blow you to hell and
back."

Johanna hurried Bucko into the attic room and closed the
door, shutting out the sound of angry voices downstairs. She
led him to the chair beside the window and pulled him onto
her lap. He snuggled his face into the curve of her neck
and she held him tenderly, stroking the hair back from his
forehead, wet with sweat, and she realized the effort he had
made to climb the steep steps so quickly.

"You don't have to be afraid of old Mack, darling," she
said. "It's best to face the fact that he's old and sometimes

says cruel things.'' Johanna spoke softly in Spanish. "Old Mack is a sad old man. He has no one to love him, so he says mean things, trying to act as if he doesn't care. But he must care, and for that reason we should feel sorry for him. You have many people who love you, Bucko. I love you and Jacy and Luis love you. You know that Burr loves you.''

"Burr give ponies for me.'' His voice was muffled and drowsy in the soft folds of her dress.

"He must have wanted you very much to give ponies.''

"He give five.''

"That many?''

"I wish old Mack die!''

"No, we don't wish that. We wish he would be nicer, but if he isn't, we'll have to try harder to close our ears when he says bad things.''

The room darkened and Bucko fell asleep. Johanna gently rested his sagging head against her. Her eyes were accustomed to the darkness, and she studied the child's face. It was delicately formed, and she couldn't see a feature she could attribute to the Macklins except for the blue eyes. They were exactly the color of Burr's and slightly slanted. Now dark lashes lay on the child's cheeks. The boy's slight frame had none of the big-boned, rugged construction of Burr's body. *Such a little boy*, she thought, *carrying the burden of living in this house of dissension and with a misshapen foot*. She looked at it now in the loose-fitting moccasin; it turned awkwardly at the ankle, and she wondered how he managed to walk on the side of it. He should have a special boot. She thought of the harness maker and decided he would be the one to make the boot if she made the pattern.

It was much later when she heard the creak of footsteps on the stairs. She had been holding the boy for so long that her arms were numb, but the child and the comforting quiet had a soothing effect on her. She had come to realize that her life would have more meaning with this small human being to love and to teach. He would help to fill the spot in her life that Jacy had held all these months.

There was a rap on the door. Johanna rested her head against the back of the chair and ignored it. If it was her sister, she would come in; anyone else could go away. Ben would understand. The rap came again, insistent this time. After a long pause the door opened.

"Ben?" Johanna turned her head and saw the outline of a large frame. "What do *you* want?"

Burr came quietly into the room, his footsteps muffled by the moccasins he wore. He carried a lighted candle and set it down on the table beside the chair.

Without looking at him, she said, "Why haven't you had a boot made for this child's foot?"

There was silence, then the creak of the rope springs as Burr lowered himself onto the side of the bed.

"I didn't know it would help," he said simply.

"It needs support from soft leather that can be laced tightly. In time it may force the bones to straighten somewhat. It seems to me his ankle was broken and never set," she said accusingly.

"Have you seen such a boot? Can you show me how to make one?"

"I'll make a pattern." Her words were short and abrupt.

They sat in silence until Burr asked quietly, "Do you like Bucko?"

The question was so ridiculous that she glared at him. He was sitting on the bed, his arms resting on his thighs, his big hands clenched between his knees. He was staring at the floor.

"You must certainly have a great opinion of me," she said

sarcastically. "Why wouldn't I like a child whose parents were not of his choosing and who is forced to live in this vile house with a fiend in human form? His mental anguish must be great each time that old man sneers at his limp. This child and Ben are the only things in this house I do like."

Burr lifted his head, and Johanna saw a forlorn expression on his face, but her heart was so hardened against him that she refused to acknowledge her feelings for him.

"Bucko has as much right here as I do," he said slowly.

"Which only confirms what I thought. It's his due, you said. But you don't think it's his due—you just want to flaunt him before the old man. It's your pride that keeps him here, not what's best for the child."

Burr drew in a ragged breath. "Your tongue's got a sting like a scorpion!"

"I'll need it if I'm going to survive in this house."

"It doesn't have to be this way."

Johanna didn't answer. The child in her arms stirred, and Burr got to his feet and lifted him from Johanna's lap. He held Bucko upright in his arms and eased his sleeping, dark head to his shoulder. On his way to the door he paused, turned slowly, and looked down at Johanna standing behind him holding the candle.

"It doesn't have to be this way," he said again. When she silently looked away from him he said angrily, "What do you want, for God's sake?"

"I want peace in this valley without having to marry you. That's what I want."

"No!" His voice bellowed above hers.

"I'll not live in a house where my husband's whore comes and goes as she pleases," she said shrilly.

"You mean Isabella?"

"Who else would I mean for heaven's sake!"

"If Isabella bothers you so much I'll tell her to stay away."
He glared down. "But don't you mistreat her. She's not had
the easy life you've had. Do you understand?" She backed
away from his fury. "Don't cringe from me, damn you!" he
ordered.

She stood immobile, and he went on in a voice more
menacing because his tone suddenly became quiet. "The
*padre* is here. Paco brought him in tonight. I'm going to wed
you, and I don't want to hear any more about it."

He turned on his heel and strode out the door, then turned
back. "There's something more that you have the right to
know. The Apaches are pouring into the lower valley. From
the looks of things, it will be the largest encampment that's
ever been here. I'm going with Luis to bring in his breeding
stock, and we'll drive the *remuda* up in the morning. I want
you women and Bucko to stay in the house. I'll have a man
here to stay with you while I'm away." That said, he turned
to leave, then once again changed his mind. He turned and
searched her face intently. "I expect my orders to be
obeyed." He flung the words at her and left.

Johanna kicked the door shut behind him.

Later that night Johanna awoke from an uneasy sleep. At
first she didn't know what had awakened her; her muscles
were tense and her skin prickled with fear. The wind tearing
at the tin roof, so close to the bed tucked beneath the sloped
ceiling, moaned like a woman in pain. The phrase *death wind*
slipped into her mind.

Far away she heard the sound of horses' hooves on
packed earth. She raised her head to listen. Soon the familiar squeaking of the gate and the soft, calm voices of
the men reached her. She got out of bed and went to the

window. A dozen horsemen were returning from the corral at the base of the mountain. A rider took off his hat to wipe his face and the moonlight shone on his white-blond hair. A feeling of relief washed over her, and she returned to her bed, sank down into its softness, and dropped into a deep sleep.

# CHAPTER
## *Fifteen*

The sturdy squaw reached out and viciously pinched the scrawny arm of her husband's third wife. Sha-we-ne showed no sign of the pain that traveled up her arm, but inwardly she cringed and prepared herself to accept the blows from the willow switch held by the shorter, round-faced woman. Her cruel eyes offered no mercy. Sha-we-ne was to be punished for taking so long to bring firewood to their husband's fire. It did not matter that she had had to range far to find the sticks. It mattered only that she had caused the delay and Black Buffalo's meat would not be the first to be cooking over the fire. It was a matter of pride with Moon Rising that the smell of her cookfire should fill the air before that of the other squaws.

Sha-we-ne was to be punished, and no appeal would move Moon Rising. Her name should have been Snake Rising, Sha-we-ne thought. If she should run, Moon Rising would only pursue her, and then her punishment would be greater. She might even call the younger and stronger second wife, Bright Morning, to administer the lash. Sha-we-ne shivered, for it seemed to her that since coming to this valley, the place of her disgrace, her spirit had left her and only the shell of Sha-we-ne remained.

The spicy smell from one of the cookpots hanging over a small fire to the left of their lodge spurred Moon Rising to action. She seized Sha-we-ne's hair, twisting it so that she was forced downward. She laughed when Sha-we-ne's tears came.

"Bitch dog," Moon Rising shouted, making sure the other squaws would hear and come out of their wickiups to watch her punish her slave. "You cannot even gather wood for my husband's fire. Take a stick in your mouth and crawl on your belly." The slashing switch punctuated her words.

Sha-we-ne let a scream escape her lips, more for Moon Rising's sake than for her own. If the squaw thought she was inflicting enough pain to cause her to cry out, she would soon stop. She cringed before her tormentor, allowing her dark, gray-streaked, straggling hair to fall on the ground so that the other woman could tread upon it. She placed a stick between her broken teeth and dropped flat on her belly to crawl painfully forward. Vaguely she heard the yipping of the other squaws, who had gathered to enjoy Moon Rising's mastery with the willow switch, but she did not care. After so many years of being prey to the viciousness of Black Buffalo and his other two wives she had become numb to humiliation. But she did dread the physical pain.

Satisfied that she had proved her dominance, Moon Rising placed a well-aimed kick to Sha-we-ne's ribs and basked in the admiring glances of the other squaws.

"Get up, slut," she commanded. "The hour grows late and my husband is hungry."

Sha-we-ne's drooping head rose and she laboriously got to her feet and swayed slightly. Her lids lowered to hide the hatred burning there.

"I will do what you command, Moon Rising," she said in a subdued voice.

Whatever she commanded! Moon Rising haughtily looked at her circle of admirers, now breaking up to return to their own fires. It was a good feeling to have a slave. She would tell Black Buffalo how the mother of the lame one crawled on her belly with a stick in her mouth. He would be glad he had never lain between her legs. When she was younger and before the lame one had been traded she had caught him looking at the firm body of Sha-we-ne with lust. Always she reminded him of the disgrace of having his strong seed returned in the form of a weak, malformed son, so he used his third wife in various perverted ways, but never so that she could be called Mother.

The range of the Apache was from the middle of Arizona through the New Mexico territory and south into Sonora and the Sierra Madre Mountains of New Mexico. This land was theirs, and within this area they lived and raided. Among their warriors were names that brought dread to the hearts of many. Mangas Colorado, Cochise, Nana, Victorio, Chato, and a dozen others; some were alive and some dead. The name Geronimo was fast becoming the most respected of all among the warriors and their chieftains. Not a Chiricahua by birth, he had married into the tribe, and his leadership had been recognized immediately. A short, thick-set man with a perpetual scowl, he had the unlikely name of Gokhlayeh, "one who yawns," but was generally called Geronimo.

In the Apache culture the men were all-powerful, the women subservient and responsible for all the work. A warrior went hunting and raiding and saw to his weapons. He took as many women as he could afford and his women saw to everything else and looked after his comforts. There were

taboos in the Apache society that prevented a man from looking at the face of his mother-in-law or conversing with her.
Geronimo took one of Sha-we-ne's sisters for a wife and had
come often to the wickiup and talked with Sha-we-ne. She
was sure he would have taken her for a wife, too, if not for
her . . . disgrace.

When she was younger she had dreamed of him often, and
her mind was still susceptible to pleasant dreams. She saw
herself young and beautiful, her flesh firm, her hair long and
shining, lying on the soft skins of his bedding. Her legs would
be wide open to accommodate him. He would enter the wickiup, gaze down at her, and tear away his breechcloth. Naked,
his loins would be hot and throbbing, and he would stand over
her, letting her admire his huge, swollen tool. She could cry
out to him to come to her and enter her, and her hands would
reach out for the object of her desire. He would kneel and
plunge into her, and she would fling her legs wide so that he
could thrust himself deep within her. She would be like a mare
and he a fierce stallion riding her. He would bite her face and
breasts and suck at her nipples. He would scream loud with
joy when he emptied his seed within her, and then he would
not leave her but would stay inside her to become hard again,
and she would buck and rear beneath him.

The dreams were very real to Sha-we-ne. Now that Geronimo was becoming so great and respected a warrior, she
dreamed that she was one of his wives and Moon Rising was
her slave. She would carry a sharp stick, and when Moon
Rising lagged behind or displeased her she would jab at the
fat flesh on her face. Moon Rising would grovel and plead,
but she would show her no mercy. Little by little, so that the
punishment would last, she would cut her until her head
looked like a hunk of raw meat, and then she would parade
her around the encampment with a thong tied about her neck.

There was one dream Sha-we-ne had that gave her more

pleasure than any other; a dream that even now caused her heart to race and her eyes to blaze with emotion. She would have the pale-skinned man, the one with hair like the clouds and eyes like the sky over a red-ant hill. He would be naked and spread out. His huge arms and legs would be tied to stout stakes. He would bellow with rage and she would laugh as the ants crawled up on his hairy chest, walked across his belly, and got into the thick hair around his man-thing. He would scream as the ants ate at him and pass water to try to wash them off. She would poke her stick into the ant hole to make then angry and they would boil up and cover him. She would stay and watch until not even a muscle of his big body jerked or twitched. She would be sad that he had died so soon, that his punishment couldn't have lasted longer, as hers had.

Sha-we-ne had been little more than fourteen summers when she first came to the notice of the white man who lived in the valley. All her life the Apache had used this place on their way south to the mountains and again when they came north in the spring. Here they would rest, slaughter cattle to fill their bellies, and prepare for the journey whatever meat they had not eaten. She was wading in the stream with a group of girls when she saw him sitting on his horse looking at her. She had thrust out her small breasts and lifted her skirts highter, as she had seen the older girls do when they knew they were being watched by the young bucks.

This was a man. Bigger than any warrior in their encampment. His hair was like a cloud. The other girls giggled and ran away when the man held a shining object up for them to see. He motioned for her to come to him, and he held out the bit of blue glass so that she could see the sun shine through it. Slowly and cautiously she approached, and she could see that his eyes were of the same color. He silently held the glass out to her and let it drop in her hand. She ran then, hiding the object in her dress so her mother wouldn't see it and ask where it had come from. When she was alone she took out the piece of sky and looked at it. It was beautiful, and it was a thing no one had but she.

Each day she went back to the stream, and each day the man came. If the other girls were there he would ride away, so she would try to slip unnoticed from the camp and go to the stream to fish. When he found her there alone he would give her another shining object. They would not always be blue like the sky, sometimes green like a leaf, or red like the sunset. She didn't run away now, and one day he got off his horse and she gasped as he towered over her. He reached out a hand and rubbed it over her breast. She felt an excitement. The next day he rubbed her breast again, and she smiled. He lifted her buckskin dress to her waist and pressed his hand between her legs, his fingers working into the soft, moist folds. She was startled at the pleasant feeling that coursed through her. She spread her legs and stood quite still, enjoying this thing the man was doing.

She went early the next day to the stream in eager anticipation of meeting the white man and having him do with his fingers what he had done before. This time he took her hand and led her away from the water and into a place surrounded by thick brush. He took off her dress, then motioned for her to lie down, and she complied, opening her legs. When he removed the big belt from around his waist and opened his clothing, Sha-we-ne saw his extended man-thing rising out of thick hair. She wanted to laugh. She'd seen this many times when the young bucks didn't know she was about. Their breechcloths would stand straight out and they would try to push them down with their hands. This man didn't try to push his down. Instead he knelt down in front of her and put the tip of it to the place his hand had been the day before. It felt good to her, and she smiled. Suddenly he thrust forward and the thing went up inside her. She opened her mouth to scream, but he covered it with one of his big hands. The pain was like none she had ever felt, and she thought the thing was going up into her belly. She looked at him with fear-filled eyes, but he wasn't looking at her. His eyes were closed and his mouth was open and he was breathing heavily as he moved back and forth. He would let the thing come almost out, then would push it back. Sometimes it touched a place in her that felt good and she forgot the pain and tried to tilt her hips so that she could feel it again. Soon he shuddered and she felt a flood of something warm inside her. The man got up at once, fastened his clothing, and got on his horse and rode away.

Sha-we-ne went back to the place beside the stream each day while they were in the valley. Sometimes the man came and sometimes he didn't. He didn't bring any more pretty things, but she didn't care; she had come to like what he did to her.

She never told anyone about her meetings with the pale-skinned man until they were deep into the mountains of Mexico. Her mother was furiously angry with her when she discovered that her flow of blood had stopped, and she beat Sha-we-ne until she told her about the white man she had let go inside her, and showed the pretty things he had given her. She was never welcome in any of the other lodges after her mother chased her through the village and beat her with a stick. Her sisters too were ashamed of her, and only the intervention of their mother kept them from stoning her.

When the white man failed to come for her to make her his woman, Sha-we-ne knew her fate. She would never be first or second wife to a husband, and only if she was lucky enough to be taken for a third wife would she have meat to eat. She clung to the hope that her child would be a big, strong warrior who one day would walk through the village forcing everyone to stand aside so that his mother could pass. This hope died when she gave birth. To add to her disgrace, her son was small and weak and one of his feet was twisted. The gods were angry, her mother said, because she had coupled with the paleskin, and this was her punishment. She hated the child. "Let him die!" she had shouted, but her mother would not and forced her to nurse and tend him.

After Sha-we-ne's mother died, her sisters no longer brought meat to the lodge; and when Black Buffalo offered to make her his third wife to be slave for his other two wives, she moved, with the lame one, to the lodge of Black Buffalo, where her position was lower than that of a cringing dog, despised and reviled. She learned to endure the sly pinches, the kicks, the spit clinging to her face, and her hair jerked so hard that her scalp bled. It was as if her mind and body belonged to someone else and the only thing about her that was alive was her hate. It was coiled deep inside, and she nourished it and it festered.

It became a matter of pride to keep the fruit of her hate alive. She fed the child, but that was all. She never held him, talked to him, or taught him. In fact, she never looked at him unless it was unavoidable, and never since the day he was born did she look into his sky-blue eyes. Sha-we-ne spent as much time away from her lame son as she could. When he was very small she hung his basket on the branch of a tree and did not go near him all day. Later he crawled in the dirt and snatched food from the dogs. She didn't know when the white man came and stared at the blue-eyed child. She was relieved when she returned from picking berries one day and found that the child had been traded for five fine ponies. Thinking the paleskin a fool, she looked anxiously at Black

Buffalo, hoping he would notice her for the wealth she had brought him, but he scowled and shoved her aside. That night he came to her and used her while she was lying on her face, and without the bear grease the pain was almost more than she could bear without screaming.

The seasons passed: winter, summer, winter summer. Sha-we-ne lost count of how many. Wearily she tended the great fire in the middle of the circle of wickiups as well as the one in the lodge of Black Buffalo. She had more and more to do as Black Buffalo's family increased. There was firewood to gather, the contents of the cookpots to stir, children to tend, and the never-ending softening of pieces of hide, which she did with her spit and the grinding of her teeth. More and more moccasins had to be made and more and more garments pounded clean on the stones beside the streams.

The Apache warriors were masters. They sat cross-legged before their wigwams, boasting of their deeds and their power with the bow and arrow, each man seeking to make himself appear braver and stronger than the others. There was talk in the encampment of an uprising, of raids against the paleface settlers of their land. Knives were sharpened, short powerful bows were tested, and new flint-head arrows were made by the older men. The braves lucky enough to possess rifles flaunted them before their poorer brothers.

The chieftains and their chosen warriors sat around the big fire in the circle of wickiups. The discussions were about whether the white man called Sky Eyes would bring the wagon with supplies to the camp. He had come for five seasons, but this encampment was the largest ever to stay over in the valley, and some said the white man would be afraid to come among them. But it did not matter, they said;

they would take what they wanted and kill all the paleskins. They would kill and eat what cattle they wanted and drive off the rest.

Geronimo sat quietly and listened to the talk. Not yet powerful enough to stand up and command, he nevertheless knew that his opinion was respected. His narrow black eyes rested often on the face of Gray Cloud. When the warrior spoke of the white man his eyes glittered with ferocious hatred. Geronimo began to wonder about that hate and about how many of the warriors would follow Gray Cloud into battle.

"We sit like women and talk," Gray Cloud said angrily. "Why do we not go and take what we want? Kill the white man and take his horses and his guns. We are many, they are few, and there are no bluecoats to come help them."

"We will drive them from our land," one brave said, his voice rising with excitement.

A murmur of approval came from the braves surrounding Gray Cloud; then a war drum was produced and a dozen warriors sprang to their feet to begin the dance.

Geronimo thought it time to speak. He stood and held up his hand. The group fell silent. "Hear me well," he said. "It is not yet time to make war on the white man. For many seasons we have come here and had cattle to feed on and to kill and take with us on our journey. We are not using the land as Sky Eyes is using it, and he brings us blankets and tobacco. If we run off his cattle, we will have none when we pass this way again. It would not be wise to kill Sky Eyes at this time. The bluecoats would come before we are ready." When he finished, he sat down.

Gray Cloud was furious. The voice of Geronimo was becoming too powerful; too many heads turned to listen when he spoke. Gray Cloud didn't dare show his hatred for the chief's favorite chieftain, so he directed it toward the whites in the valley, and to Sky Eyes in particular, who had watched and enjoyed his humiliation when he was beaten, having been caught stealing his brother's horse.

"Sky Eyes comes in friendship because he is afraid. Can it be he is not the only one afraid?" Gray Cloud had not meant for his words to be a challenge. But now that they had been spoken, he waited to see how Geronimo would receive them.

Geronimo got to his feet again. The faces of the other Indians were impassive as they watched the two men, but each knew the importance of this encounter. One of the two men would emerge a leader, the other merely a follower.

"Before I retire to my lodge there is a thing I will say to you, Gray Cloud." He pointed a finger at him. "Words flow from your lips like the water in the stream and some are as useless as the leaves that fall and are carried away. It is not words that make a great warrior, but deeds. If you wish Sky Eyes dead, kill him, if you can." He paused. "But do not take our braves to their death when it will serve no purpose but to weaken us for the war ahead."

The chieftains nodded in agreement and Gray Cloud felt a rising tide of fury that they would listen to the words of this man who was not Chiricahua. It made him uneasy . . . it was almost as if they were conspiring against him, trying to belittle him. A great hot anger toward the white man rose in him. He had not grown weak and soft. He was a man and to prove it he would meet the white man from the house of stone and kill him.


Sha-we-ne was sick. There was fever in her body, her head was throbbing, and her tongue was thick. Her brain registered the news that Gray Cloud wished to kill the white man. Her thoughts whirled in hot confusion. At first she didn't know why she was disturbed by what Gray Cloud had said; then, with a cry of despair, she realized that the white man would die quickly and honorably in battle. This must not happen. He must not die before he knew of her hate, before he suffered long, agonizing moments of pain. Perhaps she could appeal to Gray Cloud to capture him and let her torture him with burning sticks. She closed her eyes and gave herself up to the pleasure of devising ways of bringing pain to the white man.

She was going to die soon. She was in much pain and her body refused to do her will. She could accept death, even accept what torture Moon Rising and Bright Morning chose to inflict upon her, if only she could see the white man once again before she died. Looking up at the sky, she saw his face. He was bending over her. It was strange that he was there. She put up a weak hand, but encountered only air. Her swollen lips stretched into a smile. The message was clear.

# CHAPTER
## Sixteen

B urr sat hunched over the table in the cook shack, his stomach empty and grumbling, his hands circling the mug of hot coffee while he waited for Codger to cook the refried beans and eggs. He nodded to Red and Mooney when they came through the door, then turned back to Luis, who leaned back in one chair with his booted feet resting on another.

Both men were tired. After the *remuda* was safely inside the corrals, Burr had spent the remainder of the night supervising the fortification of the ranch buildings. Luis had scouted the Indian camp.

"How many men would you say were in the camp, Luis?"

"Three, four hundred, I'd guess."

"That's twice the usual number. Do you think it means anything?"

"*Sí.* I think they plan war. Perhaps not now, but later."

"Holy hell!"

"There is excitement among them. The old men make

bows, the warriors strut and talk. It could be that a leader has emerged that can draw all the tribes together.''

"Holy hell!" Burr said again.

Luis grinned. "Not to worry, brother. We will not be caught unaware.''

"I know. We got forty men we can put behind rifles.'' Burr tilted his chair back against the wall. "The trick will be to get all the people up here—"

"We will have time.''

Burr rubbed his hand across his face. "I'll take the supply wagon down tomorrow. Don't think we ought to rush it. They might get the idea we're running scared.''

"*Sí*. We will go together, as usual.''

"Not this year, Luis. I'll go alone. One of us must stay here.''

"Then I go.''

"They expect me. Be reasonable. Listen to your big brother for once. Which one of us is more capable of defending the ranch? And who is the sly fox who can sneak in and out of their camp, who trained the sentries we've got posted? Whose idea was it to organize the women—"

"He's right, Luis," Red spoke up. "Our women and kids would have a better chance with you here. I'll make the trip with Burr this year.''

"Now you wait just a doggone minute," Mooney said.

"We can decide that tomorrow. Codger, where're the eggs?" Burr yelled.

"Keep yore britches on, they're comin'.''

The front legs of Burr's chair hit the floor and he reached over and knocked Luis's feet off the chair. "What say we get married today, brother?" He grinned at the surprised look on Luis's face.

Smile lines appeared around Luis's tired eyes. "*Sí*. It is a good time. If the Apache come it will not be before they get the supplies.''

"I was thinkin' that. Besides, the *padre* wants to leave in the morning. There's sickness in a village in the mountains.''

"He will have no trouble. I will send Paco to show him the way. They will circle the big butte and go up.''

Burr rubbed the stubble on his cheeks. "Do you think I ought to shave?''

"*Sí.*'' Luis moved his chair a distance from Burr's. "And wash off that cow smell, as well.''

"Eat up,'' Burr said, taking the plates from Codger and shoving one down the table to his brother. "We'll go break the good news to the ladies.''

From the moment Burr appeared in the kitchen door to announced that the wedding ceremonies would take place that afternoon, time had ceased its meaning for Johanna. An unalterable tide of events began its course. She went through the motions of preparing for the weddings without quite realizing what she was doing. Burr had explained that there was no immediate danger that the Indians would attack the ranch; but that because the Apache were there in the valley, the weddings would take place without the festivities that usually accompany such an event. This was perfectly agreeable to Johanna.

Jacy was beside herself with excitement. She and Luis had planned to be married at his hacienda, but because of the distance from the fortified ranch buildings, they had accepted the invitation of Red and Rosita to be married in their home. Burr asked Johanna if these arrangements were suitable to her. When she shrugged, he arranged for their wedding to follow his brother's and Jacy's.

With numbed heart and shaking hands, Johanna slipped the wedding dress over her sister's head.

"I wish Mama were here," Jacy said with a catch in her voice.

"Perhaps she is, honey." Johanna blinked the tears from her eyes.

"Do you think she knows that in spite of . . . all that happened, I found someone to love me . . . and that I'm happy? The last time I saw her she was—"

"Shhhh, shhhhh . . . don't think about it. I'm sure Mama knows, and wants this to be the happiest day of your life. Now, how about your hair?"

"Luis likes it to hang loose." Jacy's eyes gleamed and her cheeks turned rosy red. "I'm glad I washed it in rainwater. Oh, Johanna! The dress is beautiful!" She ran her hands down the sides of the full skirt. Johanna had cut off the bodice of the dress and moved the full, gathered skirt up so that it fit snugly beneath Jacy's breasts. She had covered the seam with a strip of white tatting taken from a pair of pillowcases and had added a white satin bow.

Johanna brushed her sister's hair, then placed the mantilla she had made out of four white handkerchiefs edged with lace from her mother's petticoat over her head, allowing one of the corners to fall down over her forehead. She turned Jacy around so she could see herself in the small mirror.

"Oh, I really look like a bride! The mantilla! When did you make it? Oh, Johanna, thank you!" She threw her arms around her sister. "No one ever had a more wonderful sister. We'll both wear the mantilla. I'll wear it while I say my vows, then you wear it."

Johanna dressed with a heavy heart and a shaky stomach. For her wedding she was going to wear a freshly washed white shirt and her gray skirt. She brushed her hair back severely from her brow, then twisted it into a rope that encircled her head—like a noose, she reflected wryly. A noose that would slowly tighten to cut off her independence and perhaps make her as bitter as old Mack himself. Beneath the silvery crown her face was pinched and white, her eyes shadowed by the realization of the enormity of the step she was about to take. In her frozen state she dared not think too far ahead lest the composure she had striven so hard to achieve crumble and spoil this most important day in Jacy's life.

At the sound of footsteps coming up the stairs her nerves tightened and the butterflies in her stomach went berserk. She had eaten little. Not even Ben's scolding had induced her to tackle more than a few mouthfuls of food at each meal. Now she suffered waves of weakness and clutched hard on the iron rail of the bedstead, willing herself not to allow Jacy to see her in this condition. A tap on the door set her heart racing and a few seconds elapsed before she was able to call, "Come in."

Ben opened the door. "Lovely ladies." He bowed. "Your future husbands have given me the honor of escorting you to your weddings."

Both stared at him in amazement. He wore a dark suit, white shirt, and string tie. His black shoes were polished until one could almost see a reflection in them, and his hair, parted in the middle, was slicked down on each side. He limped into the room, his neck held stiffly away from his starched collar.

"Johanna," he said shyly, keeping his eyes averted from hers. "Will you give me the pleasure of seeing you wear Anna's brooch on your wedding day?"

The tears Johanna had managed to hold back all day suddenly flooded her. She went to Ben and kissed his cheek.

"Ben, I'll be proud to wear it!" She took the small cameo from him and pinned it to the neck of her blouse.

Beaming with satisfaction, he said, "If you ladies are ready, we should be leaving."

They had reached the bottom of the stairs and were waiting for Ben to take the last few painful steps out of the house when Johanna saw old Mack standing in the doorway of his room. Johanna paused. For one heart-stopping moment she thought he meant to attend the ceremony, but then she saw that he was leaning against the door frame without his sticks. The look on his face made her feel sick. It was the self-satisfied look of an animal that has made a kill and is gloating over it before tearing into its flesh. His face was flushed and his eyes were overbright.

"You said you couldn't be bought, but I bought you, didn't I, missy?"

His words had a steadying effect on Johanna. She lifted her brows haughtily.

"If you want to think so. Only a fool would turn down such a bargain for a few principles."

She looked toward the door and saw Jacy and Ben standing there. The thought flashed through her mind that she'd been cornered and would be forever branded a bought woman by this old man and his bastard son. For one wild moment she was tempted to send Jacy and Ben on without her. But she wasn't going to let Mack Macklin stand in the way of Jacy's happiness. She knew she was sacrificing her own, but that was her choice. She forced a smile and went toward them, and the three went out into the bright sunlight.

"What did he mean, Johanna?" Jacy asked anxiously.

Johanna laughed lightly. "Who knows? I think he's slightly drunk. Does he drink much, Ben?"

"Hardly at all," Ben said thoughtfully. "But let's forget about him. This is your wedding day."

Every ranch hand who wasn't on sentry duty was waiting for them when they reached the bunkhouse. They stood somberly in a half-circle, their hands awkward with nothing to do. To them, the ceremony was sacred, and each and every one of them wished to witness it. These hard-looking, hard-working men were shy to the point of boyishness, Johanna thought, and found it hard to keep her own face somber. Each wore his best, be it a colorful poncho or a clean flannel shirt. Boots had been wiped clean of dust and spurs had been removed. Some showed small cuts on their faces where they had nicked themselves scraping away a week's growth of beard. Without exception their lean, tanned faces wore expressions of solemnity.

"I didn't see Mooney," Johanna said, glancing back at the men who followed a discreet distance behind them. She almost smiled at the pained looks on their faces: cowboys despised walking!

"Mooney drew watch. He's up by the spring. Luis thought we should have extra patrols."

"Where's Bucko?"

"He went on ahead with Burr."

They walked on slowly and silently. Ahead Johanna could see groups of people standing in front of Red's small adobe house, staring intently in their direction. To Johanna's relief, Isabella was not among them. The garb of the men and women could hardly be called elegant. All had the air of practicality, of making do with what was on hand. They stood quietly and waited for the wedding party to reach them.

Jacy broke loose from Johanna's hand and hurried to Luis the moment she saw him standing beside the small, balding *padre*. Her face was radiant, and her shining eyes saw no one but him. He was breathtakingly handsome in slim tan trousers with a wide colorful stripe running down the side. Over his full-sleeved white shirt was an elaborately embroidered vest, and around his waist was wound a colorful sash. His black boots matched the shine on his carefully brushed hair. It was clear that Luis considered this the most important day in his life and had dressed for the occasion. He feasted his eyes on the beaming face of his beloved and then went to meet her with arms ourstretched.

A sense of rightness swept over Johanna as she viewed their obvious joy in each other, and the great weight she had carried for so long lifted from her heart. How wonderful for Jacy and Luis! Two people who had been so cruelly wronged had found each other, fallen in love, and would live out the days of their lives together. She silently thanked God for being so kind to her sister.

"My . . . reluctant bride has arrived at last," a voice whispered close to her ear.

"Burr, behave . . . please," Ben said impatiently.

"Ah, Ben, let me have my fun. After today I'll be hog-tied for life to a prissy, old-maid schoolteacher."

"If you're going to be sarcastic, Burr, I'd not blame Johanna if she left you flat," Ben said crossly.

"She'll not do that. I'm the only eligible bastard left in the valley."

Ben sighed in exasperation.

Johanna glanced up and caught the gleam of mockery in Burr's eyes. In spite of the devilish smile on his face, a nerve in the corner of his narrowed eyes twitched and the fingers that adjusted the silk scarf about his throat trembled. Johanna smiled and gave herself up to the pleasure of knowing that the big brute was nervous. He was not dressed as elegantly as Luis; however, he was a fine-looking man in his spit-polished boots, neat dark pants, and white shirt. The scarf at his neck matched the blue of his eyes, and without wishing to, Johanna felt a thrill of pride in his handsome appearance.

"You . . . ah . . . look very presentable," Burr said as his eyes wandered down over the unfrilled blouse and plain skirt.

"Thank you," she replied coolly and let her eyes roam insolently over him.

"Do I pass inspection, teacher?" he asked softly.

"You'll do. At least you don't smell like horse manure."

Burr let loose a shout of laughter that caused all heads to turn in their direction. "You're no prize, Johanna, but at least you won't bore me to death."

"Then I'll have to think of something else, won't I?"

She turned her back on him and scanned the crowd for Bucko. Finally she saw him standing with his back against the side of the house. She left Ben and Burr abruptly and went to him.

"I've been looking for you."

It was the same as on the first day she had met him. He stood silently, with his head bent.

"I would like very much to have you at my side during the ceremony." Dejectedly, he broke a small twig he was holding and threw it on the ground. "Bucko, please look at me."

"You be Burr's woman," he said without lifting his head.

"Burr will still be yours, Bucko. It won't make any difference in the way he feels about you, or the way I feel about you."

"Isabella say you make me go."

Johanna stood stone-still, almost speechless with anger. Why would that . . . hussy say that to Bucko? To make him feel unwanted?

"Isabella is wrong, Bucko. She's disappointed because she's not the one to marry Burr, and that's the reason she said this to you. It is *not* true. When I marry Burr, we will be a family. You will be our little boy. I could never send my own little boy away."

"You be my mama? Like Roseta and Harley?"

"Of course I will be. I thought you knew that." She grimaced as she pictured Burr's reaction if he could hear this conversation.

"Isabella say you lie, you will go away."

"Have I ever lied to you, Bucko?" Johanna lifted his chin with her fingers, forcing him to look at her. "Have I?" He shook his head. "Well then . . . ?"

"I will stand by you." He reached for her hand.

"Thank you."

Together they walked back to where Ben and Burr were waiting.

"I've invited Bucko to stand with us," Johanna said evenly, and looked into blue eyes that looked deeply into hers and then down at the small boy who held her hand tightly. He looked back at her for an instant and she thought he was going to say something, but then he shrugged and reached out and ruffled Bucko's hair.

"That suits me fine, cowboy."

"Come on," Ben urged. "The *padre* is ready to start."

"This is your last chance to bolt and run," Burr teased softly in her ear when she turned to follow Ben.

Johanna choked back a retort. If he was so determined to have the last word, let him.

Johanna played her part, as if in a dream seeing nothing of the interior of Red's small house or the people who crowded in to witness the ceremony. The service uniting Jacy and Luis was over before she realized it, and Luis, with his arms around his radiant bride, stood aside and urged Burr and Johanna forward.

She held tightly to Bucko's hand and pulled him along beside them, and the three of them stood before the *padre*. Looking calm and aloof, her slender figure erect, she spoke her vows without a tremor. Inwardly she was numb, ice-cold from head to foot, yet terribly conscious of the presence at her side uttering words with cool deliberation, deceiving every listener with promises. "With my body I thee worship . . . to love and to cherish . . . till death us do part." The soft voice of the *padre* droned on. "Do you, Burnett Englebretson Calloway, take this woman . . ."

Startled, Johanna looked up at her bridegroom to see him looking down at her with a mocking grin. Burr quickly turned his attention back to the *padre* and gave him a firm reply. When it was time for Johanna to reply, her voice was a mere thread of sound—the brave facade she had managed to pull around her had started to crumble.

Burr's steely hand clasped hers, the long brown fingers wiry and tough. He bent his head and his lips fleetingly touched hers. It was then that Johanna realized the ceremony was over. Jacy rushed to her and embraced her tearfully. Luis kissed her on the cheek and shook hands vigorously with his brother, who claimed the right to kiss his bride.

A cheer broke from the crowd when the two couples stepped out of the house. Johanna blinked, dazzled by the brilliant sunshine. A horde of well-wishers descended upon them, showering them with flowers picked from their gardens. Jacy squealed as Luis swung her up into his arms and clutched her to his heart. The women were delighted by the action and the men grinned at the color that transformed the new wife into a creature of shy enchantment. The story of Jaceta's violation had been told and retold, and the part Luis played by killing the two men responsible was fast becoming a legend. Most of those present knew the story of Luis's birth and their hearts warmed to see the glow of happiness on his face.

It was difficult for Johanna to remain aloof for long among the happy well-wishers who surrounded them. She was soon relaxed and smiling, then laughter came bubbling up as Burr was pelted with one outrageous remark after another. He glanced down at her with laughing eyes and took her hand. He gave it a comforting squeeze, a gesture so warm and surprising that it released from deep within her a flood of pleasure.

"Kiss her, señor! Kiss her!"

His hard hand cupped the back of her head and he kissed her lips, still parted in laughter, and crushed her to him in a bone-crushing and fierce embrace. So overwhelming was the wonder of the feeling that Johanna made no protest. Every nerve in her body was alive in a way she had never before known, and she knew, too, that never would she again feel quite this way. He released her lips, and she leaned against him, faintly dizzy from the excitement that churned within her. She gulped for air, and, finally, sanity crept back to calm her mind and senses. She looked at him then, fully expecting his face to show the mockery she had come to know. But Burr was unmistakably serious. He reached out and with his fingertips lightly touched the brooch fastened at her throat. Their eyes held for an immeasurable time. Someone called, and he turned to acknowledge the good-natured joshing. Johanna felt a twinge of disappointment that the moment was over.

The afternoon shadows lengthened quickly and the cool air of evening swept down from the mountains. The wedding party broke up, the men going out to relieve the patrol and the women to their homes with the children. Burr's and Luis's promise of a real celebration with a whole barbecued steer after the Apache left the valley brought a buzz of excited voices all talking at once about kettles of *frijoles,* platters of *tamales*, and vats of peppery *chili*. The men whooped with excitement on hearing that several barrels of whiskey from the locked storehouse would be opened for the occasion.

Jacy and Luis were staying in the Mexican village until they could go to their hacienda. The widow who had relin-

quished her small one-room home to the couple would stay
with Red and Rosita for the time being.

Luis, of course, wouldn't go to the stone house and Jacy
wouldn't leave him, so Johanna offered to pack her sister's
belongings, and Burr volunteered to bring them down as soon
as he dispatched the men to guard duty. He and Luis stepped
aside and talked in low tones. Luis did most of the talking
and Burr nodded in agreement.

"Burr and I will be away for a few hours, *mi corazón*."
Luis took Jacy's hands in his. "You are to stay with Rosita
and I will come for you."

Jacy started to protest, then stopped. "*Sí, mi marido*," she
said, love and gladness shining in her eyes. "I will obey my
husband."

Burr looked at Johanna with raised eyebrows. "Words I
hope to hear very soon," he murmured.

An impudent smile came to Johanna's lips. "It's foolish
to hope for the impossible."

Luis kissed Jacy tenderly and murmured to her.

Burr went to kiss Johanna, but she turned her head sharply
and his lips brushed her cheek. He chuckled.

"I'll be back," he whispered. "Your waspish temper
won't keep me away from you." He held her chin with his
fingertips and kissed her lightly on the lips. "I'll not be back
for supper, so leave something on the table. I've got to keep
my strength up now that I'll have regular . . . night duties."
He grinned devilishly, gave her chin a light pinch, and walked
away to join Luis and Ben.

Johanna watched the two tall men, one so dark and the
other so fair, as they talked quietly and earnestly with Ben.
Bucko sidled up to Luis, who without looking down at the
child held out his hand. Then something happened that Johanna wouldn't have believed if she hadn't seen it herself.
Burr put his arms around Ben and embraced him. She could

see his big hand patting him gently on the back. He stepped back and Luis embraced the small gray-haired man, and then he knelt and spoke to Bucko. The child ran off toward Rosita's. Johanna wanted to cry. The two big men, the old man, and the child were a family. It was something that hadn't occurred to her before.


Ben had been quiet during and after the weddings. He waited while Johanna said her goodbyes to Rosita and Jacy, and then they started up the path to the stone house.

Johanna didn't asked him the question that had been on her mind since the ceremony until they were well away from the Mexican village.

"Ben, there's something bothering me."

"Yes, I know, lass."

"Why did the *padre* call Burr, Burnett Englebretson Calloway?"

"Because a long time ago, when Burr and Luis were lads, I adopted them. Their legal name is Calloway. Luis uses his mother's name, Gazares, except in legal matters. Burr enjoys deviling Mack by calling himself Macklin."

"Why didn't someone tell me? Why so secret? I doubt if Jacy knew it, or she would have said something."

"I'd be surprised if Luis had thought to tell her. The boys have always kept the things that are important to them to themselves. I never told Mack. I thought if the boys wanted him to know, they'd tell him. They didn't. Both boys take special pains to keep Mack from knowing anything about their private lives. I'm sorry you weren't told before the wedding, Johanna. I reminded Burr to tell you. He said he'd handle it, but I guess he forgot."

*Oh yes, no doubt he has forgot to tell me a lot of things,* Johanna thought bitterly. She digested this last bit of news with a sick feeling that was beyond anger. The whole ghastly reality hit her now—she had married a man who didn't love her but had used her to keep control of his land. He intended to use her body for sexual gratification and he also apparently intended to continue carrying on with his mistress. He hadn't even bothered to tell her that after she married him she would be known as Mrs. Calloway, and not Mrs. Macklin.

Suddenly she hurt as she had never hurt before. And yet, she asked herself, how could she have handled the situation differently?

# CHAPTER
## Seventeen

"We'll see if the bastard's man enough to fill your belly."

Johanna pretended she hadn't heard the old man's remark and went on about her work. His hot, bright eyes had been following every move she made until she wanted to scream. He had come early to the kitchen and settled himself in the chair by the hearth to watch her prepare the evening meal. Whenever she glanced up he was staring intently at some part of her anatomy. Occasionally she could hear the hiss of a stream of tobacco juice hitting the fire.

Ben came in, and Johanna breathed a sigh of relief. He noticed her heightened color at once and tried to draw Mack's attention away from her.

"Burr thinks there are nearly four hundred Apaches in the lower valley, Mack." He paused and waited for a comment, but none came. The old man continued to stare at Johanna.

Dear Ben. Johanna realized he was striving for a civilized conversation with old Mack for her sake.

"It's been years since that many Apaches have gathered

here. Burr left about fifty head of cattle down there. That should be enough for them." Ben turned toward Johanna. "It's a matter of pride for the Indians to steal them."

"Humph!" old Mack snorted. "Where's the bastard gone to now?" His eyes fastened on Johanna's face as she brought a plate of food to the table. "He'd be a fool to wear hisself out a-humpin' one of them Apache bitches."

Johanna was sure that she had never hated anyone or anything as much as she hated this vile old man.

"Burr's out patrolling. He'll be back soon." Johanna didn't know how Ben could be so patient.

"Be a goddamn fool if he didn't." The smile on old Mack's face made his meaning clear.

Johanna shrank from the vulgar remarks of the old man and the pitying looks Ben gave her each time her face burned. Time had failed to dull the embarrassment of old Mack's tactless comments and the shocking methods he used to focus attention on himself.

She found herself wishing she could hear the ring of Burr's boot heels on the stone floor of the hall. What if something happened to him and he didn't come back? She breathed so deeply that her lungs hurt, and her heartbeat faltered, then picked up speed. The realization of that possibility brought her up short, and she stood motionless facing the cookstove. She was aware now of the truth she had tried so desperately to avoid facing. Johanna Doan, Calloway now, the woman who was sensitive to beauty and softness, books and music, a considerate person brought up to appreciate the fine arts, had fallen in love with a crude, arrogant, overbearing rancher!

The thoughts went around and around. *Stop it*, she said to herself. She must stop this obsessive thinking—must concentrate on what needed to be done. There was nothing she could do about the situation in which she found herself, so she'd best get on with her work. She picked up the copper teakettle and went to the wooden water bucket, intent upon blotting out all thought but work. Burr's face, his brilliant blue eyes, his animated features, looked up at her from the clear water in the bucket. She turned quickly and walked back to the stove.

The scraping of old Mack's chair on the stone floor sounded loud in the quiet room. Johanna paused on her way to the table. She could see his features in the lamplight, and his sharp, piercing eyes seemed to see right through her. He hobbled to the door, and she could hear him muttering to himself as he went down the hall to his room.

"He's not going to stay and eat." Johanna was so relieved, her shoulders sagged.

"We can thank God for that. Come sit down, lass. We can eat in peace."

Johanna added a stick of firewood to the cookstove, removed a lid, and moved the teakettle over the blaze before she spoke.

"Thank you for keeping Bucko out of the kitchen tonight." She poured coffee for herself and Ben and sat down at the table. "He's terribly afraid of Mr. Macklin. And when Mr. Macklin is in one of his miserable moods he'll say whatever comes to his mind."

"I've known him thirty years, lass. There's not an ounce of goodness in him."

"It isn't right that a child has to live in constant turmoil."

"There's no reason why you have to suffer Mack's presence now, either, lass. You're no longer an employee here. Remember? If Mack continues to be so insulting—and I see no prospects of him changing—Burr will have to arrange for other living quarters for you and Bucko."

"Oh, Ben, do you think he'd do that? The thought of spending the rest of my life in this house is enough to make me go mad!'' Tears sprang to her eyes and she blinked rapidly, hoping Ben wouldn't notice them.

He patted her hand. "Don't worry about Bucko for a few days. He'll stay down at the bunkhouse with Codger while the Apaches are camped here. Burr's afraid they might get it in their heads to steal him back. Codger'll keep an eye on him every minute.''

Johanna searched Ben's face with large questioning eyes. "I wish I knew more about Bucko.''

Ben continued to pat her hand. "I wish I knew more to tell you, lass, but I don't. I don't know who fathered him, but it's a sure fact he's a Macklin one way or the other.''

"If there were a chance that Bucko were not Burr's child, you'd think he'd have said so.'' A sad note crept into her voice. Ben look at her sharply. She got up from the table and carried the dishes to the pan of sudsy water she had left to heat on the cookstove.

"Let me help you tonight, lass.''

"No, Ben. You've put in a long day.'' She smiled at him fondly. "You're quite a handsome man, Mr. Calloway, when you get all dressed up.''

"I'll never get dressed up for a bigger occasion, Johanna. Both my boys were married today . . . and to two lovely sisters.'' His eyes twinkled.

Johanna put her arms around him. "Ben, thank you for letting me wear Anna's brooch. It means a lot to me that you think I was worthy of that honor. Oh, Ben!'' She hugged him tighter. "You're so much like my papa. And, Ben . . . I love you.'' She kissed his cheek and saw tears come into his eyes. "Oh, I'm sorry. I've embarrassed you!''

"Not a bit,'' he said hastily. "Not a dadgummed bit! I just can't believe my luck, is all.'' His seamed face broke into a bright smile.

"Luck had nothing to do with it, Ben. You're one of the nicest people I've ever known. And you're a tired one, too, so be off with you. I'll clear up and leave some food on the table for Burr." She walked with him to the door and watched his slow progress down the hall. A small glow of light shone from the partly open door of old Mack's room, and Johanna prayed that the old man wouldn't decide to come back to the kitchen now that Ben had gone.

Johanna was fixing bread and butter and meat for Burr when she heard his voice outside the back door. She fought the impulse to flee to her room upstairs, and then to still the trembling of her knees when she heard footsteps coming down the hall.

"Whom were you talking to?" she managed to say lightly when he appeared in the doorway.

"Mooney. I told him to get some sleep. Luis and I have been to the Indian camp, and from the looks of things they'll not ride in on us tonight." His voice was husky, as if his throat were caked with dust.

"I'm glad of that."

Burr took the teakettle from the cookstove and poured hot water into the washbasin, then ladled in several dippers full of cold water from the bucket.

"Are you afraid?" he asked just before he scooped water up with his two hands and splashed his face. He did this several times before wiping it dry with the neatly folded towel he took from the rack.

"Of course. I'd be a fool not to be," Johanna replied tartly.

"You don't trust your husband to keep you safe, eh?" He looped the damp towel over the towel bar.

She turned her back on him and took a plate of food to the table. She wanted to look at him, but she didn't dare, afraid he might read in her face her newly discovered feelings about him. She brought his coffee and sat down at the table. He caught her arm as she turned to leave.

"Sit down, Mrs. Calloway, and talk to me." His soft voice evoked even more confusion within her.

She pulled her arm away. "In a minute." Her tone was sharper than she had intended.

Fumbling with the pans on the stove gave her a few minutes to collect herself. When she could delay no longer, she poured herself a cup of coffee and returned to sit at the opposite end of the table. Burr stood, reached for her cup, and set it down on the table next to him.

"I'm not going to pounce on you, if that's what you're afraid of. I'm too goddamn tired." He glared at her with red-rimmed eyes.

Johanna sat down beside him. Her knees brushed his thigh and she quickly moved them away. She glanced at his face. He did look tired.

"Did you get any sleep last night?"

He lifted his head, and his eyes searched her face. Johanna bridged the awful silence that followed by sipping her coffee. She realized the reason for his surprised look. It was the first bit of personal, civil conversation she had directed to him.

"Not much. Luis and I drove the horses up and spent the rest of the night moving wagons to use as blockades in case of an attack."

She cleared her throat nervously. "Do you do this each spring and fall when the Apache come through?"

"No," he said honestly. "We haven't taken this many precautions for a long time. We always drive the herds from the lower valley, leaving a decent amount for them to steal. It's horses they want."

"I heard you bringing them in last night."

"We've got a good strong corral over next to the cliffs and

they'd have to go past here to get to them.'' He talked quietly, then fell silent.

The silence dragged on while he ate. He was hungry, Johanna noted, and was pleased she had prepared a satisfactory meal in spite of old Mack's disruptive presence.

Not until his plate was empty did he speak again. ''I meant to tell you about Ben adopting Luis and me, and giving us his name, but every time we talked the fur would fly and I'd forget about it.'' He grinned, and small lines appeared at the corners of his eyes. His hair was almost silver against his tanned face. It was sun-bleached, Johanna realized.

Johanna got up to refill his cup. ''It doesn't matter. I was surprised, that's all.'' She could feel his eyes on her while she poured the coffee.

''It happened a long time ago, and I don't think about it much.''

''I can understand that, but . . . why do you call yourself Macklin? I'd think you'd prefer to use your legal name, Calloway.''

''One reason I use Macklin is because I don't have to, thank God! The other reason is because it gripes the hell out of the old man. I guess I'd be legally an Englebretson, if Ben hadn't adopted me.''

''Well, it's all right with me,'' she said with a deep sigh. ''I'd rather be Mrs. Calloway than Mrs. Macklin.''

''Glad to hear it.'' He grinned devilishly. ''I thought you might be disappointed not being Mrs. Macklin of Macklin Valley.''

''I didn't want to be *Mrs*. anything,'' she said tartly, and could have bitten her tongue the moment she said it, for she was sure that with her sharp words she had put an end to their first civil conversation.

She had.

''I know,'' he replied sarcastically. ''God knows you've

told me often enough.'' He sat at the table, shoulders hunched, and rolled a cigarette with not quite steady fingers.

Johanna glanced at his bent head. *Is this the way it's going to be for the rest of our lives?* she asked herself. *Will all our conversations end this way? Down through the years when we are old, will we still be snapping at each other? He'll not make the first effort to change the pattern. All he knows to do is to hide behind sarcasm and that devil-may-care attitude. If the pattern is to be changed, I'll have to be the one to do it, and I must do it . . . for my own sanity, and for Bucko's sake.*

''I'm sorry, Burr,'' she said quietly. ''I shouldn't have said that. Circumstances that neither of us could control have forced us into this marriage. What's done is done, and no amount of wishing will change it. Our lives will be unbearable if we're constantly bickering. And . . . we have Bucko to consider. I'm willing to make the effort to be amicable if you are.''

He looked up and pinned her eyes with his. ''Suffer in silence, eh?''

''I don't mean that,'' she said patiently. ''I promised Bucko that we'd . . . be a family—''

''He told me. You're going to be his mama.''

Johanna's face reddened, but she refused to turn her eyes away. ''You don't approve?''

He shrugged. ''Whatever is best for Bucko is all right with me.''

''There will be times when we'll have to discuss . . . certain matters.'' Johanna was determined that they come to an understanding.

''Like what?''

''Well . . . such as food supplies, and clothes . . . and birthdays, Thanksgiving—''

''Birthdays?'' He looked at her as if he didn't know what

she was talking about. Then he said, "Tell Codger. He'll take care of it."

Her temper flared. "I'll not tell Codger! I'll tell you, and *we* will discuss it."

"All right. But I don't see—"

"Then you agree that we must have some semblance of harmony between us?" she insisted.

"Sure, why not?" he said flippantly.

Johanna turned away. The knife in her heart pierced deeper. She had tried. She asked herself if she had the strength to keep pecking away at this impossible situation. There was no answer.

She cleared the table and put away the food. Burr sat quietly, his arms on the table and his long legs stretched out in front of him. He watched her, but his gaze was not as disturbing as old Mack's had been. Finally, when she had done everything she could find to do, she turned and faced him, her nervousness intensifying. He had removed his neckerchief and his shirt was open, revealing an expanse of brown chest. Johanna froze as his eyes bored into hers, sending a message she was not too confused to interpret. She had hoped that he would not insist she sleep with him tonight, but she could see now that it was a futile wish. He was a man who took every single thing he thought he was entitled to take, she could see that clearly now.

As before, Johanna took refuge behind cool hauteur.

"Excuse me," she said and started for the door.

When she went to pass him, his arms snaked out and she was hauled off her feet and onto his lap. It happened so suddenly that she hadn't time to make a sound of protest, and his mouth was on hers before she could resist. He kissed her deeply, again and again, holding her tightly against his hard, unrelenting chest. His lips were hard at first, then softened and moved even more demandingly as his tongue darted forth to trace hotly the outline of her mouth before compelling her lips to open. He molded her to him as if she were a missing part of him and kissed her mouth, her eyes, and her cheeks with insatiable hunger.

"Little silver fox," he muttered against her mouth. "You're soft and sweet and smell like a . . . woman."

Startled by his words and totally defenseless, Johanna could do nothing but submit. To her horror, she found that she didn't want to resist, and a moan began deep within her and slowly rose to her throat and caught there when she felt his hand free her breast from the tight bodice of her dress.

"I knew it would be like this—that you'd feel good against me." His whispered words came from someplace near her mouth, and then his hands and his lips became bruising.

A wave of sexual desire swept her. She wanted to yield, to cast the last vestiges of restraint from her mind and body and let him carry her away again on the flood of his passion and give him all that he needed to satisfy the hunger in him.

"Hmmm . . ." He rubbed his nose against her cheek. "Who'd'a thought that behind that beautiful face and icy stare there's a hot little woman just aching to be loved."

The murmured words and the roughness of his hands as they flipped up her skirt and stroked her bare flesh set off a warning bell in her brain. She had given in to her body's demands that night in his room, and he had humiliated her. It wasn't going to happen again. Sex should be an act of love, she thought wildly. The coming together of a man and a woman should be something to cherish, to hold sacred, not merely to gratify the carnal desire like an . . . animal.

She tore herself free from his embrace. She knew instinctively that she'd never make it out the door, so she ran to the fireplace and rested her forehead against the broad mantel. She leaned there, her heart racing, her stomach churning. Her lips felt bruised and tortured and she was mortified that she had lain in his arms like a wanton and let him caress her as he would a whore. She was humiliated by her desire. With shaking hands, she restored order to her clothing and her hair.

Johanna tensed as she heard his footsteps on the stone floor and flinched when she heard his mocking voice.

"What the hell's the matter with you?" he hissed angrily. "You're my wife, goddammit!"

She did not move from the hearth. He came up behind her and pulled her around to face him.

"I said, what the hell's the matter with you? What did you expect?"

To her horror, huge tears suddenly welled up in her eyes, and despite her desperate efforts to stop them, they started to roll down her cheeks.

"If you ever come at me like that again . . . I'll kill you!"

It was seconds before he took the import of her incredible words. Then he asked in a disbelieving whisper, "You'll what?"

"I'll kill you!" she sobbed. "I mean it. I won't be manhandled as if I were a . . . were a whore!"

Seconds of silence passed while he glared at her. The look on his face clearly stated that he didn't have the slightest idea what she was taking about.

"What did you expect?" he said again, and this time there was no harshness in his voice.

The eyes that locked with his were tear filled, but her gaze was steady and her head tilted in a gesture of defiance. She jerked her shoulders from his hands.

"I expected . . . tenderness!"

The puzzled look that crossed his face was genuine.

"Tenderness?" he questioned, and then his expression changed to one of exasperation. She held her chin up and her eyes looked straight at him while his eyes roamed her face.

Finally he said with disgust, "Tenderness!" and started for the door, his broad back a blur through her tears.

In the seconds that followed, Johanna heard a bellowed curse from old Mack's room. Burr paused, a questioning look on his face, and then the sound of a shot and the impact of the bullet as it pierced the wall to strike the storage cabinet. In one swift movement he sprang to the light and squelched it.

"Stay down and back . . . away from the fire—" he commanded and bolted for the door.

# CHAPTER
## *Eighteen*

Johanna stood frozen for a second.

"Burr! Burr!" She wasn't sure if she said his name or not as fear for him surged hotly through her and lent wings to her feet. Unmindful of his command, she raced after him. When she reached the hall she saw him fling open the door to old Mack's room and disappear inside. She ran down the hall and peered in from the doorway.

The glow from lamp on the bureau illuminated the room, and what she saw made her gasp with horror. Old Mack lay on the bed, the handle of a knife protruding from his chest. He was writhing in agony, his gnarled hands pulling at the handle. Burr stood at the foot of the bed, gun in hand, his eyes roaming the room. The only sound was the weird creaking of the rope bed as the old man's considerable weight shifted as he attempted to rid himself of the torturing knife. Burr shoved his gun back into its holster and went quickly to Mack. He pried loose the frantic fingers, pulled out the knife, and let it drop to the floor.

"Oh, my God!" This wasn't happening! This couldn't be true! Johanna was nearly sick to her stomach.

"Who . . . in the world?" Johanna gasped.

Burr jerked his head toward the end of the room. In the semidarkness a brown bundle, much like a discarded rag doll, lay on the floor. Going a step closer, Johanna saw the ragged buckskin dress and the long matted hair of an Indian woman. She lay slumped against the wall where the bullet had slammed her.

Old Mack's gasps were loud in the eerie quiet of the room. Johanna went back to the bed. The old man's eyes were open and bright and he stared up at Burr accusingly.

"Goddamn dog-eatin' bitch! How'd she get in here?"

"Who is she?" Burr demanded.

"Goddamn dog-eatin' bitch!"

"Why did she come here?"

"You goin' to stand there and . . . let me bleed to death . . . you bastard?"

"Why did that woman come here?" Burr ground out, his voice filled with anger and frustration.

"It ain't no . . . goddamn business of yours!"

"You knew her. She came to find you. Why? Is she Bucko's mother?"

"Aye," old Mack whispered hoarsely. "The bitch whelped the cripple . . . bastard!"

Burr straightened and looked at Johanna. His eyes told her nothing, but her eyes revealed the fact that she had looked death in the face, and not recovered from the sight. He placed his hand on her shoulder.

"Get towels and whiskey," he barked.

Ben stood in the doorway, and Johanna brushed by him on her way to the kitchen. She could hear the pounding of heels on the stone outside the house and the excited murmurs of the men. She grabbed towels and the teakettle from the stove and hurried back to Mack's room.

Burr cut open the old man's shirt and moved aside to make room for Johanna. She willed herself not to faint at the sight of the warm, sticky blood welling up from the hole in the hairy chest. Her anxious eyes sought out Ben's and he shook his head slightly. She looked down again to see the old man staring up at her.

"Ain't no bastards goin' to have my valley. I . . . seen to it, didn't I, missy?" His eyes closed and a bloody froth came out of his parted lips.

Johanna placed the towels against the wound, then covered them with a long cloth and tucked the ends under his back. She saw Burr pull Ben back from the bed.

"Did you hear what he said about Bucko, Ben?" he asked anxiously.

"I heard. Does that relieve your mind, son?"

"More than you know," Burr said intensely, squeezing Ben's shoulder and looking him straight in the eye.

"There's not much we can do for him." Ben nodded toward the bed.

"I know, but do what you can."

The doorway was crowded with men drawn by the sound of the shot, and Mooney squeezed his way into the room.

"The men say there's nothin' out there, Burr," he said in hushed tones.

"Didn't think there would be. She sneaked in here alone, but how in the hell did she do it?" Burr motioned for the men to move back into the hall, and he followed them out. "Is Codger still with Bucko?"

"Sittin' on him like a mama hen," Mooney said. "He won't let one of them redskins get in smellin' distance. He's got a shotgun on his lap."

"Mack's done for, there's no question about that, but we've got to think about what to do with the woman."

"Who'd'a thought an Injun woman could'a come in here and done such a thing."

"Apaches have a heap of pride, Mooney. She was a woman wronged. Indian ways are different from ours. She couldn't rest until she had her revenge. Probably she was cast out by her family and made a slave after Mack ruined her. He admitted that she's Bucko's mother."

"The poor little ol' thing," Mooney said sadly.

Not a flicker of surprise showed on the faces of the men when they heard that Bucko was old Mack's son, although they had all firmly believed that Burr was his father. Schooled in keeping their thoughts to themselves, they only nodded in agreement at Mooney's pitying words.

"Ben and Johanna will do what they can for Mack. Will someone go down and get Luis? I hate to disturb him on his wedding night, but this is something he should know about." Burr ran his fingertips over his tired eyes. "I think someone should go out and tell the sentries what happened and tell them to keep their eyes peeled for the rest of the night, just to be on the safe side."

"Me, I can do it, señor." A young Mexican boy edged his way to Burr and Burr put his hand on his shoulder.

"Thanks, Ramon. But be careful and call out before you get too close. I don't want one of them to shoot you, thinking you're an Apache. Mooney, wrap the woman in a blanket and get her out of there. I'm sure her being there is upsetting to Johanna."

Mooney brought a blanket and laid the pathetically thin body of the Indian woman on it. He shook his head sadly when he saw the torture marks on her thin arms and how thin the skin was over the bones of her face. He wrapped her in the blanket and carried her down the hall to the sitting room, then returned with rags and water to mop up the blood.

Old Mack's face was deathly white now and his breathing laborious. Johanna and Ben had managed to stop the flow of blood and to get several spoonfuls of whiskey down his throat. He opened his eyes and looked into Johanna's face.

"Juanita," he whispered. "Why'd you have to go and do that for?" He stared at Johanna for a long moment, then wearily closed his eyes.

"Who is Juanita?" she whispered to Ben.

"Luis's mother," Ben said in hushed tones. "She might have been the only person in the world that Mack cared a whit for. She was a sweet, young, beautiful girl, and Mack ruined her just as he did my Anna and that poor Indian girl." For the first time Johanna heard a bitter note creep into Ben's voice.

Old Mack's head lifted off the pillow. "You shouldn't'a let the dirty greasers touch you! You . . . slut, bitch . . . whore! You was mine . . ." His breathing was hard, but there was rage in his voice.

Ben shook his head sadly. "He'd never admit, even to himself, that Luis is his son."

"Juanita!" old Mack shouted in his delirium. "Come back here!"

"Oh, Ben, how awful."

Ben reached for Johanna's hand. "When Mack discovered that Juanita was in the family way, he turned on her," Ben said. "He put her in a crumbling old adobe shack down were Luis has his house now, and forbade anyone to go near her. No one dared even to speak to her, but me. Not that she wanted anyone; she was so ashamed that she shrank from contact with anyone. I gradually won her confidence and when it was time for Luis to be born I was with her."

Mack reared up. "Don't go, little pretty thing," he cried

hoarsely. Ben eased him back down onto the bed. He looked up at Ben with an expression of pure hatred on his face. "You goddamn greasy bastard!" he snarled. After that he closed his eyes and lay still. Ben sat down.

Johanna wanted to cry for Juanita, for the poor Indian woman, for Anna and Ben, and for all the people whose lives had been been affected by Mack Macklin's ruthlessness.

"He must have cared for Juanita," Ben said in wonder. "She once told me that Mack would sit his horse, off in the distance, and watch her. He didn't go near the house, but the sight of him scared her half to death. Luis was her life, and she lived in constant fear that Mack would harm him. He despised the boy and heaped insults on him whenever he got the chance. When I told Juanita my plans for Burr, I asked her to allow me to adopt Luis. She gave me a letter to present to the court at the same time I presented Anna's letter, so I adopted both boys."

"How awful it must have been for them to live here, and how fortunate they were to have you, Ben," Johanna said.

"I was the fortunate one. After Anna died, I had Burr to think about, and then Luis. The two of them have given me something to live for."

"Does Luis ever come to the house?"

"As far as I know, he has never been inside the house. Mack doesn't recognize that he even exists. After Juanita died I thought sure he'd kill Mack, but he had promised her he wouldn't kill him unless he was defending himself."

"How old was Luis when Juanita died?"

"He was a stripling, but well able to take care of himself. Mack didn't know Juanita was dead until after we buried her. Then he went storming down to her house and stayed there, roaring drunk, for three or four days. Luis hid out in the corrals until he left. I thought sure he'd kill Mack, but he had promised his mother he wouldn't kill him except in self-defense. A week after she died he rode out of the valley. He came back from time to time to see us. He and Burr were close even as children. Then both boys went to the war and afterward they met in El Paso and came home together. I'll never forget the day Paco came riding in to tell me the boys were down at the shack where Juanita used to live, and they were home to stay. All the years I'd put up with Mack's cussedness paid off. My boys had come home." Ben's faded eyes came alive, and he clasped Johanna's hand with surprising strength.

It took Mack several hours to die. Although blood continued to ooze out of him, his tough old body clung to life. He continued to mutter, but the words now were inaudible.

Burr came in and stood beside Ben.

"Luis came up and we're going to look around. Mooney will be here with you." He glanced down at old Mack, a blank expression on his face. "I bet it doesn't sit well on his mind knowing he's been done in by a woman who was little more than a bag of bones." His voice was surprisingly free of bitterness.

"Mack lived a hard, unloved life, but that was the way he wanted it," Ben said.

Johanna looked up to see Burr's eyes on her. *What is going through his mind?* she thought. *Does he see himself in this same position when he's old: dying and unloved?* It seemed an eternity, but no more than ten seconds passed while their eyes clung. For a fleeting instant Johanna thought there was a flicker of tenderness in his eyes as he gazed at her. But when he spoke his voice was dry and impersonal.

"I dumped some coffee in the pot if you want some." He turned and left the room.

The stone house that the old man had built in his younger days was quiet except for the slight rumble of the tin roof as the wind passed over it. Mooney moved quietly up and down the hall or stood on the porch outside the door, his steps a muffled acknowledgment that death was near. Johanna left the bedside to stoke the cookstove and put a kettle of fresh water on to boil. She returned and sat down beside Ben. Together they waited for the inevitable.

Old Mack died as he had lived—violently. He reared up in bed, his eyes wild, and blood gushed from his mouth. When he fell back he was dead. Ben stood, and after a few minutes had passed he closed the staring eyes with his fingertip.

"It's over, Johanna. Go to the kitchen. Mooney and I will take care of things here."

Someone had just filled the cookstove with wood and laid fresh logs in the fireplace. Johanna didn't realize how cold she was until she felt the warmth of the room. After she had added additional water to the coffeepot and set it over the blaze, she eased herself down into a chair and stared wearily into the fire. She couldn't bring herself to be sorry that the old man was dead. She was sorry, though, that a man like Mack Macklin could live so many years, and accomplish as much as he had here in the valley, and still die without a single person to mourn him.

Johanna was drained of emotion. So much had happened so fast on this, her wedding day. She went over the scene in her mind—how old Mack had cursed the Indian woman, and then admitted that she was the mother of *his* child. So, Bucko was half-brother to Burr and Luis. How could it be that Burr didn't know this? Why was he so insistent that old Mack admit Bucko was his son? She wondered what effect the old man's passing would have on the valley, and on Burr. Would Burr simply slip into the mold of tyrant and raise another generation to live in constant turmoil in Macklin Valley? "Oh, dear God," she prayed. "Please don't let that be my fate."

Ben came in and she made a move to get up.

"Sit still, lass. I'll get a cup of coffee and join you."

"Ben," Johanna said when he'd sat down opposite her. "What do you suppose happened in Mr. Macklin's life to make him so mean?"

Ben answered slowly. "This seems to be the night for telling stories, lass. Things happen that affect people differently. I knew Mack for years and it wasn't until Willard Risewick came to the valley that I understood some of the reasons for his bitterness. I'm making no excuses, mind. And I shouldn't say unkind things about the dead—but Mack was a man totally without conscience. He never felt the slightest twinge of remorse for any of his cruelties, whether it was taking a woman against her will or forcing the Mexicans to work harder by depriving them of food to feed their children, or killing a man. Whatever Mack did, he did because he wanted to do it, regardless of the consequences."

"I don't see how he could have lived with himself. It's no wonder he was eaten up inside with hatred."

"When Risewick came to the valley, he came on the pretext of buying land. Oh, he would have bought it, if he could," Ben added hastily. "But his main reason for coming was to find out as much about Mack as he could. Mack has a half-brother back East, the son of his father's Spanish mistress. His father was never able to marry the woman he loved because his wife went into a mental decline just after Mack was born. She died many years later, hopelessly insane. The poor man was tied to her for as long as she lived."

Johanna made a pitying sound.

Ben continued, "Mack's father found love with the Spanish woman from Mexico City. She bore him a son, and tried to win Mack's affection, but he was venomously against her and her son, and eventually his father. His father was a good businessman, and wanted both his sons to take over his iron foundry, but Mack refused to have anything to do with it if the bastard son was included. The father stood firm, and after a row that left the old man battered and bleeding, Mack left home, never to return.

"Rafael Macklin, Mack's half-brother, is without family. Mack was his only blood relative as far as he knew. He sent Risewick out to get the lay of the land, to find out if perhaps the years had mellowed Mack. He wanted some idea of what kind of reception he would receive if he came out for a visit. Of course, Risewick knew right away that any reconciliation was impossible, but he was able to take back to Rafael the news that he had nephews who would one day welcome him. It seems that possibility is now closer to happening that we expected."

Silence lingered after Ben finished his story. Johanna thought back over the things she had learned about old Mack: his hatred of Mexicans was because of his father's mistress; his determination to see to it that a bastard didn't inherit his valley, because a bastard had inherited his father's fortune. But still, Johanna thought, he begot bastards of his own; and by being so extremely cruel and sadistic toward them, had he felt in some way that he was inflicting punishment on his father's bastard?

Johanna was so totally absorbed in her thoughts that she had forgotten Ben. She looked up to see his head tilted back and his eyes closed.

"Ben," she said gently. "You're tired. Go to bed. There's nothing more we can do tonight."

He got to his feet. "All right, lass. I am tired."

Johanna leaned back and closed her eyes. She was tired in body and tired in mind. She listened to the crackling fire as it ate at the firewood, and watched the sparks fly upward when a chunk of burned wood fell into the embers. Two people had breathed their last breaths in this house tonight.

But time didn't stop. It went on, and dawn would come tomorrow the same as it had today.

She opened her eyes and, completely without fear, looked into blue ones. Burr had squatted down beside the chair, his eyes level with hers.

"You all right?"

She nodded, surprised by his concern. "You know . . . ?"

"Mooney came and told us. Why don't you go to bed?"

"I will. Did you find out anything?"

"Luis and I think the woman came in alone and that she got past the spring before Mooney went up there. She must have hidden somewhere near the smokehouse all day and seen Mooney leave his post when I told him to go get some sleep."

"How did she know to find old Mack's room?"

"Mack left his lamp burning and she saw him through the window. The old fool was probably waiting to see if I went upstairs with you," he said dryly. "I don't know how she got the knife in him before he shot her, unless he was dozing. He always kept the gun right on the bed beside him. He had it in his head that Luis or I would try to kill him sometime." Burr took a deep breath and his shoulders sagged. "He wasn't too far off the mark, Johanna. More times than one, I was tempted. Anyway . . . he's dead!"

Johanna didn't think about the strangeness of their talking like this. Or how natural it was for her to reach out and touch his arm. "Don't think about it," she urged. "You did what you could for him. You have nothing to regret."

"Luis is bringing Jacy back up to the house, and he and Red will stand watch for the rest of the night," he said wearily. "Mooney and I are going to get a couple hours' sleep. We're taking the supply wagon down to the Indian camp first thing in the morning, just as if nothing's happened."

Burr got to his feet and Johanna stood as if pulled by

invisible strings, her stricken eyes on his. "You're going down . . . there?"

"I always take a wagonload of supplies to the camp. They expect it."

She reached out and clutched his arms. "But . . . they might kill you!"

"Maybe, maybe not." He lowered his eyes to her hands on his arms. She removed them quickly. His mood changed instantly. Mockingly, and with a devilish look on his face, he said, "Don't tell me you wouldn't be pleased to be made a widow tomorrow?"

A look of shock crossed her face as she reeled back a step. Her lips, red against a white face, quivered, and her voice trembled. "How . . . can you say such a thing?"

He tilted his head to the side and stared at her, his face sobering, eyes questioning, but he said nothing.

She stumbled past him and hurried to the door. When she reached it, she turned and was surprised by the look of concern on his face. She forced herself to meet his eyes and not to look away.

"Will you please tell Jacy to be careful of the steep stairs when she comes up? She's one of those people who can't see in the dark, and I'm afraid she'll fall."

"Don't worry. Go on to bed. I'll bring her up." His voice held a quality that, had Johanna been less distraught, would have made her wonder.

Johanna began to shake all over, and it was such a peculiar sensation that it frightened her. Fear ate into her very being. Burr might not come back from the Apache camp! She looked at him as if to etch his face in her memory forever, and fought an impulse to run to him and plead with him not to go. Shocked back to reality by the thought of what his reaction would be, she wondered how she could feel this way about a man who thought of her only in terms of his physical needs.

Suddenly she was ashamed. *At least he's been honest*, she thought. He didn't want her inner self. He wasn't interested in her thoughts, her dreams, or whether she was happy or sad. He had told her that her being here would save him a trip to El Paso to visit the whores. He would use her body to satisfy the age-old urge to procreate, while she hid her lust behind her pride. She was no better than a harlot! The word stiffened her resolve to do her utmost to hide her love. She would never, she vowed silently, allow him to know of it and risk his using it as a weapon against her.

Without speaking, she turned and left him.

# CHAPTER
## Nineteen

**M**orning came and with it the dread. Sleep had held Johanna's fear at bay for a few hours. This morning Burr and Mooney were taking their lives in their hands. They were going to the Apache camp.

Johanna and Jacy walked down to the corral to watch the loading of goods Burr would take to the Indian camp. There were sacks of corn, stacks of blankets, bolts of cloth, knives, dried fruit, tobacco, iron pots, and a small keg of gunpowder.

"The Apaches," Ben said, when she questioned, "are not frivolous people. They want practical things."

"I wish they didn't have to go," Johanna said worriedly.

"So do I, lass. But a man does what he thinks he must."

Burr and Mooney joked lightly about their mission.

"I'm sure a-hatin' to depend on these old clods to get me outta that camp fast." Mooney shifted his chew of tobacco to the other side of his mouth and patted one of the mules on the rump. "Sure'd like to take that old pie-eyed horse of mine along."

"They'd steal that old nag and have her butchered for the pot before you could spit, Mooney."

"I still think I should go with you, Burr." Luis lifted the large sack from his shoulder and threw it into the wagon.

Johanna heard the small gasp come from Jacy when she heard her husband's words. She gripped Johanna's arm tightly, and waited in terrible silence.

"Things are different now, Luis. You'll do more good here," Burr said, and Jacy let the breath escape from where she had trapped it in her throat.

"I'll ride with you as far as my place and wait for you there," Luis insisted.

"Stay here. You've got three good men down there. We'll stop at your place and see if things are all right. If anything had happened at your ranch we'd have heard shots." Luis looked worried, and Burr laughed. "Cheer up, brother, you got that pretty little bride over there to keep you company." When Luis didn't smile, Burr sobered. "If we're not back by the time you think we should be, you know what to do. Don't let them draw you away from the ranch . . . regardless. There'd be nothing you could do for me or Mooney if it came to that. They're either going to take our goods and treat us as usual, or they're not."

Mooney threw the last sack up onto the wagon and let loose a stream of tobacco juice. "Guess there ain't nothin' t'do but get on with it." He pulled his hat down on his head and climbed up onto the wagon seat.

Johanna stood behind the corral fence, and when Burr looked at her, she didn't look away. He climbed over the railing and took her hand. He looked at her for a moment, then led her away from the group that had gathered to watch him and Mooney set off.

"They expect me to kiss you," he said, nodding toward the watching eyes. "We'd better make it look right."

"Yes, I suppose so," she whispered, her eyes mute testament of the fear churning inside her.

He touched his lips to hers. Her arms went around his body and her lips clung. The kiss lasted a long time. She could feel the pounding of his heart against her breast as his arms pulled her to him. When they broke the kiss, she lowered her eyes in an attempt to hide her tears.

His hands gripped her shoulders and he gave them a gentle shake. "Don't cry, little wife. If your luck holds out, my hair could be hangin' from an Apache belt by night," he said lightly.

Her eyes, now sparkling with anger and tears, came up to meet his. "You're hateful! You scoff at everything. You . . . you . . ." She drew back her foot and kicked him on the shin. "You make me so damn mad!" She broke loose from him and ran toward the house.

He stood with his hands on his hips and watched her go. God, how he hated to leave her! In time things could be different between them. Ben seemed to think so. But his time might have run out. The smiling, devil-may-care expression he had worn for her benefit was no longer necessary, and in its place came a look of frustration and regret. Regret that he had allowed his pride, and his bitterness toward old Mack, to keep him from being grateful for the precious gift that had been given to him. "Goodbye, little silver fox," he muttered and climbed back over the rails.

"Hee-yaw!" Mooney shouted and cracked his whip over the backs of the team as Burr climbed into the wagon. "H'yaw!" The yell echoed in the morning stillness. The mules strained at their harnesses, and the wagon moved out of the corral and through the gate. The men being left behind stood silently, a few took off their hats and bowed their heads in silent prayer. They knew that there was a good chance Burr and Mooney would not return.

Burr's eyes clung to the slim woman who stood beside the house, her hands wrapped in her apron. Her bright hair glinted in the morning sun and he thought suddenly of the straw hat she had worn the day she arrived. Now it hung over the barn door, dilapidated, the faded pink rose a mere piece of tattered cloth. He had nailed it to the barn after the wind had torn it from the peg on the porch. *She's quite a woman*, he mused. Although he was sure she knew that he was the one who had put it there, she had never mentioned it. *I'll take it down*, he promised himself—*that is, if I come back.*

Burr looked back one more time. Johanna hadn't moved. She looked lonely standing beside the house. Burr raised his hand and waved and she answered with a wave of her arm. The picture of her stayed in his mind for a long time.

Burr squinted under the pulled-down brim of his hat and studied the terrain. Behind them and a little higher up were the ranch buildings and below them was the Indian camp. The sun was at their back and not yet high enough to give warmth. A cool breeze drifted down from the mountains and waved the long grasses alive with small birds that whirred up from under the feet of the mules. The trail ran alongside the rocky stream. A startled deer bolted when they approached. The snow peak of the distant mountain shone in the morning sun. It was all very peaceful.

The men hadn't spoken since they'd left the ranch yard. Each was wrapped in his own thoughts. Mooney finally broke the silence.

"Ain't this a mite more stuff than you usually take, Burr?"

"Yeah, it is, but I figure they'd try to take it all if they had a mind to." He glanced at Mooney and grinned. "We just might get our hair took today, Mooney."

The leather-faced cowboy took off his hat and scratched his head. Wisps of sweat-drenched hair were plastered to the near-bald pate.

"I'm a-thinkin' I got the least likely scalp any 'pache'd ever want," he said dryly. "Wouldn't be no pride in hangin' my bald scalp on a belt."

"Let's hope so." Burr took off his hat and threw it on the floor of the wagon next to the fringed Indian boots for which he'd bartered a few years ago. His work pants were old but clean, as was his dark shirt. The only weapon he carried was a hunting knife tucked into his belt. Mooney wore a gunbelt that held two heavy revolvers. Despite their light chatter, both men knew the seriousness of their mission. The Apache could kill them today and ride on to the ranch.

As the wagon rolled along, Burr thought of the Indian woman, Bucko's mother. He decided she was probably insignificant enough that she wouldn't be missed, except by the women she served. If Burr remembered right, the warrior from whom he'd bought Bucko was Black Buffalo. A surly, troublesome man, he just might think he could gain something from the woman's disappearance.

They stopped for a short time at Luis's ranch and watered the mules. Burr talked to the *vaqueros* left behind to guard the hacienda.

"Keep a sharp eye on the gap that goes into the lower valley. If a sizable force comes through, hightail it to the ranch and warn Luis. There won't be anything you can do here, and there won't be anything you can do for us. *Comprenden?*

"*Sí.*" They nodded gravely and watched the wagon roll away.

* * *

The sun was almost directly overhead when the wagon rolled up and over an incline and the Indian camp came into view.

Mooney whistled though his teeth. "That's a pretty good size camp!"

"Yeah, you stubborn old goat. I told you it would be!" Burr snorted.

The wickiups had been set up to form a large circle. Inside the circle was a ring of larger wickiups and in the center of that circle was one of tremendous size. This was the lodge of the chief, and a large fire burned brightly in front of it. He was an old man, but he had three young, powerful chieftains. Burr had talked with all of them, and he liked the one called Geronimo the best. He realized that the short, squat man would be a formidable enemy, but he was also a deep thinker and a shrewd man. Geronimo was sure to understand the need to keep the white man alive so as to ensure future supplies for his people.

"Well, let's get on down there, Mooney, and see which way the wind blows. Don't let any hotheaded buck bait you into doing anything foolish."

"Don't you worry none about that. I ain't a-makin' a move or openin' my yap."

As they rode toward the camp they heard dogs barking and children shouting. Unpleasant smells from the cookfires assailed their nostrils. From everywhere people came running to see the white visitors. A group of mounted braves charged forward, yipping, and encircled the wagon. They wore breechcloths and leggings, and their hair hung to their shoulders. Twisted bands of cloth were wrapped around their heads.

All sounds stopped suddenly, as if from a signal, Burr thought. The riders ceased yipping, the children, shy and silent, peeped at them from behind the women. There was only the sound of a single dog barking frantically, and then, after a loud yip, it too became silent. Some of the Indians gathered around the wagon, while others lined the route they would take to reach the chief. Hundreds of curious black eyes stared at the white men.

Burr and Mooney kept their eyes straight ahead, focused on the lodge in the middle of the camp. Mooney moved the mules to within a few yards of the big lodge and pulled them to a halt. Burr jumped down, and the crowd fell back. He strode forward to meet the chief, and the two men shook hands. The Indian was large, with a muscular body and flat belly. His hair was streaked with gray and fell unbound to his shoulders. His head was bare, but he needed no elaborate headdress. His majestic bearing alone distinguished him from the others.

"I greet my friend, chief of the Chiricahua Apaches," Burr said solemnly in Spanish.

"Greetings, Sky Eyes." The old Indian's voice held authority.

"I bring gifts from the house of stone, as I have done each time you pass this way. It is payment for the use of your land."

The old man nodded and went to the wagon to look at the supplies. The crowd moved back when he waved his hand. He grunted his satisfaction and raised his hand to beckon the three chieftains lined up in front of his lodge. They came forward and Burr extended his hand. They shook it stoically. The chieftains talked together in low tones and poked and prodded the bags in the back of the wagon.

Burr stood at the head of the mules and tried to read the mood of the crowd. The women and children looked well fed, but there was a tenseness in their quiet faces, an attitude of expectancy. The warriors stood in groups. Those with rifles proudly displayed then in their folded arms. One cluster showed open hostility toward him . . . and one brave in the group more so than the others. He strutted back and forth spouting bitter words, his fierce eyes never leaving Burr's face. Burr looked at him boldly and allowed a flicker of contempt to show in his expression. The uneasiness he had felt all along escalated. Gray Cloud was showing too much resentment to back down. His pride would force him into action. Burr sensed what was to come. His muscles tensed and his mouth became dry.

One of the chieftains hefted the keg of powder from the wagon and pried open the lid. Smiles appeared on their faces, and they gathered about the small keg and talked in excited tones. On a word from the chief, a warrior came forward and carried the keg into the big lodge. He spoke again, and a group of braves started unloading the wagon, then he went to stand in front of Burr.

"You brought no rifles."

"I brought powder. The bluecoats would chase me from your land if I came with rifles." Burr knew that every eye was on him, and he looked straight into the fiercely proud eyes of the old man. "I have rifles to hunt food and to protect myself from Mexican *bandidos*."

The old man nodded and looked away at last. "We will smoke," he said.

Burr moved over to the wagon, where Mooney sat like a statue. He leaned over and made extra work of lifting a small bag from under the seat so he could speak.

"Stay on the wagon, but watch that bunch on your left. If they come at you, yell out like you're yelling at the mules."

Burr took the bag to the circle that was forming in front of the chief's lodge and handed it to the chief before he sat down. The Indian sniffed at the bag, and his eyes lit up with pleasure.

"The tobacco comes from over the mountain. I will have more when you return in the spring."

A group of warriors came into the circle and sat cross-legged on the ground. Others sat close by and listened. The women and children dispersed, and the sounds of children playing, dogs barking, and women scolding could be heard once again.

The chief picked up a long pipe decorated with feathers and took several long puffs before passing it to Burr. He took a puff and passed it on. The pipe made a complete round of the circle. When it came back to the chief he carefully placed it on the ground in front of him. He looked directly at Burr and said in fluent Spanish, "You bring people to our land?"

"No. I do not want more people to come and spoil your land."

There was an ominous murmur, but Burr kept his eyes on the old man. The chief raised his hand for silence, and all were instantly quiet. He lifted the pipe to his lips with dignity, puffed, and passed it again to Burr. After he passed it on, Burr searched the faces in the circle. Black Buffalo was there, as well as Gray Cloud, whose eyes burned with passionate hate. When the pipe passed, Black Buffalo stood up, signaling his wish to speak when the ceremonial pipe completed the round.

When the pipe was returned, the chief once again placed it on the ground in front of him, then nodded to Black Buffalo.

Black Buffalo spoke in the guttural tongue of the Apache. From the tone of his voice Burr knew he was enraged. The longer he talked the angrier he got. The chief listened without looking at him. He was handed another pipe, which he puffed for a moment before handing it to Burr. Black Buffalo continued to talk, and the men listened and smoked.

Finally the chief lifted his hand in an impatient gesture and Black Buffalo fell silent. The chief turned to Burr.

"Black Buffalo say you have stolen one of his wives. She has been gone from his lodge for two sunsets. He wants her back or you come with six ponies."

"Which one of his wives is missing?" Burr asked gravely.

"The most beautiful of all his wives," the chief said. "The one that gladens his heart the most. His third wife."

Burr looked straight into the dark eyes of the chief. "I have bartered with Black Buffalo and I have seen his third wife. If I steal a woman it will not be one who has been beaten until her spirit is broken, whose skin has been pierced many times, and whose body has been starved until there is no fat."

Burr thought he saw a glint of amusement in the old chief's eyes before he turned his head and gravely repeated the words to Black Buffalo. The Indian almost jumped with anger as he listened to his chief. He opened his mouth to reply but was silenced by a sharp word from the old man.

The warrior Gray Cloud, who showed such open hostility toward him, sprang to his feet and began to talk. He addressed his words to all in the circle as well as to the chief. His angry bright eyes and his sneering face often turned toward Burr, and at times he pointed his fist toward him and spat. Several men in the circle added remarks, and a few nodded in agreement with what the brave was saying. They were arguing about him; Burr knew this without understanding their words. The skin on the back of his neck tightened. He looked fleetingly at the chief, who was smoking calmly, his face expressionless.

Several braves behind the angry speaker got to their feet and began to dance. Burr's seemingly calm blue eyes found Mooney. The old cowboy sat stone-still, his coat pulled away from his weapons. The dancers began to chant.

"Heya . . . a . . . a . . . heya!"

An excited warrior leaped up brandishing a bow. The excitement was catching; more warriors jumped to their feet.

The speaker looked gloatingly at Burr, who considered for a moment making a dash for the wagon and the rifle hidden in the compartment beneath Mooney's feet. He wished he knew what the chief was thinking.

Geronimo got to his feet. The speaker didn't wish to stop, but the chief raised his hand and the Indian stepped back, his face sullen and resentful. Geronimo spoke in dispassionate tones, his words rolling out calmly and confidently. He talked for several minutes while the circle of men and the dancers grew quiet. The chief nodded as he listened. The ugly little man stood with feet braced apart, and it seemed as if he had issued some sort of challenge to Gray Cloud, who drew himself up to his full height and looked down contemptuously at Burr then drew his knife from his belt and sank the blade into the earth.

Geronimo turned to Burr and spoke in halting Spanish. "Gray Cloud wishes to kill all the paleskins in the valley. He has braves who will follow him. If you fight him and kill him, you go in peace to bring blankets and tobacco and powder when we come this way again. If he kills you, we go to the house of stone and take what you have."

Burr got slowly to his feet. All eyes were on him. He felt a flash of elation. It was better than he had feared—at least he had a chance. He drew his knife from his belt and with a flick of his wrist sank it into the ground between Gray Cloud's feet. The Indian's eyes burned hotly.

Geronimo drew a large circle in the dirt with a stick. Gray Cloud stood proudly among his admirers, and Burr, after picking up his knife, went to the wagon.

"I'm going to fight him," he said, taking off his shirt. "If I kill him, we can go and the ranch will be left alone. If he kills me, they ride on the ranch." He grinned at Mooney. "We got a chance. It's more than I thought we had a while ago."

"Gol' damn, Burr," Mooney said, taking off his hat and wiping his face on his sleeve. "It's tight, ain't it?"

"Yup. But I'm not too bad with a blade. Luis taught me a trick or two. The only thing I can tell you, old friend, is if it looks like I'm not going to make it, whip up the mules and try to get out of here." He didn't add that it was almost a certainty he wouldn't make it, but Mooney knew that. "Give me a chaw of that tobacco, Mooney. I've got to take every advantage I can get." Glad that he had chosen to wear moccasins, which allowed him greater agility, Burr popped the chunk of tobacco into his mouth, took a tight grip on the handle of his knife, and walked into the circle.

The crowd closed in. Gray Cloud, obviously confident of his prowess with his knife, was enjoying the attention now focused on him. He was taller than the average Apache, broad in the shoulders, and thick through the chest. His legs and arms were heavily muscled, and he moved on the balls of his feet like a cat. He stood with legs apart, one ahead of the other, staring at Burr. He was surpremely confident, having fought many battles with other Apache tribes, Mexicans, and the Yaqui Indians of Mexico.

Burr gripped his knife tighter as the Apache moved in, his blade darting and thrusting like the tongue of a snake. The point of the blade ripped a small gash in Burr's forearm. He sprang forward, then Gray Cloud leaped back to escape the thrusting knife. They fell into the dirt and rolled over, stabbing and thrusting. They came up facing each other. There was blood running down the Indian's shoulder. Burr was bloody, too.

"Shit-eatin' buzzard," Burr hissed in English.

He held his knife low, cutting edge up. They circled each other, ramming and stabbing. Another fleck of blood showed on Burr's forearm. The Indian was incredibly fast. His flat, hard face and cold eyes showed no emotion. He lunged forward. Burr moved and seemed to slip; the Indian sprang to the side, and Burr swung with his left fist, catching Gray Cloud on the side of the head and knocking him to the ground. Gray Cloud came up swiftly, thrusting low for Burr's crotch, but Burr knocked the knife aside and lunged. His blade sliced a path across the Indian's chest. Gray Cloud swung around, striking rapidly with his knife; it went into Burr's shoulder. Burr struck him again with his fist, and they both fell. The blood from Burr's arm soaked the cloth tied around his knife hand.

The Indian was on his feet first and lunged. Burr sidestepped and caught Gray Cloud's wrist, throwing him over. He moved in to step on the knife arm, but the Indian rolled and came up slashing. Burr circled to the right, forcing the Indian to turn. Blood ran down his chest, and he could feel it, wet, in the bottoms of his moccasins. He moved his foot forward, gaining a step, then crouched. The Indian feinted, then came in fast. Burr struck the knife arm and the blade entered his side. He grunted with pain and clamped his hand on the Indian's arm, his fingers seeking the funny bone, to find it and paralyze it so that he would drop the knife. For a moment it was strength against strength, straining every muscle, then the Indian suddenly yielded and stepped back, throwing Burr off balance. He lost his grip on his knife when his fist hit the ground. The Indian sprang up, and Burr rolled over and came to his feet empty-handed.

Gray Cloud leaped at him, and Burr sidestepped, his left forearm taking the tip of the blade, his right fist smashing into the face of the Indian. The second Gray Cloud hit the ground, Burr was on him, his powerful arm straining to hold the Indian's knife away from his body. Burr hammered him with his fist while Gray Cloud's clawlike hand grabbed for the soft parts between his legs. Wildly, bitterly, and desperately they fought, their bodies slick with blood. They rolled in the dirt, their faces close. Burr got his hand into the oily hair and jerked Gray Cloud's head back. The hate-filled eyes blazed up at him. It was the chance he had been waiting for. He spat a thick stream of tobacco juice into the blazing black eyes.

The Indian let out a yell, and Burr's two hands closed over the knife in Gray Cloud's fist and plunged it into his throat. A well of blood gushed up, covering Burr's hands. Dazed, he looked at Gray Cloud, expecting him to spring up again. He got to his feet and backed away.

The shrill keening of the women made him aware that the fight was over. He looked at the chief and the old man nodded slightly. Burr picked up his knife and staggered to the wagon. Mooney reached down, grasped his hand, and hauled him up onto the seat.

"Hee-yaw! Heee-ee-yaw!" Mooney shouted to the team and cracked the whip over their backs. The crowd parted and the wagon rolled out of the village.

Mooney walked the mules at a fast pace until they were over the rise and out of sight of the camp, then he stood and cracked the whip hard over their backs, whipping them into a run. Burr swayed dizzily on the seat, his chin on his chest, blood dripping from his side and from a dozen cuts on his arms, chest, and back. Realizing that he could tumble from the seat, Mooney slowed the mules again to a fast walk and held on to Burr with one hand. After a few miles he pulled the mules to a halt and tried to stanch the blood coming from Burr's side.

"I'm all right. Go on," Burr said weakly. "Just . . . let me lie . . . down."

Mooney stood and eased Burr down on the seat. "Hold on—we ain't far from Luis's place."

Still, progress was slow. Mooney was afraid to run the mules, afraid Burr might bounce off the seat. A rough ride might even cause more bleeding. The late afternoon sun was riding the crest of the mountains and Burr had been unconscious for some time when Mooney spotted a rider in the distance. He signaled by waving his hat, and soon the rider came at a fast gallop.

Luis pulled his black stallion to a halt beside the wagon and sprang from the saddle. He let out an astonished oath when he saw his brother's white face and the number of wounds on his body.

"Get up here and hold on to Burr so I can whip up these mules," Mooney said. "It ain't more'n a couple a miles to your place."

Burr roused when Luis knelt beside him to lift his head from the hard seat.

"Tobacco did the trick, brother. God . . . I'm sick—" He vomited.

"Swallered too much juice, I reckon," Mooney said.

When they reached the hacienda Luis brought out a straw tick, put it in the back of the wagon, and laid Burr on it. He bound the wound in his side and covered him with a blanket. They talked about him staying at the hacienda and Mooney going to fetch Ben and Johanna. Luis decided the care he needed would come faster if they took him home.

On the way to the ranch, Mooney told Luis what happened.

"That Burr fought like a wildcat," he said with pride. "And that Indian buck was ugly—ugly as a mud fence. He shore did want to take our hair and ride on the ranch. Don't think we'll have no trouble now. That one feller, that Geronimo, told that to Burr. He's got a powerful lot to say 'bout what goes on. He said if'n Burr killed the buck they'd leave us to bring 'em goods when they come again. I swear to God, Luis, that's what he said—"

Mooney told Luis every detail of what had happened from the time they reached the Indian camp to the present. Luis listened patiently through the second telling of how Burr had spat in the Indian's eyes. He knew Mooney was just getting warmed up to tell the story when they reached the ranch.

# CHAPTER
## *Twenty*

It would be the longest, most miserable day in Johanna's life. She came to this conclusion before mid-morning. She moved nervously from one chore to another, her mind dulled with dread as it had been from the moment Burr's wagon had rolled out of the yard. At first she was angry because of the flippant attitude he had taken about going to the Indian camp. After thinking about it, however, she decided that the flippancy was probably to conceal his own apprehension, because surely no man in his right mind *wanted* to go there. And he *had* turned and waved at her.

At high noon they buried old Mack and the Indian woman. It was decided shortly after the old man died not to ask the *padre* to stay over for the burial because Mack would have scorned a service and because the *padre* was urgently needed elsewhere. The good man, with several gold coins in his purse and escorted by Paco, left before dawn for the village in the mountains.

Johanna and Ben rode on the tailgate of the wagon that carried the bodies to the small cemetery. Red drove, and two of the ranch hands followed the wagon on horseback. Bucko and Jacy were left in Codger's care. Under Ben's instructions a grave for Mack was dug at the far end of the burial ground, as far as possible from the graves of Anna Englebretson and Juanita Gazares, although the final resting place for the mother of Mack's third bastard son would be near that of the mothers of his two other sons.

They buried the Indian woman's body first. Red carried her slight, blanket-wrapped body and placed it in the grave. Johanna was pained when she looked down at the pitiful bundle. She wished she knew the woman's name, and if it mattered to her that she was being buried here, or if she'd rather be with her own people. As the men covered the body with earth, she softly recited the Lord's Prayer, knowing it would mean nothing to the woman, but somehow she felt better for doing it.

The men were sweating profusely by the time they lifted the crude box containing old Mack's corpse out of the wagon and into the grave. They stood with hats in hand while Ben read from Scripture, then shoveled the soft earth over the box, ensuring that the old man's dust would remain forever in the valley he had loved.

The men went back to the wagon, and Johanna and Ben walked over to the other graves. She read the inscriptions on the markers in a hushed voice: "Juanita Gazares, beloved mother of Luis Gazares." She moved on to Anna's grave. Her eyes filled with tears. Anna had been only twenty years old when she died. She had been even younger than Jacy when she was introduced to Mack Macklin's cruelty.

Ben reached out and caressed the top of the board marker on his beloved's grave. Johanna looked at him through her tears and saw that his face was serene. His eyes had a faraway look, as if he were seeing once again the fragile, golden-haired girl with the enormous blue eyes. As Johanna moved away to leave him alone, she heard him say softly, "It's going to be all right now, Anna."

Ben's words stayed with her on the way back to the house. She clung to them for reassurance. She imagined that if Burr lived to come back to her, her life would be a series of crises that would run from ecstasy to despair. God help her! She loved Burr Macklin and would be more miserable without him than with him. She reached out and grasped Ben's hand, needing physical contact with someone else who loved Burr.

"I'm scared, Ben."

"I know. So am I, but it's going to be all right. I feel it. It *is* working out." He patted her hand.

Red pulled the team up in front of the house, and Johanna and Ben went up the path to the porch. Johanna couldn't help thinking about the day she'd arrived, and had walked up this same path to be met by such hostility. She almost expected to hear the old man shouting profanities. She thought about how during the weeks that followed she had cringed each time he had bellowed, "Girl!" What a strain it had been to steel herself each time she walked out onto the porch to face him.

The enormous cowhide-covered chair was empty, and the bucket old Mack had used for a spittoon was gone, although the tobacco-juice stains remained. The door to his room stood open, an eerie silence emanating from it. Johanna walked slowly down the hall to the kitchen. Rosita was busy with the noon meal while another Mexican woman cleaned. They were laughing and talking but fell silent when they saw Johanna in the doorway. Bucko and Harley, Rosita's little one, sat at the table stuffing themselves with warm buttered bread sprinkled with sugar.

"Señora," Rosita said, "Señor Burr tell me to come and bring Sofia, she have no family, she stay and help you, no?"

"*Sí.* I would like Sofia to stay and help."

The short, plump woman's face broke into a wreath of

smiles. She dipped the mop into the bucket of water and scrubbed the floor vigorously.

Jacy and Luis were across the hall in the sitting room. Johanna stood quietly in the doorway and watched Luis nervously pacing the length of the room. It was undoubtedly the first time he had been inside the house.

Jacy jumped up from the comfortable chair. "Johanna, you're back! Can't you feel the change in this house already? Oh, I don't . . . I know it's wicked to be . . . not sad. It's not that I'm glad, but—"

Luis looked at her with an indulgent smile. "*Vida mia*, sit down and rest. You've been like a small drop of water dancing on a hot stove." He continued pacing.

"When do you think they'll be back, Luis?"

"I do not know, *hermana*, perhaps not till the sun goes down."

It was comforting to hear him call her sister, but his anxiety increased her nervousness.

"Not before then?" The anguish in her voice brought Jacy to her side.

"Burr will be all right, Johanna. Luis says Burr knows the chief. He thinks he's got a good . . . chance."

"What kind of chance? One in ten? Nine in ten?" Johanna's voice rose, her mind riddled with fear.

"A good chance, *hermana*," Luis said.

Johanna wanted desperately to believe him, but couldn't.

Jacy grabbed her husband's arm and her eyes sought his. "Didn't I tell you she loved him, Luis? Didn't I tell you Johanna wouldn't have married him if she didn't love him?"

"Yes, little one, you told me." Luis gazed down at his wife with such love in his eyes that Johanna felt a stab of profound longing. "I'll leave you two together," he said abruptly.

Jacy threw her arms about his waist and buried her face against his chest. "Are you going . . . there?"

"I will not do anything foolish, my pet. You are not to worry. I will be here to spank life into our *niño* when it is time for it to face the world."

"Be careful," Jacy whispered.

"Of course." He raised her face with gentle fingers. "My first concern is for you, my love, my life. My next concern is for my brother and," he looked at Johanna, "his wife."

Jacy and Luis walked out of the room together, their arms entwined. Johanna slumped down into a chair and sat for a few minutes before jumping to her feet. She went out into the hall in search of Ben, passed the old man's room, then slowly went back and looked in. It seemed so strange for him not to be there. The mattress was missing from the bed and the floor had been scrubbed. It seemed bare, lonely. Even the unpleasant odor that had always permeated the room was replaced by the scent of lye soap and damp stone slabs. Again she felt sorrow for the man who had been so lacking in feeling for those around him, and who was so disliked that they couldn't wait to remove all trace of him.

Deep in thought, Johanna wandered onto the back porch, only to be startled by the sudden appearance of Isabella, on her way into Burr's room. Cold anger surged through her and propelled her into the room in time to see the woman toss some freshly washed shirts onto the bed. Isabella turned to face her rival, her eyes challenging, her mouth curled in contempt. Johanna, however, faced her down, and Isabella finally lowered her eyes and, with spiteful arrogance, attempted to sweep past Johanna. She did not get far before Johanna grabbed her arm. Isabella whirled like a tigeress, her teeth bared, her eyes spitting hate.

Surprised by the girl's sudden ferociousness, Johanna

stepped back, but did not yield. "You are never to come into this house again." She issued the command with cold dignity.

"Only Señor Burr tell me that!" Isabella hissed, confidence blazing in her eyes.

Johanna smiled coldly. "I am mistress of this house." The very words now brought with them a new confidence. "If you wish to remain in the valley you will do as I say."

Isabella, not unlike a brazen child, placed her hands on her hips and thrust her small pointed breast forward, the dark nipples showing brown beneath the thin material of her blouse. She glared at Johanna with dark eyes flashing with fierce volatile lights, and then in a gesture of defiance she tossed her head to one side, her long black hair whipping out and over her shoulder.

"*Gringa!*" she spat. "You not woman enough for Señor Burr! He no want your pale skin and body sharp with bones. You go from here!"

Johanna's anger turned to wide-eyed disbelief at the incredible nerve of the girl. "I'm here to stay. You'd better understand that right now. You are not to come here again. *Comprende?*"

There was such loathing and violence in Isabella's eyes that had Johanna been less angry she might have chosen her words more carefully.

"You never have Señor Burr's *niño*. I swear it! Señor Burr my man! You know nothing of how to please him." Isabella spat out the words with vengeance. As if to inflict further pain, she said arrogantly, "Luis not wed your *puta* sister, if not for rape *niño* in her belly. He do it for his mother."

"That's enough!" Johanna said sharply.

"What I say is so, *gringa*!" The Mexican girl was panting with anger. She spun around and was through the door before Johanna could say another word.

Johanna followed her out of the room and from the back

porch watched her race down the path toward the adobe houses. She stood there long after Isabella was out of sight and played back their conversation in her mind. Calmer now that Isabella was gone, Johanna recognized Isabella's threat. Finally she realized there were more immediate problems—the main one was getting through the day.

She went to the front porch, where she found Ben sitting in a chair he'd brought from his room and looking off down the valley. He took the pipe from his mouth.

"I see Luis couldn't stand it any longer," he said quietly.

"Is he going to the Indian camp?" she asked with some alarm.

"No, lass. Luis knows where his responsibility lies. He'll just scout around. He won't do anything foolish. Sit down, we'll wait together."

"Is it always like this when he goes to the camp, Ben?" Johanna asked after she was seated.

"There's always worry when the Apaches come to the valley."

"Why is this time different? Why is Luis so edgy? Is it just because it's such a large encampment?"

"Not exactly. For some time now the braves Luis trades with have been getting bolder, more resentful of our being here. You have the right to know, lass—Luis thinks the Apaches may go to war against the whites. That don't necessarily mean against us," he added quickly. "The Apaches are a people of their word. If they say they will leave us in peace, they will."

"You could have kept Burr from going," Johanna accused bitterly. "Why didn't you?"

Ben looked at her sharply and silently questioned the reason for her outburst. He took his pipe from his mouth and tapped the bowl on the heel of his shoe.

"Johanna," he said slowly, "Burr is a man who makes

his own decisions and does what he must. I wouldn't presume to tell him what to do, and I advise you to do the same."

At first Johanna was slightly resentful of the advice, and then she saw the wisdom of it. She sat quietly and the afternoon, which she thought would last forever, wore on. She strained her eyes toward the horizon, watching and waiting for a moving speck, a puff of dust, anything that would mean that Burr was on his way home. Neither she nor Ben exchanged another word. For once, the man beside her didn't wish to visit.

The shadows of the mountains crept down over the ranch buildings and the air became cooler. Rosita brought a warm shawl for Johanna, and Jacy, wrapped in a blanket, joined them on the porch, her usual exuberance dampened by worry. Across the porch, Sofia came out of Burr's room. She was lighting fires in the hearths to take off the evening chill. Food smells came from the kitchen, where Rosita was preparing the evening meal, but they went unnoticed by the people waiting on the porch.

At first Johanna wasn't sure she had seen anything. She waited a moment, then slowly moved to the edge of the house, all her senses willing the image for which she hoped. The speck was too large to be a horseman; still she waited. She thought her heart would burst. Dread, fear, and a wee bit of hope kept her feet rooted to the spot on the porch and her eyes on the horizon. The speck disappeared down an incline, and it was a long while before it appeared again, larger this time. It was the wagon, and her heart leaped with relief.

"They're coming, Ben!" She wrapped her arms about the heavy post that supported the roof, and her eyes clung to the wagon. As it drew nearer, her happiness dimmed. Only one man sat on the seat, and it was unmistakably Mooney. Her heart plummeted to the pit of her stomach. *Oh, God!* she prayed. *Please don't let Burr be dead!*

Drawn by an irresistible force, her legs moved her out onto the path in front of the house. She could see Luis's horse tied behind the wagon and his black sombrero bobbing up and down behind the wagon seat. She stood very still, fighting the despair that threatened to overwhelm her.

Red's big sorrel shot past her. Johanna watched him ride to the wagon, wheel his horse, and look down into the space behind the seat. He spoke to Luis for a moment that seemed an hour to Johanna, then galloped his horse toward the house.

"They're all right!" he shouted. He pulled his horse to a skidding stop beside the porch. The animal danced around nervously while Red said, "Burr's been cut up some. You'll need hot water and lots of clean cloth."

Johanna was suddenly intoxicated with relief. Burr was alive! Burr was alive! The words repeated themselves in her mind as she ran to the kitchen, calling out orders to Sofia and Rosita, then went swiftly to Burr's room to stoke the fire and turn down the bed. She went back outside and waited anxiously while Mooney pulled the wagon to a stop at the edge of the porch.

It took three men to carry Burr's limp body into the house and place it on his bed. He was almost totally covered with blankets, so Johanna saw only the top of his head and the soles of his moccasins.

"Johanner," Mooney was at her side, "Burr'll be fine as a fiddle in a day or two. He done lost a parcel of blood, and you'd best wait and let Ben and Luis clean him up a bit."

"What's the matter with him? Why don't you want me to see him?"

Sofia bustled by her, carrying the teakettle and an armful of clean cloths. Rosita came along behind with whiskey and a large washbasin. Johanna moved to follow them into the room. Luis barred her way.

"In just a few minutes, sister. No man wants his woman to see him so."

"What did they do to him?" Her voice rose to near hysteria.

"He throwed up, is what he done, Johanner," Mooney said. "C'mon over here, 'n' I'll tell ya while they clean him up. Ya see, thar was this big buck that Burr was goin' t'fight. So he took a big chaw of tobaccy in his jaw, and he swallered the juice and it made him sick. He's the biggest mess ya ever did see."

They were standing outside the door to Burr's room. The ranch hands, who would not have dared set foot on the porch while old Mack was alive, gathered around. Mooney was in his glory. They hung on every word he spoke.

"I tell you, that Indian buck, the one what wanted to kill Burr and go on the rampage, was meaner than a steer with a crooked horn. He was big, too. Big as Burr, and madder than a cow with her tit caught in the fence. That feller, Geronimo, had put him down some and that went against the grain. He shore thought he was a goin' to cut Burr up and use him for dog meat. But that Burr was steady. He stepped into the ring they drawed on the ground like he done it ever'day. He give that buck a fight. Then he lost his knife and I thought he was a goner." Mooney paused, enjoying the crowd's suspense. "Then I knowed why he took the chaw. He spit right in that buck's eye and killed him with his own knife. The women folk let out the keening cry and Burr come a stumblin' to the wagon. It were the purtest sight I ever did see. We drove outta that camp jist as purty as ya please, till we got over the rise." He laughed. "Then we high-tailed it. Luis met us a couple miles from his place. You can bet yore bobbed tail I was glad to see him."

Mooney described every detail, leaving nothing to the imagination. The men stayed clustered around him, awed by his and Burr's bravery, and Mooney basked in their admiring glances.

Not until later did Johanna remember that not a word about old Mack had been spoken all day. From outward appearances, at least, it was as though he'd never existed.

Jacy asked Johanna if she and Luis could use the room at the top of the stairs, as she was sure Johanna would want to stay near her husband. There was no way Johanna could deny that fact without letting her sister know the true situation between her and Burr. She watched Jacy and Luis go up the stairs, their arms around each other, and she wondered if the happiness they shared would ever be hers.

Johanna and Ben sat for a long while beside Burr's bed after everyone had left. The flickering light from the lamp showed the cuts and bruises on his face. He slept deeply. Soon the sleepless night and the stress of waiting for him to return made themselves known to Johanna's tired body, and she nodded.

"Go to bed, child," Ben said quietly.

"You don't mind?"

"Not at all. I'll go soon, myself. I'm just so relieved to have him back that I want to be with him for a while longer."

"I'll lie down in Bucko's room so that I can hear Burr if he calls." She kissed Ben's cheek. "We've managed to weather one more crisis, Ben," she said tiredly.

"Life is a series of crises, Johanna. And you done just fine with this one. It was a lucky day for me and my boys when you came to the valley."

*And for Jacy, too*, Johanna thought as she left the room. *But as for me—only God knows.*

# CHAPTER
## *Twenty-one*

I n the late afternoon Johanna stood in the doorway of the kitchen, breathing in the aroma of the cooking food and smiling with satisfaction. Sofia was preparing the evening meal. Meat and thick broth, Johanna had told her, were the quickest way to replace blood. As she went down the hall she silently gave thanks that Burr had returned and for the gift of peace he had brought back from the Indian camp.

Johanna, about to tiptoe into Burr's room, held her finger to her lips in an attempt to silence the giggles coming from Jacy and Bucko, who sat on the porch with a book. It was as though someone had swept the gloom from the stone house, leaving it shiny and bright; even Bucko attacked his studies with less grumbling. She entered the room and glanced at the bed. Burr's eyes were closed. Johanna paused to look at him. His face was softer, his mouth gentler in sleep. His light hair curled down over his ears, making him look younger. Looking at him, Johanna almost forgot what she'd come for. She went to the mantel and lifted the chimney from the lamp to clean it.

"I'm hungry."

Johanna turned to find him looking at her.

"You're awake." She said no more, because her voice was shaky, as were her legs as she went to the bed.

"I feel like somethin's gnawing a hole in my belly."

"Well," she said, with a casualness she did not feel, "you've already got enough holes in you, and you sure don't need another. I'll bring you some broth."

He pushed back the cover and lifted his head, his hand seeking the bandage on his side. He closed his eyes and moaned against the pain that shot through him. His head fell back on the pillow, and he looked up at her with that familiar, irritating, obstinate look on his face. Damn know-it-all woman! She was so damn confident, so . . . haughty, and so goddamn . . . beautiful. She stood there like a queen looking down at a peasant! He couldn't even look at her without feeling inferior. He didn't like that feeling. It brought out the worst in him.

"I don't need any damn broth. I need meat. Where's Ben?"

Johanna felt like throwing his chimney into the fireplace. She breathed deeply, clenched her teeth, and glared down at him. He was back to his true self: demanding, ungrateful, and crude. How could she have possibly thought the two of them could manage any kind of peaceful existence together?

"I'll call Ben and tell Sofia to bring you your meal."

"You bring it. You're my wife," he called as she left the room.

She stuck her head back in the door. "Unfortunately, but I'm not your servant."

Johanna went swiftly down the porch to Ben's room. She rapped on the door, then opened it when Ben called out. He and Luis were looking over a stack of papers found in the bureau in old Mack's room.

"He's awake," Johanna announced, "and cross as a bear."

She walked briskly down the hall to the kitchen, grabbed a plate and forked a piece of half-done meat from the skillet, and slammed it down on it. She added two large half-cooked turnips and several cold biscuits. On her way to the door she snatched a knife and fork from the table, completely unaware of the puzzled look on Sofia's face. She kicked open the door to Burr's room as she had when she'd taken food to old Mack. Without looking at the man on the bed, she hooked a chair up close with her foot, put the plate on it, and walked out.

"Come back here!"

She pulled the door closed with a loud bang. She heard him laugh and his mocking voice reached her through the roar in her ears as she walked away.

"Why don't you slam the door, Johanna?"

She went to the end of the porch and around the house toward the smokehouse. Hateful, hateful man! Her eyes found her hat nailed above the barn door. She clenched her jaw in frustration and turned her back on the symbol of her humiliation. She looked out over the peaceful valley, felt the cool mountain air fan her flushed cheeks, and gradually became calm. She wished desperately that she'd never need return to the house, but she knew it was an impossible wish. Dwelling on the situation would not change things, she told herself sternly. With her face a mask of cool composure, she went back to the kitchen to help Sofia.

When the evening meal was over, she and Jacy settled down in the sitting room with a lamp between them, Johanna knitting stockings for the baby, Jacy unraveling a shawl that had been their mother's and rolling the yarn into a ball. Jacy had spent time with Burr while Johanna had helped Sofia. Johanna hadn't gone near her husband since she had left his room shortly after he had awakened, and Jacy, although puzzled by her sister's behavior and sudden loss of cheer-fulness, didn't ask any questions.

Until the Apache left the valley, Jacy and Luis were going to stay at the house. Having them there, so obviously in love, made Johanna more aware than ever of her position as unloved wife. The thought kept coming back to her that if the *padre* had come one day later there would have been no need for her to marry Burr. Old Mack was dead, and surely it could be established that Burr, Luis, and Bucko were his heirs.

Luis came for Jacy. He, Burr, and Ben had been together in Burr's room for more than an hour.

"Come with me, *querida*." He pulled her up and out of the deep chair. "Ben wishes to talk with your sister, and you need to rest."

"Is he in his room?" Johanna asked.

"No, sister, he's with your husband." Luis's eyes flicked to Jacy to see if she had noticed the tightening of Johanna's lips and the way her body had stiffened.

Johanna picked up the shawl, her movements stiff and jerky, and flung it about her shoulders. She went down the hall to the porch. *The arrangement of this house, with outside doors to the end rooms, is ridiculous*, she thought, *just like everything else in this blasted valley.*

She pushed open the door to Burr's room and stepped inside. Two lamps were lit; the one on the table beside the bed cast a glow on Burr's scowling features, the other was on the wide mantel shelf. Burr said nothing to her, but his eyes met hers the moment she walked through the door. Silence, taut and chilling, stretched between them.

Ben got to his feet. "Come sit here, Johanna. There's something Burr and I wish to discuss with you."

Johanna advanced slowly, pulling the shawl closely about

her; although the room was warm, she suddenly felt cold. Burr was propped up on the bed, and several papers lay on the quilt beside him.

Ben cleared his throat. "We found a paper among Mack's things, Johanna, that concerns you."

Startled, she looked at him questioningly.

"Mack left a letter to let us know, in case of his death, that when Willard Risewick left the valley he carried with him a will making you his heir. You are to receive the total bulk of his estate—money and land." Ben's eyes went from Johanna to Burr and back.

The full meaning of Ben's words did not take root in Johanna's mind at first. When they did, shock and confusion took over. Finally she gasped, "No! He couldn't have."

"But he did," Burr said with a sardonic grin. "You played your cards right, little fox. He liked the way you stood up to him and told him how the cow ate the cabbage. I'm surprised he didn't try to marry you himself—guess he knew he wasn't the . . . stud he once was."

"That's not necessary, Burr," Ben said sharply.

"You're rich. You could go to town and buy your own saloon. There's only one hitch—my wife is staying right here. The old man kicked off just a day too late for you, didn't he, little fox. Just a day too late."

"Burr . . ." Ben's voice was filled with exasperation. "I wish you wouldn't talk like this. Tell her all of it, or I will."

Johanna jumped to her feet. "I don't want it! I never did. I'll go to Fort Davis and talk to Mr. Cash and sign it over to you. It belongs to you, Luis, and Bucko." She looked pleadingly at Ben.

"Don't get so worked up, little wife. You didn't get it all. You got a pile of money, but not all of the valley. The house is on your land, and you can throw me and Ben out of it anytime you take a notion. But we'll just go out to the other side of the corrals and build ourselves another one—on *our* land.''

"Burr, there are times I wish you were small again. I'd take a stick to you.''

"Let me have my fun, Ben. It's not often a little fox gets outfoxed.''

"Johanna, come sit down, lass. I want to tell you something you should have been told long ago, and would have except for this stubborn boy of mine.''

Johanna wrapped the shawl tighter around her trembling shoulders and went to stand at the foot of the bed, keeping her eyes averted from the man lying on it.

"I don't want to know any more, Ben.''

"Please, Johanna. I'll make it brief.'' His kind face was so troubled that she nodded agreement, and he continued hurriedly, as if afraid she would leave. "As I told you before, I legally adopted the boys long ago. Well, back in 1853 the United States bought forty-five thousand square miles of land from Mexico. It was called the Gadsden Purchase, and this valley was included in the land that was bought. All title to the land had to be reestablished in Sante Fe. Mack went there and filed his claim. A year later I went to Sante Fe and discovered the law had allowed Mack to file on only a certain number of sections and that he had left money with a land investor to buy up the rest of the land when it became available. I filed on the allotted number of sections and took out tentative titles to sections in the names of the boys. That meant that if no one else filed on the land, when they came of age they could go to the land office and claim title if the required improvements had been made. We also bought up the land that adjoined ours. The three of us own all the land surrounding Mack's. Mack never knew that. He assumed he owned the whole valley, and that land man let him think that. He was probably too scared of him to tell him that the rest of the valley was unavailable to him and that he'd lost the money in land speculations of his own."

Ben looked down at the paper in his hand, then looked up at Johanna. Her face was coolly composed, and it was impossible to tell what she was thinking.

"And you let Mr. Macklin believe he owned the valley. Why?"

"Why?" Burr answered harshly. "Because I wanted it that way. It pleased me to run this place the way I wanted, running roughshod over his orders. The old bastard didn't own anything but this house and a few outbuildings."

"And you wanted those, too." Johanna kept her eyes on Ben, refusing to look at Burr.

"You're damn right I did. But they're yours now."

"So there was no question of selling the valley to Mr. Risewick. There was no danger of its being turned into a battlefield. There was no danger that the workers would be driven off, and no danger to Jacy." She spoke the words fatalistically.

"Not by . . . no, Johanna," Ben said haltingly.

"So there was really no need for me to sacrifice my future happiness in order the keep the valley safe for Jacy, and to save the land for Mr. Macklin's *bastard* sons?" She spat out the word deliberately, raised her brows, and waited for Ben's answer.

"Ah . . . no, Johanna."

"I see." She went to the end of the room, stood with her back to the men, and closed her eyes. She wasn't even angry, her hurt went too deep for that. She felt betrayed . . . used. Turning back, she retraced her steps to the foot of the bed and asked Burr, "Why did you marry me? Why did you go to all the trouble of making up the lie about the land being sold, when you knew it would never happen?"

Burr grinned but in no way was it an embarrassed or sheepish grin. He appeared enormously pleased with himself and wanted her to know it.

"I wanted Luis to have what he wanted. If your sister was happy, Luis would be happy. I wanted you to stay here and teach Bucko." He looked at her now with eyes that mocked. "There's a couple more reasons. You're a bit on the skinny side, but not a bad-looking woman, and I get tired going to El Paso to visit the —"

"Burr!" Ben's voice thundered in the quiet room.

"I'll be leaving as soon as Jacy has her baby," Johanna said to Ben. "I'll see to it that the land is put in Bucko's name—he's deserving of his share the same as Mr. Macklin's other two sons. I'll divide the money between the three of them, but I will keep enough to see me through to California and a teaching job. I'm entitled to that much after all I've been through here. My main concern is for Jacy. I don't want her to know of my plans or about any of this . . . sordid affair. Distress at this time wouldn't be good for her."

"Lass, don't make plans yet. I know how you feel, but give yourself a little time—"

"You couldn't possibly know how I feel," she said scornfully. "Being victimized by old Mack's sons doesn't surprise me, but you . . . I thought you were my friend, Ben. I'm disappointed in you."

"Hold on." Burr swung his legs off the bed and sat up on the side with a grunt of pain. "Don't go blaming Ben for any of this. It was my idea."

Johanna didn't look at him.

"Yes, lass, he knew you wanted to leave here, and he thought . . ." Ben's words hung in the silence while his eyes pleaded with her.

"For once he was right, Ben. I only wish I didn't have to

spend another night in this ghost-ridden, hate-filled house. Thanks to Mr. Macklin, I no longer have to stay and accept your charity." She started for the door.

"Charity! Damn you! You'll stay here, by God! You're my wife, like it or not, and you'll stay here!" Burr's angry voice filled every corner of the room.

At the door Johanna turned and looked at him. "Demands and curses. Old Mack's legacy lives on in his son," she said sadly as if to herself. With a pitying glance at Burr, she turned and went out the door.

As she walked down the darkened porch she could hear Ben's raised and agitated voice as he talked to Burr.

Almost three weeks passed before the Apache dismantled their camp and started the long trek to the mountains of Mexico. During that time Johanna went about her daily work calmly and efficiently. She and Sofia made preserves from dried peaches, sliced cabbage for kraut, caught clear rainwater, set several casks of vinegar working, and gathered herbs, onions, and garlic and hung them in bunches from the rafters in the kitchen. They scrubbed everything in the house, washed clothes, and aired bedding.

Johanna never admitted it, even to herself, but the strain of keeping up a cheerful front for Jacy had taxed her nerves to the limit, and only with hard work could she keep control.

It was a relief to Johanna when the day finally came when Luis brought the wagon to the door and loaded Jacy's belongings. By the time they were ready to leave, the wagon was full of supplies from the storage shed and foodstuffs Johanna and Codger had boxed up from the root cellar and smokehouse. Burr brought a milk cow from the barn and tied it behind the wagon. He had been up and about since the day after the fight, but he still moved slowly and painfully. At the last minute while the goodbyes were being said, Mooney came from the bunkhouse proudly carrying a cradle. It was small but expertly made. The bare wood had been rubbed smooth and a coat of wax applied. Jacy was ecstatic, and after Mooney carefully set the cradle in the wagon she insisted he come around so that she could plant a kiss on his weathered cheek. He was all grins and embarrassment. Johanna watched and for the first time in weeks tears came to her eyes.

"Do not worry, sister," Luis said softly from behind Johanna. "All will be well."

"I know, Luis. And I'm happy for both of you."

"All will be well for you too."

"Of course."

"Sister . . ." There was an edge of worry in his tone.

Johanna turned and smiled brightly. "I'll be down soon. I've yet to see your home."

"You will always be welcome." He saw the dark circles beneath her eyes and the way the skin stretched over her cheekbones. She was deeply unhappy, as was his brother, and it grieved him.

Johanna watched the slowly moving wagon until it was out of sight, then went to her room beneath the sloping roof. What would she do during the long days ahead? Sofia relieved her of much of the work and was so happy doing it that she hadn't the heart to tell her she'd rather do it herself. If she had her choice she would work from dawn until dark, so that her tired body would demand that she sleep. Thank God, she still had Bucko.

Thankfully, Burr had been busy away from the house the last few weeks. She hadn't spoken to him directly since the night Ben had told her about old Mack's will. At the supper table he listened to the conversation between Luis and Ben and left the kitchen as soon as he had finished eating. Johanna had been distantly polite to Ben. She did not seek him out, as she had before. The closeness she had once felt to the little man was gone. He had contrived with Burr to deceive her and she couldn't forgive that.

Johanna stretched out on the bed and stared at the tin ceiling. She counted on her fingers. Jacy should have her baby in less than six weeks. Six weeks! How was she going to endure staying in this house for that long?

# CHAPTER
## *Twenty-two*

The days sped by faster than Johanna had thought possible. The occupants of the stone house settled into a routine. Burr was up at first light and gone from the house, not to return until just before evening. He had retreated behind a wall of polite silence. At times Johanna would search his face for a sign of softness. She saw only eyes hard as steel, a firm outthrust jaw, and an implacable mouth. Ben breakfasted early, and went either to his room or over to the bunkhouse, leaving Johanna and Bucko to have their meal alone.

Johanna was constantly surprised by Bucko. The little boy was very bright and even witty. They spent the morning hours at the table in the sitting room working on reading, numbers, and penmanship, and in the afternoon, if the day was warm, they sat on the porch. Bucko seemed unaware of the tension between Johanna and Ben and Burr. A kind of unspoken truce existed during the evening meal, after the awkwardness of the first few meals without Luis and Jacy. Ben and Burr discussed ranch work and Johanna encouraged Bucko to talk.

He was opening up more and more, eager to share his new knowledge with the others. His English was improving along with his confidence, and occasionally his choice of words brought a smile to Burr's grim face.

One day Bucko put down his book and asked Johanna the question she had been waiting for him to ask.

"Why did the woman kill old Mack?"

Johanna thought for a moment, then sat down and pulled the boy down on her lap. "Long ago old Mack did a cruel thing to the woman. She was young, a beautiful young Apache girl, who came to the valley with her people. He shamed her. It's terribly hard to be shamed before your family and friends. She must have thought it right to kill him."

"What did he do to her?"

Without hesitation Johanna answered. "He mated with her. He put a baby in her stomach and then went away and left her. Her family scorned her and cast her out. She didn't have anyone to take care of her and she had to work hard so that she would have food for herself and her baby. She wasn't strong, and much of the time she was tired and hungry."

Bucko was quiet for a long while. "The baby was me, Johanna. I was hungry, too, before Burr bringed me here."

"The word is *brought*, Bucko, and, yes, I'm sure you were hungry, too."

"I'm glad she kill him," he said fiercely. "She was brave."

"Yes, she was brave to leave her village and come here alone. But killing a man is never right unless he is trying to kill you." She hugged him close. "That woman was your mother, darling. Remember her with kindness. She gave you life. Forget old Mack. You have two brothers who will take care of you. Now let's get back to the lessons."

That evening at the supper table, during a lull in the conversation, Johanna encouraged Bucko to talk.

"We had a history lesson today. Bucko, tell Ben about Christopher Columbus."

Bucko looked proudly around the table. He was beginning to enjoy the attention of having everyone listen while he talked. He spoke in halting English.

"The woman kill old Mack for he put me in her stom . . . chy. She was tired with shame and hungry. She was very brave." His eyes searched the faces of the two men to see their reaction to his news. They were speechless.

Burr carefully set down his mug and glared at Johanna.

Although as astonished as the men, Johanna said calmly, "Your English is much better, Bucko, but the word is *stomach*. Some call it *belly*, but I don't think it's as nice a word as *stomach*. We'll learn to spell it tomorrow, if you like."

Burr was waiting for Johanna when she left the kitchen after helping Sofia. Somehow she had known he would be.

"Why did you tell Bucko a thing like that?" he demanded.

Johanna lifted her head and drew her dignity around her like a blanket. "Because he asked me, and I don't lie." She emphasized the *I*, and saw his fists tighten with anger.

"I told you I didn't want him to know anything about that."

"You told me nothing of the kind; and if you had, I would still have used my own judgment and told him the truth."

"I didn't want him to know until he was older."

"How old were you when *you* knew?"

"That was different. I had Ben."

"Bucko has you and Luis, and me . . . for a while."

"Another thing. I don't want you spending so much time with him. He's getting too attached to you. You'll leave here and he won't understand."

"All right, but *you* tell him, Mr. . . . ah . . . Calloway. You tell him to stay away from me. Try to explain *that* to him, if you can. But I'm going to teach him while I'm here, and when I go, Jacy will take over the lessons. He's too bright a child to let remain ignorant.'' Her voice was cold and distant. "The other children in this valley should be taught, too," she added bitterly. "You brought them here; it's your responsibility to see to it.'' She turned away from him and made her way up the dimly lit stairs to her room.

Aware that he stood below watching her, she firmly closed the door, felt her way in the darkness to the table, and lit the candle. She heard the pounding of boot heels on the stairs, and by the time she turned he'd flung open the door. He ducked his head and stepped into the room.

"Don't walk away from me when I'm talking to you . . . like I'm something beneath your contempt!"

Johanna raised her brows. "You put your own value on yourself, Mr. Calloway."

"And don't ever again go to my men and ask them to take you away from here! I won't be shamed in front of those who work for me. Is that clear? When the time comes for you to go, I'll take you myself and be glad to be rid of you!'' His loud, angry voice boomed against the tin ceiling.

"Very well. That sounds like a reasonable request. Now, please leave my room.'' Her body was so tense that she felt as if her heart would stop beating, but her eyes caught his and held them defiantly. It was the first time in weeks she had looked him full in the face. It was a face she didn't know. His eyes were sunken and blazed with bitterness. His cheekbones stood above hollowed cheeks shadowed with several days' growth of beard, and a vein in his temple stood out prominently and throbbed with each beat of his heart. It was the boniness of his face and the wolfish snarl of his twisted mouth that held her attention.

He scowled, then ran his fingers through his unruly hair, but he didn't move.

"I asked you to leave.'' Her voice was as icy as her eyes.

He stared at her as if he had not heard her.

She put her hands behind her to hide their trembling and encountered the hairbrush on the table. Her tense fingers gripped the handle and her cool control broke.

"Get out!" she shouted and flung the brush. It bounced off his chest and fell to the floor with a loud clatter.

He looked at her searchingly for a moment, his eyes probing her angry ones. Then he backed out the door, closing it behind him.

Johanna threw herself on the bed and sobbed. She hated him, she told herself, and she hated herself for what she'd just done. "No," she moaned aloud in her misery. "I don't hate him. God, help me—I love him!"

The week before Thanksgiving the weather turned cold. The pumpkins were gathered and put in the cellar and corn was husked and shelled. Some was set aside for hominy and some ground into cornmeal. Johanna was grateful for the extra work to fill the hours.

Now she spent an hour each morning with Bucko before sending him down to the bunkhouse or over to Rosita's. She did her best to explain to him that she was spending too much time on his lessons and neglecting her housekeeping duties. The little boy accepted the new routine but seemed dejected and was less talkative than before. Reluctantly Johanna admitted to herself that Burr was right—Bucko was becoming too dependent on her company. It would be easier for him when she left the valley if she gradually weaned him away from her now.

Jacy's baby was due in a week or two. She had settled nicely into her new home and was so glowingly happy that Johanna was sure she would be content with Luis and the baby when she was gone. Two familes had moved to Luis's ranch, and one of the women came in each day to help with the work and to be with Jacy while Luis was away. Johanna's heart was lighter each time she returned from a visit with her sister. It had worked out well. Their coming to the valley had been right for Jacy . . . but oh, so wrong for her.

One afternoon Johanna wandered down to check the almost bare garden plot and paused at the corral to watch the cowboys break a dun-colored stallion. A whoop went up from the men as she approached, and she climbed onto the rail just as the stallion broke away from the opposite fence and bucked his way to the center of the corral. His sharp hooves stirred up a cloud of dust in his frenzy to rid himself of the man clinging to his back. One moment the cowboy was there, the next he was arcing high in the air before crashing to the ground. Seconds later he was up again and scrambling over the fence, slapping his floppy-brimmed hat against his leg and enduring the good-natured joshing of his friends.

"I don't see you galoots a-tryin' him. All you're doin' is a-runnin' off at the mouth and a-ridin' the fence." He climbed onto the rail and sat beside Johanna.

"That was a hard fall. Are you hurt?"

"'Twarn't nothin', ma'am. Would'a been if he'd'a got a hoof on me. He's a wild 'un. Never lets your get settled in, just takes off a-rompin'. He'll make a good 'un once he gets whapped in shape. He can turn on a dime and give ya a nickel to boot."

Several cowboys were still trying to rope the bucking horse. Finally they had the mustang caught between two ropes. They held him fast while a bowlegged *vaquero* ran to his head, tied a handkerchief over his eyes, then grabbed one of his ears between his teeth.

"I feel sorry for him."

"Ma'am," the cowboy snorted, "that grulla ain't the one t' feel sorry fer. He's a heller, that 'un."

Paco called down from where he was perched on the fence, ''Señora, your man, he gonna try him.''

Burr settled himself firmly in the saddle, his long legs locked against the heaving sides of the animal and his feet planted in the stirrups. His work shirt was open to the waist, revealing his hard-muscled chest and a binding of white cloth about his middle. *Oh, God*, Johanna thought frantically, *that wound isn't healed enough to take this kind of punishment!* For a fleeting second his eyes locked with hers, then he wound the reins around his gloved hand and tugged at his hat. Not a flicker of surprise showed on his face at seeing her at the corral fence. He said something to the cowboy who was holding the horse's head. The man leaped back and dived for the fence, taking the blinder with him. The grulla stood for a fraction of a second, then exploded into the air like a coiled spring released. The animal twisted in midair and came down on all four feet with a bone-jarring crash that set off a convulsion of frenzy.

A whoop went up from the men on the fence. The longer Burr stayed in the saddle the louder they yelled encouragement. With cold-blooded determination the mustang went into a frenzy of contortions, and Johanna held her breath as Burr was whipped back and forth. Through the swirling dust she saw the horse leap up, his hind legs lashing out to splinter the rail behind him. He landed on the run and circled the corral, wheeled, and headed around before charging the fence once again. Burr yanked the mustang aside before he crashed into the rail. The eyes of the beast were wild and rolling, and he screamed with rage and shot into the air again, then stood on spraddled, quivering legs.

Burr sat the horse for a moment, then called softly, ''Come get me off.''

Two loops were put over the horse's neck and pulled taut. Slowly and painfully Burr climbed from the saddle. The white

binding around his middle was stained with blood and his
jaw was clenched with pain. His squinted eyes passed over
Johanna without expression. The cowboys whooped and exchanged money. Not until the air escaped from her tortured
lungs did Johanna realize she had been holding her breath.

Johanna walked past the house and up the path toward the
smokehouse. She needed a quiet place where she could gather
her thoughts and calm her nerves. It seemed to her that she
had been living in limbo for the past few weeks. She and
Burr did no more than acknowledge each other when they
met for meals. At first Ben had tried to heal the breach
between himself and Johanna, but days ago he had given up
and retreated behind a polite silence. Now it was the waiting
period. Waiting for Jacy to have her baby. Waiting to know
her sister was well and happy. Waiting to leave the valley
and make some order of her life.

Isabella stood close to the wall of the smokehouse. She
could faintly hear the shouts of the men at the corral, and she
could see the dust rising as the vicious hooves of the horses
being broken raked the soft earth inside the enclosure.

Her heart pounded. The *gringa* was coming up the path.
The pale *puta* who had taken her man was walking straight
to her death. Isabella was glad. Let the bitch go unsuspecting
to the stream and the Apache warrior who waited there!

Isabella's sharp, experienced eyes had spotted the Indian
standing in the shadows, as still as the large boulders that
lined the stream. Her eyes had passed over him twice before
the outline of his head alerted her to his presence. Uncon-
cerned, she veered off and circled back to the smokehouse.
Her intention at first had been to report to Señor Burr; for
since the Apache seasonal camp had broken up, the vigilance
had relaxed. Surely her discovery would make him proud of

her, make him realize that she was better fit to be his wife, have his sons, but . . . no!

She quivered with excitement now as she watched Johanna approach. Señor Burr had scorned her, forsaken her, cast her out for the pale, haughty *gringa*! Señor Burr, the man she loved with all her heart and soul, had even suggested that she marry Paco, the wiry *vaquero* who had been making cow eyes at her for months.

She drew her rebozo closer about her shoulders and braced herself against the hurt as she remembered the warmth of the señor's kisses. That was all she had to remember, for never would he go further, never would he enter her, always laughing at her insistence, at her passion for him, telling her she was but a child. A child! She was a woman—a woman not to be ignored and ordered away from the stone house like a *puta*. She laughed lightly to herself and her eyes gleamed triumphantly. Let the Apache kill the *gringa*! And then the heat in the señor's loins would force him to take her and give her his *niño*. Then he would be hers.

Isabella hesitated, reluctant to leave the shadow of the building, yet knowing she should go on down the path and pass the *gringa*. A small fear leaped into her mind. What if Señor Burr should find out that she knew the Apache warrior was lingering by the stream and she had allowed his woman to walk, unwarned, up the path? His rage would be terrible! She tossed her head. It was foolish to think he would know, but suppose he did find out that she had been to the stream; he would never believe she was a traitor. Shoving herself away from the wall, she started down the path toward the woman who walked slowly toward her, her head bent as if deep in thought. Isabella's hatred burned deeply as she passed Johanna, her dark, smoldering eyes straight ahead, her chin lifted defiantly.

Johanna looked up and saw Isabella coming down the path

toward her. It was the first time she had seen the young Mexican girl since she had ordered her out of the house. No doubt Burr was meeting her somewhere else now. Johanna was thankful that she no longer had to suffer her presence. She looked directly at Isabella as she passed her, but the girl clutched her full skirt in her hand and swept past, her face set, her eyes never leaving the path ahead.

Going on down the trail, Johanna let her thoughts wander. She was legally married to Burnett Engelbretson Calloway. Would he divorce her when she left the valley? She knew it could be done, especially by a man with money to pay the high court costs. She searched her mind but could think of only one woman she knew who had been divorced. No respectable man or woman in San Angelo had had anything to do with her. Was that to be her lot in life? Johanna wondered. A divorced woman wouldn't be allowed to teach school, so the only option open to her would be to sing in a saloon. Of course, Burr had said that he would never let her go. But now he had told her he would be glad to be rid of her. She closed her eyes as the pain of his words pierced her heart.

There was no movement and no sound that she could recall. Abruptly she was swept off her feet. A hand came from behind and clamped over her mouth and nose, and a greasy arm tightened about her throat. She had only a moment of panic before she lost consciousness.

Isabella went to the corral and stood for a moment watching the activity. She passed a word here and there with the *vaqueros*, making sure a number of them knew she was there. When she left the corral she went to the stone house, crossed the porch, and walked off the other side. Sofia was taking the dishtowels off the line on the porch and looked at her coolly. *Another bitch*, Isabella thought. *When I am mistress of this house, she will bow and scrap to me as she does to the pale puta.*

As she crossed the path leading to the stream she saw Bucko running toward her. He was falling, picking himself up, and running again. She waited for him and grabbed his arm as he attempted to pass her and almost jerked him off his feet.

"Where do you go so fast? Did I not tell you your feet are not made for running, stupid boy?"

"I get Burr . . . Let me go . . . I go get Burr . . ."

"Why you get Burr, you silly mule?"

"Apache . . . at the stream! He . . . get Johanna—" Bucko choked out the words, pulling on his arm to get free of the hand that held him.

"Ha! Yes, you are a silly mule. Apaches are gone. You see nothing, hear?"

"I did see it. Let go, Isabella. I get Burr!"

"You tell on your Apache brother? Ha! They skin you like a rabbit." Isabella twisted his arm. "Burr beat you when you tell him lie."

"I no lie. I see him hit Johanna." Sobs tore at Bucko's throat, but he choked them back.

"When Burr beat you I will laugh," Isabella said spitefully and turned, blocking the boy's view of the corral. "Go. Go tell the señor the lie. He go to the windmill."

Isabella watched him run away with a gloating expression on her face. The days were short at this time of year. She glanced at the sky above the mountains to the west. Already it had started to darken. It would take many minutes for Bucko to reach the windmill and many minutes more to get back to the stone house. Isabella ran down the path toward her home. It mattered not if Bucko found the señor. The hair of the blond *puta* was already hanging from the Apache's belt.

Bucko ran stumbling down the sandy path, tears streaming down his face. Why didn't Isabella believe him? He didn't lie! His ankle gave way and he went sprawling. He picked himself up and wiped the sand from his face with his hands and hurried on. *Oh, Johanna, if I was a man the bad Indian wouldn't hurt you*, he cried silently. He came to the path that cut off toward the Mexican village and it occurred to him that it would take a long time to get to the windmill. He knew someone who would believe him. He turned down the path calling as loud as he could, "Rosita! Rosita!"

# CHAPTER
## *Twenty-three*

B lack Buffalo stood over the unconscious woman. It had worked out better than he'd planned. Sky Eyes had caused the council to laugh at him and the chief to rule against him. He would do what Gray Cloud had failed to do: he would take the woman of Sky Eyes to be his slave and Sky Eyes would have to travel to their winter home deep in the mountains of Mexico to find her—there he would kill him.

A look of gloating satisfaction crossed his face. Once again he had outsmarted the white man. His first victory over the white man had been when he demanded and received six ponies for Sha-we-ne's lame, weak son who was due to die soon. Sky Eyes had stolen the slave woman to replace her dead child, thinking he, Black Buffalo, would swallow his pride and allow his possession to be taken. He would show all the Chiricahua Apache that he was a man of pride, of vengeance.

Black Buffalo's dark eyes gleamed. His long wait beside the stream had paid off. He was glad the dark woman had not come on down the trail; he would have taken her, and missed the chance to get this woman with hair like a cloud. How envious the other warriors would be when they saw his white slave. He pictured her in his wickiup. He would forbid his wives to mark her skin and make her ugly, but he would allow them to beat her until she cringed before him. He would fling her white body on the blanket and go inside her. She would give him many sons, all with eyes like the sky, to remind the Apache Nation of his brave and daring mission.

He nudged her with his foot. She would awaken soon. He had cut off her air for only a short time—time enough to stuff her mouth so that she would make no sound. He bound her hands with a thong, then looped the strong string of rawhide about her neck so that he could lead her.

Johanna was now conscious. Her eyes flew open and she found herself staring into the pockmarked face of an Indian. Her head throbbed viciously and the hide that bound her wrists behind her back cut cruelly into her flesh. Her heart pounded with fear. The sound was so loud that she felt sure the Indian could hear it. He didn't move and she wished fervently that she had not awakened. Why hadn't he killed her? If he was going to, why not now, and get it over with?

Several minutes passed. A frog croaked. Leaves crackled as a breeze stirred through the trees. The Indian stood as still as a statue, waiting. Johanna shifted about. Her throat was dry and her mouth foul, tasting of the filthy cloth stuffed in it. She desperately needed to swallow but was afraid she would strangle on the wad of cloth. She closed her eyes, feigning unconsciousness, but the Indian kicked her in the side, seized her by the forearms, and hauled her to her feet. He picked up her shawl and tied it tightly around her, binding her arms to her sides. He jerked viciously on the thong looped around her neck. It bit into her throat, and she frantically fought to breathe. He wrapped the end of the leash about his hand, then knelt and carefully removed all trace of his having been there with Johanna. When satisfied that such signs were erased, he tugged on the leash and jerked his head, indicating that she was to follow.

Slowly at first, the Apache moved down the rocky bank, looking back often to see if they were leaving a trail. Johanna followed on shaky legs, keeping within the distance the leash allowed. She had no doubt that if she couldn't keep up he would strangle her, leave her, and fade away into the distant mountains.

When they were some distance from the stream, the Indian increased his pace to a slow trot. Johanna staggered behind him, her lungs afire. She stood the pace as long as she could, then halted suddenly and let the leash jerk her to the ground. The Apache turned and kicked her in the side. Pain tore through her, and she felt herself sinking into darkness. When her vision cleared, she saw him standing over her with a knife in his hand. She closed her eyes in resignation as she felt the blade touch her cheek, then swiftly the gag was gone, and great gulps of air were coming in through her open mouth. The heaven of it! She breathed deeply, then looked up with pleading eyes. He placed the flat side of his knife over his mouth, indicating silence, then drew the sharp edge of the blade across her throat, plainly telling her what to expect if she made a sound. Johanna nodded and got to her feet, grateful that the foul rag was out of her mouth and she could breathe sufficiently to keep pace with the Indian.

Black Buffalo continued at a trot. They were in the foothills now. Grimly determined not to break stride, cry out, or fall, Johanna anesthetized herself with a rhythmic inner whisper of the name of the man whose arms would never hold her again, whose memory of her would not be with sweetness and love as Ben's was of his Anna, but with bitterness and scorn. Burr . . . Burr . . . Burr.

In the cool of the evening, the emotional shock of the kidnapping wore off and Johanna appraised her situation. No one, she realized, would know that she was gone until she failed to appear at supper, and then they would think she had gone to visit Jacy. She had to believe that she would eventually be missed and someone would come looking for her. If not Burr, perhaps Luis, for Jacy's sake, would search for her. She had to believe it.

Fatigue, physical and spiritual, struck when darkness fell. Each step was torture. Thirsty, hungry, and tired beyond her wildest nightmare, she doggedly held her pace. Her hair, pins long gone, streamed down her back and stuck to her sweat-covered face and neck.

Evening came quickly. In the semidarkness she stumbled often. She let herself imagine Burr's face, but now, when she wanted to remember each and every detail, his image was hazy. Her eyes focused weakly on the back of the Indian and she trudged on. A night bird whistled shrilly, and she heard the swish of his wings as he left his perch. The wish to fly with him moved fleetingly across her mind.

When Black Buffalo stopped, Johanna's mind and body were so numb that she didn't register it and stumbled into him. He put his palm over her face and pushed hard. She tumbled over backward, falling against a tree trunk. Her head seemed to explode, and for a few moments she whirled in a black void. She lay exhausted against the mesquite trunk until her vision cleared. Her legs and ankles throbbed; her wrists were rubbed raw by the rawhide. Her stockings hung by threads to her garters, and she tried to cover her scratched and bitten legs by pulling them up and under the now ragged skirt of her dress.

They were not going to rest there; that faint hope vanished when the Indian jerked her to her feet and led her to a horse concealed amid the thick brush. He motioned for her to mount. She looked at him stupidly and then at the horse. There was no way she could get on the horse with her hands bound behind her back. She shook her head, holding out her bound wrists. He curled his lips scornfully and drew his knife. Johanna was sure he would kill her, but he sliced through the thong. Pain knifed through her shoulders as her arms fell to her sides. The Apache jerked on the leather looped around her neck, letting her know he could cut off her air if she caused him any trouble. He jumped on the horse, reached down, and hauled her up behind him. She emitted a quick shriek before she knew it was coming, then threw her arms around the oily, foul-smelling body to keep from tumbling off backward as the horse took off at a run.

Hours of riding, and pain that would have been insufferable had not nature provided her with that curious blanking of the mind that carries one through extreme suffering. Trees, sky, streams, huge boulders, the crackle of brush and leaves, cold night wind, the movement of the horse, the rocking motion— she was conscious of them all, but with the remoteness of an ill-remembered dream.

They rode on through the night. At first the pain had been excruciating, but now her legs were numb. Her head hung forward, lolling and jerking, but she had not the strength to straighten her neck. She had, hours ago, passed the desperate need to lie down. She would go on forever like this, there would be no end—

Johanna was not aware that the horse had stopped until the Indian slid to the ground and jerked on her arm. She fell in a heap at his feet and lay there. He grunted with disgust, moved the horse away, and tied it to a downed log. When he returned, he stood over her while she pushed herself up into a sitting position. Then he took a pouch that hung from his belt and with his eyes on her face lifted it and squirted water into his open mouth. Johanna's tongue was swollen and her mouth felt as if it were stuffed with cotton. More than anything she wanted a drink of water, and he clearly wanted her to beg for it, but her pride would not allow it. She curled her lips scornfully and looked away. However, she was not so brave on the inside, and she silently murmured a prayer.

*Oh, God, whoever and wherever you are, please help me! Don't let me lose my mind and plead with this savage for a drink of water. Help me, God! If you must take my life, do it now while I have some dignity left.*

She lay back, pride doing battle with thirst and her aching body. There would be no compassion and no water for her, she knew that now. Perhaps it was just as well: her ordeal would be over all the sooner.

With his wiry fingers the Indian rebound her wrists, checked the loop about her neck, and twisted the leash about his hand to shorten it. The rancid smell of the man sickened her. He settled himself with his back to a tree, but his eyes remained open and staring. Johanna struggled to sit erect, to keep her leaden eyelids from closing. Pain knifed through her back, hips, and legs. The insides of her thighs were raw and bleeding. Weariness crawled through her veins, and she was stricken with terror that he would kill her while she slept. If only she could stay awake. Perhaps if the Indian slept she'd have a chance. Minutes seemed hours. She imagined she could see his burning black eyes gleaming in the dark. Finally fatigue conquered her mind, her fear, and her body. She lay down in the grass and surrendered to sleep.

Johanna stirred in her slumber; sometimes she stayed half-awake for a few seconds, then dropped back into unconsciousness. Sometimes she stirred and imagined faces staring down at her. She saw Burr's face close to hers, willing her to get up; the next instant his face was far away, his voice calling her name. A man with bright beady eyes and a face like a rat was trying to pull Jacy away from her. She screamed and the shadowy figure of Luis loomed against the sky and enfolded Jacy in his arms. She dreamed that her papa and her mama were walking around her, wondering why she was lying in the grass. She tried to get up off the ground, but she drifted back into darkness again.

She was in old Mack's room. He had locked the door and his back was to it. He was young and quick and his face was evil. The look in his eyes told her plainly what was in his mind. She backed away; the room seemed enormous, and she kept backing away, farther and farther away. Still he continued to stalk her, never letting his eyes leave her face. His mouth moved, spouting silent obscenities. She had her back to the wall, and huge clawlike hands were reaching for her. She eluded them and ran down the hall of the stone house, trying to reach the door that seemed miles away. She heard Luis's voice. Was he cursing old Mack? Killing old Mack?

There was a struggle beside her. She opened dazed eyes and saw the Indian grasp his chest, a look of startled anguish on his face. His eyes bulged and gurgling noises came from his throat. The thong about her neck was jerked cruelly; she fought for air, then blackness came rushing up to envelop her.

Someone was holding her tenderly and lovingly, cradling her against his chest. She wasn't afraid. Her eyelids lifted, but she saw only darkness. *I'm still dreaming*, she thought tiredly. But, no, her hands were free. She tried to raise her arms, but they fell lifelessly to her sides. Her face was wet and her mouth was full of water, delicious water. It was running down her parched throat. She wasn't dreaming, because she could taste the water and smelled a familiar tobacco smell. She heard a beloved voice crooning to her. Burr's voice!

"Johanna! Johanna! Open your eyes. Oh, darlin' girl, I thought you were dead!" His hoarsely murmured words were whispered against her face. The strength of the arms holding her reminded her of the fierce strength that was in him. Was that his heart thumping against her breast? He was kissing her hair, her lips, her face, and wiping the dirt from her eyes.

She pulled back to look at him, but her eyes were flooded and she couldn't see.

"Don't cry. You're safe now. You're safe with me and Luis." His voice was strained, but soft and amazingly gentle.

"I can't stop!" she croaked. His arms tightened around her and he rocked her as if she were a baby.

"I've been so afraid you'd go off and leave me!" His arms relaxed a little. "I never thought about someone stealing you away."

"I'll not leave you, unless you want me to go." Johanna tried to put her arms around him, but they were too heavy.

He kissed her again, burrowing his face into her hair, mumbling words she couldn't decipher. The stubble on his cheeks and chin scratched her skin as he kissed every inch of her face. "You don't hate me? Say you don't hate me!" He spoke in a kind of desperate whisper, then lifted his face to look closely at hers.

"No. No. I don't hate you!" Her arms reached for his neck and he helped her place them there. "How could I hate you when I love you so?"

She must have drifted back to sleep, for suddenly he was carrying her, trying to kiss her eyes open. His voice was strange, as though he had been crying.

"Help me on the horse, Luis. We've got to get her home."

Other arms held her for a moment, and she heard the creak of the saddle. Then she was lifted up and she lay against him again, feeling the strength of his arms as he took the reins. Every part of her body throbbed with pain.

"How did you find me?" she asked.

"Luis tracked you. Didn't you know I'd come? I told you

you'd never get away from me.'' He wrapped her in a coat and tucked her skirt about her legs. "Are you all right? Do you want more water?'' His questions were anxious, loving.

"I'm all right, now.'' She snuggled her face in the curve of his neck. "Burr!'' She tried to sit up. "The . . . Indian?''

His arms tensed and he held her tightly to him. "Dead. Nothing will ever hurt you again. I swear it.''

# CHAPTER
## Twenty-four

They were approaching the stone house. Johanna knew it as soon as she opened her eyes, for light shone from every window and long streaks of it fanned out into the darkness. As her eyes began to focus she could see two figures standing on the porch and two coming across from the bunkhouse. The place was alive with activity. Anxious voices called out to Burr.

"Is she all right?" Ben's voice was trembly.

"She's worn out," Burr called, "but all right."

"By gol', Burr, we been mighty itchy. It didn't seem right, us jist a-sittin' here doin' nothin'."

Johanna looked down into Mooney's worried face and began to cry.

"What's the matter?" Burr whispered, his neck and chin hiding her face.

"I'm . . . just glad to be . . . home."

"Where's Luis?" Ben asked.

"He turned off and hurried home. He didn't want Jacy to know Johanna was missing until she was found."

Arms reached up to help her down. Her body ached all over and her legs were too weak to hold her. Burr was by her side almost as soon as her sore feet touched the ground, and he picked her up as if she weighed no more than a child. She let her head fall to his shoulder, and he cuddled her to him. He started walking very slowly, then stopped.

"The son of a bitch 'bout run her to death," he said huskily. "Sofia," he called sharply, "bring water to wash her and a gown of some kind. She's got to have something to eat, too. Ben, I promised Bucko I'd not come back without her. If he's sleeping, wake him and bring him in."

"He fell asleep about a half-hour ago, Burr. Poor little tyke was worried sick."

Burr waited in the doorway for Ben to light a lamp, then carried her into his room and lowered her onto the bed. Her eyes questioned his.

"Our room and our bed, Mrs. Calloway," he whispered in her ear.

Johanna sank into the soft bed, hardly aware that Burr was removing the shoes from her swollen feet. Her eyes rested on the curtainless window, the stark walls, and the crude pieces of furniture. A well of pity, pushed by nerves taut as a bowstring, surged up within her. This poor house! This poor, sad house was just sitting here waiting to come alive. Too exhausted to move, she gazed into the corners of the room. The sadness of the house and those who lived in it, and the gentle ministerings of the crude, hard man who bent over her, suddenly overwhelmed her. She turned her face into the faded quilt and wept silently for the house, for the small motherless boy, for Ben and his lost love, and for herself.

"Johanna." Burr's hand was gentle on her shoulder.

She looked up to see Bucko standing beside the bed, his big, solemn eyes bright with tears. She held her arms out to him, and he clutched her tightly, burying his face in the warmth of her body.

"Bucko, darling—"

"Me no . . . cry . . ." he sobbed, denying the obvious.

"It's all right for you to cry if you feel like it. Because you're a boy doesn't mean you don't have feelings."

"I saw the bad Indian hit you, Johanna. I stand by the tree so still he couldn't see me. I saw him tie you up and kick you. I run to tell Burr. Isabella saw too but she say I lie. Isabella say Burr at the windmill. I hate Isabella!"

"Bucko's been following you ever since . . . well, for days now," Burr told Johanna. "He's been like your shadow, trailing you everywhere. Thank God he was." Burr's voice became husky. "He told Rosita and she rang the bell to sound the alarm. He took me to the place where he'd seen the Apache take you. I sent Paco for Luis and started tracking, but lost the trail. Luis got there while it was still light and picked it up again. If it hadn't of been for Bucko we'd not have had any idea where you'd gone."

"Thank you, Bucko. I'm proud of you and I'm proud of the part of you that's Apache. It was your Apache blood that let you stand so patiently and wait until it was safe to go to Burr."

His lips trembling, his eyes ashine with tears, Bucko looked up at Burr. "I no want Johanna to go," he said in his halting English.

Burr squatted down on his heels and Bucko, beaming with pride, threw his arms around his neck. "Neither do I," he murmured and stood with the boy in his arms. "Let's get you to bed. After Johanna's rested you can talk to her again."

Later, when Johanna was washed and in a clean nightdress, she drew the quilt up to her chin and stretched her legs in sheer luxury. The kindness and concern of everyone made her realize how fond she had become of all of them. It was pure heaven to feel so wanted, so cherished and loved.

When she awakened, evening was approaching once again. She could hear the ring of boot heels on the stone porch and Sofia's high musical voice talking to the men. Through the window she could see that almost all the light had gone from the sky. It was the golden time of day, as her papa used to say.

"Do you feel better?" Burr came through the door and stood beside the bed. He reached down and tucked the quilt about her shoulders. He spoke gruffly and did not look at her.

"I'm hungry. I feel like something is gnawing a hole in my belly." His head jerked up and he saw the teasing laughter in her eyes. His face broke into a grin and his eyes were brilliant as he gazed down at her.

"Sofia!" It was a shout of jubilation. "She's awake."

"Burr! I'm sure they heard you down at the bunkhouse." There was laughter in her eyes and on her lips.

"Just so Sofia did. I told her to fix you some broth."

Johanna couldn't decide if he were teasing her, but laughter bubbled up, and she held her palms against her bruised ribs. "Please don't make me laugh. I'm too sore."

Sofia came in carrying a bowl on a wooden tray and set it down on a chair beside the bed. "Señor Burr say you no need broth, you need meat."

Johanna couldn't force her eyes to leave his smiling face. "Señor Burr is right, Sofia. It smells delicious, and I'm so hungry I could eat shoe leather."

"Shoe leather? Aye-yi-yi!" Sofia rolled her eyes and scurried out of the room.

"Burr, about Jacy . . ."

"Luis was home before she awakened."

"I'm glad." She reached up and took his hand. "Thank

you for coming for me—'' Her tear-filled eyes looked like twin stars shining up at him.

"God, Johanna, did you think I *wouldn't*?"

She looked away from him. He dropped her hand and turned to leave. "Burr—stay and talk to me."

"You've got to eat," he said gruffly. "I'll be back."

Johanna felt so much better after she emptied the bowl of meat and potatoes that she asked Sofia to bring her hairbrush and to light the lamp on the mantel. She sat up in bed and brushed her hair with long, even strokes, pulling it forward and holding a great handful so she could brush the tangles from the ends. It was calming to her nerves to be doing something. Now that she was stronger, she didn't know what Burr expected of her. She was in *his* room, in *his* bed. She vaguely remembered him telling her it was *their* room. Had she dreamed the soft endearments he'd whispered during the ride back to the ranch?

He came into the room and closed the door behind him. Their eyes met and held. His eyes were bleak, hers questioning. He stood at the foot of the bed looking at her.

"Do you want me to go?"

She carefully placed the hairbrush on the chair beside the bed. "No." The word came out on a breath of a whisper.

The lamplight cast shadows on his cheeks and softened the lines of his mouth. He looked younger and so vulnerable that a pain clutched Johanna's heart. She thought of the small, motherless boy growing up with only Ben's love to protect him from old Mack's hate.

Caught in sudden yearning, she wondered how he truly felt about this marriage. Her own emotions were so mixed. She was scarred from the battles with both Macklins. Her love for this man had come slowly, and the new harmony between them was fearfully fragile. As Johanna mulling over the situation, she realized that this relationship was as new to Burr as it was to her. She held out her hand and struggled to find a subject they could talk about.

"Sit by me and tell me about finding Bucko in the Indian camp," she said.

Burr sat on the side of the bed and studied her with an intensity that puzzled her. He dropped his eyes for a moment to look at her hand, now resting so naturally in his, then met her eyes again, willing her to understand what he was about to say.

"When I first saw Bucko he was lying alone under a scrub oak on a piece of dirty blanket and making a weak, mewling sound. Camp dogs surrounded him, sniffing at the filth." Johanna drew in a trembly breath and tightened her fingers on his. His compassionate tone affected her as much as did his words. He continued, "I thought, *Oh, God, how can they treat their little ones like this?* Then it occurred to me that this one was an outcast, a male child with a less than perfect body. When I got closer to him he looked up at me with big blue eyes and I almost fell off my horse." Burr stopped speaking; the telling was painful to him. He looked down at the slim hand engulfed in his, then met her eyes and spoke firmly. "It didn't seem possible he could belong to one of us, but I had to get him and give him his chance." Johanna felt her heart swell with love for him as he continued the story and told her how he had traded ponies to Black Buffalo for the boy. "He'd not have made it if not for Rosita and the other women. I didn't know anything about how to take care of him, and Luis and Ben didn't know much more."

He sat silently, his fingers gripping hers. Johanna felt compelled to ask, "Why didn't you tell me you weren't his father?"

"It was a matter of not knowing," he said simply. "About ten or twelve years ago, when Luis and I were just a couple of young scutters and just finding out what it was all about,

Mack took me to El Paso. He turned me over to a couple of women . . . you know the kind. I came back, and, boylike, I told Luis all about it. Now that I think about it, I know we didn't have any more brains than a couple of fleas.'' He lowered his head and looked at the floor. ''The Apaches came down that year. They were a small, friendly bunch. We were out one day and came onto these two girls down by the creek . . . and they were willing. Both of us regretted what we did. That spring we saw them again and they didn't seem any different, so we figured nothing had happened. We swore then that we'd never father a bastard.'' He got up and went to the fire. Johanna followed him with her eyes. His voice lowered on a sigh. ''Thank God the old man lived long enough to admit that Bucko was his.''

Burr was a curious mixture of compassion and bitterness, Johanna thought. He had carried the guilt all these years of not only looking like the man who had raped his mother, but perhaps of having done the thing he had sworn not to do—fathered a bastard. Her heart went out to him, and she wished she could think of something comforting to say.

Burr sat in the chair and stretched his long legs out toward the fire. It seemed hours but could have been only minutes before he broke the silence.

''Isabella will be leaving the valley.'' He paused, glanced at Johanna, then looked away. ''She's never been in my bed, Johanna. It was pure cussedness on my part that let you think she had. Paco knows she's a feisty little thing, but he wants to marry her. I'll see that they have a start somewhere.'' Johanna started to tell him about ordering Isabella from the house, but he was speaking again. ''I'm right sorry you don't like it here, Johanna. I realize that because Luis and I think it's the best place to be don't make it so for everyone.'' He cleared his throat nervously. ''What I want to say is . . .

well, what's done is done. We're married . . . all legal and binding . . . and I want my wife with me."

He looked at his feet, shifted them nervously, then, for lack of anything else to do, he drew the makings of a smoke from his pocket. His fingers were shaking so badly that he spilled some tobacco on the floor.

"You know," he said, trying to roll the smoke, "there's never been a woman in this house before, except my mother, and Ben tells me she stayed in that one room of his. It's been good having the house like it is and a meal ready . . . and knowing there'd be a pretty woman to look at while you ate it."

"Now that Mack's gone there's no reason why one of the Mexican women can't come and clean house, and Sofia is an excellent cook. They'll keep your house neat and running smoothly." The words were softly spoken, but his head jerked up as if she had shouted.

"Goddammit, Johanna! That's not what I mean, and you know it." His voice boomed impatiently, but not angrily, and she smiled.

Johanna got up out of bed, fully aware that only a thin nightdress covered her naked body and that his eyes were on her. On sore, bare feet she walked around behind him and stood looking down on the top of his head. Her glance found the crushed paper and tobacco in his tight fist. She closed her eyes tightly in an effort to still her pounding heart.

"Have you ever wondered why Jacy is so open with her expressions of affection, Burr?" Once she started talking, the words came easier. "She learned it from Papa. Every day, from the time she was old enough to understand to the day they died, Papa would tell Mama he loved her. Sometimes it was at the supper table, or when she was working about the house. He would say, 'Have I told you today that I love you?'

and she would say, 'Yes, *querido*, but tell me again.' '' Burr sat rigidly in the chair; the only movement was that of his two big fists opening and closing. Johanna hurried on before she lost her nerve. "If love is nourished it will grow strong. Fail to feed it and it will wither and die. Burr, I cannot stay here as an . . . unloved wife."

Boldly she moved around to the side of the chair, so that she could see his face.

"Unloved? What are you talking about?" His voice was strained, husky.

Her dancing nerves made her voice almost a shout. "Do you want me to stay to keep your house and take care of Bucko, or do you want me to stay because you . . . love me? You acted as if you did when you brought me home last night."

A brief silence ensued, and Johanna colored as the enormity of her words hit her. Slowly his expression changed from shock to wonderment and his eyes and mouth became tender. His voice, when it reached her, was deep and sincere.

"I want you to stay because I love you." He clasped her arm and pulled her onto his lap. "If loving you means not being able to sleep without seeing your face, and not being able to eat unless you're at the table, and not speaking to you unless I'm either sore at you or acting the fool . . . and being crazy out of my head when you . . . were gone!" He leaned his head back against the chair and studied every feature of her face, his eyes lingering on her softly parted lips. "The first time I saw you, you were standing in that dirty, cluttered kitchen. You were bright and shiny as a new silver dollar— the sun coming through the window shone on your hair. I thought you were a vision. You were too beautiful to be real; too beautiful for the likes of me. I knew you'd never see me as anything other than the old man's bastard son, so I wrapped myself in bitterness to keep from hurting so much." He gave her a tender, apologetic look. "Ben knew, and understood that I wanted you to take to me like Jacy did to Luis, but you didn't, and I told myself I didn't care. Then the idea fell right in my lap . . . the way to get you to marry me, for Luis's sake, I told myself, so Jacy would be happy in the valley."

Johanna tried to speak but failed. She lifted trembling hands and stroked the hair back from his face, then with palms against his cheeks she leaned forward and tenderly kissed his lips, before resting her head against his shoulder. Gently, he adjusted her on his lap, and pulled her nightdress over her bare feet. She snuggled in his arms, and felt his heart beat as wildly as her own.

"I love you," she whispered.

Her voice was the softest of sounds. He searched her face for reassurance and when she smiled radiantly at him he saw the love in her eyes and believed it. With a thankful groan that came from deep inside him, he rested his face against hers. All that mattered was their newly declared love and the need to be close to each other. At first he didn't seek her lips, but nestled his warm mouth close against her face with a gentle reverence that made her heart turn over.

"That time in my room . . . I hated myself for what I did to you. Can you forgive me?" With restrained passion, he caressed her face and threaded his fingers through her hair. "I've been such a fool," he whispered huskily. "Tenderness is . . . much better."

Her arms tightened and she moved her mouth to his. "Not all the time, Burr . . . darling."

His lips found hers in a kiss of deep dedication and promise. She knew they would always be together and her happiness was overwhelming. Their lips met and met again, each kiss sweeter than the one before. His hand moved down her back and over her hips, stroking, caressing. Gradually his kisses became more forceful and he whispered endearments against her lips, which she offered so eagerly. They kissed and murmured to each other and were lost in the wonder of their new intimacy.

Finally Burr lifted his head. "This is our wedding night, Mrs. Calloway. I know of a more comfortable place to spend it."

She nuzzled her nose against his face before shyly slipping off his lap. Her face, arms, and legs were scratched and her hair was hanging down her back, but she'd never felt more beautiful.

"Go along," he said, giving her a gentle push toward the bed. "I'll add more wood to the fire."

As if in a dream Johanna moved the one pillow to the center of the bed and slid in under the quilt. It seemed a long time before Burr came to the bed, and when he did it was silently. She looked up and he was there. He removed his shirt and his powerful shoulders and chest were white in the semidarkness of the room. She closed her eyes when his hands went to the buttons on his pants. Cool air hit her body when he raised the covers, and the bed sagged as he lowered himself in beside her. She went into his arms eagerly. His powerful heart thumped furiously against hers.

"Sweetheart . . ." he murmured, holding her against his trembling hardness. "You're tired and sore. I'll just hold you."

"Not *that* tired and not *that* sore, darling," she whispered before he found her parted lips and caressed them with the tip of his tongue.

"Can we get rid of this?" he asked urgently, his fingers plucking at her gown.

She drew away from him and quickly wriggled out of the nightdress, then stretched the length of her naked body against his. He drew in a ragged breath, whispered an endearment, and clung tightly to her. She wound her arms about his neck and the sweet burning pressure of his lips on hers fused them together, blotting out everything except their passion.

What happened between them was wondrous . . . miraculous . . . incredible. His velvety touch between her thighs sent involuntary little shudders of delight surging through her. He spoke to her in tender words, soothing her, quieting her.

"You're mine," he whispered. "You're mine forever. Oh, love, you don't know how much I wanted you to love me, how much I hungered to hold you, taste you, feel your arms around my neck." His hands shook as they moved over her and into her hair, catching the silver strands and bringing them to his face. "It's like sunshine," he whispered.

Burr entered her slowly and reverently. His great body trembled violently with the effort it took to hold back. He penetrated deeper and deeper, making no sharp or hard thrusts. Only slow, sensuous motion, deliberate and controlled. He lifted his head to look at her when he rested snugly against her pelvis, embedded to the hilt. The long release of his breath warmed her mouth.

"Look at me," he whispered hoarsely. "I swear to give you my love until the day I die."

"And I . . . you, my beloved," she vowed. They spoke mouth to mouth, sharing breaths and quick, hard kisses.

His hands held her face in a vicelike grip, his body, muscular and hard, delighted her senses beyond belief. She clutched him tightly and ran her slender fingers over the warm skin of his back. The heat radiated from his body to hers, sending her into a rapture of love so exquisite she felt as if her soul had left her and joined with his.

Unable to further articulate his feelings with words, Burr did so with his body. She kissed him with fiery sweetness. Needing desperately to ride the crest of his own urge, Burr slowly and deliberately plunged and withdrew until her excitement spiraled and she clasped him tightly, resisting his withdrawal. The movement of her hips drove him over the edge into his own blazing rapture. Then the joyous fulfillment raced through Johanna, alive, pulsating, taking her breath.

When they reached earth again he gazed at her with intense delight, glorying in the loveliness of her face. Again and again he kissed her soft mouth. Her laugh was low and wonderfully happy. She wriggled and released a soft, purring sigh as she spread her fingers behind his head and pulled his mouth down to hers.

"I love you," he said, and listened while she echoed his words. "I've finally caught my little silver fox."

"I'm so happy I could cry." Tears brimmed at the corners of her eyes. "I was so envious of Jacy and Luis. Oh, Burr, I didn't think you'd ever . . . love me—"

Soft murmurs came from his throat and he kissed her lips and siped at the tears on her face.

"Don't cry. I never want you to cry, again," he whispered. "I love all your proud courage."

Hours later, as dawn broke, Johanna caressed her husband's face with her fingertips. She lay on her back, contented, with the weight of his head on her shoulder.

"Are you awake? Please wake up, darling. There so much to say, I can't wait to say it." He stirred and grunted a reply. She giggled. "Burr, can you imagine what our children will look like?"

He raised his head. "I know what they'd better look like," he growled.

"I want to start a school, Burr—and fix up the house. May I have a sewing machine? I saw one in a catalog. I'll make curtains and we'll put rugs on the floors—cowhides will do. We'll have a wedding feast on Thanksgiving and invite everyone. Oh, Burr, darling, won't Luis and Ben be pleased? They love you, but not as much as I do!" She sounded amazingly like her young sister. Burr laughed and kissed her nose.

"I can see that I'm going to be clay in your hands, Mrs. Calloway. How many turkeys do you want?"

Johanna laughed with delight. "You'll never be clay in anyone's hands, Burnett Englebretson Calloway." She clutched his face between her hands. "You're a fraud! You're not one bit as mean as you want everyone to think you are!"

The chuckle came from deep in his chest; she could feel the vibration against her heart.

"You just try to leave me and you'll find out how mean I can be!"

She gave the hair at the nape of his neck a little jerk.

"What was that for?" He lifted his head and looked inquiringly into her laughing blue eyes.

"That was for nailing my beautiful hat over the barn door!"

The throaty laugh came again, and he gazed at her with all the love she'd ever hoped to see in his eyes. "Have I told you today that I love you, Mrs. Calloway?"

"Yes, *querido*," she whispered, "but tell me again."

# EPILOGUE

Around her was silence, utter and complete except for the wind that raced down the valley, stirring the tall grasses and whispering through the pine trees. A cone fell now and then without a sound to the grass-cushioned earth. It was a beautiful morning and this was a beautiful place. Johanna walked slowly through the gate and approached the graves reverently. For the past twelve Septembers she had made this pilgrimage to the cemetery. Not only did she enjoy the serenity of the place, but it was one of the few places she could go where she could look down on her home.

Turning now, she saw the stone house, surrounded with its split-rail fence, and shrubs, flowers, and hanging baskets trailing their bright blossoms. The morning sun shone on the tin roof of the new addition, on the sparkling, curtained windows, and on Grandpa Ben sitting on the porch. A smile played around the corners of Johanna's mouth as a small, blond figure raced out of the house and climbed up onto his lap. *Dear, dear Ben*, she mused, *how he loves his grandchil-*

*dren!* She should hurry on back before the scamp had him worn out.

There were scarcely more than a dozen graves inside the piled-stone enclosure, but at one end three markers stood straight and solid. Johanna walked over to read the inscriptions.

ANNA MARIE ENGLEBRETSON
1827–1847
Farewell, my love, your life is past,
My love for you through life will last.
I'll grieve for you and sorrow take,
And love your child, for your sake.
B.N.C.

Through the years the headboard had weathered, but dabs of stain outlined the letters and they were as easy to read as the day they had been put there.

She walked a few feet away to another headboard.

JUANITA GAZARES
Beloved mother of Luis Gazares
1828–1860
Kind angels watch this sleeping dust,
Till Jesus comes to raise the just,
Then may she wake with sweet surprise,
And in her Savior's image rise.

The markers were identical, except that one was much more weathered than the other. The thought crossed Johanna's mind that Mack Macklin had probably never come to this cemetery and read the inscriptions. He would have scorned such sentiment.

Johanna stood beside the Indian woman's grave for a few

minutes. Before Bucko left five years ago to go East to school he had carved a headboard. The words were his. It read simply:

MOTHER
Shamed in life.
Brave in death.

Bucko had a brilliant mind indeed. Uncle Rafael Macklin had come to the valley for a visit and he had taken Bucko back East with him. The young man had finished his studies at the university in record time and joined his uncle in business.

Johanna passed on to another grave. The headboard was as neatly carved as the others.

O. MOONEY
1825–1875

*Dear Mooney*, Johanna thought with a smile. No wonder he had always said, "Just call me Mooney." It was after his death that they had discovered his name was Only. Mooney had died with an arrow in his back, but he had lived long enough to fire warning shots that alerted the roundup camp where Burr and the men had been working.

Several times during the last few years there had been small Indian raids in the valley. Geronimo and another colorful chief, Victoriano, were raiding and causing havoc in southern New Mexico, Arizona, and southeastern Texas, but they had kept their word, so far, and had left Macklin Valley in peace. Burr still took supplies down when the Indians came to the valley, but now they came in small pitiful groups, made up mostly of women, children, and old men.

Johanna went toward a small mound. The marker was newer than the others.

NATHAN CALLOWAY
3 months, 2 days
son of
Burnett and Johanna

Tears filled her eyes. Four years had failed to dull the pain of losing her second son. She and Burr had had a daughter the first year of their marriage and three years later a son. Both children were blond, blue-eyed, and bounding with energy. Little Nathan was born with a yellowish tinge to his skin, and they had known almost from the first that he would never grow up to be as healthy as his brother and sister.

Two weeks ago Johanna had presented her husband with a third son, and from the way he had pulled on her breast when she fed him this morning she was sure he was going to be as robust as her other two children. She had left him with Anna, her eleven-year-old daughter, who was fascinated with him and had vowed she was going to have dozens and dozens of babies of her own.

Luis and Jacy had three children and another on the way. Tiny Marietta was almost a year older than Johanna's Anna, yet barely came up to her shoulder. She had long, shiny black hair and large black eyes and was as shy as Anna was daring. Both girls had the same lament; their fathers were overprotective.

Johanna passed Codger's grave and that of Red and Rosita's little one and moved on to stand beside the grave at the far end of the cemetery. At her insistence a marker had been placed there.

## MACK MACKLIN
### He found the valley

She never lingered beside the old man's grave, but passed on, as if by doing so she had somehow done her duty. Looking down toward the ranch house, she saw a rider come out of the corral and head up toward the hill. She knew who it was before he took off his hat to wipe the sweat from his forehead and the sun glistened on hair yellow as cactus blossoms. She leaned against the stone fence and waited for him.

From her vantage point the land fell away, sweeping down to the sparkling stream whose waters threaded their way across the valley carpeted with waving knee-high grasses. She let her glance wander to the mountain peaks where the green timber gave way to rocky, snow-covered towers. She remembered Burr's words on that night, so long ago, when they had declared their love. "'Cause Luis and I think this is the best place to be don't make it so for everyone." It *was* the place she wanted to be, she thought. The only place in the world she wanted to be.

"Johanna." Burr's voice drifted up the hill.

She waved to him and laughed when she saw the scowl on his face and knew she was in for a scolding. The instant he got off his horse she hurried to him, and his outstretched arms welcomed her. He kissed her tenderly at first, then roughly, almost savagely.

"I've missed you," she whispered.

He held her away from him and looked down with mocking sternness. "Don't be tryin' to get around me with honeyed words. You shouldn't've walked all the way up here. It's only two weeks tomorrow since you had the baby. You're not strong enough yet."

"I've missed you," she said again with sparkling eyes.

"What am I goin' to do with you, woman? You don't have

the brains of a flea, but I . . . love you, love you. And I've missed you, too." He folded her to him lovingly, and she raised her mouth for his kiss.

"How much longer do I have to wait?" He breathed the words in her ear.

She drew back and laughed up at him. "Two weeks."

"Two weeks!" His face twisted with pain, then the old roguish grin she adored claimed his features. "I'll have to go to El Paso and visit the—"

She drew back her foot and kicked his shin.

"You just try to get out of this valley without me, Burr Calloway, and you'll soon find out how mean *I* can be!"

His laugh was rich and satisfying. "Come on, you mule-headed shrew. I'll give you a ride home."

He lifted her gently up onto the saddle, placed her hands on the pommel, and cautioned her to hold on, then jumped up behind her. She leaned back against him, feeling loved and protected, and reveling in the strength of his arms as he took the reins. The horse moved on down the slope.

"Have I told you today that I love you, Mrs. Calloway?" The soft, familiar words were whispered in her ear.

"Yes, *querido*," she murmured, "but tell me again."

# IF YOU ENJOYED
## *GLORIOUS DAWN*

### *look for*

# *A GENTLE GIVING*
# by Dorothy Garlock

Set in the Bighorn Mountains of Wyoming during the late 1800's, *A GENTLE GIVING* is a hauntingly beautiful love story. Smith Bowman is a lonely guilt-ridden man; Willa Hammer, a gentle, giving woman. The story will make you laugh, love, cry, and hate, but most of all, it will make you turn pages.

Coming January 1993
from Warner Books

# CHAPTER
# 1

*A*wakened by the heat beating against her face, she leaped from her bed. Fire had enveloped the table and the bureau where she kept the pictures of her mother and the few mementos she had managed to save over the years. Suddenly, the straw mattress on the bed erupted into a ball of fire.

Over the sound of crackling flames, a murmur of angry voices reached her. She ran out the door as the fire, turning into an inferno, roared angrily into the room where her stepfather made his beautiful clocks.

Was this a dream—the roof ablaze and flames dancing a queer rigadoon against the dark sky?

Willa Hammer faced the angry crowd. Why had they come here to the edge of town to set afire the little shack she had so lovingly made into a home? A dirt clod struck her cheek. She cried out in surprise and terror, and lifted her hand to shield her face.

"Slut! Spawn of the devil!" The woman who threw the clod had spoken to her just that morning when she went to post a letter. She had not been friendly but she had been civil. "It's because of you—"

"We don't want ya here!" yelled another.

"It's evil ya 'n' that deformed monster brought to this town," a man shouted. "Nothin's been right since ya come here."

"Get the hell out of Hublett or . . . we'll tar 'n' feather ya!"

A sixgun fired into the air made an unspoken threat clear to even Willa's befuddled mind.

Pelted with clumps of dirt, she raised her arm to protect her head and turned toward the road. A man with a hickory switch in his hand blocked her way.

"Uppity whore! Whelp of a thievin' murderin' hunchback," he shouted, his sneering face so close to her she could smell his sour breath. Willa tried to edge around him, but he caught her nightdress at the neck and ripped it, leaving an arm and shoulder bare. Then he lifted his arm again.

She heard the breathy hiss of the switch slicing through the air just before it sent a serpent of flame writhing across her back.

"Ya ain't got no shotgun now."

Unremitting terror engulfed her. This was the man she had turned away a few nights ago when he had come pounding on their door, drunk, and showing off for his friends. He had wanted to know what she would charge for an hour in bed. She had endured the shouted insults until he had attempted to break down the door. Then she had flung it open and faced him with the shotgun. With fear making her stomach roil, even though she had been through this many times before in so many towns she had even forgotten the names, she had ordered him to leave.

"Bitch! Ever since ya come here ya've been looking down yore nose at us decent folks." The switch came down on her back again.

In a daze of pain and confusion, she cried out, stumbled, regained her balance and tried to run. Again and again she felt the bite of the switch. The end of the pliable bough curled around her neck and stung her mouth.

Too numb to cry, too frightened to think, she ran to escape the agony of the switch and the clods and stones being thrown by the angry crowd. The light from the fire and the bright moon sent her shadow dancing crazily in front of her as she ran barefoot down the path. She reached the end of the lane to find it blocked by a canvas-covered, high-wheeled, heavily constructed wagon. Unsure as to what to do, she paused.

When a stone, thrown harder than any of the others, hit her in the middle of the back, the pain forced a scream from her lips. She staggered and grabbed the wagon wheel to keep from falling to her knees.

"Up here, girl! Quick!"

She had no idea who was on the other end of the hand that was extended to her. She grasped it gratefully, placed her foot on a thick spoke and was pulled up onto the seat. The instant she was in the wagon, a long whip snaked out and stung the backs of the mules.

"H'yaw! Hee-yaw!" The driver shouted at the team as he cracked the whip over their backs. The wagon lurched forward. It made a wide loop and headed for open country.

"Papa! Wait for Papa and Buddy—" Willa cried.

"Too late fer yore pa, girl. They already hung 'em."

"No! Oh, God—"

Then in the wavering light of a bonfire, she saw the body of Papa Igor hanging from a tree in a grove between their house and town. His shirt had been torn away. The white skin on the large hump on his back shone in the light from the fire. His head, oversized in proportion to the rest of his body and covered with thick dark hair, was tilted back as if he were looking at the heavens above.

There, abandoned and lifeless, was the only person in the world whom she loved and who loved her. The scene was burned into Willa's mind. It would stay forever.

There is a time when a human being has taken all that can be endured; a time when strength and logic are burned away. This was that moment for Willa Hammer. The physical pain was so intense it was scarcely to be borne, but within her the awareness of her loss seared far more deeply.

She screamed, and screamed, and screamed.

It was the cry of a soul in agony—a sound most of the crowd would never forget. It pierced the cool night air, shattering the silence, moving like a cold, desolate wind, sweeping down from the mountains, raking the mob with fingers of ice, chilling and awesome.

As the screams died away, a sorrowing voice spoke from among the hushed throng standing in front of the burning house.

"Dear God. What possessed us to do such a terrible thing?"

But it was too late for regrets. The deed was done.


"What the . . . hell!"

To the west in the Bighorn Mountains, Smith Bowman, startled out of a half-sleep, dropped the empty whiskey bottle and leaped to his feet. Screams, wordless, terrified, unearthly screams blasted the silence. They filled every crevice of the mountains and sent a shiver of terror pouring through him.

The screams stopped suddenly and all was quiet again.

Smith shook his head to clear it. He must be drunker than he thought. The cries he'd heard must have been a cougar's mating call, but he would have sworn they were a woman's primeval screams of grief.

An hour earlier he had awakened abruptly from a

tortured sleep, reared up out of his bedroll, his eyes wide open, his face drenched with sweat, his hands reaching. A wave of sickness had washed over him, as it did each time the nightmare forced him to relive the horror of that dreadful day. Would he ever forget the pleading look in Oliver's eyes as he reached for his hand just before— just before—he had just coaxed sleep back again when the shrieking began.

Smith's shaking fingers combed through his thick blond hair before he pulled another whiskey bottle from his saddlebag. He took a long swallow, then cradled the bottle in his two hands. When he was a boy, he had yearned for a horse of his own, but when he was left alone after his family was lost in a flash flood, he wanted nothing more than to see another human face. Then when he went to Eastwood, he had a desperate desire to belong. Now, all he wanted was to be free of the invisible chains of guilt.

A tear slipped from the corner of Smith Bowman's eye and rolled slowly down his cheek.

Dear God, would it ever end? It had been six long years since Oliver's death—and guilt still clung to his back like a leech.

He drank from the bottle again. This was all the whiskey he had to last him until he reached Byers' Station. He would stop there and buy more before he crossed the river and headed for Eastwood ranch.

He lay back down on his bedroll. Long ago he had developed an awed affection for the Bighorn Mountains, marveling at their trickery, their beauty, their valleys and their towering trees. Tonight they wore a crown of a million stars. Smith watched the shadows and listened to the sounds of the forest, wondering if there were another human being in the world who felt as desperately alone as he did.

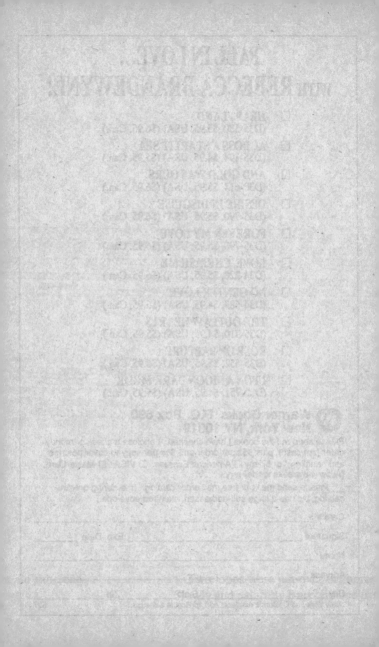